THE CONCORDIAN CHRONICLES

JONAH'S AWAKENING

JOHN DAROUS

Published by John Darous

www.johndarous.com

ISBN

978-0-6459248-2-4 (Hardcover)

978-0-6459248-1-7 (Paperback)

978-0-6459248-3-1 (Paperback Draft2Digital Distribution)

978-0-6459248-0-0 (ebook)

978-0-2288-8075-2 (Audiobook)

ACKNOWLEDGEMENTS

I wish to thank the following people for assisting me on my publishing journey:

For editorial services – Lamonte W., Lauren H., Mikaela S., and Kim M.

For photography – David Mundy

For the cover design – Ryan Montigny

ACKNOWLEDGMENTS

CHAPTER 1

The Middle Astral Realm

I'm finally ready, Master Jakeel thought to himself.

It had been several decades, from the perspective of Earth time, since Jakeel had lived a life on Earth. As he sat in a corner of a temple set amongst the Middle Astral Realm—where souls of the highest vibrational frequency reside between incarnations—Jakeel spent time evaluating his previous life. He reflected on the many lessons that had been learned and the karmic debt that needed to be repaid. Although Jakeel had evolved significantly, he knew there was room for even more growth. Learning and evolving was the perpetual task of every soul in the universe. It was the only expectation God had for every soul.

A big part of Jakeel's evaluation involved him sitting with the Review Council to conduct a life review. The Review Council consisted of a group of advanced souls, known as Elders, who would sit down with a soul after completing their human incarnation to help them assess their life. Together, they would examine all the ways in which their human form had interacted with other humans and the impact of their existence. The Elders never judged someone's actions on Earth during a review; it was up to the soul to determine what they had learned and what they could have done better.

Now that he'd had plenty of time to consolidate everything learned during his last life review, Jakeel was ready for another visit. For this to happen, he had to speak to the Elders about his decision. This was another one of the many responsibilities the Elders had—to help souls plan their incarnations on Earth and guide them on their path to evolution. It was, therefore, imperative that Jakeel speak to his Elders so they could collaboratively map out his next journey into the Physical Realm.

As communication amongst souls in the Middle Astral Realm was by means of telepathy, Jakeel telepathically requested an audience with Elder Ezekiel and Elder Baldel. They obliged and emerged before him instantly, materializing initially as small orbs of light that expanded very quickly to reveal their entire soul bodies. Jakeel immediately stood to attention.

Although they appeared before Jakeel resembling transparent human figures, all beings in the Middle Astral Realm could transform into any shape or form they wanted.

"Greetings, Elder Ezekiel and Elder Baldel," Jakeel said before bowing.

"Greetings, Master Jakeel. You wanted to speak to us?" Elder Ezekiel asked.

"That's correct. Thank you for agreeing to see me. It's been some time since my last life on Earth, and I'm ready for another visit. There are a few things I want to go back and experience. And a few things that I need to revisit that I haven't quite mastered yet."

Both Elders looked at each other as if they weren't surprised about what Jakeel wanted to discuss. After a previous conversation, where Jakeel mentioned some lessons he wanted to learn during his next incarnation, the Elders suspected he was considering returning to Earth for another visit.

"Well then, let's go somewhere quieter and begin preparations for your journey. We have a lot to discuss," Elder Baldel said.

All three dematerialized and reappeared in a different area in the temple that was less crowded. A soul's ability to dematerialize required nothing more than a single thought. It was easily accomplished as they didn't have dense, physical bodies like humans. Rather, they had energy bodies—made up of white light—that could move freely across time and space as required.

Jakeel and the Elders stood beneath ceilings that soared overhead, filled with brilliant golden spheres of light that radiated throughout the temple below. The temple walls glowed white, while the floor reflected the light from the ceiling. All light in the temple was from one source: God. God's energy powered the entire Middle Astral Realm.

As they were about to begin the discussion, they all sat on the floor, hovering slightly above the ground with their legs crossed in the lotus position. Although the area was less crowded, Jakeel could see other souls in the nearby surroundings. They, too, were in the midst of preparing for their next human incarnations on Earth, with their Elders. One soul in particular, Jakeel noticed, was being counseled by Elders Ezekiel and Baldel at the same time he was; this ability, for souls to be present in multiple locations at once, was known as omnipresence.

"You know, you have the potential to make this your last visit," Elder Ezekiel said. "If you can learn these last few lessons well enough, you may not need to go back again, which means you'll be able to evolve into other realms of existence and new levels of consciousness."

"But I still have quite a lot of karmic debt I need to repay. Is it possible to do so in just this next life alone?" Jakeel asked.

The Elders paused for a moment to consider his question, assessing Jakeel's karmic debt and his ability to pay it back.

"There's a way, if we plan your life correctly," Elder Ezekiel said.

Jakeel looked at Elder Ezekiel and leaned in a little closer. "What exactly do I need to do?"

"Have you ever heard of a realm of people called the Concordians?" Elder Ezekiel asked.

Jakeel thought about it for a moment. "I don't believe I have. Who are they?"

"The Concordians are a realm of people tasked with protecting all parallel universes, from invasion by opportunistic entities outside their universe," Elder Baldel explained. "Certain evil beings, known as Infringers, like to find ways to escape the dimension they're from and invade other dimensions, for various sinister reasons. The Concordians are responsible not only for intervening when this happens but preventing it from occurring in the first place."

"What do these Concordians look like? Are they human?" Jakeel asked.

"Yes. Concordians are humans; however, their DNA has been altered so they can possess magical powers," Elder Ezekiel said. "Powers such as the ability to teleport between parallel universes with just a simple thought, communicating telepathically, and being able to levitate. Similar to what we can do as souls, but in human form."

Elder Baldel explained that Jakeel needed to go to Earth first and live there for several years before he could take up his role as a Concordian Guardian. Concordians lived in a separate dimension from Earth but could go back and forth between the two.

"You will have the opportunity to protect and serve dimensions from Infringers, which in turn, will pay off your karmic debt quicker," Elder Baldel suggested.

"The other thing about Concordia is that it is a place where only the most advanced souls go. So, you should consider it a privilege we are sending you there. Please don't abuse it. I say that because some souls have, which has led to even more karmic debt being accumulated," Elder Ezekiel said.

"I promise you I won't."

"That's good to hear. Now, let's sort out some of the finer details," Elder Ezekiel said.

Going to Earth to live a life required complex planning. The first of these planning tasks was for a soul to select the family they would be born into. Elder Ezekiel explained that he already had a suggestion for Jakeel, which he was hoping he would like. After all, they were a part of his soul family, which, in The Middle Astral Realm, is a group of souls energetically connected and on a similar frequency with each other.

"You will know them as Master Ranyul and Master Unlal. On Earth, they are currently known as Mason Michaels and Aurora Michaels."

Jakeel remembered them straight away. They were his children in one of his previous lives. "You know, that sounds like an excellent idea. They gave me so much trouble as children; now they can understand what it's like to be the parent of a difficult child."

"This isn't about payback, Jakeel. Nonetheless, it will give each of you a different perspective of the parent and child relationship." Elder Baldel grinned.

"Yes, I know. I was just kidding." Jakeel laughed, which made his energy body glow brighter.

Now that this important aspect had been agreed upon, the next item on the agenda was to pick his Earthly name. Jakeel had thought about it a lot and had chosen his name already: Jonah.

"Why did you select Jonah?" Elder Baldel asked.

"I can't give you a logical reason other than I was drawn to that name for some reason," Jakeel said.

The Elders agreed with his name choice and noted it down in his soul contract—an energetic book used to record all the information they were gathering for Jakeel's life. His soul contract would be what Jakeel would abide by during his incarnation on Earth and form the basis of what he would accomplish throughout his journey.

"So, tell us, what are you wanting to learn during your next life?" Elder Ezekiel asked.

"First on my list is grief. Surprisingly enough, through all my incarnations, I haven't had the chance to experience this emotion very much. I've seen so many people on Earth experience this when someone dies. I've always been so fascinated by this emotion," Jakeel pondered. "I can't understand all the sorrow surrounding the feeling when we all end up coming back here and reuniting. Yet humans seem to get so caught up in the heaviness of grief like it is somehow the end of the road for an individual when nothing could be further from the truth. So, I need to understand why they get caught up in the drama of grief."

"Yes, grief is a difficult emotion to deal with on Earth. So, we'll need to plan some life events that will lead you to a better understanding of it." Elder Ezekiel took note of it on Jakeel's contract.

"We will have to leave it there for now. Before we can continue working on your list of lessons, we need to start the creation of your physical body," Elder Baldel said.

"Of course. I look forward to our next meeting to discuss the other details," Jakeel replied.

With that, the Elders departed, while Jakeel went to the temple gardens to contemplate what else he wanted to accomplish on Earth. The garden was a tranquil place with a small river, surrounded by a bed of magnificent flowers not available on Earth. Gentle music that could soothe the harshest of souls played in the background. The flowers never died and had fluorescent colors of yellow, red, blue, and purple that were mesmerizing and difficult to walk away from.

Preparing for an incarnation on Earth was a complex task that would take several meetings with the Elders to arrange. The temple garden was the perfect space for Jakeel to begin compiling the list of experiences to be included on his next journey.

CHAPTER 2

The Physical Realm

"Jonah, get up! You're going to be late! Again!" Aurora yelled to her son from the kitchen for the second time.

Aurora was preparing breakfast, dressed in jeans and her favorite red T-shirt. Her hair was tied up in a ponytail so it wouldn't annoy her while she cooked. As she wasn't working that day, Aurora was eager to get everyone out of the house so she could have the day to herself. She had an appointment at the hairdresser's to trim her curly, mousy-brown hair, which cascaded over her shoulders and was getting way too long for her liking.

As a special treat, Aurora also had an appointment for a massage. It wasn't often she did that, but she'd had a busy last few weeks and felt she deserved a gift to herself for her hard work. Now the only thing standing in the way of her pampering time was her lazy son, Jonah.

Aurora turned to her father-in-law who was sitting at the kitchen table. "Luke, did you want more toast?"

Luke, whose head was staring down at the newspaper he was reading, tilted his head up briefly. "No thanks."

As she continued preparing breakfast, Aurora became more aggravated with Jonah's lack of response and sense of urgency to get to university on time.

In recent months, Jonah had made a habit of waking up late, resulting in him not getting to his morning classes on time. Then there were days when he didn't go to university at all.

"I'm up." Jonah staggered into the kitchen and walked past Aurora, picking up a piece of cooked bacon from a plate that his mother was preparing for him.

Aurora raised her eyebrows and shook her head when she took one look at Jonah walking toward the kitchen table. "I gather you haven't shaved?"

Jonah rolled his eyes as he was chewing on the bacon. Jonah was quite a tall young man with a well-toned body and normally quite pleasing to the eye. However, that particular morning, Aurora could see he was unkempt. His dark, straight hair—about three inches long—was disheveled and his brown eyes were noticeably bloodshot. Jonah's shirt, which was from the day before, displayed a couple of food stains.

Jonah's father—Mason—who was at the kitchen table eating breakfast alongside his father, Luke, wrinkled his nose as Jonah walked by. "Have you run out of body wash?"

Jonah sat at the kitchen table and ignored his father. A moment later, Aurora placed Jonah's breakfast in front of him: scrambled eggs, crispy bacon cooked just the way he liked, sausages, and a small stack of golden-brown toast.

Jonah pushed the plate away. "I'm not hungry. Just gimme a cup of coffee."

"What did your last slave die of?" Aurora asked as she went to make him coffee.

"Not doing what I asked," Jonah snapped back.

Aurora didn't respond. She pursed her lips and gave Jonah a fiendish stare with her dark-brown eyes when she thought he wasn't looking.

Mason slapped his hand onto the kitchen table. "Hey! Show some respect to your mother—a 'please' wouldn't go astray, you know."

Mason's typically good nature had changed dramatically in an instant. Mason was about the same height as Jonah, but his piercing brown eyes, along with his stern face, and dark beard, radiated his lack of patience for Jonah's insolence.

"Please," Jonah said snidely as he rolled his eyes at his father. He was not in the mood to be polite.

Aurora, from across the kitchen, could see Mason clench his fist, trying not to get angrier at Jonah's response. She grabbed a mug from one of the kitchen cupboards and banged the cupboard door shut. After pouring Jonah's coffee, she walked over to him and placed the cup on his table mat.

"You can't just live on coffee alone," Aurora said as Jonah added cream and sugar to his coffee. "You need to have a good breakfast to think properly and focus during your classes. At least have a few bites. C'mon, make your mother happy."

"I said, *I'm not hungry*. If I get hungry later, I'll grab something from the cafeteria." Jonah drank a mouthful of coffee and took a couple of painkillers for his headache, which he'd grabbed from the bathroom before entering the kitchen.

Jonah was tired from having stayed up late. He had only walked into the house at three that morning after spending the night at a frat party with his friends. He could barely keep his eyes open.

Jonah's grandfather, Luke, chatted with Mason, trying to alleviate some of the tension in the room with lighthearted conversation. Luke—who was in his seventies—always tried to be the peacemaker in the family, especially these days between Jonah and Mason.

As Jonah finished his coffee, he got up from the kitchen table and grabbed his backpack, making his way toward the front door of the house.

"See ya, Pops!" Jonah said to his grandfather.

"Bye, Jonah. Have a nice day!" Luke shouted back, brushing a strand of white hair from his face.

"You too." Jonah waved to his grandfather before leaving the house, ignoring his parents.

"Love you, too," his mother whispered to herself as he shut the door behind him.

A few seconds later, Aurora could hear Jonah's car starting and reversing out of the driveway before he drove off to university.

Luke grabbed Jonah's plate and ate the breakfast he had left behind. He couldn't bear the thought of wasting good food.

"Don't be so harsh on the boy," Luke said to Mason.

"That's the point, Dad. He's not a boy anymore. He's twenty years old! He'll be twenty-one in a few months. He needs to pull himself together and start acting like an adult . . . and you need to stop defending him!"

"I'm not defending him," Luke countered as his blue eyes narrowed. "I'm just showing him a little understanding. Don't forget, you weren't exactly a saint at his age either. Your mother and I used to worry sick about you. But you eventually came through in the end."

Luke paused for a moment and took a deep breath. "Look, he's just having a bit of fun. He'll grow out of his partying and drinking ways eventually. I'm sure of it."

"Well, he better hurry up!" Mason got up from his chair. He took his last sip of coffee before he pounded the cup on the table in frustration and left the kitchen to get ready for work.

Luke sat there and didn't say another word. He continued eating his breakfast, trying to read his newspaper.

As Aurora began clearing some of the breakfast dishes from the table, she sensed Luke's frustration with Mason as he sat quietly, slumped in his chair. Throughout her marriage, she had witnessed similar scenes play out many times between father and son. Deep down, Aurora knew the two had a profound respect for each other, and their arguments normally resolved themselves quicker than they had started. It was the reason she never interfered. One way or another, they would always sort it out.

Once Mason was ready to leave for work, he walked out the front of the house without uttering a word to anyone. From the kitchen window, Aurora could see Mason step into his van and drive off.

Mason was a carpenter, a trade he'd told Aurora he enjoyed very much, as he was able to earn a reasonable living and be his own boss, working as a contractor. Mason had learned the carpentry trade from his father. Although Luke was retired now, he would occasionally help Mason, especially if he was working on a big project.

On the other hand, Aurora worked part-time as a yoga teacher. Since the mortgage was paid off and they lived a reasonably simple life, there was no need for her to work full-time.

Their home was relatively modest. Located in Chicago, the single-story timber home with three bedrooms contained simple furnishings. It wasn't a very big house, but it was adequate for all of them to live comfortably and for everyone to have their own space—especially for Jonah, who spent a lot of time in his bedroom watching TV, listening to music, and wasting time on social media apps. He managed to do some studying if he felt like it.

Luke finished his breakfast and took his last sip of coffee. He got up from the kitchen table and picked up his plate and coffee cup so he could take them to the kitchen sink.

"Luke!" Aurora screamed after she heard a crash of crockery. She ran toward him to see what was wrong. His left hand was clenched over his chest, and his breakfast dishes were shattered around him.

Aurora ran to her cell phone to call 911. After frantically explaining to the operator that she thought Luke was having a heart attack, they quickly dispatched the paramedics. Immediately after the call, Aurora rang Mason.

"Mason, it's your father—"

"What's happened?"

"I've called the paramedics; they are on the way . . . I think he's having a heart attack."

"I'm turning around now and coming back home."

Mason hung up and returned home within a matter of minutes. He arrived just as paramedics were pulling up in front of the house.

Aurora tried to ring Jonah. Since he was at university, Jonah's cell phone was on silent and he couldn't be reached. She left him a voicemail message and sent him a text to call her immediately on her cell phone.

Mason ran into the house and saw Luke on the kitchen floor with his eyes open and still conscious. Mason dropped to his knees beside Luke and grabbed his hand.

"Dad, are you ok? I'm so sorry I yelled at you before—"

"Sir, you need to get out of the way," one of the two paramedics said as he got on the floor to help Luke.

Mason backed away while the paramedics began treating Luke. Mason and Aurora were beside themselves. After a few minutes, Luke was stabilized and put on a stretcher. He was wheeled into the ambulance and driven to the hospital with Mason by his side; meanwhile Aurora got into her car and drove there on her own.

They all arrived at the hospital together, where Luke was rushed into the Emergency Department. Aurora's eyes were swollen and red from crying on the way to the hospital. Luke was like a father to her. She could tell Mason was frantic by the way he was pacing the corridors. Although Mason and Luke occasionally had disagreements, Aurora knew Mason loved and respected his father.

"I'm so scared," Mason whispered to Aurora as he sat next to her and clutched her hand, waiting to hear from the doctor. "I'm not ready for Dad to go yet."

Aurora hugged Mason tight as he cried on her shoulder. The possible loss of his father overwhelmed him. Aurora didn't know what to say to make things better. All she could do was be there and share his pain.

After some time, a doctor came out to speak to Mason. He approached Mason with a solemn expression.

"Are you Mr. Mason Michaels?" the doctor asked, looking at Mason.

"Yes." Mason stood and composed himself.

"I'm Dr. Livingstone, and I've been treating your father. He suffered a massive heart attack and—"

"Heart attack? Is he all right? Please tell me my father is going to be okay?"

"We attempted to do everything we could to save him, but I'm very sorry to say he didn't make it."

Mason and Aurora broke down in tears again. Aurora put her arms around Mason and hugged him tightly.

Both of Mason's parents were now gone. Losing his mother, Evelyn, many years earlier had crushed Mason. Aurora knew losing his father would be heart-wrenching for him; he never got the chance to say goodbye or tell him how much he loved him, especially since their last conversation had been full of anger.

While they were still in the hospital grieving the loss of Luke, Aurora's phone rang. She looked down at the display and saw it was Jonah. Aurora was at a loss for words. As she wiped away tears with a jacket sleeve, she took a deep breath. How was she going to tell him?

CHAPTER 3

L uke's funeral was conducted three days after his passing. Jonah was heartbroken. He couldn't believe his grandfather was gone. For as long as he could remember, his grandfather had been a constant presence in his life. To lose him now left Jonah with an indescribable feeling of emptiness.

It felt so strange to Jonah that his grandfather wasn't there anymore when he came home from university. Luke wasn't there to talk to when Jonah wanted to share something amusing that happened during the day or to have a general chat. The house felt empty. Jonah thought back to when he was a young teenager and would come home from high school after being bullied, and Luke was there to console him and wipe away his tears. Now, as a young adult, even though Jonah wasn't being harassed at school, he still missed having Luke to vent with when he was having problems dealing with his parents.

Jonah struggled to come to terms with it all. When he had first heard of Luke's passing, he became numb. His mother had to tell him over the phone, which Jonah sensed was difficult for her. Aurora had tried to compose herself, but her shaking voice betrayed how affected she was to Jonah.

Mason, on the other hand, tried to be strong. However, there was no denying he, too, was overcome with sorrow. He felt so alone now that his father was gone. Mason could always count on Luke to have a chat about anything. Sometimes it was just to have a laugh. Other times it was more serious, particularly when he needed his advice. Whatever the reason, he always appreciated what his father had to say. Even though Mason was in his mid-forties, he still longed for his father's presence.

"Hey Jonah, are you ready?" Aurora shouted from her bedroom, while she was sitting on an armchair putting on her shoes.

Jonah was sitting on a couch in the lounge room, dressed in a black suit and was playing with his cell phone. "Yes!"

"Great, we're almost ready too," Aurora shouted back. She then turned and looked toward Mason. "How are you feeling?"

Mason was grappling with his tie in front of the mirror. "I don't know. I'm still trying to get my head around all of this. I just want this day to be over. Plus, I'm not very good at giving public speeches."

"Don't worry, your eulogy is going to be just fine." Aurora stood up and walked over to Mason to help him straighten his tie.

"I hope so." Mason took a deep breath and exhaled. "I'm really going to miss him."

Aurora wrapped her arms around her husband and gave him a comforting hug for a few moments. Mason smiled. Aurora then gave him a kiss and looked him in the eye. "Come on . . . we need to get going, or we're going to be late."

After grabbing her handbag, Aurora walked over to the lounge room, where she found her son playing a game on his phone. "C'mon, Jonah. Let's get going."

The funeral was held at a local church minutes away from where they lived. Aurora and Mason weren't particularly religious. They only attended church on festive occasions like Christmas and Easter.

When Jonah and his parents arrived at the church and parked the car, Jonah observed that there weren't many vehicles in the car park. As such, he figured there would only be a small group of people in attendance at the funeral service. For Jonah, that was reasonable. From what he knew, Luke didn't have many friends, and as their family circle was small, he didn't expect a huge turnout.

As they got out of the car and approached the church, Jonah could hear lots of people talking from inside. To his surprise, Jonah noticed hundreds of people when he walked in. In fact, the church was almost full and it looked as if he and his parents would struggle to find somewhere to sit. However, they managed to find seats in the front row that were deliberately left empty for them.

As they approached their seats, Jonah was immediately greeted by the scent of flowers. Looking out toward the front of the church, he observed a sea of roses laid out on the floor. He couldn't believe how many flowers people had brought in and how gorgeous it was. Out of something so heartbreaking, Jonah was able to find something beautiful.

Jonah initially didn't recognize many people from the huge crowd of mourners, leaving him somewhat baffled. However, after he surveyed the crowd a few times, he spotted some familiar faces, including family friends and a few neighbors. Luke had gotten to know these people over the years while living with Mason and Aurora. Out of the people he could recognize were some close family friends, Lucy and Jordan, and their son, Max, who approached him.

"Hey, Jonah, I'm really sorry about your grandad." Max, who was of similar height, with brown hair and blue eyes, wrapped his arms around Jonah and gave him a consoling hug.

"Thanks, Max. I really appreciate it."

Max removed his arms and stepped back after a few seconds. Max was three years younger than Jonah and in his final year of high school. Jonah and Max were once good friends. As each of them was an only child and their parents were close, growing up together meant they'd formed a strong, brotherly bond. However, they started to drift apart when Jonah began college, and as such, they now saw much less of each other.

"How are you holding up?" Lucy asked with a gentle voice.

"I'm okay," Jonah said, even though he seemed withdrawn and not his usual self.

"We want you to know how sorry we are about your grandfather's passing. He was a wonderful man. We really are going to miss him." Lucy rubbed one of her hands on Jonah's shoulder.

Jonah noticed Lucy's blonde hair was tied up in a ponytail that day, and she wasn't wearing any makeup. It was unusual for Lucy, as she usually liked to leave her hair down and wear scorching-red lipstick.

"Thanks, Lucy. You too, Jordan. I'm glad you guys came today. It means a lot. Especially when I don't really know everyone here. It's kinda weird. I didn't realize Pops knew so many people."

"It just goes to show how much your grandfather was loved and what a good man he was. So many people chose to come and say goodbye to him. I hope you can take comfort in that," Jordan said.

"I really appreciate that, Jordan."

"You're gonna be all right, kid." Lucy gave Jonah a heartwarming smile.

She then grabbed Jonah and hugged him for quite some time while gently patting him on the back. Jonah could hear some of Lucy's bracelets rattling. Tears welled in her eyes during the embrace. Lucy thought about what it must be like for Jonah to lose his only living grandparent. Jonah adored Lucy and Jordan tremendously and treated them like family, as if they were his aunt and uncle. Their attendance at the funeral, along with Max's, was comforting for him and much appreciated.

When Lucy eventually let go of Jonah, she, Jordan, and Max gave their condolences to Mason and Aurora, who were grateful for their presence and heartwarming words. They had all been family friends for years. They often spent time together on weekends, whether at each other's homes for dinner or meals at a local restaurant. They had even vacationed together over the years and spent major holidays like Christmas and Thanksgiving together.

After chatting for a moment, everyone sat, at which point the minister came out and the funeral service began.

Jonah sat next to his parents and kept to himself. He was trying to process everything that had happened over the previous few days. During that period, he'd spent a lot of time in his room in deep mourning. Jonah wanted to believe that somehow it wasn't real; however, looking at the coffin on display and seeing his grandfather's lifeless body, which looked almost like a mannequin, made Jonah face reality. This made him even more despondent.

Mason got up during the service and delivered a heartfelt eulogy. He talked a little about Luke's life story and how Luke met Mason's mother, Evelyn.

"My father and mother met in 1972. My father was a carpenter; one day, he went to my grandparent's house to fix a broken floor. My mother was there. She was quite young at the time and had just started learning how to cook. She'd made a chocolate cake that day and offered some to my father when he had finished with the floor. I remember my father saying it was the worst cake he had ever eaten in his life."

The church erupted in laughter for a few seconds.

Mason continued, "But he did say to me that whatever she lacked in cooking ability at that time, she made up for it with her adorable smile, great sense of humor and joyful spirit, which melted his heart. He knew then and there that he wanted to marry her. And two years later, to the day, they did."

He went on to talk about how his parents started a family, as well as the life they had as Mason was growing up. In speaking, the unmistakable love he had for his father was evident to everyone in the church, especially during moments when he had to pause and hold back tears.

At the service conclusion, everyone in the church approached Mason, Aurora, and Jonah to give their condolences. The number of people who expressed sympathy for Luke's passing overwhelmed Jonah.

As people left the church, Jonah spotted many of them going through a side door. He assumed it was an exit. As it was all getting a bit too much for him, Jonah decided to step outside for a moment and get away from it all. He approached the side door and opened it, finding a small storage room filled with brooms, mops, and cleaning supplies. There were no other doors and only two small windows located high up the wall toward the ceiling. The windows were not large enough for anyone to fit through.

How could this be? Jonah thought to himself. He stood there for a moment, baffled. *All the people who came in earlier, where did they all go?*

Jonah walked into the room to double-check if there were any exits that led outside, which might have been overlooked. There weren't any. Jonah stood in the room for a few moments, perplexed.

"Hello!" Jonah called out. There was no response.

He then turned around, stepped out of the storage room, and closed the door behind him. After shrugging it off, Jonah walked back to his parents. By then, everyone had practically left, and it was time to leave the church.

"That's bizarre," Jonah said to himself.

"What's bizarre, Jonah?"

"Oh . . . never mind Mom. Let's go."

They walked out of the church and headed to the car park, where they all got into Aurora's car and drove home.

By the time they arrived home and walked into the house, they were all emotionally exhausted. Jonah went to his room and closed the door behind him. He had worn a suit and tie for the funeral. As soon as he shut his bedroom door, Jonah yanked on his tie and pulled it off. He quickly changed into something more comfortable and lay on his bed, thinking about the funeral and what a long day it was.

Jonah couldn't stop thinking about all the people that came to the service to pay their respects to his grandfather. He also wondered where all those people went whom he saw go into that little room with all the cleaning supplies.

A few moments later, there was a knock on his door. It was Aurora. She slowly opened the door and went into his room; she left the door open and sat next to Jonah on his bed.

"I just wanted to see how you were doing," Aurora said in a soft, nurturing tone.

"I don't know Mom. I'm sad, I guess. I'll be okay. I just need to be left alone."

"Your dad and I are here for you if you need anything." Aurora rubbed Jonah's right hand to comfort him. After a few seconds, Aurora got up from the bed and left the room, before she closed the door behind her.

Jonah rolled onto his side, facing away from the bedroom door. It was the first time in his life he had ever felt the loss of someone so close to him. When his grandmother died, Jonah was only two years old and didn't understand what was going on. Now, being much older, he understood the loss of his grandfather all too well. He didn't know how to deal with it and whether he would ever get over such a loss. He wanted to cry, but for some reason, he couldn't. Jonah didn't understand why. Surely, it was natural to cry and express that emotion if he was so sorrowful.

"How is he?" Mason asked Aurora as she entered the kitchen. Mason had just put on a pot of coffee and was waiting for the percolator to finish.

Aurora could smell the nutty aroma of fresh coffee being brewed as she walked in and thought it was perfect timing. After the emotionally draining day with the funeral service, a cup of coffee was just what she needed to unwind.

"Jonah seems okay on the surface, but I can tell he's hurting. I'm sure he'll be all right. I guess we need to give him some time and space."

"You know, things are going to change for him very quickly. I hope he can handle everything that's about to happen," Mason said.

Aurora looked at Mason with concern. "I don't know if he's ready. But, ready or not, he'll have to grow up fast and deal with the challenges ahead of him."

Mason poured his wife a cup of coffee and then another for himself. They both sat at the kitchen table, drinking their coffees in silence, pondering what would happen next. They were nervous for Jonah, but there wasn't much they could do apart from support him and help make the transition as easy as possible.

After Aurora and Mason finished their coffees, they went and sat in the lounge room and watched TV. They weren't particularly hungry that evening, so they didn't bother with dinner. Aurora checked on Jonah and asked if he wanted anything to eat, but he wasn't hungry either. After watching TV for a couple of hours, Mason and Aurora went to bed. Emotionally drained from everything that had happened that day, they weren't in the mood to do anything else.

CHAPTER 4

F or two days after the funeral, Jonah didn't attend university. He spent
the most of the time locked in his bedroom. During that period,
Jonah didn't drink alcohol, which did wonders for him. His mind seemed
sharper, and his face looked refreshed. He could now recite pi to fifty
decimal places. When he drank, he couldn't remember anything past ten
decimal places.

Aurora and Mason left him alone during his self-imposed sabbatical to
allow him some space. They didn't give him any grief about not attending
classes. They only interacted with Jonah when Aurora checked on him to
see if he wanted anything to eat. If he was hungry, he would briefly leave
his room and eat, then quickly return.

Three days after the funeral, Jonah woke early in the morning for some
unknown reason and couldn't get back to sleep. He decided to get up and
get ready for school. Jonah had a shower and put on some clean clothes. He
also combed his hair and sprayed some aftershave on, leaving him feeling
rejuvenated. Although he was still quite heartbroken over the passing of
his grandfather, he at least felt rested.

Jonah walked into the kitchen and managed to make some coffee. While
he wasn't much of a cook, he did know how to use the coffee machine.
As he poured himself a cup of coffee Aurora entered the kitchen, dressed
in her nightgown and robe. She was a little surprised to see Jonah already
awake and dressed. While Aurora walked toward the coffee machine, she

noticed Jonah's hair was wet and could smell wafts of the spicy aftershave he had sprayed on.

"You're up early," Aurora said.

"Yeah, I woke up a couple of hours ago and couldn't sleep again. I thought I'd drive to campus early and try and catch up on what I've missed over the last few days."

"I see you've also showered. That's a bit different." Aurora scoffed.

Jonah laughed. "Snap! You're on fire this morning."

"Did you want something to eat?"

"No thanks Mom, I'm just going to have some coffee."

Aurora went to the fridge and grabbed a loaf of bread. She put a few slices in the toaster for herself and grabbed some peanut butter from the pantry while she waited for the toast to finish.

"How are you feeling today, Jonah? Are you all right? You've been awfully quiet the last couple of days, and I'm worried about you."

"I'm fine, Mom. I'm still trying to get my head around everything that's happened."

"It's perfectly acceptable to be sad and to grieve. To show some emotion and even shed a few tears. I'm concerned you're holding everything in and not dealing with your grandfather's passing."

"I'll be all right. I just need a bit more time."

"Okay, Jonah. But talk to me if you need to. I'm always happy to listen."

"Yeah, I know, Mom."

"Here, let me give you a squishy hug." Aurora embraced Jonah, which was her way of letting him know she cared for him and that life would get better.

"That's enough now. I need to breathe." Jonah chuckled as he let go.

"At least you still have a sense of humor," Aurora said, as she walked over and collected her cooked slices of toast.

After he finished his coffee, Jonah grabbed his backpack and said good-bye to his mother, before he left the house and drove off to university.

Jonah was studying to become an aerospace engineer. From an early age, he had always been fascinated by airplanes. He would constantly read books about plane designs. Whenever Jonah was at an airport, he would sit at a window for as long as possible and watch planes taxi and land. He would often imagine being a pilot and then pretend to contact air traffic control centers to advise them of his approach toward the runway to land.

In the last few months, however, his interest began to wane. Jonah had met two new friends, Jason and Shane. They all attended the same university and were studying engineering. Initially, Jonah thought it was great, because he had met some like minded individuals.

However, Jason and Shane were heavy drinkers, which soon rubbed off on Jonah. As a result, he became more interested in partying and drinking rather than studying. Jonah's parents worried he was heading down a dark path due to Jason and Shane's bad influence.

When Jonah arrived on campus, he parked his car and began walking to the campus library. On the way, he spotted Jason and Shane and approached them to have a chat.

"Hey, Jonah, how's it going?" Jason asked.

"I'm all right," Jonah said with melancholy in his voice. "Had my grandfather's funeral a few days ago, so I've just been laying low at home ever since, not doing much."

"Well, the best cure for sadness is a party. In fact, there's one tonight. What do you say, Jonah?" Shane asked as he slapped Jonah on the back.

Jonah thought about it for a moment before responding. "I don't know. I'm really not in the mood to go out partying and—"

"Oh, hell yeah you are boy! Tonight, at ten, I'll pick you up," Jason said, as he and Shane walked off to their classes before Jonah could refuse their offer.

In truth, Jonah wanted to go home and have dinner that evening, put his pajamas on, curl up in bed, and watch TV. Subconsciously, he wanted some time and space away from his friends and the party scene he had become accustomed to lately. He wanted to cocoon himself and allow the healing process for his grandfather's loss to begin.

As Jason and Shane weren't going to take no for an answer, Jonah rolled his eyes and accepted his fate. He was going to a party that evening, whether he wanted to or not. He took a deep breath and continued on his way to the library.

The problem with Jason and Shane was that they would constantly think about the next party or club they could go to and drink the night away. Even though Jonah was only twenty and not allowed to drink legally, it didn't stop him from doing so using his fake ID. Being so young, they could drink until the early morning hours and somehow get to classes hours later with little sleep.

Generally, it wasn't that Jonah loved going to parties with Jason and Shane so much; it was more that he didn't want to be left out of the group. He just wanted to feel like he belonged somewhere. Like he was part of "the boys."

Later that evening, Jonah was at home in his room, playing on his phone, while waiting for Jason and Shane. Then, without warning, he heard the rev of an engine as Jason's car pulled up. Seconds later, he saw a text message come through on his phone. The message was from Shane, telling him to come out quickly. Jonah texted him back immediately to say he was on his way.

So he wouldn't wake his parents, he quietly and swiftly walked to the front door and opened it gently; Jonah stepped out of the house and slowly closed the door behind him. Running to Jason's car, he jumped in, and they drove off.

About twenty minutes later, they arrived at the party. The house where the party was being held brimmed with young college students. Loud music played in the background as all three of them walked inside. Jonah stopped just past the entrance and took stock of what was happening. In one room, a group of young guys played drinking games to find out who could drink the most shots before passing out. In another room, people were dancing. The rest of the house, meanwhile, was littered with lots of couples passionately kissing.

The three classmates stood inside the house surveying the scene.

"Over here, guys." Jason spotted some alcohol and led his two friends to where the drinking games were.

"Tequila! Hello, my old friend . . . You guys want a shot?" Jonah asked as he started pouring himself a shot.

"Line them up!" Shane demanded.

Jonah poured some more shots and gave one to each of his friends. They simultaneously gulped them down, and once they recovered from the burning sensation of the alcohol running down their throats, all three slammed the shot glasses onto a table. They gave each other high-fives.

"Next!" Jason shouted, waiting for Jonah to pour more shots.

Jonah's short-lived dry spell was now officially over.

The drinking continued, with one shot after the other being swallowed in quick succession. They lost count of how many they drank. After they finished with the shots, soon after came the beer. Within an hour of being there, all three had degenerated into a drunken stupor. As they continued to drink nonsensically, they laughed hysterically for most of the night and talked trash to each other to pass the time.

Two other friends of Shane, Chris and Elijah, arrived at this time and sat down with the group. Jonah had met them a handful of times during previous outings but didn't know them very well.

"Did you leave any Tequila for us?" Elijah asked in jest as he walked up behind Shane and patted him on the shoulder.

"I'm sure there's a few drops left!" Shane shouted back, slurring.

The whole group laughed as Elijah poured himself and Chris some shots. Elijah was eager to catch up to Shane, Jonah, and Jason.

An hour later, Shane walked away from the group to find the bathroom. Along the way, he walked into a bedroom by mistake. He looked around the bedroom for a moment and saw a Wonder Woman outfit lying on a chairback. The guy hosting the party had a younger sister who had gone to a costume party the previous week dressed as Wonder Woman. After looking at the outfit for a few moments, Shane came up with an idea.

Shane turned back and stumbled out of the room as quickly as he could, heading back towards his friends. When he reached them, Jason and Jonah were both drinking and talking, before he grabbed them both by their arms and dragged them into the bedroom.

"What the hell! Why did you drag me in here?" Jonah asked

"Don't ask questions!" Shane screamed back.

Standing in the bedroom, Jonah took notice of a bed in front of him. As he was feeling a little nauseous and lightheaded, he decided to climb onto the mattress and lie down. Within seconds, he passed out and began snoring.

"He is so wasted," Jason said.

"I've got an idea. Let's dress him up as Wonder Woman!" Shane said.

Jason was confused. "Wonder Woman?"

"Yeah, look!" Shane pointed out the Wonder Woman outfit.

Jason laughed. "You're an idiot, but I like it."

"Then we'll put on him on the couch in the lounge room for everyone to admire his sexy legs," Shane said.

Jason, like Shane, thought it would be equally funny, so they went about undressing Jonah and adorned him with the Wonder Woman costume. The two found it challenging at times, as Jonah was tossing and turning a little, even though Jonah had no sense of what was going on.

Once they'd finished dressing him up, Jason grabbed some cherry lipstick he found on the dressing table and covered Jonah's lips in a thick layer of it. Jason also applied lipstick around Jonah's mouth to make his lips look similar to a clown's. He stepped back to admire his work while Shane pulled his phone out of his pocket and took a few photos to post on social media.

"I've got another idea. Let's take him to the football field and leave him in the middle of the grounds," Jason said.

"That's messed up." Shane paused for a moment. "Let's do it!"

With the help of Chris and Elijah, Shane and Jason carried Jonah from the house and into Jason's car. They all jumped into the car along with Jonah and drove to a football field at their college campus, which was only a short drive from the party. All four of them managed to haul Jonah to the middle of the football field. It was a full moon that night and a clear sky, making a spectacle of all the stars in the universe. The football field had a few lights on, so they could see where they were going. After dropping Jonah off, Shane pulled out his cell phone again and took some more photos before they all ran back to the car. Leaving Jonah behind, they drove off and headed back to the party.

Meanwhile, back at Jonah's house, Aurora and Mason were sound asleep in their bedroom. Suddenly, there was a flash of light in the room, and a figure appeared before them. At that moment, Aurora and Mason both awoke from their sleep and saw Guardian Ezra—a stocky man in his mid-fifties with silver-gray hair and a beard—standing at the end of their bed. The pair weren't shocked to see him; it was as if they already knew who he was and why he was there.

"I've just spoken with the Grand Guardian. She said it's time for Jonah's transition," Ezra said. Aurora and Mason jumped out of bed, put on their wardrobe generators—metallic band bracelets that clothe people—and changed into their teal-colored Concordian robes.

Aurora walked to Jonah's bedroom to wake him up. When she saw Jonah wasn't there, she ran back to her room in a panic.

"He's not in his room!"

"I spoke to Wyatt at the Observatory just before I arrived here. He showed me where Jonah is. I can guide you both there," Ezra said.

Within moments, Ezra, Mason and Aurora teleported to where Jonah was. He was right where Jason and Shane had left him minutes earlier.

"What the hell is he wearing!" Ezra said, dumbfounded.

Looking down, Ezra could see smeared lipstick on Jonah's face as he slept peacefully. The silver stars on the blue skirt of his Wonder Woman outfit sparkled in the moonlight.

"Are you sure it's him?" Ezra continued to look over Jonah, lying in the middle of the football field.

Mason approached Jonah; after he stared at him for a few seconds, he sighed and rolled his eyes. "Yes. It's him, all right."

"Good grief! I gather he's had a few too many drinks tonight. For everyone's sake, let's just go with that, shall we?" Ezra shook his head.

Aurora, perturbed by Jonah's condition, wasn't sure whether she wanted to laugh or smack her son's head.

"All right, then. Well, I'm glad it's you who has to train him and not me." Ezra laughed.

As Ezra spoke, he raised his left arm, which made Jonah's body levitate. He grabbed Jonah's right hand, and within moments, they both teleported away to a different dimension. Aurora and Mason followed him in quick succession.

CHAPTER 5

J onah had been asleep for many hours. As he awoke, he immediately
felt heaviness in his head, alongside an excruciating headache. The first
thing Jonah noticed as he opened his eyes was the unfamiliar surroundings.
He could tell he was in a room, but it wasn't at home; he couldn't recognize
where, though. Jonah tried to remember what had happened the night
before, but he struggled to do so.

As he looked around, Jonah could see he was lying on a bed; however,
the pillow and sheets felt different. They felt softer and more luxurious as
though he was staying at an expensive hotel.

Jonah shut his eyes again. Brief flashbacks of going to some party with his
friends Jason and Shane began flooding his mind. He also recalled drinking a considerable amount of alcohol with them but couldn't remember
anything past that.

As he opened his eyes once more, Jonah took another look at his surroundings, trying desperately to think where he could be.

Familiar voices whispered in the background of the room. Jonah tried
focusing on the conversation but couldn't quite make out what was being
said. Soon enough, he recognized it was his parents.

"Mom, is that you?" Jonah asked with a strained voice.

The sound of his voice hurt his head even more. As he spoke, Jonah tried
to lift his head but couldn't due to the unbearable pain.

"Hey, Jonah, how are you feeling, honey?" Aurora asked as she walked toward her son and sat next to him on his bed. Mason followed suit and stood beside her.

"I feel awful." Jonah strained to look at Aurora as he held a hand to his head. He felt drained. A few seconds later, he put his hand down away from his head and looked at his mother again, and then his father. "Why are you both wearing onesies?"

Mason and Aurora both chuckled.

"These aren't onesies, Jonah," Mason said. "These are robes, and it's customary to wear these robes here in Concordia."

"They sure look like onesies to me," Jonah said flippantly. "What . . . Concordia. What did you say?"

"Son, do you really think you should be making fun of our clothes right now, considering how you're dressed? Have you looked at yourself lately?" Mason asked.

Jonah looked at himself and saw he was dressed as Wonder Woman. His face grimaced and went red as he pulled a blanket over him. He was lost for words. Jonah had no idea how he'd ended up in those clothes. Aurora giggled at Jonah's abashment.

"And where did you say we were again?"

"Concordia." Aurora paused briefly to give Jonah a chance to comprehend her words, then handed him a big glass of water. "There's a lot we need to explain to you, but I think you need to sober up first because you're going to need a clear head. The best way to sober up right now is to drink plenty of water. So, drink up."

Jonah drank the water as his head was held up with one of Aurora's hands. With each sip he took, Jonah became thirstier. Water had never tasted so good to him before; he guzzled it down within a matter of seconds.

"That was great. Can I get some more, please?" Jonah said as he took a few deep breaths and handed the cup to his mother.

"You actually said 'please' for once. In that case, of course, you can." Aurora gave her son a warm smile as she got up from the bed to refill the cup.

While she was getting more water from an adjoining bathroom, Jonah noticed the room was very unusual. The bed he was lying on had a rounded shape and floated about a foot off the ground. It wasn't a typical mattress like he was accustomed to; however, it was very comfortable. He also saw that the room had holographic images on the walls, littered with information. Jonah started to wonder if he was hallucinating or perhaps in a dream.

Aurora gave Jonah the glass of water, which he drank until he felt full.

"Have you got any painkillers, Mom?"

"No, I don't, honey. How about you rest up and let your body recover naturally? That will help clear your head."

"Okay," Jonah said as he lay down and fell asleep again.

Jonah slept for a few more hours and woke up again. He felt a lot better, and his headache was almost gone. He sat up on the bed and saw his parents were standing on the other end of the room. They noticed he had awakened and walked toward him. Clearheaded, Jonah began to wonder where he was. This was definitely not his room, and he certainly wasn't at home.

"Are you feeling better?" Mason asked.

"Yes, Dad, definitely feeling a lot better. But I need the bathroom, though."

Mason pointed Jonah in the direction of the bathroom, which directly adjoined his room. A few minutes later, he returned with a perplexed look on his face.

"This place is weird. Where did you say we were again?"

"Concordia," Aurora said.

"Concordia? Is this place some expensive hotel or something? Or a retreat? Do they have massages here? Mom, I could really use one right now."

Mason and Aurora briefly grinned at Jonah's response before they glanced at each other and then looked back at Jonah.

"Son, this might be a little difficult for you to understand but . . ." Mason said.

"But what, Dad?"

"You see, we are no longer on Earth. We're actually in another dimension," Mason said.

"Okaaay. . ."

At this point, Jonah thought it was some elaborate joke, or he was in some peculiar dream. After a moment, he could see from the look on his parents' faces that they weren't joking. He grew a little nervous and felt his heart racing.

"Are you serious? What exactly do you mean when you say this is 'another dimension'?" Jonah asked.

"Look, Jonah, I know this might sound like science fiction, but here's the thing—there's an infinite number of parallel universes that exist," Mason said. "And many of them are similar to the one you've lived in all your life. Each one is a little bit different and unique. Perhaps in another universe you aren't going to university to study engineering. Maybe you're training to be a pilot. Remember when you were a kid, and you loved planes and you'd go 'Wooshi Wooshi! Wooshi Wooshi!'?"

Mason put his arms up, perpendicular to his body, and pretended to be a plane and fly around the room.

"Dad, now is not a time for Wooshi Wooshi!"

Aurora laughed and turned her head away from Jonah to avoid laughing in his direction.

"Okay, Jonah, so no Wooshi Wooshi. But going back to the different dimensions concept—this one we're in right now is called Concordia. It's the center point of all parallel universes. What that means is you have Concordia right in the middle, and it's surrounded by millions of other dimensions with their own universes."

"Okaaay. . ."

Jonah's jaw slackened, and his eyes were wide open, staring in disbelief.

"What it all boils down to is this: our sole purpose here is to protect all parallel universes from being invaded by evil entities, known as Infringers. Do you understand?" Mason asked.

"Aaaa . . . no!" Jonah looked bewildered.

He struggled to come to grips with what his father had just told him. Deep down, he understood what Mason was saying but refused to believe it. How did he and his parents end up in some other dimension?

"Jonah, I know it's a lot to take in," Mason continued. "And it's probably a little overwhelming. It was for me when my parents had to explain all of this. But in time—"

"Your parents? Your parents had to explain this to you? You mean Pops was from this place, too?"

"Yes, he was. As was your grandmother and your mother's parents as well," Mason calmly explained.

Jonah stopped speaking and thought about that for a moment. His mind went back to Luke's funeral.

"Now it all makes sense, all those people from Pop's funeral that I didn't recognize. Were most of them from here?" Jonah asked as he started pacing around the room.

"Yes, many of them were Concordians. Some were from Earth as well," Aurora said.

As Jonah cast his mind back to the funeral, he thought about the moment after the service had concluded, when he had decided to get some fresh air and be alone.

"You know what I found odd?" Jonah asked his parents. "When a whole bunch of those people went into a storage room. I thought it was an exit, but when I went inside, I discovered it was a storage room with no exit door. I found it strange at the time and couldn't figure out where they all went. Now I'm starting to realize that they had disappeared into some other dimension."

"Yes, that's right. They would have all come back here to Concordia," Aurora said.

"It's true," Mason said. "They were all Concordians. In our family, we come from a long line of Concordians as well. Although we were all born on Earth, we have been charged with protecting and upholding the utmost greater good of all parallel universes in existence."

"Oh, okay! Is that all?" Jonah quipped. He stopped speaking for a moment and continued pacing the room a little before taking a deep breath.

"So, you're saying we *are* human. But at the same time, we're part of some cult protecting the universe? A cult. Oh my God! Are we part of a cult?"

"We're not part of a cult, Jonah! Get it together, kid!" Aurora took Jonah by the shoulders and shook him momentarily. She then took a moment to calm down before almost laughing at the suggestion that they were part of a cult. "We are Guardians of Concordia. We protect and serve all universes. I assure you, it's far above and beyond any cult you could ever imagine. It's an extraordinary responsibility, in every which way you can imagine. And now that your grandfather is no longer with us, you must take his place as a Guardian. It is your duty."

"My duty! You can't tell me it's my duty! I never asked for this! No one told me I had to become a Guardian!" Jonah paused for a moment to think. "Now riddle me this my darling mama—what if I don't want to become a Guardian?"

"But you have to; it's your duty and your birthright," Aurora said.

Jonah felt like he was being backed into a corner. His stomach sank.

"And by the way, if Grandpa was a Guardian, how come he died?"

"Because we aren't immortal, Jonah," Aurora said. "You need to remember we're from Earth, which means we still have human weaknesses. Although we have special powers, we can still become sick and get wounds, and we can die."

"Mom, what do you mean we have 'special powers'?"

"We'll get to that a bit later," Mason said.

"So, Dad, how did we get here then?"

"We teleported you here," Mason said.

"Teleported?" Jonah scrunched his eyes at what Mason had suggested.

"Let me show you, Son."

Mason grabbed Jonah's arm. In an instant, they both disappeared. They were back on Earth, in their home's kitchen. Jonah didn't know what to say or think. A moment later, Mason and Jonah disappeared again, back to Jonah's room in Concordia. Aurora was still there, standing where she had been before they left.

After they returned, Jonah sat on the bed with his hands to his head. Not only was he overwhelmed, but he felt a little nauseous from the teleportation and needed a moment for his stomach to settle down.

He didn't want to believe any of this was true. Up to this point in his life, Jonah had thought he was a normal young man—just a typical college student who liked to party and drink with his friends, listen to music, spend hours online, and study engineering every now and then. Now, suddenly, he was some Concordian being that had to protect the universe?

Jonah needed time to process everything. He already had enough on his plate. Like many young men his age, he was trying to complete his studies and balance his social life. At the same time, he endeavored to tackle his way through life and the world at large, seeking to "fit in" while also trying to process the grief of losing his grandfather. And now this. How was he to make any sense of it all and try and function as a hybrid Human-Concordian being?

Aurora and Mason looked at Jonah as he put his hands down and looked back at them, feeling a little lost. Both of them understood Jonah's unease with everything that was going on. They, too, had felt unnerved when this was all revealed to them many years before and could sympathize with him.

"So, what now?" Jonah asked.

"Well, let's get you out of those clothes and cleaned up; I've got a wardrobe generator for you to put on and use," Aurora said as she handed Jonah the wardrobe generator. "Then we can show you around Concordia, and you can see what an amazing place this is."

"Mom, what exactly is a wardrobe generator?"

"You fit it around your wrist like a watch." Aurora pointed to Jonah's left wrist. The wardrobe generator was a metallic wristband with a digital display. "Press the button on the front. Within moments, it will clothe you in your Concordian robe. In fact, it can clothe you in just about any form of clothing you can think of. You just need to learn how to utilize its more advanced features. For now, let's just use it for your Concordian robe. Okay?"

Jonah walked into the adjoining bathroom with the wardrobe generator, removed his Wonder Woman outfit, and showered. The bathroom was quite different from the ones he used on Earth. It was grand and elaborate, yet very futuristic. There were no taps that needed to be turned on. As he stepped into the shower cubicle, the water started running immediately and was at the perfect temperature. The water, although similar to Earth's, felt softer and purer. It didn't have any harsh chemical smells of fluoride or chlorine like the water on Earth. It somehow smelled sweeter. In fact, it was so cleansing that he didn't need to use soap to wash himself. The water was more than ample.

Jonah cleansed his body and washed all the lipstick off his face. He spent some time in the shower, partly because the water was so warm and comfortable and partly because it helped him sober up. Jonah eventually had enough and stepped out of the shower cubicle. The water switched off by itself. He took a deep breath and felt so awake and reinvigorated. It was unlike any other shower he'd ever taken.

As Jonah stood there feeling energized, he tried to find a towel to dry himself with. At that point, a machine, seemingly out of nowhere, appeared and hovered over his head: a body dryer. Jonah stood for a moment, frightened and alarmed, not knowing what to do next. It formed a force field around his body, followed by an intense wind that blew the moisture off him and onto the force field. The body dryer then sucked up all the water, and once finished, the force field and body dryer disappeared. After a few seconds, he had a chuckle and marveled at how well the machine dried his body.

Jonah grabbed the wardrobe generator and placed it on his wrist while standing naked in front of the bathroom mirror. The strap stuck to his wrist like a magnet, which he could barely feel on his skin. Jonah pressed the button on the generator like Aurora had told him to. Within milliseconds, a robe grew over him and covered his naked body from head to toe. It started as a small patch on his left arm, which expanded to the rest of his arm, his chest, and his right arm, then continued on to cover his torso, waist, and legs.

Once he was fully clothed, Jonah grinned. He couldn't believe what he had seen. It was magic. The robe, which was teal in color and resembled a long Indian kurta that went all the way to his ankles, fitted him perfectly, and accentuated his well-toned body. It wasn't exactly skintight but was tight fitting with sleeves that had a slit running through the middle. He rubbed his hands over his arms and chest. The robe felt so comfortable, almost like velvet. It was identical to his parents' robes. He didn't feel hot or cold wearing it. The wardrobe generator had a special quality, whereby it helped with heat regulation so that whoever was wearing the garment, stayed at a comfortable body temperature.

Jonah eventually stepped out of the bathroom and walked back into his room. Mason and Aurora looked at Jonah and both smiled. They admired how angelic Jonah appeared. He had a sweet, innocent smile which Aurora adored—it had been a while since she had seen her son with such a smile. In that moment, Jonah melted her heart.

"Jonah, repeat after me. Hello, Amica," Aurora said.

"Hello, Amica," Jonah repeated with a confused look on his face. "Who's Amica?"

"Good morning, Jonah. I'm Amica," a loud voice responded, which could be heard throughout the entire room.

"Hi. Who are you?" Jonah asked as he spun around, trying to find the person who was speaking.

"I'm Amica, an artificial intelligence system. I'm voice-activated and can assist you with a whole range of things from switching off the lights in your room to answering any general knowledge questions from any planet in any universe. Just ask me a question whenever you want, and I will help as best I can."

"Amica, can you make the windows transparent?" Aurora asked.

"Of course."

"Thank you, Amica," Aurora said.

"You're welcome."

Within seconds, the windows—which were pitch-black—became crystal clear, allowing an instant burst of radiant morning sun to light up Jonah's room, which was previously softly lit. Jonah's eyes squinted against the light; he covered them with one of his arms until his eyes were able to adjust. Then he stepped forward and approached the windows to see what was outside.

Jonah saw the skyline of a futuristic city light years more advanced than anything he ever remembered seeing back home. Nothing on Earth compared to what he could see before him. Buildings constructed of metal and glass were all interconnected with intriguing patterns. Some of the buildings were triangular in shape, while others were conical or circular.

Some of them sparkled like diamonds against the morning sun. Now, he couldn't wait to go and explore the land.

"Wow! Let's get the hell out of here!"

Mason and Aurora laughed. They couldn't wait to show him the rest of Concordia. Now that Jonah looked like a Concordian, he was ready to venture out of his room. As he stepped out, his parents looked at each other with glee; they were thrilled the day had arrived. Although Jonah had a long journey ahead of him to completely actualize his role as a Guardian, there was an inner knowing in both parents that Jonah would eventually settle into Concordia.

CHAPTER 6

As Jonah walked around Concordia, he observed its breathtaking architecture with a never-ending array of interconnected buildings that seemed to continue for miles. As an engineering student, he was fascinated by cutting-edge structures. The buildings were a combination of what appeared to be glass and metal, which reflected the majesty of the sun. The Concordian sun was similar to the one Jonah was accustomed to on Earth—brilliant, warming, and soothing.

Surrounding all the buildings were beautiful lakes and waterfalls that continued infinitely around Concordia in alluring patterns. The water was radiant and pristine. Alongside countless trees, Concordia had the most astonishing flowers and vegetation Jonah had ever set eyes on. Their colors were remarkably vibrant with different shades of yellow, orange, red, and blue.

Jonah, who normally wasn't all that interested in nature, touched a flower and smelled it. It had an incredible aroma. So much so that he remained there for some time repeatedly smelling it. Jonah couldn't satisfy his craving for that scent. To Jonah, the smell was an unusual mixture of citrus, cinnamon, and caramel with a hint of peanut butter. He lifted one up to his mouth, as the peanut butter scent made him hungry. However, Jonah thought twice about it in case it was poisonous. Being in a different dimension, he wasn't too certain.

After he finished smelling the flowers, Jonah looked at the sky. Few clouds billowed overhead. The sky was a brilliant mauve color with hints of deep purple on the horizon. It was extraordinarily pristine, unlike the polluted skies back on Earth. Jonah was so captivated by Concordia's beauty that he realized this place wasn't so bad.

As Jonah continued walking around with Mason and Aurora, he encountered a large building which looked like a state-of-the-art gymnasium. He glimpsed inside and observed several people doing some sort of martial arts training. Wearing clothes similar to spandex, some learned to fight using just their bare arms, while others learned using electrically charged batons. The batons could throw someone from one end of the building to the other with the slightest touch.

"What are they doing there?" Jonah asked. "Why are they fighting?"

"Every Guardian here in Concordia has to learn how to fight," Aurora said.

"But why?"

"Well, Jonah, sometimes we have to go on missions—"

"What sort of missions?"

"These missions we go on, to put it simply, are to help protect one dimension from being invaded by another," Aurora said. "Remember how we mentioned Infringers earlier? When they invade a dimension, our encounters with them sometimes turn into battles and can get physical. And we need to be ready so that we can fight back."

"Oh, I see." Jonah began to feel uneasy.

Although he was in reasonably good shape, Jonah wasn't much of a fighter and worried he could get seriously hurt. He didn't realize that was part of the deal. When Aurora had mentioned that being a Guardian meant protecting and serving all universes, he didn't understand. Now, Jonah felt a little uneasy. He tried to conceal his concern; however, Aurora could see by the stunned look on his face that this was making him anxious.

"But don't worry about it just yet. You have other things to learn first." Aurora wrapped one arm around Jonah's shoulders, giving him a reassuring hug. Not that her embrace made Jonah feel any better.

As Jonah and his parents continued strolling through Concordia, Aurora and Mason suddenly stopped walking. Jonah looked at his parents, who had tilted their heads slightly, trying hard to focus. It was as if they were listening to a distant sound. He couldn't understand what was going on initially. Jonah also noticed everyone else in the vicinity had halted what they were doing. A small group of people, who were talking a few feet away, had stopped.

Attention all Concordians. Please report to the Council Stadium immediately for a General Assembly.

Jonah was unable to hear the communication. Soon after the broadcast, everyone headed toward the Council Stadium.

"What's going on?" Jonah asked.

"We've just received a telepathic message from Ezra instructing us to go to the Council Stadium. So, we need to head over there now. And that includes you, Jonah," Mason said.

"Okay. You can hear telepathic messages?" Jonah asked, intrigued by the idea.

"Yes, we can," Aurora said as they hurried toward the Council Stadium. "We'll explain later."

General Assemblies were held regularly in Concordia. These were sometimes used to discuss routine Concordian matters. However, most of the time, they were used to communicate any breaches in interdimensional travel and plans to combat those breaches.

Jonah and his parents arrived at the stadium. It was about a ten-minute walk from where Jonah was staying. The stadium was centrally located with a Community Center nearby. Jonah could see a river running beside it that headed toward some mountains in the distance.

Once inside the stadium, they walked for a short while until they found somewhere to sit. As Jonah looked around, he noticed that although it looked like the modern stadiums he had seen on Earth with thick concrete blocks, there were large, protruding squares built into the walls. From a distance, they resembled square fish scales that were able to flip backward and forward in a synchronous, wave-like pattern throughout the entire stadium. Jonah's head tried to follow the wave around the stadium until he eventually got dizzy and had to sit down.

After they all sat and Jonah had overcome his vertigo, he spotted his parents' friends, Lucy and Jordan, seated farther away. They waved at Jonah, and he waved back, as did Aurora and Mason. Jonah was in disbelief.

"Lucy and Jordan are Guardians as well?" Jonah turned to his parents with his mouth wide open.

"Yes, they are," Mason said.

Aurora giggled when she observed Jonah's stunned look.

Jonah thought about it for a moment, and as he did, it all started to make sense. He realized why his parents were so close to Lucy and Jordan on Earth. As he thought about it, Lucy and Jordan approached him. Jonah and his parents stood.

"You made it, kid!" Lucy blurted out with a huge smile. She gave Jonah a big, welcoming hug and laughed. "We all knew this day would come. And now, here you are! And you look so darn cute in the robe."

"Doesn't he?" Aurora squealed.

"Absolutely!" Lucy shouted in agreement as she stared at Jonah in adoration. "Now, come on, give us all a big spin!"

She made Jonah twirl so she could take a good look at him. Jonah wasn't a big fan of the attention and felt a little uncomfortable.

"Can everyone stop looking at me now?" Jonah asked, trying to divert attention away from himself.

"Oooh . . . I think the ladies over here are going to like you a lot, young man!" Lucy laughed.

Jonah, being a little shy, went visibly red in the face. Mason and Aurora laughed. They knew what Lucy's sense of humor was like, which was mostly harmless and always in good fun, so they were never offended by her actions.

Jordan, on the other hand, rolled his eyes. He understood Lucy couldn't help herself and could sometimes get carried away. Yet Lucy's boisterous nature was one of the qualities Jordan loved so much about her and found so charming.

Jonah tried to change the subject. "I had no idea you two were also from here. I'm so confused right now."

"It's a little overwhelming, for sure," Jordan said. "You just need to give it some time for it all to sink in. You don't need to worry. Trust me. You'll settle into Concordia in no time. Lucy and I are always here for you if you need anything. And I promise I won't spin you around every time I see you."

Lucy smiled at Jordan's tongue-in-cheek mockery, knowing his sense of humor could sometimes be a little dry.

Jonah found the banter between the two quite endearing. His own parents, although they loved each other very much, didn't have the light-hearted approach to life Jordan and Lucy had. This was one reason Jonah was so fond of them and thought of them as his own family.

"Thanks so much, Jordan. I really appreciate that," Jonah said.

"You're welcome, Jonah. By the way, Max doesn't know about any of this just yet. He's still in the dark about Concordia. So please don't say anything to him if you ever see him. At least, not for now."

"Oh, okay. Of course, Jordan. I didn't even think of that."

"Anyhow, it was great to see you. And welcome to Concordia! We'll catch up with you later." Lucy waved goodbye as she and Jordan walked back to their seats.

Jonah and his parents sat again. Jonah spent a few moments looking around the stadium. It astonished him how magnificent and grandiose it was. The colossal building could fit hundreds of thousands of people. One end of the stadium had a stage close to where Jonah and his parents were seated. In the middle of the stage were some opulent chairs reserved for Executive Council members.

Within a matter of minutes, the stadium had reached full capacity. However, people continued to pile in. Jonah looked around and noticed there were no seats left. He wondered where they were going to sit. As soon as he thought that, the stadium started growing. The walls began expanding in length, making a rumbling noise as they grew. As they did, more seats became available so new people coming into the stadium could be seated. Jonah's eyes blew wide open. His parents looked at him and chuckled.

There is so much for Jonah to learn, Mason said to Aurora telepathically. *I know. And this is just the beginning,* Aurora responded.

After some time, the Executive Council entered the stadium—from an entrance on Jonah's left side—and took their places on the stage. Everyone became quiet and stood to attention. Grand Guardian Omiya, Concordia's ruler, was the last to step up onto the stage. She immediately approached the podium.

From the moment Jonah first looked at her, her regal manner mesmerized him. Her robe was different from everyone else's, being crimson in color. She wore a headpiece identical in color, resembling an isicholo, adorned with various precious stones like rubies and diamonds. The Grand Guardian's hair was a dark color with a few strands of gray running through it, from what Jonah could ascertain out of the small patch of hair that wasn't covered up. When Jonah looked at her face, he could tell she was in her mid-fifties by the lines around her eyes and on her cheeks.

The Grand Guardian's eyes, however, were her most distinguishing feature. They were dark in color—complementing her exquisite dark skin—and piercing in nature. With her regal stance, her eyes connected with the audience. She commanded respect. Everyone in the Council Stadium obliged without question before the Grand Guardian began to speak.

"Please be seated," Grand Guardian Omiya began. "I welcome everyone to this General Assembly. Today we begin with some very sad news. A few days ago, one of our beloved Concordians transitioned out of his physical form and began his journey into ascension. He was our much beloved Luke Michaels. To his son, Mason, his daughter-in-law, Aurora, and his grandson, Jonah, who are with us today, we offer our condolences and deepest sympathies on behalf of the Executive Council and all of Concordia. Words alone cannot mend your broken hearts right now. Please know his presence will be deeply missed."

As Jonah sat in his chair, he listened intently to Grand Guardian Omiya's calming words. He became emotional and put his head down, trying to hold back tears, hoping no one would see him—especially the Grand Guardian. The loss of his grandfather was still raw.

"There are many things Luke accomplished during his physical incarnation that we can celebrate. I hope you can take comfort in that." The Grand Guardian looked at Mason and Aurora. "To pay our respects, we will now have a moment's silence to honor his memory."

The Grand Guardian signaled with her arms for everyone to stand up. A loud shuffling noise reverberated throughout the stadium before it became quiet again. Mason's eyes welled up with tears. He was touched that the

Grand Guardian had chosen to honor his father's memory. Aurora, who stood next to Mason, gently grabbed his hand to comfort him.

"Long live his memory!" Grand Guardian Omiya shouted, concluding the period of silence. She turned and looked toward Mason, Aurora, and Jonah, then bowed her head at them, as a mark of respect. In return, Mason and Aurora bowed their heads.

"Long live his memory!" the entire stadium shouted in unison.

An overwhelming wave of tranquility immediately filled the stadium.

"Please be seated," the Grand Guardian said.

As everyone sat again, Grand Guardian Omiya moved on to the next agenda item: Jonah's empowerment ceremony.

The Grand Guardian looked at Jonah. "As we all know, according to Concordian custom, when someone leaves us, it's necessary for them to be replaced. Today, Luke's grandson, Jonah Michaels, will take his place as a Guardian. A role filled with immense responsibility. For this to happen, he must undergo the empowerment ceremony. I will now ask Jonah to come up onto the stage."

Jonah raised his eyebrows in surprise. He wasn't prepared for this moment. Clearly, it was something his parents had neglected to tell him.

"Go on, Jonah. You can't keep the Grand Guardian waiting," Aurora leaned over and whispered to Jonah.

Jonah hesitated for a few seconds. After a little coaxing, he stood and walked to the stage. As he approached the Grand Guardian, the eyes of the entire stadium were focused on him.

"It's okay. There's no need to be scared," the Grand Guardian said with a gentle smile. Her eyes, which Jonah found so piercing, were now very comforting and helped to allay his fears. "Jonah, this is a most important day, not just for Concordia but also for you. You'll now be given the powers you need to carry out your duties as a Guardian. This is a great responsibility and one I hope you will take on with great pride and devotion. Do you agree to take on such an enormous responsibility?"

Jonah didn't know what to say. He paused for a moment and looked at the Grand Guardian blankly. Jonah turned to his parents and stared at them briefly before looking at the entire stadium of people glaring at him, waiting for his answer.

Drawing his shoulders, Jonah answered, "Yes." There was a slight hesitation in his voice. With everyone in the stadium focused on him, he felt he had no choice. The truth was he *did* have a choice. He didn't have to accept his powers or his role as a Guardian. However, something inside of him told him to go ahead with it anyway. Jonah had an inner knowing that compelled him to accept the Grand Guardian's offer. A knowing that it was the right decision for him to make.

The Grand Guardian smiled at Jonah after he finished speaking. She raised her hand and put it on Jonah's head. Her hand glowed and grew brighter. The energy in the Grand Guardian's hand pulsated throughout Jonah's body, causing him to shine and convulse. This lasted for several seconds; it filled the entire stadium with light and ended with a thunderous sound. Jonah passed out and collapsed on stage.

Jonah was unconscious for a short while before waking. He initially felt confused and thought he might have been dreaming; once he saw the Guardian-filled stadium, he remembered where he was.

Mason, who was on the stage by this point, helped Jonah get back up. Jonah remained dazed for a brief period but managed to regain his balance. He felt a little different and sensed a strange energy pulsating through his body—one he'd never experienced before. Jonah wasn't sure what to do. As Mason supported him to stand upright on stage, the entire stadium stood and cheered for him.

"Long live Jonah!" they chanted in unison, repeatedly.

While Jonah stood on the stage, the audience could see the Concordian emblem tattooed on his neck. The emblem tingled on Jonah's neck for a brief period while he was standing. Every Concordian had the tattoo emblazoned on them during their empowerment ceremony automatically. It was only visible to other Concordians—it was an identifying marker used amongst Concordians to recognize each other, which was sometimes useful in battle. It was a brilliant blue color that shimmered brightly, resembling a mathematical infinity symbol.

Mason and Aurora decided to teleport Jonah out of the stadium and take him to his room, so he could rest and adapt to his new powers. Having gone through the process many years before, they both knew how Jonah felt and what he needed to recover. They also understood he would need a bit of training to understand his powers and how to use them. This was going to fall on Mason and Aurora to deliver. The two Guardians would act as Jonah's mentors.

"I feel so weird after that ceremony, like I have electricity running through my veins," Jonah said as he lay on his bed.

"You need to take it easy, Son. Now that your powers have been unlocked, you'll feel like you want to fire lightning bolts out of your hands," Mason said.

"What do you mean my 'powers have been unlocked?' What powers do I have?"

"Jonah, you've had powers from the day you were born," Aurora said. "All Guardians do. Your powers were locked down soon after you were born until Grand Guardian Omiya unlocked them for you now. In fact, it was the Grand Guardian who locked them in the first place. This was done so you wouldn't accidentally use your powers until you were ready. Now that you finally know who you are and your true purpose, they've been unlocked."

"You still haven't answered my question. What sort of powers do I have? How do I use them?"

"Before we get to that stage, I suggest you rest for a little while and take it easy. Your body needs a little time to adjust. It's common to feel nauseous after an empowerment ceremony," Mason said.

As Mason spoke, Jonah drifted off to sleep. It was as if Jonah's body had shut down, like a machine being switched off. Mason and Aurora weren't too concerned, as they had seen many other Guardians faint after receiving their powers. They expected that after a little rest Jonah would be up again and back to normal in no time.

After a few hours, Jonah awoke. As he opened his eyes, nausea overwhelmed him. He sprang from his bed and ran into the bathroom. Jonah just managed to make it in time, avoiding vomiting all over his bedroom and bathroom floors. Aurora, who was in the room monitoring him as he slept, ran after him to help. Once he was finished, Aurora helped him get up, at which point Jonah took a moment to compose himself.

As Jonah returned to his room, with Aurora, not only had his nausea subsided, but he felt an unparalleled radiance.

"I'm definitely feeling better now. That nap really did wonders for me."

"See? Occasionally your parents *do* have good advice to give," Aurora said.

"Emphasis being 'occasionally,'" Jonah retorted.

"Now, come on, you two. That's enough," Mason interjected to avoid a war of words.

"Okay then. So, tell me, Dad, what are my powers, and how do I use them? What do I do?"

"Well, today, we'll begin with teleportation."

"You showed me that before. You mean I can do that, too?"

"Yes, you can, Son."

Jonah's face lit up. "Wow! That is so cool. So how do I do it?"

"Like all your powers, you need to concentrate. If you want to transport yourself somewhere, focus on where you want to go and in an instant, you'll be there. It just takes a bit of practice."

With that explanation, Jonah took matters into his own hands and gave it a try. He concentrated on a place he wanted to go and within seconds, he disappeared. Mason and Aurora looked at each other and were simultaneously shocked and impressed. Teleportation took a little practice for most new Guardians, including themselves when they first received their powers. Mason and Aurora couldn't believe Jonah was able to teleport with such ease during his first attempt. They could see where Jonah went, so they followed him.

Jonah had transported himself to his home on Earth. His parents arrived shortly after, where they found him lying in pain on the coffee table in their lounge room. Being inexperienced, Jonah hadn't considered the fact that he needed to transport himself somewhere free from obstructions. When he had landed, he hadn't seen the coffee table; he fell onto it and smashed his torso, which led to agonizing pain. As he tried to get up, his parents laughed.

"Quite impressive for a first try, but you obviously need some more practice. We should've warned you to scout the area first, but you were just too quick," Aurora said.

"We'll give it another try. Let's head back to Concordia. Only this time, you need to look out for objects first." Mason said.

"How do I do that?"

"Before you imagine yourself being transported somewhere, think of the place first and visualize you're looking through a telescope," Mason explained. "You'll see an image of where you want to go. Next, survey the location. See what's around and find a spot where you can safely land. Then imagine being transported into that spot. So, let's try it."

As Mason spoke, Jonah envisioned his room on Concordia. He pictured an image of the room in front of him and looked for a suitable location where he could land.

"Okay. I found a spot. Here I go!"

Jonah teleported to his room in Concordia, to a location a few feet away from his bed where there was open space and no obstructions. He landed without incident. His parents followed immediately after.

"Yes!" Jonah punched the air.

Mason smiled. "That was much better!"

"Thanks. I feel a bit funny, though. Lightheaded. I need to sit." Jonah walked over to his bed and sat for a few moments. His stomach had become nauseous again.

"Don't worry, honey, that's perfectly normal the first few times you teleport. Your body will get used to the sensation soon enough; then the process won't bother you anymore," Aurora said.

As Aurora said that, Jonah scurried to the bathroom. An overwhelming feeling that he was going to be sick again surfaced. He reached the toilet just in time as he began to vomit. Jonah's parents ran after him to check that he was okay. He stood and walked to the sink to rinse his mouth with water. Jonah looked at himself in the mirror, trying to catch his breath and settle his stomach. In doing so, he spotted the blue Concordian emblem on his neck.

Jonah rubbed it a few times to try and get it off, but he couldn't remove it. He turned his neck to one side slightly to get a better look at it in the mirror. Jonah recognized it as an infinity symbol from his engineering training but couldn't understand why it was there and why he couldn't remove it.

"What's this on my neck?"

"That's the Concordian emblem. Now that your powers have been unlocked, it's become visible. We have it on our necks too." Mason pointed to his own neck.

"You will be able to see it on other Concordians as well. Only Concordians can see the emblem. Non-Concordians can't. So, if you were to show the emblem to your Earth friends, they wouldn't see it," Aurora said.

"Oh . . . okay," Jonah said.

Jonah stood in front of the sink, leaning toward the mirror to get a good look at the emblem. As he viewed it, he tried to make sense of everything. A few days ago, he was a typical, run-of-the-mill university student. Now, he was a Concordian Guardian. He had magical powers that enabled him to teleport between dimensions. He had a blue emblem on his neck that only he and other Concordians could see. His life had taken an unexpected turn.

CHAPTER 7

"Governor Ragnar, Lieutenant Lomar is here to see you," Amani, the governor's personal assistant, announced.

"Let him in," Governor Ragnar responded in his typically blunt manner as he sat behind his desk.

Moments later, Lieutenant Lomar walked into the governor's chambers. As he entered, Governor Ragnar immediately noticed Lomar's glum face.

"Leave us alone, and ensure we're not disturbed," the governor said to Amani.

Amani exited the chambers and closed the door behind her, while the governor motioned for Lieutenant Lomar to sit on a chair in front of his desk.

"What is it, Lieutenant?"

The governor noticed that Lieutenant Lomar was twiddling his thumbs and tapping one of his feet. A tall man in his mid-forties with blond hair and green eyes, Lieutenant Lomar was one of the governor's most loyal workers. He was also known for not mincing his words when it came to crisis talks.

"I have just come back from our Power Generation plant. I've been told our supplies of Chrimatide are running dangerously low. At our current rate of power generation, our existing supplies will last five or six months at best. If we don't find a new reserve of Chrimatide soon, we will cease being able to generate power for our planet. We must act swiftly!"

"We will find more Chrimatide, Lieutenant. We always do."

Governor Ragnar looked at the lieutenant with arrogance and indignation.

"But Governor, we don't need to use Chrimatide. We have alternatives. Some of our planet's best scientists have developed alternative sources of power that are cleaner and more efficient and—"

"That is enough!" Governor Ragnar slammed his fist on the desk. "Chrimatide is superior. I don't want to hear this nonsense about alternative sources of power ever again!"

The lieutenant recognized the governor's typically cold demeanor was descending into a depth of malevolence he was all too familiar with, and knew better than to challenge the governor further.

"I suggest now would be a good time to leave lieutenant."

Without uttering a word, Lomar arose from his chair, turned around, and left. As the lieutenant walked away, Governor Ragnar shouted out to Amani to enter his chambers.

Dressed in a gray pantsuit, Amani was a short woman in her mid-thirties with dark hair tied back in a ponytail. She had worked for the governor as his personal assistant for ten years. During that time, she'd learned that whenever Governor Ragnar called for her, she had to drop everything and see him immediately. He was always the number one priority, without fail.

"Amani, contact Master Sinai and tell him to come and see me at once."

"Yes, Governor."

Amani ran out of the chambers, not only to fulfill the governor's request as quickly as possible, but also to get away from his terrible mood.

The governor sat at his desk while he waited for Master Sinai to arrive. His grey hair, the wrinkles on his face, and the dark circles under his eyes were accentuated by the anxiety of having to look for Chrimatide yet again. He didn't share his emotions with others and internalized everything, leading to his premature aging. The governor was forty-five years old but looked closer to sixty-five. The stress of being his planet's leader had taken a visible toll on his tall, slender body. It was also the reason he had digestive issues, which required him to take regular medication.

Governor Ragnar was aware there were alternative methods to create power. Some of the best scientists on Planet Zareet had managed to find creative alternatives to Chrimatide. However, they were all silenced and locked away by the governor so they could not release that information to the rest of the planet.

These methods were clean processes that didn't generate any pollution and didn't need mining or processing of raw materials from the ground. They created just as much energy with less effort, which meant they were relatively inexpensive when compared to Chrimatide.

The issue with these other methods was that they weren't lucrative for Ragnar financially. Life for the governor was always viewed through the lens of a cost-benefit analysis. If there was no financial benefit, it was not worth the investment. Also, these alternatives didn't require the use of his power plants, which had run in his family for decades. This meant he would have no control over the generation or distribution of this new energy.

For Governor Ragnar, maintaining the current ways of power production was about domination. Control of Planet Zareet and its people. By controlling power generation and using Chrimatide as the primary source, he was able to create a reliance on it. Not only for financial gain but for conformity to his regime.

Anyone who did not abide by his rule was cut off from power—a cruel practice that safeguarded the overwhelming success of his evil reign over Zareet. It ensured he was unopposed. No one dared to challenge or attempted to overthrow him. Since the population of Zareet was ignorant about alternative sources of power, due to the suppression of information by the governor, they had no choice but to comply.

Although Planet Zareet was under tyrannical rule, it was a technologically advanced planet. Everything that its inhabitants relied upon for their day-to-day living ran on power. Communications, transportation, household appliances, as well as major industries and agriculture to produce food, all required the use of power from Governor Ragnar's plant. Hence, why the planet's inhabitants could not afford to be cut off from power.

An hour later, Master Sinai arrived at Ragnar's chambers. He was wearing his usual exuberant, bright-colored silk pants and shirt with multiple beaded necklaces—some adorned with crystals and stones. The governor thought Sinai looked ridiculous as always. However, he quickly overlooked his attire, as he needed Master Sinai's help.

"Governor Ragnar, you wanted to see me urgently."

"Yes, I did. Take a seat." Governor Ragnar pointed to the chair in front of his desk. "Sinai, I have been advised that our reserves of Chrimatide are diminishing. I need you to tell me where I can find more and tell me quickly."

"Governor, as I said, the previous reserves we found were the last in this universe. I have searched using my psychic powers many times over and haven't been able to find any more." Sinai crossed his legs and brushed back his silver hair.

"That's not good enough, Sinai! You *must* find more!" Governor Ragnar got up from his seat, approached Sinai, and grabbed him by the throat. "If you cannot find any in this universe, look elsewhere. There must be other universes you can search."

Sinai had a look of fear in his eyes. He struggled to speak due to the tight grip of the governor's hand over his throat.

"But I wouldn't even know how to look outside our universe. There's possibly infinite universes—"

"Then start searching. Even if it's one-by-one. Do not test my patience because you will find I have none. Go home and start looking *now*! I expect an answer by tomorrow when I see you again!"

Governor Ragnar pulled Sinai out of his chair, dragged him across the chambers, and threw him out.

Amani, who was sitting at her desk, observed Sinai land on the ground nearby. She tried not to react. Instead, she turned her head to look the other way. She was used to this type of behavior from Governor Ragnar after having worked for him for so many years.

After a few moments, Master Sinai, having recovered from the shock of being thrown out and humiliated, stood and composed himself, dusting down his pants. He took one brief look at Governor Ragnar and saw his wrathful grimace. It left him with a feeling of terror in the pit of his stomach. He left and began making his way home.

CHAPTER 8

The day after Jonah's empowerment ceremony, he woke early in the morning after having a good night's sleep. He lay in bed for a while, trying to dissect everything that had occurred over the previous two days. Jonah started experiencing mixed feelings about what was happening. Although a part of him felt excited about his new powers—just thinking about being able to teleport wherever he wanted to go was so exhilarating—and his role as a Guardian, he also thought about his life prior to his empowerment ceremony.

Did this now mean he had to abandon his engineering studies to become a Guardian? Or would he be able to incorporate both activities into his new life? If so, how? Was he meant to keep all of this a secret? Was he perhaps overthinking it?

As all these questions swirled around his head, he tossed and turned in bed. Feeling overwhelmed, Jonah got out of bed and freshened up with a hot shower. After getting dressed, he decided to go for a walk to find something to eat. Jonah hadn't eaten anything the previous day and was now ravenous. He wondered if Concordia had any cafeterias or supermarkets so he could eat something during his walk. Surely, Concordia had somewhere to get food? Otherwise, what was he to do?

"Hi, Amica, can you tell me where I can get some food here in Concordia? I'm so hungry right now."

"Good morning, Jonah. You don't need to go anywhere to get food. Just think about what you want to eat, really concentrate on it, and it will appear before you. It's called *instant manifestation*. This is only available in Concordia. Give it a try."

"Oh. Okay."

Jonah was a little skeptical. However, because he was so hungry, he was willing to give it a try.

Jonah had an intense craving for bacon and eggs with toast and sausages on the side. This was a breakfast his mother had lovingly cooked for him so many times as he was growing up. It made him think about all the occasions over the years where Aurora had cooked him breakfast in the morning and he hadn't eaten it. Sometimes it was because he was in a rush to get to school, and other times because he had a hangover. Jonah began to feel a little guilty, thinking of his mother spending so much time making breakfast for him that he never ate. For the first time ever, he felt terrible and realized how impertinent it was.

No sooner had Jonah thought of what he wanted that the food emerged before him on a plate, resting on a round table draped in a nice tablecloth and adorned with fine cutlery.

"Yes!" Jonah threw a fist pump in the air. "Thanks for the tip, Amica. I would never have known unless you told me."

"You're welcome, Jonah. Enjoy your breakfast."

Jonah bolted to the table and sat. He smelled the food first. It smelled so fresh as the steam that was emanating from the dish hit his face. The plate was exactly what he wanted, at the right temperature too, as he was feeling a little cold that morning and needed something hot to warm him up.

Within minutes, he devoured every morsel on his plate. Jonah ate so fast that he didn't chew his food properly, almost choking at one point. The dish was a generous serving, and everything was exactly the way he liked it, perfectly cooked and delectable.

When he finished eating, he felt satisfied and full. He placed the cutlery on the plate in front of him and held his stomach, taking a deep breath. He couldn't eat another thing. However, his mouth was a little dry, and Jonah wanted some orange juice to wash it all down. A glass of orange juice appeared on the table before him as he thought about it. Jonah laughed. He was really starting to enjoy this and figured he could easily get used to it.

Jonah drank the orange juice, which was so delicious and refreshing, with just the right amount of sweetness.

As he was drinking the juice, Jonah paused for a moment to take in a breath. He swirled the glass around in his hand and noticed the bright orange color. In that moment, Jonah wondered if his mother ever actually cooked anything. Surely, if she had this sort of power, she wouldn't need to. Jonah remembered when Aurora scolded him for not eating the food she had supposedly cooked, after allegedly spending many hours slaving over a hot stove. Was this the biggest lie ever?

While sitting at the table, having his last few sips of orange juice, Jonah could see Aurora and Mason walk into the room. They both had smiles on their faces.

"So, you've discovered a new power all by yourself, I see?" Mason said.

"Well, actually, Amica told me about it. Thanks again, Amica!"

"You're very welcome, Jonah."

"And I can see you've made very good use of it as well. That's quite a feast you just had," Aurora said.

"Mom, it was incredible! The best breakfast I've ever had. I've never had anything so delicious in my life. I swear. I've never felt so satisfied after a meal."

"The food is pretty amazing here, so I'll overlook your backhanded comments about my cooking skills just this once." Aurora pursed her lips.

"So, Mom. Tell me. Have you actually ever cooked a meal in your life?"

"I beg your pardon? Now, you listen here, Jonah—"

"Surely, not. All those times you 'slaved over a hot stove' to cook dinner was a big fat lie!"

"No, it wasn't!" Aurora shook her head in disbelief. "What you don't understand is that instant manifestation—which is what this is called—can only be done here in Concordia. On Earth, we don't have that power. That's why we must work and earn money to buy food, live in a house, and pay bills."

"Oh . . . yes, that's right. Amica said so before. This doesn't work on Earth."

"No, it doesn't! And let me tell you something. The only time I didn't cook was when I bought take-out or when we went out for dinner. And another thing—I had to cook so you didn't find out who we were. And before you ask, Concordia doesn't do takeaways or deliveries. You can't create food here and take it with you to Earth. It doesn't work that way. Trust me—I've tried. So, don't you try giving me any lip, Jonah. I'm still capable of giving you a smack on the head, regardless of how old you are!"

"Apologize to your mother!" Mason hollered, pointing his finger at Jonah.

"Okay, okay. I was just kidding, Mom. I'm sorry. Take it easy. Can't you take a joke?"

"A joke? Hmm . . . we'll see who gets the last laugh today, my boy."

Aurora gave Jonah a brutal look. She wasn't going to tolerate his brashness. Especially not now. Aurora had put up with Jonah's bad moods and attitude when he was a teenager and up until recently, when he was at university. He was old enough now to know much better and treat her with the respect she deserved. If he hadn't learnt this by now, he was about to do so very quickly.

Aurora walked over to Jonah's bed and sat for a moment, taking in a couple of deep breaths to calm herself while Jonah finished his orange juice in silence.

"Today, you're going to begin combat and defense classes. We'll head to the Training Center we saw yesterday. That's where you'll learn to fight like the Concordian you are. It's a good thing you ate a big breakfast because you're going to need all the energy you can muster. Let's go!" Aurora commanded.

Jonah stretched his arms and stood. As soon as he walked a few steps away from the table, it all disappeared. The table, the chair, the plate and cutlery—all gone. Not only did he not have to cook, but he didn't have to do any dishwashing either.

"Sweet!" Jonah said.

"Yes. That's another perk here. You don't have to clean up after yourself when you finish eating. Not that you ever did any of that on Earth," Aurora said.

"Touché, darling. Touché," Mason said to his wife as she quietly snickered to herself.

Moments later, Aurora and Jonah started heading to the Training Center, a five-minute walk away. Jonah was a little apprehensive about the training. He wasn't sure what to expect.

"What sort of training is this going to be? Is some big burly drill sergeant going to throw me around the room and break every bone in my body?" Jonah asked.

"You'll see," Aurora said with a wry smile.

When they arrived at the Training Center, Jonah saw other young Guardians training and learning how to fight. He looked at them for some time and observed them doing various intense training drills. Standing there, Jonah was in awe of how fit they were and the great skills they had.

"C'mon, Jonah, if you spend all day staring at people training, you won't get any training done."

Aurora, who was standing behind Jonah with her arms on his shoulders, forcefully pushed him to the other end of the Training Center. She took him into a separate room where no one else was training. During this session, Jonah was going to get one-on-one training. Since he was new to Concordia, Jonah needed private coaching sessions before he could train in a group setting.

After they entered the room, Aurora instantly changed outfits by pressing a couple of buttons on her wardrobe generator. She changed into a blue outfit resembling spandex gym clothes seen on Earth. She got Jonah to change his outfit by showing him what buttons to press on his wardrobe generator. Jonah looked at her, puzzled.

"Mom, why did you change outfits?"

"I need to wear something more comfortable, seeing as I'm going to teach you how to fight."

"What? You're my mother; you can't fight. You're a woman."

"Women can't fight? Is that what you think, my darling son?"

Aurora slowly walked behind Jonah. When Jonah wasn't expecting it, Aurora grabbed his neck in a chokehold for a few seconds. Jonah panicked;

the chokehold constricted his breathing. Jonah tried desperately to release his mother's grip, using his own arms to try and pull Aurora's arms away, but he couldn't. Aurora then released the chokehold and shoved Jonah to the ground. She did it with such force Jonah was almost knocked out cold. He lay on the floor for a moment in shock; he was speechless. He looked up at his mother, who was staring at him with the most fearsome expression. It unnerved him. Jonah couldn't believe his mother had such physical strength.

"Would you like to reconsider your previous statement?" Aurora asked.

Jonah continued looking at his mother in horror.

"Let me give you an education. The concept of men versus women is nothing more than a human construct on Earth, made up by humans to imprison each gender into a stereotype for the convenience of the status quo," Aurora said.

"Ah . . . okay. Whatever that means. Are you, like, some feminazi or something?"

"Jonah, this isn't about feminism. In Concordia, we are above gender discrimination as are evil Infringers from other dimensions, who couldn't care less that I'm a woman. They wouldn't think twice about hurting me or killing me in a heartbeat. But they've never succeeded because I'm an incredible fighter. And that's what my son needs to be too. Now, get up!"

As Aurora raised her voice at Jonah, she gave him a slight kick in his side to force him upright. Jonah stood as quickly as he could. As he tried to get his balance, Aurora shoved him to the ground again.

"What the hell, Mom! Are you crazy?"

"Have you not heard anything I've said, Jonah? When you're in a fight, your opponent doesn't care about anything other than hurting you. When you fall, you need to get on your feet and fight back. Get up!"

As Jonah continued to get up, Aurora continuously tackled him to the ground, time and time again. He was starting to get fatigued. Jonah's anger toward his mother escalated. Her constant beatings bruised both his body and ego. Aurora was trying to knock out of Jonah what he thought fighting was and drill into him what fighting *really* was. Fighting was brutal. Vicious. It was pure rage.

"For the love of God . . . I need a break."

Jonah begged his mother, almost in tears, after about twenty minutes of training.

"No." Aurora was not going to let Jonah give up so easily.

Although Aurora loved Jonah deeply, she knew he would have to learn the hard way how to fight his enemies. It was going to be the biggest challenge of his life, but it was the only way to guarantee he would have a life. Aurora knew all too well what Jonah could potentially face in his duties as a Guardian. She had seen her fair share of the Infringers that existed in other dimensions. Jonah had not. He had no clue. Aurora's only hope was that one day, Jonah would be ready to fight back and live to tell the tale if faced with an adversary. Right now, he was nowhere near ready. As a mother, she was anxious. As a trainer, she knew there was a long journey before him.

The training went on for several hours. He was not prepared for this physically. It took a lot out of him and by the end, he was spent. Jonah lay on the ground, drenched in sweat and feeling completely battered. There were a couple of bruises on his face and some blood dripping from his nose as he had hit his nose hard on the ground during one of his falls. Jonah took a moment to stop the bleeding with his sleeve, while trying to catch his breath and muster the strength to get up and leave. As he lay there, Aurora, covered in sweat, sipped some water.

"You've got a lot of work to do, Jonah. I'm not kidding. This training is going to be the difference between life and death. So, you'd better take this seriously and work hard because I won't be able to protect you in battle. Now, get up, go back to your room, and get plenty of rest. That was just an introduction. There's way more to come."

Jonah eventually stood and left the Training Center, slowly limping his way out. He was sore and bruised all over and struggled to walk. He desperately needed to lie down and have a rest. Aurora, on the other hand, still had plenty of energy. Although she was a little tired and drenched in sweat, she was still in great form. Jonah didn't know how Aurora did it. He couldn't understand how she could fight for so long and still be able to stand strong. Jonah was now in awe of his mother. Who would have thought his mother was some fierce combat trainer capable of fighting like a martial arts warrior? Certainly not Jonah.

As Jonah was walking back, there came a point where he collapsed to the ground. He couldn't move any further due to the pain. Every muscle in his body ached. He wasn't sure how he was going to make it back to his room.

During that moment, it dawned on Jonah that he had the ability to teleport. He wondered why he hadn't thought about it before. Jonah took a couple of deep breaths and concentrated on his room, visualizing where he could teleport to. Before he knew it, Jonah was in his room. He managed to get there without hurting himself, unlike one of his previous attempts the day before.

Jonah walked a few steps before slowly climbing onto his floating bed. He closed his eyes as he sank his head into one of the soft pillows. He stretched out his tired, aching body on the mattress, trying to get some rest. Although he was hungry, he was too tired to eat. All he could think about was the throbbing pain all over his body until he eventually fell asleep shortly after.

Jonah woke the next morning and found himself on his bed back on Earth, wearing his regular clothes. He glanced from left to right. He couldn't recall teleporting back to Earth. The last thing he remembered was falling asleep on his bed in Concordia. He got out of his bed and walked around the house to see if his parents were also there.

"Anyone home?"

There was no response.

Moments later, a knock rumbled at the door. He panicked. He didn't know who was at the front door. He stood there for a moment, not saying or doing anything. As he was doing so, the knocking continued. He thought about ignoring it and heading back to Concordia, but his gut told him otherwise. Jonah ran to the door and opened it; he saw two police officers standing before him, which made him a little nervous. They filled the doorway with their towering bodies and blue uniforms. He was puzzled as to why they were there.

"Good morning officers, can I help you?"

"I'm Officer Fernandez, and this is Officer Conroy. We want to speak to a Mr. Jonah Michaels."

Jonah gulped and became a little anxious. *Why do they want to speak to me?*

"I'm Jonah. What's going on?"

"We received a missing person's report from a friend of yours—Jason Henderson—claiming you went missing two days ago, so we're investigating what happened," Officer Fernandez said.

"Well, I'm here, and I'm okay, so no need to investigate anymore." Jonah laughed nervously.

"Where have you been for the last two days?" Officer Conroy asked.

"I've been home, resting. I was feeling a little under the weather the last few days, so I thought I'd take it easy."

"Who else lives here?" Officer Fernandez asked.

"Just my parents. They're not home right now. Not sure where they are at the moment."

"Are they perhaps in Concordia?" Officer Fernandez asked.

Jonah felt a rush of goosebumps all over his body and remained silent. How did he know anything about Concordia? Was he a Guardian also? Could Jonah talk freely about it? Jonah wasn't sure what to do.

"What are you talking about?" Jonah asked, pretending as if he was unaware of what they were talking about.

Without warning, Officer Conroy seized Jonah's left arm and turned him around, slamming him up against the front door of the house. The impact was so strong; it stung his face as he made contact with the wooden front door. Officer Conroy grabbed Jonah's other arm and proceeded to handcuff him.

"What are you doing? Why are you handcuffing me?"

"You're under arrest for crimes against humanity and for illegal interdimensional travel. We arrest your powers and suspend you from Concordia," Officer Fernandez shouted.

"I haven't done anything wrong!"

Officer Fernandez unholstered a titanium gun from his jacket and pointed it at Jonah's neck. Before Jonah had a chance to even think about teleporting, Officer Fernandez pressed a switch on the gun and proceeded to drain the powers from Jonah's body. The pain of the extraction was so unbearable, he screamed uncontrollably.

After a few seconds, Jonah woke up. He was back in Concordia, and it was very early in the morning. On his bed, he sat up, confused and covered in sweat. His heart raced uncontrollably. After catching his breath, Jonah slowly laid back down on his bed. He managed to calm down and realize it was all a bad dream. It seemed so real. Especially the pain he felt when his powers were being drained from his body.

Aurora rushed into his room.

"Are you okay, Jonah? I heard you screaming!"

"Yeah, I'm okay. I had a bad dream . . ."

"Do you remember what it was about?"

"I dreamt I was on Earth. And in the nightmare, I woke in my room at our house, and these police officers showed up knocking on the front door. When I opened the door, they arrested me for being Concordian. And something to do with 'crimes against humanity,' and they were trying to drain my powers. It felt so painful and so real."

"It was only a dream, Jonah. I can assure you that no one can take away your powers. Except for Grand Guardian Omiya. She's the only one with that kind of power." Aurora brushed Jonah's hair off his sweaty forehead, trying to calm him as she sat on his bed.

"So, what do you think that dream meant?"

Aurora thought about it for a moment. "Well. . . maybe deep down, you feel a little uneasy about this whole Guardian role you've come into, which is understandable. You only just discovered this about yourself, so it's all very new to you. And because you need to keep all of this a secret, you're afraid you might accidentally tell someone about it or reveal your powers to someone on Earth. I'm not a dream interpreter, so that's the best I can come up with in the middle of the night."

"It kind of makes sense, I suppose."

Jonah was still uneasy about the dream. However, it did get him thinking about his life on Earth and about his friends. He was still unsure about what to do with his studies and whether he should continue being friends with Jason and Shane. It also got him thinking about all the partying and drinking he had been doing in recent months. Now that he was a Guardian, it didn't seem appropriate behavior for someone entrusted with protecting lives.

"So Mom, do we have to keep all of this a secret? You know . . . about who we are?"

"Absolutely, Jonah! We cannot reveal our identities to people outside of Concordia. People on Earth wouldn't understand who we are and what we do. They'd probably think we were witches and warlocks. Regular humans are too closed-minded about what exists in the vast universe. They just aren't ready to understand us yet. And besides, it's forbidden to disclose who you are. You must keep your true identity a secret at all costs."

"So, I shouldn't tell my friends anything. Got it."

"That's right, Jonah. You can't say anything. It's prohibited. If you really need to tell your friends something, make up whatever you need to get them off your back. Personally, I think you should get rid of your friends altogether. They're not worth your time. I mean, they left you on a field after you passed out drunk. Some friends they are!"

"You have a point there. They shouldn't have left me out there all alone. The more I think about it, the more it irritates me. Especially leaving me in a Wonder Woman outfit . . . but what about my studies? Do I have to give that up?"

"That's something you'll need to figure out in your own time. You're an adult. You're responsible for your own choices, so I really can't answer that for you. You will need to figure out if it's possible to balance both. If you really like what you do, you'll make it work. Your father found a way to combine his carpentry work and his responsibilities here. I'm sure you'll figure it out soon enough. Anyhow, let's leave that for another day. Get some sleep and lots of rest; you'll need it."

"Mom, can we skip training tomorrow? I might need to go to Earth and tie up some loose ends. I think I've figured out what I need to do."

"Okay. But I'm only giving you a day. You must continue with your training. You have a long way to go before you are ready to fight in a battle. Do we have a deal?"

"Deal."

"Okay, then. Good night, Jonah."

"Good night, Mom."

Aurora got up from the bed. She kissed Jonah on his forehead and walked back to her room.

Once Aurora left the room, Jonah drifted off to a sound sleep.

CHAPTER 9

On Planet Zareet, as Master Sinai arrived home, he quickly closed the front door to his house. With his back against the door, he took a few deep breaths. He was glad to finally be in the comfort and safety of his own home. Sinai knew Governor Ragnar was a tyrant, but this was one of the worst outbursts from the governor he had ever been a victim of. It shook him to the core of his being and left him feeling degraded. Sinai burst into tears and fell to the ground on his knees. He continued crying for a few minutes to release his shame and fear. Once he finished, Sinai dried his eyes with a handkerchief.

After gathering some incense and sage, he set the two ingredients alight, burning them for some time to help cleanse his aura from Governor Ragnar's darkness. After a few minutes of quiet meditation, he calmed down and began to feel like his normal self again.

Now that Sinai was in a better state of being spiritually, he spent the rest of the day scanning universes, one by one, trying to locate worlds that had enormous reserves of Chrimatide. For Sinai, it was a laborious task and not as simple as Governor Ragnar thought. It involved entering into a deep meditative state so his soul could travel into other dimensions and perform a psychic scan of different planets and their compositions to see if Chrimatide—a mineral—was available.

At some level, he enjoyed doing this, as he was able to visit other universes and their associated planets that were unlike anything he could have ever imagined. He appreciated how fortunate he was to be able to do this, as not many people on his planet had this ability. Sinai came from a long line of mediums and psychics, all with different abilities. In addition to being a medium, he was blessed with the ability to astral project at will and travel through space and time at his leisure. It was a skill he'd discovered at a very early age when he was nine years old. Although it frightened him at the time, Sinai began to appreciate it as he grew older and was able to master his craft.

As he began his meditation, Sinai realized his responsibility in giving Governor Ragnar an answer, which inhibited his extensive enjoyment of these visits. After meditating and astral projecting for many hours, he finally stumbled upon a dimension he believed was worth exploring—one that seemed to have a rich supply of Chrimatide that could power Zareet for many years to come.

Finding this planet, though, was physically taxing on Master Sinai. At the end of his search, Sinai returned to his conscious state. With his head and shoulders slumped, he was constantly yawning and could barely keep his eyes open. He knew the governor would interrogate him for many hours and ask him numerous questions about this new discovery. Sinai needed to be well rested and in top form before enduring such intense scrutiny. As such, he decided to have a good night's sleep before visiting Governor Ragnar again.

The next morning, Master Sinai awoke feeling refreshed and well rested from his sleep. He spent the morning mentally preparing himself—with a brief meditation session while burning incense—for an arduous day ahead before leaving his home to go see Governor Ragnar.

On his approach, Sinai began sweating profusely, and his stomach ached. When he arrived, Amani let him into the chambers. Walking in, he found Governor Ragnar sitting behind his desk. He had a steely look on his face, eagerly awaiting to hear what Sinai had to say. The governor was hoping not to be disappointed.

"Master Sinai. I hope you have some good news for me."

Sinai stood in front of the governor's desk. "Yes, Governor. After we spoke yesterday, I went home and meditated. After many hours of scanning and searching, I found what you're looking for."

"I knew you would," Governor Ragnar said with an unnerving tone, despite being pleased with what Master Sinai had to say. "You may now sit and tell me what you have found."

As Master Sinai sat, he felt a little relieved, though he was still very uneasy. He could never relax and be comfortable whenever in Governor Ragnar's presence and always approached their encounters with apprehension.

"Yes, Governor. I've found a planet called Ebris, located in a dimension called the Occulus System. For some reason, Planet Ebris is particularly rich in Chrimatide. I estimate they have enough Chrimatide to power Zareet for many years. Possibly decades. The only issue you'll have is that the planet is densely populated. You will encounter a bit of resistance in trying to mine the planet for Chrimatide, as the process will displace thousands, if not millions, of people."

"You don't need to worry about the indigenous population. My army will take care of them."

"But the other thing you will have to figure out is how to get there. You will need to find a way to cross over into that dimension. That, I don't know how to do. Physically traveling between dimensions is out of my realm of expertise," Sinai said.

"Again, you don't need to worry about those details."

Governor Ragnar spent the next few hours getting as much information from Sinai as he could regarding the location of the dimension and planet. He also wanted to know everything about Planet Ebris itself, such as details about the planet's inhabitants, its terrain, geology, climate, and even right down to its air composition.

Governor Ragnar could see Sinai yawning, getting tired from all the questions. He didn't care. At one point, Sinai was unable to answer some of the questions, and Governor Ragnar forced him to meditate in front of him to find out. Although he found it a little difficult to relax in Ragnar's presence and meditate effectively, Sinai did what he could to appease him.

Once Sinai had provided all the details he had asked for, the governor dismissed him.

"You can go now. I don't have any more use for you."

"As you wish, Governor."

Sinai stood and left the chambers to make his way home.

When he walked away from Governor Ragnar's headquarters and was halfway to his home, Sinai stopped for a few moments. He took a few deep breaths and exhaled. He couldn't believe he had managed to get away unscathed. Sinai smiled and instantly felt like a heavy load had been lifted off his shoulders; he was relieved it was now all over.

Governor Ragnar sat in his chamber for some time, contemplating how to solve his next problem. He now knew where to find a new reserve of Chrimatide. However, he had to cross over into another dimension to extract the Chrimatide he so desperately needed.

This was not something that had ever been done before on Zareet. While he suspected there were many other dimensions in existence—from a growing body of evidence produced by some of the great scientific minds on his planet—it was only now being confirmed by Master Sinai. As such, he'd never had to consider crossing dimensions before. This would be a considerable challenge for him and his new mission.

Governor Ragnar called Amani into his office.

"Yes, Governor."

The governor had his back to Amani as he stared out into the distance from the window of his chambers. "I want you to contact Professor Lyndon and ask him to come and see me immediately."

"Right away, Governor."

Amani ran out of the chambers and went to her desk so she could contact the professor.

Professor Lyndon was one of the governor's advisors and Zareet's most senior physicist. The governor was aware Professor Lyndon had been undertaking some studies into parallel universes. His research was specifically on travel between dimensions. The governor was eager to know how he had progressed in his research. Especially since the governor had just been told there was a vast amount of Chrimatide in the Occulus System.

Governor Ragnar also called for his son, Zyaire, to attend and participate in the meeting. As Zyaire was now in his mid-twenties, the governor felt it was time he started taking on more responsibilities. Specifically, this next project he had in mind.

Professor Lyndon, who was of average height and wore unusually dark, thick glasses, arrived and was led into the chambers by Amani. The professor sat down in front of the governor's desk at his invitation. Lyndon was clueless about why he had been summoned into the chambers at short notice.

Moments later, Zyaire walked in. After Amani left, Governor Ragnar got straight to the point and began questioning Professor Lyndon about his research into inter-dimensional travel.

"Professor, we have discussed this a few times before. The idea of inter-dimensional travel. I want to know how you've progressed in your research. And by progress, I mean have you figured it out? When can we expect to travel into other realms? You've been researching this for years now. My patience is wearing thin."

Governor Ragnar intently stared Professor Lyndon in the eye.

Lyndon could see the governor was not willing to accept anything other than an affirmative answer. After contemplating his response for a moment, Professor Lyndon took a deep breath.

"Yes, Governor. I've made significant progress. In fact, I figured out how to bridge a gap between two dimensions. I've even done some experiments with small objects, moving them from one place through to another using a wormhole. I've built a machine that can do this on a small scale, but I'm still working on a much bigger machine that can enable people to move through a wormhole. It's called a teleporter."

"Professor, how soon can you build this 'teleporter?'"

"It would take twelve to eighteen months with—"

"We don't have that amount of time, Professor! I need it built in four months."

Governor Ragnar slammed his fist on his desk.

"But Governor, I haven't finished the teleporter's design yet, let alone started building it. The teleporter is going to take more than four months for me to finish the design, then get all the necessary materials together for its construction and—"

"I don't want to hear any more excuses!"

Governor Ragnar got up from his chair and walked over to the professor. The governor grabbed Professor Lyndon by his shoulders and continued to shout at him. "Just get it done. You have four months. Zyaire will help you. He will oversee the project and help you gather whatever team you need, however big that is. Just get this teleporter built quickly! Do you understand?"

"Yes, Governor."

Professor Lyndon's head hung low and his body was shaking a little.

"Now get out!"

Governor Ragnar released the professor from his grip and pushed him away with such force that Professor Lyndon was slammed to the ground. Amani could hear the thud from outside. Once he got up again, the professor regained his composure. Shocked by what happened, the professor hurried toward the chamber's exit and left as promptly as he could. He had no time to waste.

The governor asked Zyaire to stay behind to discuss the project further. Zyaire rarely saw his father get angry in front of him. After seeing the governor's display of fury, he felt a little shocked and unnerved.

"Zyaire, I know you haven't done anything like this before, but I think it's time for you to take on some responsibilities and learn how to be a leader. You will one day inherit my rule and this entire planet. This means you must learn how to lead. That's why I want you to work with Professor Lyndon on building this teleporter to start getting some experience. Do you understand?"

"Yes, Father. But I don't know how."

Governor Ragnar briefly looked at his son, who stood before him, terrified. For all of the governor's flaws and lack of empathy toward most of the people on his planet, he held an inexplicable love and affection for Zyaire. Being orphaned when he was a young child, Zyaire was taken in by

Governor Ragnar and raised by him ever since. The governor treated him as if he was his own flesh and blood. As he'd never married and had children of his own, adopting Zyaire fulfilled a parental need in the governor he never knew he had.

Now, looking at Zyaire—with his long, straight black hair, dark skin, and brown eyes, wearing his soldier's outfit and an innocent, timid look on his face—Governor Ragnar felt somewhat sympathetic.

"You will learn, my son. I didn't know anything about leading when my father died, so I had to learn quickly on the spot. At least this way, you can learn gradually, and you will inherit everything I have when the time comes. You are my only son, so you won't have to share the power with anyone."

"I see."

"Zyaire, I want you to give me regular reports on what is happening and the construction status of the machine. Any problems that you come across, you come to me immediately."

"Understood."

"Now go and speak to the professor and get started. Learn whatever there is to know about the teleporter and keep an eye on Lyndon. You need to be my eyes and ears on the project."

Governor Ragnar motioned for Zyaire to leave.

Governor Ragnar sat alone in his chambers, contemplating what would happen if his planet ran out of Chrimatide before he could get to Planet Ebris. It meant his rule would be in jeopardy, and he would lose control of his planet.

Power was the driving force behind all his decisions. His ghastly desire to overpower and rule was indoctrinated into him by his father, Governor Vanu. An equally vicious and tyrannical leader, Governor Vanu had ruled Planet Zareet for many decades before his death. He'd instilled into his son the desire to rule with fear and hatred. As Governor Ragnar had yearned to please his father and gain his acceptance, he complied.

Governor Ragnar had learned never to question his father. Governor Vanu ensured the desire to question anything had been knocked out of his son at a young age with physical abuse every time he dared do so. Eventually, Governor Ragnar stopped asking questions and just accepted whatever his father wanted him to do. He never again questioned the idea of ruling with fear and hatred as opposed to ruling with fairness and a desire for equality and justice for his people.

Now, as he sat thinking about his diminishing Chrimatide supplies, all he was left with was a blind yearning to rule. He never thought for himself what the purpose of his irrational desire meant and why he was doing this. Was he a product of his tyrannical father's upbringing, or was he now responsible for his poor choices? Was Ragnar too broken to undo the damage his father had inflicted on his mind and soul?

Governor Vanu had died over twenty years ago, and ever since, Governor Ragnar ruled Planet Zareet. During that time, he never questioned what he was doing and the direction he took his planet in. He justified his actions by claiming his rule created order on his planet. By controlling people with fear, there were no crimes committed, and everyone had jobs and homes to live in and food to eat. Provided they didn't go against his rule, that was. In his mind, Governor Ragnar thought he was doing the right thing, even though the population of his planet felt otherwise.

CHAPTER 10

J onah woke from his broken sleep in the early morning hours. Immense pain from the training session the previous day crashed through him. Although he was in agony, Jonah managed to slowly get up from his bed. With every muscle in his body aching, he made his way to the bathroom to have a long, hot shower, which helped loosen his stiff body so he could move around with some ease.

Feeling refreshed and a little less sore, Jonah decided to have some breakfast. He quite enjoyed the instant manifestation process he'd discovered the previous day, and as such, he conjured up a sizable meal of waffles, eggs, bacon, and hash browns. He figured he needed to eat a vast amount of food as it would assist in the rejuvenation of his aching body.

Once he finished eating, Jonah teleported to his bedroom on Earth and spent some time getting dressed in his regular Earth clothes. Once dressed, Jonah went to the bathroom and found some painkillers in the medicine cabinet. He took a couple of tablets to help ease his pain and sat in the kitchen, waiting for the tablets to take effect. It was still too early to go to school, so he was in no rush to leave.

As he sat in the kitchen, Jonah had a good look around. After spending a few days in Concordia, witnessing its astonishing architecture and all of its advanced technologies, he now found his Earth home rather dull. In Jonah's eyes, the kitchen now looked primitive, something from the dark ages. The appliances, such as the fridge, stove, and oven, looked like they hadn't been changed in the last fifteen years. The kitchen table was wearing out with several chips and scratches that had accumulated over time. The walls looked a little dirty and needed a new coat of paint, while the linoleum on the floor had several tears and required replacing.

Previously, Jonah loved living there, as he found it very comforting. Growing up, he treated his home as his sanctuary in the world. During his time at high school, home was where he could be himself, surrounded by the warmth of his family, especially his grandfather, Luke. He was shielded from the bullies that plagued him and from the kids he never seemed to quite fit in with.

Now, though, it felt dreary. It was as if he had outgrown it. Jonah was starting to realize Concordia was quickly growing on him and becoming his preferred home. At least from a livability perspective. With its clean living and technologically forward way of life, Earth felt backward to Jonah. He found this rather amusing, as he'd known nothing of its existence days before, yet now, it was where he wished to be.

Looking around, Jonah saw a framed photo sitting on the kitchen bench. The picture was of himself posing with his grandfather. It was one of Jonah's favorite photos. He was in his early teens at the time, being embraced by Luke on a bright, sunny day at the park. Jonah had a smile that beamed with sheer joy. Luke was a little bit younger and had a cheeky yet warm smile. The photo encapsulated his personality and essence perfectly.

Gazing at the picture, Jonah smiled for a moment before tears welled in his eyes. Jonah missed Luke terribly. He tried to hold back his tears, but a couple of drops escaped his eyes and trickled down his face. He quickly wiped the tears away with one of the sleeves on his shirt. He'd never felt so alone before. The house, without Luke, felt dull. Cold and lifeless.

After some time, the painkillers started to kick in. Jonah stood and grabbed his backpack from the floor. He walked out of the house, got into his car—that was parked in the driveway—and drove to university. He felt it best to drive there, rather than teleport, to be less conspicuous.

When Jonah arrived at college, he parked his car and headed to the cafeteria on campus, Maurie's Cafe. He wanted to buy his favorite coffee—a caramel latte. Although Concordia's food was incredible, Jonah loved the cafeteria coffee. There was something about the way it was made—as well as the barista, Cora, who usually made his coffee—that Jonah liked.

Cora always gave him a warm-hearted smile and handed Jonah his coffee with a certain affection that melted his heart, regardless of how tired he was or whatever bad mood he was in. He had always wanted to ask her out but never had the courage to do so due to his lack of confidence with women. Besides, as pretty as she was—with her hazel eyes, heart-shaped face, and dark wavy hair that cascaded around her shoulders—Jonah figured she most likely had a boyfriend or girlfriend, and it would be a waste of time asking her.

"Here you go, Jonah, your caramel latte."

Cora handed over Jonah's coffee with that warm smile he was accustomed to.

"Thanks, Cora."

Jonah—with an awkward, goofy grin—took the coffee and began heading to class.

"Have a nice day, Jonah."

Cora continued looking at Jonah as he walked away, until he was no longer in view.

"Girl, he'll be back tomorrow for you to drool over. Now start making those orders!" Cora's boss, Jeana, clicked her fingers and pointed to the orders coming through on the screen.

Cora snapped out of her longing gaze and continued to make the rest of the orders in the queue, which were quickly starting to pile up.

When Jonah arrived at his class, he sat, waiting for the professor to come in and begin the lecture. The coffee was just what he needed to help wake him up. As he took his first sip, he could taste the perfect blend of the sweet caramel combined with the robustness of the freshly brewed espresso coffee. It was particularly cold that morning and the heat of the takeout cup helped warm his hands. He was still feeling a little tired and needed a pick-me-up to help him focus during his class.

Other students, as well as the professor, slowly walked in, and the lecture began a few minutes later. As the professor spoke, Jonah sat, unable to focus or make any sense of what was being said. He was distracted by what he had experienced over the last few days. What he had seen was far more fascinating than anything the lecturer had to say (who was talking about ramjet engines). Jonah wanted to get up and tell everyone about his adventures. He wanted to share with the world what existed beyond humanity's limited understanding of the universe.

As he mulled that over, he recalled what his mother had told him previously. Jonah had to keep all of this a secret. How could he do that, though, when he so desperately wanted to tell someone? Anyone. Deep down, he knew his mother was right. People on Earth weren't ready to understand something so advanced.

When the lecture was finally over, Jonah left. He continued with his other classes and remained on campus for the rest of the day. At the end of his final lecture, Jonah raced out of the lecture theater. He just couldn't deal with any more classes.

While walking around campus, Jonah lingered in a pensive mood. Part of him knew university was no longer the right choice for him. As much as he was in love with the idea of finishing his degree one day and working as an aerospace engineer, the reality was that he was no longer in love with his studies. Being on campus for most of the day made him see that perhaps it was time to make a new choice. Was it best to leave college behind completely, or perhaps take a break from his studies to think things through and reassess his position later?

Jonah was confused. He decided to go to one of his favorite spots on the campus: a rooftop of one of the main buildings several stories high. It was a quiet place not many people knew about. Jonah only discovered it through Jason and Shane, who would often take him there when they wanted to get away from their classes. To get there, Jonah had to walk up the internal fire escape stairwell, which led to the rooftop's entrance.

As Jonah got to the top of the building and opened a door that led to the rooftop, a gentle, refreshing breeze brushed against his body. The sun had come out after an overcast morning and warmed the day to a pleasant temperature. He took a deep breath to inhale some fresh air and relax.

Jonah then walked over to a familiar spot where he and his friends would normally hang about. As he stood there quietly, he took in a broad view of the campus. Being alone, he was able to spend time appreciating the building's architecture. The design of the campus buildings was something he had never noticed before, as he was normally distracted by his friends' meaningless conversations about trivial topics. If Jonah abandoned his studies, he'd miss the campus and the atmosphere of university life.

As Jonah basked in the fresh air, trying to contemplate what to do next, someone tapped his shoulder. He flinched slightly before turning around in a panic. Shane and Jason stood in front of him.

Both of Jonah's friends were shocked to see him. For the last few days, they'd wondered what had happened to him. There was a sense of relief seeing him now.

"Hey, Jonah!" Jason shouted. "You're alive! Where have you been the last few days? We haven't seen you and started to worry."

Jonah stood there for a moment, before looking at Shane straight in the eye. "You were worried about me?"

"Yeah . . ." Shane said.

"Worried about me?" Jonah repeated, sarcasm lacing his voice. "What, did the guilt sink in from leaving me on the field at night by myself dressed as Wonder Woman?"

Jason and Shane burst out laughing.

"That was hilarious. And just a harmless prank. No need to get upset, sunshine," Jason said.

"Harmless prank?" Jonah paused for a moment. "Dumping me on a football field by myself, passed out drunk, late at night isn't what I call a harmless prank. That was really stupid. Anything could have happened to me. I could have been kidnapped, attacked by wild animals, murdered. God knows. Did you think about that? I thought we were friends, and friends don't do that to each other."

Jason laughed. "Listen, you're overreacting. There are no wild animals in this area."

Jonah wasn't amused. "It still wasn't funny."

"Take it easy," Jason said.

"Well, now that you're feeling better, how about we go to a party tomorrow night?" Shane asked. "There will be—"

"No, I can't. I'm busy."

"Busy doing what, Jonah? Washing your hair?" Jason asked.

"I don't know. I'll figure something out." Jonah turned around and began walking away.

"What the hell! Are we not good enough for you now?" Shane asked.

"No, you're not!" Jonah yelled as he spun around to answer Shane's question, then turned his back again and continued walking to the exit.

Jason and Shane looked stumped for a moment. They couldn't believe what Jonah had just said.

"Screw you!" Jason screamed back.

Jonah ignored them. He reached the exit and opened the door to leave the rooftop. He ran down the stairs to get away.

As he descended the staircase, he missed a step and tripped. He fell and was about to land at the bottom of the stairs at great speed. As Jonah panicked, he suddenly stopped falling. He floated in the air about three feet away from the ground, looking on in horror and confusion. Jonah's face was close enough that he could see every crack in the concrete floor. He started waving his arms around, trying to touch the ground, but he couldn't reach it as he was unable to move.

As Jonah floated, voices approached the door at the top of the stairs—it was Jason and Shane. Jonah began to panic even more. He was unable to stand or get to the ground. The more distressed he became, the higher he levitated. The door began to open. Just as Jason and Shane were about to walk through the threshold, Jonah had to think quickly. Not being able to move or get to the ground left him without any other option. He teleported out of the building to the first place he could think of—his parents' home.

Within moments, he reemerged in his bedroom on Earth, still airborne. Now that he was home, safe and sound, he was able to take a few deep breaths and relax, after which he abruptly fell to the ground on his torso.

Jonah lay on the floor for a short while, winded and in severe pain. When he stood, a sense of dread shot through him. What if Jason or Shane saw him levitating, or worse, they witnessed him teleport? What if it was captured on camera with CCTV?

Jonah changed into his robe and teleported back to his bedroom in Concordia. He rushed out of his room to find his parents and tell them what had happened.

As he hurried around Concordia trying to find his parents, Jonah wondered why no one explained to him that he could levitate. Now, he desperately wanted to know everything about his powers so he wouldn't encounter a situation like that again.

Within minutes, Jonah managed to find his father, who was talking to another Guardian outside in an open walkway.

"Dad, we need to talk!" Jonah pulled his father aside from the conversation he was having with the other Guardian so they could talk in private.

"Jonah, what are you doing? I'm in the middle of a conversation." Mason felt embarrassed by Jonah's rudeness.

"Dad, I might've got myself into trouble. I was on Earth earlier, talking to my friends Jason and Shane at university. I ran down some stairs and tripped. The next thing I knew, I was levitating. In a panic, I teleported away. I'm not sure if they saw anything or if it got caught on camera. I'm scared I might have exposed my powers and who I am."

"Okay. Let's not panic, Son."

"Don't panic? Didn't you hear what I said? I might've been exposed. Mom told me I had to keep my powers and my identity a secret." Jonah's voice sounded frantic.

"Son, before you have a meltdown, come with me. There's only one way we can find out for sure."

Mason grabbed Jonah by his right arm and teleported with him to the Observatory.

The Observatory was a long distance from Concordia's main area. Jonah was uncertain where Mason had taken him, as there wasn't any mention of where they were going. Once they arrived outside the Observatory's perimeter, Mason took Jonah inside. When Jonah walked in, he took note of the colossal building. It had big columns, similar to an ancient Roman building, and long hallways with marble floors that seemed to go for miles.

"Where are we, Dad? Why did you bring me here?"

"You'll see shortly, Son."

For security reasons, Guardians weren't able to teleport directly into the building—it was the only place in Concordia shielded from teleportation. The only way in and out of the building was to walk there.

What was also unique about the Observatory was that not everyone was able to enter, as entry was conditional on having security clearance. Mason, who worked in the Observatory, had the required clearance and was able to take Jonah inside with him. Even though Mason had spent most of his time on Earth over the last couple of decades since Jonah was born, he did manage to find time to work in Concordia as well during that period. When he wasn't working on any carpentry jobs on Earth, he would spend time in Concordia carrying out various duties in the Observatory, which is why his clearance was still current.

Everything that was going on puzzled Jonah, especially the fact that security clearance was required to walk inside. He didn't understand why that was necessary. All he could surmise was that there must've been something serious going on in the building that was sensitive in nature. Mason was tight-lipped, not saying anything during the walk, which made Jonah a little nervous.

As they walked farther along, Jonah was taken through secret passages and corridors until they eventually entered a large observation area. Thousands of Guardians sat in long rows in front of what appeared to be glass screens with holographic images.

Mason approached a workstation he normally worked at and sat. He pulled another chair close and asked Jonah to sit with him.

"What's going on here? What is everyone doing?" Jonah turned to his dad with a perplexed look on his face.

"This place I've brought you to is called the Observatory. Here, we're essentially a big surveillance area. We're similar to an intelligence agency like the CIA or the FBI back home on Earth. Here, we monitor the activities of other dimensions and look for suspicious behavior and potential threats. This is a critical role in Concordia. The groundwork performed here is the foundation for all the other work that Guardians do to help protect all universes in existence from calamity."

"What kind of threats?"

"Well . . . from time to time, we have situations where beings from one dimension will teleport and travel into another dimension. Sometimes, it can be completely unintentional, where portals open up between dimensions by accident. People walk through them without even knowing it and end up in a completely different dimension. It's rare, but it happens. But most of the time, it's much more sinister. In those situations, you have individuals or groups of people, whom we call Infringers, who deliberately figure out how to open portals so they can travel into other realms and cause harm and chaos. And we, as Concordians, need to intervene."

"And by intervene, do you mean battle?" Jonah asked.

"Yes, that's right, Son. We do whatever it takes to stop Infringers from causing harm. So, do you see how all of this fits?"

"Yes I do, Dad. It's starting to make sense now."

As Mason continued talking, he showed Jonah the equipment they used. Concordia's technology was far more advanced than any spying agency on Earth. It emphasized for Jonah how much effort went into Concordia's surveillance and the importance of the work they did. This also helped reinforce in Jonah what Concordia's core mission was.

As for his father, Jonah couldn't believe he was a quasi-spy. To Jonah, Mason was Dad. Growing up in Chicago, he looked like any other suburban father Jonah used to see on the street. He was a carpenter by day and in the evening, he would come home and be Mason Michaels, the man who sometimes took Jonah to football games when he was growing up and the amusement park on special occasions. The guy who mowed the lawn on the weekend and washed his car—just your typical run-of-the-mill American father.

As much as there was a learning curve for Jonah to truly understand everything about Concordia, the same also applied to his parents. He now knew his mother was a combat trainer and his father a spy. Jonah saw his parents in a completely different light. After living with them for over twenty years, what Jonah thought he knew of his parents was just superficial. On the surface, they appeared to be your typical garden-variety Earth humans with boring, simple lives. Although it was now starting to sink in a little, Jonah still had a long way to go before he really got his head around it all.

"So, Jonah. I've brought you here to answer your questions and alleviate your concerns. I'm going to show you a replay of what happened during your encounter with your friends on Earth."

Jonah raised his eyebrows. "You can do that?"

"I sure can."

Mason began to track the material in question. The technology used in the Observatory was cutting edge. It continuously recorded and stored vast amounts of footage from all the surveillance activities carried out in the Observatory. It also allowed for easy recall and retrieval of those recordings at lightning speed. Mason was able to scan through an enormous amount of footage by hovering his hand over the screen and home in on the time Jonah encountered his friends at their college campus. Once found, both Jonah and Mason began examining the recordings.

The technology amazed Jonah. He was surprised how his father was able to view the recordings at different angles and rotate the views with incredible ease, using virtual controls on the screen. The process was unlike anything he had ever seen before.

Mason and Jonah spent quite a bit of time reviewing the recording until they were both satisfied they'd seen everything they needed. After this exhaustive examination, they concluded that no one had seen Jonah levitate or teleport from the university campus. They also couldn't find any cameras in the stairwell. This was a huge relief for Jonah, leaving him feeling much calmer.

This whole incident made Jonah realize how close he came to almost exposing his Concordian powers. Only now did he appreciate how crucial it was to be vigilant with concealing his Concordian identity.

What was most disturbing to Jonah, though, was his friends' behavior. He thought he'd known Jason and Shane well. Now he realized they didn't necessarily have his best interests at heart. They were quite happy with Jonah when he came along with them to parties and drank until late into the night, but if he deviated from that script, he wasn't worth their time. They were even willing to hurt him. He formed the view that he was much better off without them. Besides, he now had much more important things to focus on.

Now that this whole fiasco had been resolved, there was one question outstanding in Jonah's mind that Mason hadn't addressed.

"So, Dad. Is there something you need to tell me?"

"Such as?" Mason asked with a puzzled look.

Jonah laughed. "Such as the fact that I can levitate! You never mentioned the levitation part."

"Ah. Yes, that's right. You can levitate. Surprise!" Mason lifted his arms in the air.

"Yes, I was surprised, all right!" Jonah said.

They both laughed.

"Your mother and I didn't tell you about it as we didn't want to overwhelm you with information."

"What kind of a lame excuse is that, Dad? Had I been told earlier, we could've avoided this whole mess to begin with."

"No harm was done. Son, it will take time for you to learn everything you need to know. When I get a chance, I will sit down with you and show you how to use your powers properly. The last few days have been hectic. With your grandfather passing away, and you finding out about being a Guardian, the existence of Concordia, and your role here in Concordia . . . it's quite a bit to take in. Your mother and I were worried it might've been a bit too much, so we have taken things slowly. It wasn't done to keep you in the dark. I promise you that much."

Jonah looked at this father and accepted his explanation. Although Jonah was learning a lot about Concordia, he realized there was a lot more he didn't know.

What else are my parents hiding that they're not telling me about? For now, he had no other option but to trust their wisdom and guidance. He had to trust they would train him in the best way possible to be ready when the time came for battle. Right now, he knew he wasn't.

At that point, Jonah remembered he had another training session with his mother the next day. He grimaced at the thought as he was still recovering from the last session.

"Thanks, Dad. I really appreciate your help."

"You're welcome, Son."

Mason hugged Jonah, letting him know everything was going to be okay.

Mason escorted Jonah from the Observatory so he could teleport to his room. As they were walking out, Mason came up with an idea.

"Jonah, before you go to your room, how about we go outside and practice your levitation skills?"

"That would be nice, I suppose."

"Great. Actually, I might ask your mother to join us. She's good at teaching others levitation."

Hey, darling, can you meet Jonah and me outside in the clearing by the river? I want to teach Jonah how to levitate, Mason telepathically asked Aurora.

Ok, sure, Aurora responded.

She had just finished a combat class with some students and was about to head back to her room. Within a few seconds, Aurora teleported to the meeting point and found Mason and Jonah.

Mason explained to Aurora what happened with Jonah earlier that day and how lucky he was that no one saw him.

"Although it's kinda funny, I do agree it would be best to practice it a few times so something like that doesn't happen again." Aurora smiled.

"Agreed." Jonah nodded.

"So, first thing. I need you to close your eyes, take a few deep breaths in, and slowly exhale." Aurora instructed.

Jonah closed his eyes and began to relax with each breath in and out.

"Jonah, levitating is all about raising your frequency so you can lighten your body. Now, I want you to imagine that you are a wave and slowly oscillating through space."

Jonah squinted his eyebrows. He thought it was a strange request but nonetheless followed his mother's instructions.

"I want you to start visualizing the wave getting faster and faster until you can only see a straight line."

Jonah continued listening to Aurora's directions. He was visualizing in his mind a wave that was continuously oscillating more rapidly. In tandem, he started to feel lighter with each passing second and began to feel a breeze over his head and shoulders.

"Now open your eyes!" Aurora shouted.

Jonah opened his eyes and saw that he was floating several feet high up in the air. He was shocked. Jonah's mouth was wide open, and he could feel himself getting nervous. His parents were on the ground, excited and cheering him on. After a few moments, Jonah relaxed and enjoyed the view from up in the sky. It was an incredible feeling of lightness that he had never felt before. He felt free. The view of the surrounding buildings and the river down below was from a different vantage point, and it was something different Jonah hadn't experienced before.

"So, Mom, how do I get back down again?"

"Just do the opposite . . . Imagine your wave is slowing down and becoming slower and slower!" Aurora shouted back.

Jonah closed his eyes again, and visualized a wave slowing down. As he did, he began to descend closer toward his parents until his feet eventually touched the ground again.

"Wow, you did it!" Mason hugged Jonah with excitement.

"That was amazing! I never thought I would be able to do that!"

"That's my boy. I taught you well," Aurora said with a hint of pride in her voice. "Just remember to practice this when you get a chance so you can get better at it. Eventually, it will be as easy as breathing."

"I will. But for now, I definitely need something to eat." Jonah grabbed his stomach, feeling how empty it was.

"Sorry to burst your bubble, Son, but before you get a bite to eat, is there something you've forgotten?" Mason asked.

"Like what, Dad?"

Jonah stood there and couldn't think what his father was alluding to.

"Such as . . . you left your car at the university campus."

"Oh . . . oh, yeah I forgot about that."

With everything that had happened earlier during the day with Jason and Shane, the investigation with his father, and then learning how to levitate, Jonah had overlooked picking up his car.

"You make a good point, Dad."

"Of course, your father makes a good point. How about you go back to Earth, get your car from university, and drive it back home. Then come back here and we'll all have dinner together?" Aurora suggested.

"Sounds like a plan, Mom."

With that, Jonah teleported back to Earth while his parents went back to their room to wait for Jonah to come back for dinner.

CHAPTER 11

After Jonah finished eating dinner with his parents, he returned to his room and lay on his bed for a while. He thought about what had happened earlier that day with Shane and Jason and began to laugh. Now that his stress and panic had subsided, Jonah could see the funny side of it all. He also recalled the prank his friends had played on him days earlier, making him wear a Wonder Woman outfit. He laughed even more.

Jonah then turned his attention to his studies. While he had earlier decided it would be best to leave all of that behind, he was now starting to reconsider. Jonah thought it might serve him best to take a break from university, for now, to focus on his new role as a Guardian and reassess the situation later. He figured it would be nice to complete his engineering degree at some point in the future, especially since he had come so far and was close to finishing. If he ever needed to live on Earth again, it would be nice to have a qualification and an Earth job to fall back on.

While Jonah lay on his bed contemplating his future, there was a knock on the door. He went to see who it was. Before he could get to the door, it opened, and a head poked through. It was his mother, wearing a friendly smile.

"Hi, Jonah."

"Hey, Mom."

As his mother walked into the room, Jonah spotted a man standing in the hallway outside. Aurora invited him to come in. As the man walked a few steps into the room, Jonah looked at him and instantly thought he was some kind of hippie. Appearing to be in his fifties, he had long, matted hair and wore some weird necklaces around his neck and bracelets on each hand. The man's Concordian robe was red, a different color than the ones Jonah and his parents wore. The most striking thing about this man, though, was his face. His joyful expression beamed with serenity. He had a warmth in his smile that made Jonah feel at ease.

"Jonah, I'd like you to meet Ishwa. He has been assigned to be your spiritual counselor."

"It's nice to finally meet you, young Jonah," Ishwa said as he shook Jonah's hand.

"It's nice to meet you, too," Jonah said, a little unsure about what was happening. "Ah . . . what exactly do you mean by spiritual counselor?"

"Well, Jonah, think of it like this. Your Concordian journey is made up of three components—the mind, body, and soul. I'm looking after the physical aspect of your journey, which is your body. Your father will teach you how to control your powers, which is the mind. Then, you've got Ishwa. He is going to guide you on your spiritual path, the soul part of your journey."

"Okay . . ." Jonah was skeptical about what his mother had just told him.

"Your mother has told me a lot about you already. I really look forward to working with you," Ishwa said.

"Now, Jonah, please be nice to Ishwa. He's been my spiritual counselor for many years. Apart from being a dear friend, he's someone I respect enormously. He's a man of immense wisdom. He'll be able to guide you on your spiritual journey just like he's done with me."

"You never said anything about a 'spiritual journey' when I first came here a few days ago." Jonah grimaced at Aurora.

"Well, I'm telling you now, my darling child. As I've said before, coming here, there was a lot for you to take in, so your father and I have gradually told you what you need to know. Anyhow, I'll leave you two alone to have a chat. Have a good night!" Aurora walked out of Jonah's room, waving her right hand.

"Goodnight, Mom." Jonah waved to his mother before turning to Ishwa.

"So, what's this all about? Are you going to make me do weird stuff? Like chant 'Kumbaya, my Lord' during a full moon and burn incense? Maybe sprinkle holy water for good measure?" Jonah asked.

"Not quite, young Jonah. At least, not for now." Ishwa chuckled. "What we are going to do, though, is take a little journey. Somewhere far away from here, so we can talk freely."

"Okay."

Ishwa put his palms in front of Jonah. He sensed Jonah was apprehensive about where they were going.

"Don't worry Jonah; there's nothing to be afraid of. Just hold my hands for a moment."

"All right, I guess." Jonah's nerves tingled with anxiety.

Jonah proceeded to place his palms over Ishwa's palms. Ishwa took a deep breath and within moments, they left Concordia for an adventure.

Ishwa and Jonah re-materialized in a place Jonah had never been to before. It resembled a forest unquestionably not on Earth or Concordia. The tree trunks were a pale lilac color, and the leaves ranged in various shades of yellow, violet, blue, and green. Wherever they were, it was eerily quiet. There were no birds or animals. In fact, after a few moments of being there, Jonah thought he had lost his hearing.

"Where are we?" Jonah asked.

"Welcome, Jonah, to Planet Amabilia," Ishwa said with immense enthusiasm as he spread his arms out. Jonah, on the other hand, didn't share the same excitement.

"This is my favorite place to visit out of all the dimensions I've traveled to. And I've been to quite a few in my time! Now, here are some fun facts. First, you won't find this place on any map or GPS system in any universe." Ishwa laughed while Jonah gave a polite smile in return.

"Second, there are no inhabitants on this planet; third, this planet is located in a dimension called Anstaria. And fourth, it's the only planet in this dimension, and as you can see, the environment is breathtaking. The air is the cleanest you can ever breathe." Ishwa inhaled a couple of times deeply. "Go on, take in a few deep breaths, Jonah. You'll feel better. It will do you some good. Trust me."

Jonah reluctantly inhaled deeply a few times. With each breath he took, Jonah relaxed. The air was at a comfortable temperature and had an enjoyable floral scent to it, which Jonah found very pleasing.

"See, Jonah, you're starting to look more at ease already. Now, you may have noticed it's also very quiet here. It's one of the reasons I love this place so much. Amabilia gives you the space to hear your thoughts and focus."

"Yes, I noticed that."

"What I'll do now is give you a moment to look around. There's no rush to get back, so take your time Jonah."

As Jonah glanced around, he realized they stood in the middle of a small clearing surrounded by trees, shrubs, and flowers. In the distance, a waterfall ran into a river, which in turn ran across the clearing. By this stage, Jonah could hear the faint sound of water gently rushing down the river. Although the sky was a blue color, it had a fluorescent tone to it, giving it a luster which he hadn't seen on Earth before, nor in Concordia. The sheer beauty surrounding them amazed him.

While Jonah continued to look around, intense emotions filled him, which were warming and comforting at the same time. He also felt a tingling sensation in his skin. Jonah wasn't sure why, but the overwhelming urge to cry overtook him. He attempted to hold back tears until he couldn't anymore. Jonah broke down as he stood opposite Ishwa.

"Why are you crying, Jonah?"

"I don't know," Jonah said, his lips quivering.

"What are you feeling right now?"

"I just feel this overwhelming sensation of love," Jonah said, still trying to hold back his tears. He felt a little embarrassed that he was crying in front of another man, which Ishwa could sense.

"There's no need to feel embarrassed, Jonah. I wasn't judging you when I asked why you were crying. I was just curious. You see, this place I have brought you to is unique for many reasons. One of those reasons is to do with this planet's vibrational frequency. The vibrational frequency here is very high, and if you are not used to existing at this high frequency, it can be quite overwhelming. And the reason why this dimension operates at such a high frequency is because of the abundance of unconditional love that exists here.

"As you can see, there are no inhabitants on this planet to mar its vibrations, which gives this existence the space to be without judgement and without fear. It's why I brought you to this place. So, we can talk openly, and you can tell me anything you want, without fear and without judgement. Is any of this making any sense to you?"

"Ah . . . maybe. Sort of. Not really," Jonah said as he continued crying.

Ishwa felt compassion for Jonah and appreciated his honesty.

"That's perfectly okay, Jonah. Let's have a seat."

Ishwa motioned for Jonah to sit on the grass they stood on, which was a vivid lime-green color. They sat opposite each other and made themselves comfortable.

"Let me ask you this: when you said you felt 'this overwhelming love,' is that why you cried? Was it a bad thing to feel that?"

"I just never felt that intense level of love before. I didn't know how to react to it," Jonah said, wiping tears from his eyes with his robe.

"Have you ever felt any kind of love before? From your family, friends, people you've dated?" Ishwa asked.

"Well, from my parents, I suppose. I've never really had a girlfriend, though, and I wouldn't say I have a lot of friends."

"Okay. So why is the love from your parents so different from what you feel here?"

"Because my parents are always telling me I've done something wrong. Or somehow, they make me feel like I'm a disappointment. They don't approve of my friendship with Jason and Shane or being out late drinking."

"So, you believe their love is conditional on your behavior?"

"Well, my parents sure as hell don't love me when I'm irritating them."

"Could it be they love you, but they don't like particular actions you take? You know, Jonah, there's a difference between disliking someone's behavior and loving them. It's quite possible to love someone but not like certain actions they take, or not like certain behaviors they exhibit. Have you ever heard the expression 'Love the sinner but not the sin?'"

"Well, then . . . that's not unconditional love."

"Have your parents ever abandoned you? When you've done something they've disapproved of, have they ever kicked you out of their home or told you they never wanted to see you again?"

Jonah thought about it for a moment. "No."

"*That's* unconditional love. No matter what you've done, your parents have continued to love you. Your parents have never abandoned you. They have never demanded you leave their home regardless of how you may have upset or disappointed them. Loving someone unconditionally doesn't mean you have to accept their bad behavior."

Jonah sat for a moment in silence. He looked at Ishwa, surprised by what he just said. He didn't have anything to refute Ishwa's advice. He was speechless for the first moment in a long time. Jonah thought about how his parents had always been there for him no matter what. No matter how many times he had been moody or belligerent toward them, they continued to love him.

"Jonah, your parents have always given you unconditional love. It's your ego that has told you otherwise. Instead of taking responsibility for your actions when you've made a mistake, your ego has projected that responsibility onto others and told you it is their fault for you not feeling an abundance of love. But the truth is, the responsibility lies with you. You are responsible for your actions. You are responsible for your mistakes and successes. And you are responsible for the love you feel. So, in a way, your ego has misled you. It has indirectly made you feel unworthy of love by blaming others for your choices and actions."

"I never thought of it like that," Jonah said, twirling some grass around his fingers, trying to understand what Ishwa meant.

"Well, truth be told, Ego is pretty good at not making you see things from a different point of view."

"Ishwa, what do you mean by Ego?"

"Ego is the part of yourself that believes you are separate from God because of your physical body. It believes you are nothing more than your five senses. That your existence is limited to your physical body." Ishwa held up his hands, then hit them against each other for effect.

"Ego makes you believe you are unique and distinct from universal consciousness," Ishwa continued. "In actual fact, though, you are much more than the totality of your senses, mind, and body. You are much greater than that. You need to understand that you are a spiritual being having a temporary human experience. Your body is just the vessel you are using to navigate your current reality. We'll learn more about this in due course. For now, just realize you are much greater than the body you see and feel. Not because you're Concordian and have special powers, but because you have a soul. And your soul is more powerful than all your Concordian powers put together."

Jonah tried to comprehend what Ishwa was saying. It was a lot for him to take in. This was something his parents had never taught him, and the lesson presented a new way of thinking about himself and his existence. He needed time to absorb what Ishwa had told him, especially about what it meant to be a powerful soul.

"Jonah, when you came into existence in your physical form the day you were born, you incarnated with an unblemished soul. But as you grew up, life happened, and you forgot who you really are. You forgot your life's purpose. This journey we will embark on together will be about you remembering who you really are. It will be about discovering your truest and most authentic version of yourself. It's going to be an exciting journey for you, with some challenges you will find rewarding in ways you cannot imagine yet."

"But isn't my purpose to be a Concordian?"

"I'm sure that's a part of it, but I'm also certain there's more to your life's mission than what you currently understand, Jonah."

"Like what, Ishwa? Do you know something you're not telling me? Actually, you know what? Don't answer that question. I've already learned so much these last few days; my head is going to explode. I need a break."

Ishwa smiled. "Well then, seeing as we've covered quite a bit of ground today, how about we call it a day and go back to Concordia? I'd like you to think about what we have discussed, and if you have any questions, you can ask me next time we see each other."

"Okay. Will do. So, when are we going to see each other again?"

"In a few days time. I won't tell you when I'm coming. I'll just arrive when you least expect it, but when you're completely ready," Ishwa said with a cheeky smile.

They both stood, and Ishwa put his hands out, asking Jonah to hold onto them. Jonah grabbed his hands. Moments later, they teleported out of Planet Amabilia and returned to Concordia, ending up in Jonah's room once again.

"Thank you for the chat tonight, Jonah. I hope you found it interesting and got something out of it. Many blessings to you. Good night."

"Thanks, Ishwa. See you next time."

Ishwa left Jonah's room. As he departed, Jonah was left feeling very different from when he was first introduced to Ishwa. Something inside Jonah had awakened. He didn't know what. Almost like Ishwa had ignited a spark in his mind that was never going to die out. Jonah wasn't going to be the same again. He also began to see Ishwa in a new light. Instead of a hippie, Ishwa was someone who could help give him a new perspective on life. Something he very much needed.

Emotionally drained, Jonah went to bed soon after he got back from Amabilia. His eyes were a little swollen from crying. Jonah tried to sleep, but he couldn't. All he could think about was what he had discussed with Ishwa on Amabilia and how he felt during his visit there. He tried to comprehend everything Ishwa told him. After some time, though, Jonah fell asleep—but not before wishing he could go back to Amabilia.

CHAPTER 12

After waking early the next day, Jonah showered and got dressed. He sat in his room and enjoyed a hearty breakfast in preparation for another grueling training session with his mother. Although he felt a little tired due to having a restless night's sleep, his body had recovered considerably. After finishing his breakfast, he waited for his food to settle and made his way to the Training Center.

When Jonah arrived, Aurora was there waiting for him. This time, he was surprised to see three other students with her. Jonah was under the impression his training would be one-on-one; however, Aurora had arranged a group training session. These other students were relatively new to Concordia but had been there longer than Jonah. They had already completed several training sessions with Aurora and were a little more advanced in their abilities. Nevertheless, Aurora thought it would be a good idea to have Jonah train with them. As they were around his own age, she figured Jonah might be able to make some new friends.

Aurora introduced the other students to Jonah, who were all from other dimensions. What Jonah found remarkable about them was that they looked like humans. He initially thought people from other dimensions would look like the aliens he had seen in so many movies back on Earth. However, that wasn't the case.

"First up, we have Caleb." Aurora pointed to her right.

Caleb was from Planet Kenarios. He had curly, blond hair and was of a similar height to Jonah, with slightly darker skin and brown eyes. He was the most athletic of the group and had a muscular, solid physique to match. His robe was a peculiar mustard color, which Jonah found strange, as he hadn't seen anyone else on Concordia with that same-colored robe.

"Over here, we have Haven." Aurora pointed to her left.

Haven was from Planet Fasmeon. She had long, opulent auburn hair. Her flawless complexion and piercing violet eyes made her strikingly beautiful. She was tall and slender but looked quite strong from what Jonah could discern, especially from her well-toned arms. Haven was the most serious of the three but also one of the most fiercely intelligent. Jonah was immediately smitten by her but tried not to show it.

"And finally, we have Zak, who thinks he's God's gift to all females in every parallel universe!" Aurora teased while everyone else laughed. Zak took a bow. "Unfortunately, his success with women doesn't quite match his huge ego."

Zak was from Planet Maldoa. He had black hair and an exquisite flawless dark skin tone that accentuated his orange eyes. Taller than Haven, Zak wasn't as muscular as Caleb.

After the introductions were completed, Aurora paired them up.

"Let's begin our session with some basic combat moves and drills. Haven, you'll work with Jonah," Aurora said.

Last time Jonah had his training session, he'd made a snide remark about his mother being a woman and that she somehow couldn't be a trainer. Aurora figured she had knocked that idea out of his head last time; however, she thought it would be nice to reinforce the notion with Haven, who was quite tenacious and tough.

"Caleb, you'll work with Zak," Aurora said as she directed them to work on the other side of the room.

Matching Caleb with Zak was a pure testosterone match. Aurora knew what they were like and how competitive they were, so she figured they would aggressively challenge each other.

They began the training session with basic combat moves and drills, then moved on to more complex fighting techniques. Haven was really giving Jonah a workout like no other. Before Haven arrived in Concordia, she was a fit, athletic woman. She needed to be in shape because her home planet was a brutal land. Conflict between opposing factions was rampant on that planet, and only the fittest survived. Accordingly, Haven had adapted into a strong fighter to stay alive. Her ability to fight was truly on display as Jonah struggled to keep up with her. Fighting Haven was just as challenging as fighting his mother.

Caleb and Zak began sparring like a couple of teenage brothers who got into a fight. As the training went on, their combat became increasingly more competitive and aggressive. It was as if their life depended on it—which it would one day. They really challenged each other, and just as it looked like one of them had a hold on their opponent, they would break free and get a hold of the first. This continued for quite some time until Aurora eventually called for everyone to stop and take a break.

While they were catching their breath, Aurora retrieved weapons for their training that looked like silver batons, thick and strong and about a foot long. One end had grooves for someone's fingers to slot into. As Aurora demonstrated, they were designed to be easily carried on one's body around the hip and picked up as required.

Aurora gave each of them a baton and kept one for herself. She demonstrated how to use them. With a quick flick, one end became pointy. With another quick flick, it transformed into a five-foot-long spear. Another flick of the spear turned the weapon back into a baton. Jonah thought the batons were remarkable. The others had seen these before and weren't as excited as Jonah. These batons were a serious weapon to behold. If, during battle, a Guardian encountered a challenging opponent that proved too difficult to handle, these were the next line of defense.

"Jonah, stand over here for a moment," Aurora commanded, pointing to a spot away from the group.

Jonah moved to where Aurora instructed. A moment later, she pressed a button at the base of the baton, swung it toward him, and knocked him on his shoulder. Jonah felt an electrical surge throughout his body for a few seconds, before he collapsed on the ground unconscious.

After about ten minutes, when he regained consciousness, Jonah opened his eyes and looked around. His mother towered over him, grinning, while the other students sniggered. His mother checked to see if he was okay. After a few moments, Jonah slowly stood up with a helping hand from his mother. The other students had already experienced the feeling of being stunned by the baton, so they were glad they hadn't been chosen for the demonstration.

"What the hell was that?" Jonah asked, confused and a little sore.

"You were shocked by the baton," Aurora said, almost laughing at him. "The baton can be used as a physical weapon to defend yourself, but it can also jolt people and knock them out cold, which might be necessary if you ever come across a tough opponent.

"The bottom part of the baton is inert and won't harm you when you hold it. It's the pointier end that's active. So, make sure you hold the baton by its bottom part so you don't hurt yourself."

"You could've warned me first!" Jonah said with an edge in his voice. The other students burst out laughing.

Aurora smirked. "But that wouldn't have been as much fun."

"I'm glad you all had fun at my expense! I'll remember this. You mark my words!" Jonah exclaimed as he shook his index finger in the air.

After Jonah had recovered from being shocked, Aurora decided to call it a day and finish the training. They got to keep their batons, which, when shrunk, easily fit into their training outfits or robes, hidden away for an emergency. Jonah and the other students walked out together, while Aurora stayed behind to tidy a few things up.

"How about we get some Shankani from my hometown on Kenarios?" Caleb suggested as the group was walking toward the Training Center exit. "I know this great place that makes some seriously awesome Shankani."

Caleb was originally from a town called Darjon. A town he still cherished. Whenever Caleb had the chance, he would lovingly visit. Although Caleb was quite fond of Concordia, there was something about Darjon he couldn't let go of. For all of Caleb's flaws and bravado, he was quite sentimental.

"That sounds like a great idea." Haven, since she became a guardian, was always eager to explore other dimensions.

Zak was equally keen to go. "You can count me in!"

"I think I'll have to pass on the offer for tonight, but thanks anyway," Jonah said as he was about to exit the building.

Jonah was shy around new people and wasn't sure if he was ready to make friends. His experience with his Earth friends, Shane and Jason, made him wary.

"Like hell, you will!" Caleb cried.

Before Jonah could think about walking away, Caleb grabbed Jonah's hand and teleported him to Planet Kenarios. Zak and Haven followed them soon after.

Caleb teleported to his family home, still owned by his parents. He figured it was best to take everyone there first so they could change into Kenarian attire before going out to eat.

Although no one lived in the home anymore, Caleb and his family—who now lived in Concordia—would still visit and spend time there every now and again. At that point though, no one else was home, just the four of them.

Caleb's forcefulness took Jonah aback. His initial reaction was to punch Caleb's face. He couldn't believe Caleb was so reckless, and that he completely ignored his wishes.

"What the hell, Caleb! I said I wasn't interested and you brought me here anyway! That's kidnapping. On my planet, you can get arrested for that," Jonah shouted as he tried to push Caleb.

Caleb burst out laughing.

"I didn't kidnap you! I escorted you here. And besides, you have free will. You can go back if you like. It'll take you less than a second. No one is going to stop you. I sure won't. But you're here now, so why don't you just stay and live a little? Have some fun. Experience something new! What else are you going to do? Go back to your room and knit a sweater?"

After a brief silence and a couple of deep sighs, Jonah managed to calm down and rethink the situation. Apart from Amabilia, he hadn't been to other planets before, especially in other dimensions. He figured maybe Caleb was right.

"Fine! But this Shankaki better be good!" Jonah snapped.

"It's called Shankani! And you bet it is! All those amazing spices and flavors will dance in your mouth."

In Caleb's excitement, he put his arm around Jonah's neck in a headlock and held Jonah's head down as if he were wrestling Jonah. He rubbed his knuckles over Jonah's head as two brothers would do. Although Caleb was mischievous at times, he never meant any harm. For Caleb, it was all a bit of fun, even though it was at other people's expense. Zak thought it was funny and laughed. By the vexed expression on Haven's face and her eye-rolling, she wasn't impressed by their immaturity.

Jonah eventually got himself out of the headlock so they could all get a move on. He managed to catch his breath and fix his hair, which Caleb had messed up in the frivolity. Since they were all wearing Concordian robes, they had to change into regular Kenarian clothes to blend in and not look conspicuous. Caleb showed them how to use their wardrobe generators to program them for Kenarian attire, which was different from the clothes Jonah typically wore on Earth—mostly jeans and T-shirts. Here, Jonah had to wear tight-fitting, tailored navy-blue pants and a cream-colored dinner jacket with a white casual shirt that had a V-shaped neck and no collar. Caleb and Zak wore similar clothes with different color palettes.

Haven was wearing a navy-blue jumpsuit with a fabric belt, the ends tied up into a bow on one side just above her hip. The top part completely covered her up to her shoulders; however, her arms were exposed, showing off how well-toned she was.

Once dressed, Caleb grabbed them and teleported the group to another location on Kenarios. They landed in an alleyway not far from Caleb's favorite Shankani restaurant, Yianni's Shankani Bar.

"They make the best Shankani in town. Actually, the best in the universe." Caleb, with a huge grin, walked with gusto to get to the restaurant as quickly as possible while the others staggered behind, trying to keep pace.

As they were walking, Jonah could hear the sound of cars driving in the distance, along with chefs working frantically to prepare food for their diners, as they were passing the back kitchen of another restaurant.

The restaurant was a short distance away. It was mid-evening; however, the streets were well-lit. Jonah observed everything and was captivated. He couldn't believe he was on another planet. It looked very similar to

Earth: the architecture of the neighborhood, the cars, the people walking out and about, some with their families, while a few were walking their dogs. Further down the road, there was a small crowd surrounding a street performer, who was more like a contortionist, as he moved his body into various unusual positions perfectly timed to some drum-based music.

However, Kenarios had a different vibe than Earth's even though it looked remarkably similar. The atmosphere felt very comforting, giving Jonah a feeling of safety on this planet. It had a sense of homeliness that immediately made him feel at ease.

When they reached the restaurant, they walked inside. Caleb found a table and directed everybody to take a seat. He chose a table where there weren't too many people around. Caleb didn't want people to hear what they were saying so they could talk freely. A friendly waitress, who was dressed in a maroon, collared shirt with long sleeves and a black skirt, came around and gave each of them a menu.

"I'll give you all a few minutes to have a look through the menu and see what you would like, and I'll be back to take your order," the waitress said with a smile.

The waitress walked away so the group could mull over the menu. After all their training that day, they were famished and ready to eat the entire restaurant.

"Caleb, what exactly is Shankani?" Jonah asked.

Caleb looked at Jonah, puzzled. "Don't you have it on Earth?"

Jonah thought about it for a moment. "No, I don't think we do."

"Well, in that case, we are going to have the Shankani Deluxe. That's the best way for a newbie like yourself to experience it."

After a few minutes, the waitress returned to take their order. Caleb ordered four Shankani Deluxe for the whole table. He also ordered a number of different sauces to accompany the Shankani and a mixture of different drinks for everyone to wash it all down.

"So, are you expecting more people?" The waitress looked at them strangely, thinking they had ordered way too much food.

"No, it's just the four of us," Caleb said.

"Okay, it looks like you all have big appetites tonight!" The waitress chuckled as she started collecting the menus.

They laughed and waited patiently for the food and drinks to arrive.

While they were waiting and chatting, Jonah looked at Haven a few times and noticed a scar on her neck he hadn't seen before. It looked old, as it was a faint brown color, and ran downward from the left side of her neck.

"If you don't mind me asking, how did you get the scar on your neck?" Jonah asked.

"It's just an old injury from a fight with a soldier," Haven answered hesitantly. She seemed reluctant to talk about it, putting her hand on her neck to cover the scar, so Jonah figured it would be best not to continue asking any more questions about it.

"So, what do you all think of Kenarios so far?" Caleb asked the group, trying to change the subject.

"Well, it seems quite different from where I'm from," Haven said.

"What do you mean, Haven?" Zak asked.

"Well, firstly, this place seems a lot more peaceful than Fasmeon. People appear to be more subdued and calmer. On Fasmeon, we have a lot of civil unrest and conflict. You can never be at peace on that planet. I'm lucky because I can escape from all that and go to Concordia as I please. But for millions of people that live on Fasmeon, they don't have that choice."

A tear gleamed in Haven's eye. In that moment, Jonah began to see her in a different light. Up to this point, he'd seen her as a little cold and hardhearted; however, now he was starting to see he had perhaps misjudged her. He sensed that deep down, she was an emotional young woman. Jonah thought about how difficult it would have been to live in a dimension under such harsh conditions. Perhaps she had a difficult time expressing those feelings. Jonah tried to comfort Haven by putting his arm around her. She pushed back and gave him a strange look.

"What are you doing, Jonah?" Haven gasped.

"I was trying to comfort you. That's what we do on Earth when someone is upset. Don't you do that on Fasmeon?" Jonah asked.

"No, we don't! Please don't do that again. That was weird and uncomfortable." Haven grimaced.

"I'm sorry." Jonah put his hands up—to concede—and moved away from Haven to give her some space.

The atmosphere had grown awkward and tense. Zak and Caleb knew Haven well enough to know they shouldn't get too physically close to her. The customs on Fasmeon were different from those of Earth, Maldoa, and Kenarios.

On Fasmeon, people didn't use physical contact to express joy or comfort to one another. This was an unfortunate byproduct of the planet's constant unrest. They didn't have many occasions to celebrate or to express joy and love to one another. It wasn't that Haven was particularly strange; it had more to do with the circumstances of her home planet and her upbringing that made her behave that way.

An uncomfortable silence lingered for a brief period. Afterward, Haven excused herself from the table and went to the bathroom. She was wearing shoes with small but mighty heels, so as she walked away, they drummed against the floor, reinforcing her annoyance with Jonah. As Jonah watched Haven walk away, Caleb and Zak smirked at him.

"Look, don't take what just happened with Haven too personally. She's just a little different from us. It's not a bad thing, but you need to be a little more mindful around her. She'll be fine. Don't worry about it too much," Zak explained.

"I hope she doesn't stay angry at me for too long. I don't want things to be unpleasant between us." After a brief period of silence, Jonah tried to change the subject. "So, tell me, Zak, your eyes are orange. I've never seen anyone with orange eyes before. Is that common on your planet?"

"On my planet, Maldoa, it's actually quite common. We also have people with purple and pink eyes too. It just adds to the charm. Trust me; women go crazy for my eyes."

"I don't," Haven interjected as she returned to the table. She had regained her composure and no longer seemed upset. They resumed talking as if nothing had happened while they waited for their food to arrive.

"Do you come here often?" Jonah asked Caleb.

"Yeah, I do. I used to come here with my ex-boyfriend a lot as well. It was one of our favorite places to eat and hang out."

"How long ago did you break up?" Zak asked.

"About six months ago. Trust me; I'm over it. He was a complete waste of time and space. I'm so much better off without him. Besides, I'm sure I'll find someone who's way better."

Four waitresses came to their table to deliver their food and drinks as Caleb finished speaking.

There were over ten different platters of food that arrived on the table. From what Jonah could see, the platters consisted of lots of different types of grilled meats and vegetables along with salads, breads, and sauces. The breads were flat and blue in color. Jonah also saw something that resembled grilled carrots; however, they were green; and what resembled roasted potatoes were purple.

The meat on the platters resembled food Jonah was familiar with from Earth, such as meatballs, chicken wings, ribs, shrimp, and squid. The salads contained vegetables Jonah thought were weird in color, such as yellow cucumbers and white tomatoes. Everything was somehow similar to what Jonah had seen on Earth but varied in color and texture.

As the food was placed on the table, one of the waitresses could see there wasn't enough room for all the platters. She grabbed a nearby empty table and connected it to where the group was sitting, so they could fit everything. Jonah looked at all the food and was amazed at the quantity. However, with the appetite Jonah had, he was ready to take on the challenge.

As the waitresses walked away, Jonah and everyone else started eating. They spent the next thirty minutes devouring every morsel of food. For Zak and Caleb, it became a competition to see who could finish their food first. On the other hand, Haven and Jonah preferred to take their time to savor their food and enjoy its flavor.

"This is a bit weird." Haven picked up a small white tomato, pressing it gently between her fingers to test its firmness and texture. "We don't have tomatoes like this where I'm from."

Moments later, Jonah's eyebrows rose. "Wow . . . that was spicy!" Jonah took a sip of his drink to calm down his mouth after eating what looked like a chicken wing that was too hot for his tastebuds to handle.

They each continued eating until the entirety of their platters were consumed. Caleb managed to finish eating first by a fraction of a second.

"That's how it's done!" Caleb boasted.

"Oh, please. We finished at the same time," Zak said, trying not to give Caleb the satisfaction.

Haven and Jonah finished several minutes later.

"I am so disgustingly full," Haven uttered as she sat back in her chair.

"So, what's your verdict, Jonah?" Caleb asked.

Jonah was holding onto his stomach. "That was amazing. The flavors danced in my mouth with all those amazing herbs and spices. Even though the wings almost burnt my mouth. And yes! I'm glad you brought me here tonight!"

"I'm glad you're glad!" Caleb laughed. "Do you have anything like this on Earth?"

"Well, the closest thing I can think of that resembles Shankani is this thing called Tapas. It's a similar sort of concept. Lots of platters with different foods on it," Jonah said.

"I think you might have to take us some time so we can compare," Caleb said enthusiastically.

"Just not right now; I'm way too full!" Jonah laughed.

"So, do you kids have any room for dessert?" One of the waitresses interrupted as she began clearing their table.

"Not tonight. I think we're done here." Caleb smiled. The waitress laughed and walked away with a stack of dirty dishes. They sat for a few minutes, talking while trying to digest their food.

As they chatted, a man sitting at a table on the other side of the restaurant stared at Haven. He had taken a bit of a fancy to her and was struck by her beauty. He had drunk a few beers during the evening and was now intoxicated. The man—in his mid-thirties, tall, well-built and with facial stubble—thought he would try his luck with Haven, thinking he could get lucky. Not paying attention to the three other young men she was with, he approached their table, stumbling a couple of times along the way, and struck up a conversation with Haven, who looked at him, repulsed.

"I'm Donzo. What's a little lady like yourself doing with these three chumps?"

Donzo's speech, notably slurred, was accompanied by an unnerving smile and brash attitude.

"Having a great time. Without you." Haven, with one eyebrow raised, gazed at Donzo.

Caleb and Zak chuckled while Jonah sat with a worried look. Donzo's smile instantly changed to a scowl.

"What are you two laughing at?" Donzo asked, looking at Caleb and Zak.

"Look, I think the young lady wants to be left alone. None of us wants any trouble. So how about you go back to your table and leave us alone to have a pleasant evening. And while you're at it, you can do the same," Caleb said calmly, trying not to irritate Donzo.

"Who the hell are you to tell me what to do, boy?" Donzo took a step forward toward Caleb, leaning in on him in a threatening manner.

"You should listen to what he said and go back to your table." Haven glared at Donzo with a vicious look in her eye.

"What are you gonna do about it if I don't, little lady?" Donzo taunted.

The 'little lady' comment enraged Haven. She loathed men that belittled her simply because she was a female. Haven grabbed Donzo's neck, banged his head against the table she was sitting at, and then threw him to the floor. Everyone in the restaurant gasped. The man was knocked unconscious.

Caleb, Zak, and Jonah looked at Haven, dumbfounded.

"We need to get the hell outta here!" Caleb shouted.

Caleb grabbed his wallet, quickly pulled some money out, and threw the bills on the table, hoping it would be enough to cover the cost of the food and drinks they'd consumed. Caleb grabbed Haven in a panic and instructed Jonah and Zak to start running out of the restaurant. They headed toward the alley Caleb had brought them to earlier. Once there, they all teleported back to Caleb's home.

"That was crazy Haven! You sure as hell took care of Donzo!" Zak shrieked.

"He was being a drunk jerk. He deserved what he got," Haven said.

"Listen, we need to change and get the hell back to Concordia quickly. Let's move it, people!" Caleb yelled.

They changed into their robes and teleported back to Concordia. Once they arrived safely, the group took a moment to catch their breaths.

The guys burst out laughing. Even Haven had a chuckle. They gave each other high fives and decided to call it a night. As they were about to go their separate ways for the evening, Jonah's father unexpectedly approached them from behind.

"Where the hell do you think you're all going?" Mason boomed.

Everyone turned and gawked at Mason's ominous look. His piercing eyes looked like atomic bombs ready to explode. While the group originally planned to head to their respective rooms, Mason had other ideas.

"You've got a lot of explaining to do!" Mason screeched.

"About what exactly?" Jonah asked with a meek smile, pretending nothing had happened that evening.

"I've just come from the Observatory, where I was watching you on Planet Kenarios. I saw everything!" Mason raised his voice. He faced Haven, who looked at him with dread-filled eyes.

"Haven, your behavior was simply unacceptable." Mason's face had become red with rage. "Injuring that man on Kenarios and banging his head on a table was nothing short of barbaric. Maybe that's acceptable on your own planet, but not on Kenarios, and certainly not by a Concordian. You've been here the longest; you should've known better. I also thought you were the most mature out of this group. I'm absolutely shocked at your actions. I expected better from you. And to make matters worse, you all came back here, gave each other high fives, and laughed like dimwits."

"But, Dad, that guy was going to assault Haven. All she did was protect herself," Jonah said.

"You don't know what that man was going to do," Mason said. "We deal with facts here, and the fact is Haven assaulted and injured someone without trying to diffuse the situation. Your response was way over the top. While I am not in a position to punish you, the Grand Guardian is. And you'll need to explain yourself to her tomorrow morning. Until then, I suggest you think very carefully about what you're going to say to her.

"As for the rest of you, I recommend you think about what happened and why it was inappropriate. Thank your lucky stars that you don't have to answer to the Grand Guardian. Now, off you go. It's getting late and you should all be in bed."

None of them said another word. Everybody walked back to their rooms.

Jonah was shocked by how livid his father was. He hadn't seen his dad get that angry in a long time. A perfectly good evening had now been tainted by a silly mistake. Perhaps his father was right; they could have tried better to placate Donzo. That way, Haven could have avoided getting physical with him, which in turn would have averted the whole situation.

As Jonah returned to his room, he didn't really feel like doing much. Partly because he was tired and partly because he felt emotionally exhausted from being yelled at. He hopped into bed and drifted off to sleep, hoping a good night's sleep would make everything better.

CHAPTER 13

"**G**overnor, Lieutenant Lomar is here to see you." Amani said.

"Very well, send him in."

A moment later, Lieutenant Lomar walked into Governor Ragnar's chambers while Amani remained outside and sat at her desk. The governor was expecting his son for an update on the teleporter project and wasn't in the mood to discuss frivolous matters. Lomar stood to attention opposite the governor, who was standing, facing the window and staring into the vastness outside.

"This better be good, Lieutenant. My son will be here soon, so I don't have time to waste."

"Governor, we have detained an individual who has been trying to spread panic amongst the population. He was demonstrating in Huron and espousing the use of alternative sources of energy, telling everyone the planet is running out of Chrimatide and that we will run out of power soon. And if we don't use these alternative methods, the planet will be left in the dark, and we'll all starve to death."

As Lomar was speaking, the governor turned around to face him. Governor Ragnar's face fumed. His eyes bulged and lips tightened as his anger festered, ready to explode at any moment.

"And where is he now?" Governor Ragnar asked.

"We're holding him in a prison cell. What would you like us to do with him?"

The governor paused for a moment, thinking about what to do with the detainee. However, one question burned in his mind: *How did this individual know that the planet was running out of Chrimatide?*

"Take me to him. I'd like to have a word with him," Governor Ragnar said with gritted teeth.

Lomar escorted the governor down to the prison cells located one floor beneath the governor's chambers. Every footstep the governor took was filled with rage. The sound of each step reverberated throughout the corridors. He had little tolerance for anyone who tried to defy the use of Chrimatide as an energy source, especially for people who tried promoting alternative power supplies. Governor Ragnar had to deal with these situations occasionally, which he saw as a huge waste of his time. However, the governor also saw them as an opportunity to showcase to everyone around him, as well the world at large, why he shouldn't be challenged.

When they arrived at the prison cell, Lomar unlocked the door and Governor Ragnar barged in. The prison complex was located underground and had no natural light coming in. There weren't many lights inside either, making the complex feel grimly dark. Due to poor ventilation, it was dank and the air had an unpleasant musty smell to it.

The governor could see the handcuffed detainee was sitting on a chair in the cell. He was a slender man in his mid-thirties with long brown hair and a lengthy beard. He had multiple piercings on his face, and his arms were covered in tattoos. Governor Ragnar took one look at him and immediately thought he was just like the rest of the insurgents he had to deal with in the past—an imbecilic piece of garbage.

"What is your name?" Governor Ragnar asked.

The detainee didn't answer. He stared at Governor Ragnar with contempt for about thirty seconds. The governor slapped him across the face several times and grabbed him by the neck in a chokehold.

"I said, *what is your name?*" Governor Ragnar asked again with rage in his voice.

"Levi," he responded, struggling to speak.

"There you go. That wasn't difficult," Governor Ragnar said, releasing Levi's neck. "Now, explain what you were doing earlier today. Why were you telling people we need alternative energy sources and panicking people into thinking we are running out of energy?"

Levi coughed a couple of times and tried to catch his breath before answering.

"Because we are! We're running out of Chrimatide again, and soon we won't have any left. And we won't have any power, and eventually, without power, we won't be able to produce food, and we are all going to starve to death!"

"And where did you hear this from?" Governor Ragnar asked.

The governor was now even more furious. Who told this insurgent the planet was running out of Chrimatide? Was someone leaking information outside of Governor Ragnar's inner circle? If so, who could it be? That was a matter to be dealt with later. For now, he had this insurrectionist, Levi, to deal with.

"I'll never tell you where I heard it from! We have so many other alternatives to use instead of Chrimatide, and you won't use them because you're so damn greedy and want to control this whole planet with your leadership. Using stupid Chrimatide! To hell with you!" Levi screamed.

"Is that your final answer?" Governor Ragnar asked.

"It sure is." Levi spat in the governor's face.

The governor had reached his limit. He was no longer willing to deal with Levi's mutiny or foul-mouthed explosions of hatred directed at him. After wiping his face with a handkerchief from his pocket, the governor reached to grab his gun located on the right side of his tool belt, which he always wore. He pulled it out of his holster, aimed it at Levi's head, and shot him without hesitation. Levi died instantly. His corpse remained in the chair, lifeless and bloodied.

Governor Ragnar used his handkerchief and began wiping blood spatter from his face.

"Lomar, clean up this mess and get rid of the body."

"Yes, Governor, right away," Lomar said. Having witnessed the governor's violence many times before, Lomar didn't have any discernable reaction. He simply followed the governor's orders.

Lieutenant Lomar called for someone to assist in removing the body from the prison cell and to organize for the mess on the walls and floor to be cleaned up. Governor Ragnar turned around and walked out of the prison cell and back to his chamber, satisfied his planet had one less radical to deal with.

When he returned to his chamber, Governor Ragnar found his son, Zyaire, waiting for him. His cold demeanor quickly turned into that of a loving father in the blink of an eye.

"Sorry to have kept you waiting, Son. I had a matter to attend to," Governor Ragnar said.

"It's okay, Dad. I know you're a very busy man. I'm just here to give you an update on the teleporter project." Zyaire was sitting on a chair in front of the governor's desk. He turned his head slightly to look at his father as he walked in.

"Wonderful, so how is that all coming along?" Governor Ragnar asked with a smile as he sat on his armchair behind his desk.

Zyaire went on to talk about how the project was progressing while Governor Ragnar sat there pretending as if nothing had happened. He had no remorse for killing Levi. To the governor, Levi was nothing more than a distraction. A mere nuisance that had been dealt with, never to be a bother to anyone again.

Meanwhile, Zyaire was completely oblivious to his father's actions, which was what Governor Ragnar preferred. He never divulged to Zyaire the majority of his cruel actions; the governor preferred for his son to think his father was good.

After updating his father on the progress of the teleporter project, Zyaire left Governor Ragnar's chambers and walked to an underground garage located within the same compound. Ensuring no one was watching him, he approached one of his father's hovercrafts—used as a mode of transportation over long distances on land—and pulled out a dark brown velvet cloak from the storage compartment of the vehicle. He put the cloak on and covered his head with the hood so he wouldn't be recognized.

As he boarded the vehicle, Zyaire pressed the ignition button and started the hovercraft. The hovercraft levitated ten inches off the ground before he began making his way to the garage exit, where Zyaire waited for the closed gates to open. Once the gates opened and there was a sufficient gap for him to move through the exit, he quickly fled.

Zyaire travelled for about thirty miles to a nearby town known as Tepsey. When he approached the town, he disembarked the main highway and took lesser-known streets and alleyways; Zyaire was hoping to not draw any attention to himself.

Arriving at his destination, Zyaire parked his hovercraft in an alleyway not far from the home he was visiting. When he disembarked, the hovercraft settled on the ground quietly, and Zyaire walked the rest of the way to an apartment building ten stories high. He entered the building and walked down a flight of stairs to the underground level.

Zyaire approached one of the apartment doors and knocked. Moments later, the door opened. It was Ava, Levi's sister. She quickly grabbed Zyaire and pulled him into the apartment, closing the door before she said anything.

"Is Levi here?" Zyaire asked.

"No, he's not!" Ava replied, wild-eyed and speaking quickly. "He went to a demonstration earlier and hasn't come home yet. I'm really worried about him. I haven't heard from him and have tried calling him several times, but he's not answering. I think something has happened to him."

"Where was he demonstrating?" Zyaire asked.

"It was over in Huron, ten minutes from here."

"Okay, you stay here; I'll go and look for him."

Zyaire walked out from the front door and ran to his hovercraft. He boarded the vehicle and started heading toward Huron.

When he arrived in Huron, Zyaire went to the center of the town, where he saw a small group of people cleaning the mess left behind from the demonstration. There were leaflets all over the ground, along with abandoned signs emblazoned with words such as "Chrimatide is dirty!" and "There are alternatives!" He parked his hovercraft and walked over to a man helping with the cleanup effort.

"Do you know someone by the name of Levi? He was here earlier leading a demonstration."

"Yes, I know who you're talking about. He was swarmed by Governor Ragnar's soldiers, and they took him away from here. I can only assume it was to slaughter him," the man said.

Zyaire gasped. Without saying a word to the man, Zyaire rushed back to his hovercraft. He frantically started it up and headed back to his father's headquarters. Zyaire prayed he wasn't too late.

Although his father acted nice to him and treated him like a loving son, Zyaire knew there was a dark side to Governor Ragnar. He had been told of some of the grotesque things his father had done over the years and the way he governed Planet Zareet. Zyaire understood what the governor was capable of and feared the worst for Levi.

After he arrived at headquarters, Zyaire parked his hovercraft in the underground garage and hurried into the main building. He rushed toward the prison cells to see if Levi was there. As he approached one of the cells, Zyaire glimpsed a filled body bag lying on the ground in the corridor. His jaw dropped.

Zyaire paused for a moment, not knowing what to do. After a minute of staring at the body bag, he approached the entrance to the jail cell and quickly looked inside to see if anyone was there. Two people were cleaning the blood stains off the walls and floor of the jail cell. Zyaire stepped away from the entrance so they wouldn't see him.

He pressed himself up against a wall for a moment, collecting his thoughts. Then, looking at the body bag, Zyaire knelt down and slowly opened the bag, being as quiet as possible to avoid being noticed by the cleaners. He opened it up just enough so he could see the head of the body. It was Levi.

Zyaire put his left hand over his mouth so he wouldn't gasp and be heard. Tears welled in his eyes. He gently closed the body bag and gradually got up. He slowly took a few steps back from the corpse and scurried away from the prison cell. Zyaire continued running, leaving the compound to get as far away as possible. The shock of seeing Levi dead gave him an adrenaline rush that helped power his escape.

Running, the only thing that Zyaire kept repeatedly asking himself was, *Did my father have anything to do with this?*

After ten minutes of running, Zyaire stopped in a forested area. It was a quiet area that he frequented when he wanted to get away from his father and be alone. Surrounded by trees and a stream, Zyaire waited to catch his breath. When his breathing normalized, he screamed as loud as he could. It was an abominable scream filled with rage.

When he finished, Zyaire collapsed on the ground and cried uncontrollably. Levi—the man he had fallen in love with over a year ago, his best friend and lover—was now dead.

Crying for almost an hour, Zyaire could only come up with one conclusion. Governor Ragnar had killed him, or he'd commanded one of his soldiers to do so. Either way, his father was to blame—something he could not forgive.

Zyaire wasn't foolish. He was well aware of what a ruthless ruler the governor was. Levi had opened Zyaire's eyes to everything Governor Ragnar did. Zyaire went along with his father's game to help Levi fight for his cause. Now that Levi was gone, was there any reason to still pretend? Zyaire decided to continue the status quo until he could figure out his next move. For now, he'd give himself a few moments to grieve before giving Ava the terrible news.

CHAPTER 14

J *onah. Get up!* Mason shouted.

Jonah didn't respond. He was lying in bed, on his back, sleeping peacefully.

Jonah . . . get up! Mason commanded again.

Jonah opened his eyes and abruptly sat up in bed, overcome with shock from having his sleep unexpectedly interrupted. He glanced around his room and couldn't see anyone. Jonah presumed it must've been a dream. He figured perhaps his subconscious was playing tricks on him, especially after what had happened with his father the previous night. Jonah laid down again, taking in a few deep breaths to pacify his racing heart.

As he lay in bed, Jonah heard his father's voice.

Jonah, can you please come to my room at once?

Jonah didn't respond. Instead, he lay in his bed and rolled his eyes, trying to ignore his father.

I said, 'can you come to my room at once?' Mason asked again, frustrated at Jonah's lack of response.

"Okay, okay. I'll be there shortly." Jonah feared the request had something to do with what had occurred the night before. Perhaps Mason was about to give him another lecture about what had transpired on Kenarios.

Jonah paused for a moment. He couldn't see his father in his bedroom, and there was no microphone system in the room either. So, where was Mason's voice coming from?

He walked from his bed and went to check the bathroom. There was no one there. He checked under the bed. Again, no one was there.

Hurry up, Son, I don't have all day! Mason was growing impatient.

"Dad, where are you?"

I'm in my room.

"But how can I hear you?" Jonah glanced around in confusion.

I'll explain everything when you get here.

Did I just hear Dad's voice in my head? Jonah walked over to his parents' room. When he arrived, he knocked on the door and entered the room. His father stood alone, waiting for Jonah.

Well, it's about time, Mason said. However, Jonah noticed Mason's lips weren't moving. His mouth was shut tight, yet Jonah could hear him loud and clear.

"How can I hear you?" Jonah asked.

Jonah, this is another gift you have: the ability to communicate telepathically. This is an important power you should master. It can be a useful tool when you need to communicate with another Guardian outside of Concordia. We mainly use it during combat when we need to speak with each other and don't want our opponents to hear. So, this gift is beneficial.

"Okay. So how do I use this gift?" Jonah asked.

Well, it's going to take practice. You'll need to focus on what you want to say. That's the hard part, as your mind can easily wander in so many directions and get distracted. If that happens, it can disrupt your communication. I want you to give it a try. Really focus on me and attempt to say a word. Any word you'd like.

As Mason finished his telepathic conversation, Jonah tried to focus and respond. His father, in turn, tried to channel what Jonah was saying. Unfortunately, other thoughts kept running through Jonah's head, which he unwittingly projected to Mason.

Son, I don't need to see your fantasies about Haven. I just want you to project a conversation to me!

For some reason, Jonah had fantasized about Haven, remembering a time when he looked at her running her hands through her hair. She was standing in the Training Center, gazing outside a window into the main

Concordian city. Jonah had inadvertently projected this to Mason. His cheeks heated as he averted his father's gaze.

Jonah tried for several minutes to communicate something telepathically. He focused hard to the point that his head started trembling as if he was having a seizure. After his head quivered for a few moments, he stopped and took a few deep breaths.

I can't do this! Jonah thought.

Yes, you can, Jonah. You just did it. I heard you say, 'I can't do this.'

Oh, okay. Dad, I'm hungry. I need breakfast!

You're hungry, and you need breakfast. I heard that! Very good, Jonah.

Finally. That was hard work. Jonah grinned.

"It won't be that difficult from now on. With some practice, it should become rather effortless."

"Awesome. I meant what I said: I really am hungry!" Jonah laughed.

"All right, point taken! Before you go, I can't emphasize enough how important it is to practice this new skill. Perhaps try it out with your friends and see if you can fine-tune it. For now, you should go eat something before you wither away. Besides, I've just been called into the Observatory, so I'll catch up with you a bit later."

"Sure. Thanks, Dad. I really appreciate it."

"You're welcome, Son."

Jonah and his father left the room with Mason heading toward the Observatory and Jonah heading to his own room. On the way, Jonah encountered Caleb and Zak. They both had worried looks on their faces.

"Jonah, have you seen Haven?" Caleb asked anxiously.

Jonah was curious why Caleb and Zak were agitated. "No, I haven't seen her this morning. Why?"

"We're just a bit worried about her. We've looked everywhere on Concordia and can't find her. After the lecture she received from your father last night, we think she might have gone into hiding," Zak said.

"You don't suppose she's gone to her home on Fasmeon?" Jonah asked.

Caleb thought about it for a moment. "Maybe. Who knows? I just hope she's okay. I mean, she should be. She's quite resilient. But it would've been nice to speak to her and know she's all right."

Zak echoed Caleb's sentiment.

"It could be that the Grand Guardian is talking to her. My dad did mention Haven would have to speak with her today," Jonah said.

Caleb concurred. "You're probably right. I hope the Grand Guardian isn't too harsh with her. Anyhow, who's up for some breakfast? I know this great place on Kenarios that makes some of the best waffles. You guys up for it?"

"You're crazy! After what happened last night, I'm going anywhere you recommend!" Jonah was irritated by the suggestion.

"I'm with Jonah on this one," Zak said.

"You guys are no fun. How about we go to the Community Center, then?" Caleb suggested.

"The Community Center? What's that?" Jonah asked.

"It's not too far from here. It's this big place where people can hang out and eat, that sorta thing," Zak explained.

Jonah was excited. "Okay. I've never been there before, so I wouldn't mind checking it out."

While Jonah wasn't ordinarily much of a social person, he somehow felt comfortable with Caleb and Zak and was willing to try something new. On Earth, when he'd attended parties with Shane and Jason, it wasn't because he really wanted to go to those parties. Rather, his friends had dragged him along. With Caleb and Zak, he genuinely wanted to spend time with them and looked forward to the experience.

They walked to the Community Center and entered the building. On the inside, it was adorned with comfortable armchairs and plush royal blue couches. To the left of that area were lots of dining tables and chrome chairs with comfortable padding for people to sit and eat. Zak spotted a free table and pointed it out to Caleb and Jonah. They all walked to the table and sat.

Jonah noticed a lot of Guardians present; it was a lot busier than he had expected. Nonetheless, the Community Center was inviting and cozy, which made everyone feel welcome. Jonah felt like he belonged there, despite being in the midst of a large crowd of people.

Everyone was sitting down at tables in small groups, eating and talking to one another. One table, a few feet away from where Jonah was sitting, had a large group of people that were laughing. There was one individual at the table, a man who looked to be in his forties with black hair that was starting to go grey, who was particularly boisterous.

"There always has to be the loud one," Jonah whispered to Caleb and Zak, trying not to get the other table's attention. They all smiled at each other.

After talking for a few minutes, they each started manifesting their own breakfasts to eat. In typical fashion, Caleb and Zak tried to outdo each other with the amount of food they were manifesting to eat.

"Guys, that's enough!" Jonah hollered. "We're running out of room on the table. How about we first eat all this food, then, if you guys are still hungry, you can create some more."

"All right, all right. Stop howling," Zak said.

Zak and Caleb created everything from omelets to pancakes, French toast to croissants, fresh fruit, bacon, sausages, hash browns, cereal, and waffles. The list went on and on. There was no way they were going to eat all the food they conjured. Jonah felt that manifesting more food was going to be incredibly wasteful.

They devoured their large meals with gusto. People sitting at tables nearby stared at them and the amount of food on the table.

"You must be new to Concordia?" a woman from a nearby table commented to Jonah and his friends.

"Yes, we are. How did a beautiful young lady like yourself deduce such a thing?" Zak asked in a flirtatious tone.

"My *husband* and I can normally tell. Usually, new Guardians like to get carried away with the amount of food they like to manifest." The young woman deliberately mentioned her husband, sensing that Zak was trying to hit on her.

"I see." Zak's face immediately changed from hopeful to dejected as he realized he didn't have a chance with her.

Haven was at her parent's house on Planet Fasmeon. After what had happened the previous night and the lecture she'd received from Mason, Haven had felt the need to retreat and escape to a place where she could spend time in solitude with her thoughts. She felt terrible about what had happened. Not only for knocking the man unconscious in the restaurant but also because she got her new friends into trouble. Haven couldn't shake the image of Mason yelling at everyone for something she'd done.

Haven had spent the night at her parents' house, managing a few hours of sleep after dozing off on the couch in the living room. Soon after waking, her mother, Elina, and Guardian Ezra teleported in front of her. Unable to find her on Concordia, Elina figured she might find Haven in their family home.

Seeing Ezra and her mother in the living room, both with somber looks on their faces, Haven could only guess why they were there.

"There you are, Haven. I've been looking for you all morning around Concordia. I figured you might be here," Elina said.

"Yes, I needed some time alone. Something really bad happened last night."

"Yes, I heard. Ezra informed me earlier."

Haven sensed the disappointment in her mother's voice.

"Oh, I see. So why is Ezra here?" Haven asked.

"Grand Guardian Omiya has personally asked me to find you. She has requested you go and see her in her chambers as soon as possible," Ezra said.

"That doesn't sound very good." Haven's stomach sank.

"No, it's not good at all." Ezra's eyebrows furrowed. "And may I suggest we see her immediately? She doesn't appreciate being ignored, nor having to wait lengthy periods of time for people to respond to her summons."

"C'mon, Haven, let's go. It's time to face the music." Elina grabbed Haven's hand.

They teleported back to Concordia, where Ezra escorted Haven and her mother to the Grand Guardian's chambers. As they entered the chambers, Grand Guardian Omiya was there to welcome everyone in. Haven and Elina were directed to sit on chairs in front of the Grand Guardian's desk, while Ezra remained standing.

Haven was impressed by how lavish the chambers were, with the opulent throne-like chair the Grand Guardian sat in covered in a blue microfiber, which not only looked very comfortable but seemed pleasant to the touch. The desk the Grand Guardian sat behind was large, about ten feet wide, and made from a dark timber that had ornate carvings sculpted into it. The chamber was adorned with various trinkets. Haven assumed the Grand Guardian had collected these from her extensive travels, throughout the many dimensions she had visited during her lifetime. Ornaments of animals were featured prominently in the trinket collection, which led Haven to believe that the Grand Guardian had an immense fondness for animals.

After a few moments of looking around, admiring the chambers, Haven remembered why she was there and began to feel numb. She wasn't sure what to expect.

"Haven, thank you for coming to see me so promptly," the Grand Guardian said.

"Yes, Grand Guardian." Haven's voice was laced with fear as she bowed her head to the Grand Guardian.

"It has been brought to my attention that last night you and some friends visited Planet Kenarios for a meal. During that visit, there was an incident in which you got into an altercation with a drunk man, and you physically injured him. Is that correct?" Grand Guardian Omiya asked.

"Yes, it is, Grand Guardian," Haven responded timidly, her eyes facing the floor.

"Haven, I have to say, I'm very disappointed in your behavior. While I'm glad you all got out of there unharmed, what you did was reckless and irresponsible."

Although the Grand Guardian was incensed, she remained calm and restrained in her tone. Haven felt dismayed, not only in herself but in the fact she'd also disappointed the Grand Guardian and her mother. She looked up to the Grand Guardian as a role model, which was why her disapproval stung Haven's conscience so much.

"I'm so incredibly sorry," Haven said, almost in tears.

"Haven, you're a Guardian. As such, you need to be more discerning in your choice of physical battles. You're meant to use your abilities as a last resort for self-defense, not in the first instance. That's an important lesson you're going to have to learn. As Guardians, we have a strict code of conduct, and any breaches could result in you being suspended from Concordia, or even worse, you could be expelled altogether."

As the Grand Guardian mentioned the words 'suspension' and 'expelled,' Haven's eyes opened wide. A wave of fear shrouded her, and she was petrified about her place in Concordia.

"But since you are relatively new, we are prepared to give you some latitude. The Executive Council and I have decided to let this go with a warning. But I caution you: this latitude won't last forever. This type of behavior will not be tolerated again."

"Once again Grand Guardian Omiya, I'm immensely sorry."

Haven's heart sank. She hadn't realized the gravity of the situation and was now even more remorseful.

"Haven, whatever is done is done. It's now in the past. Sitting around moping about your past actions isn't healthy. You must learn from this experience and move forward. To do otherwise is to become a victim, which will not help your spiritual development."

"Yes, Grand Guardian."

"And another thing—the man you injured on Kenarios is okay. I have been told by Mason from the Observatory that the man did have to go to hospital, but his injuries were relatively mild and he has made a full recovery. Luckily for you, it wasn't any more serious than that. Otherwise, we'd be having a very different conversation right now. Consider yourself very fortunate in that regard."

"Yes, Grand Guardian."

"Anyhow, I think I've reprimanded you enough. Hopefully, what I've told you has sunk in. You may now leave. And remember—you need to learn from this and move forward."

As she said that, the Grand Guardian rose from her seat and motioned for Haven and Elina to leave her chambers. They got up and left. Haven was relieved it was all over. Elina was pleased Haven was only given a warning. She believed it could have been much worse.

"Haven, please don't put me through something like that again!"

"I'm so sorry. I didn't intend for this to happen. I can't believe I did something so stupid and it got me into so much trouble."

Haven's eyes stared at the ground.

"Haven, it would pay to listen to the Grand Guardian's wisdom and counsel. Now, go and do something productive. Do you have any training today?"

"Yes, I'm meant to be there now."

"Good. Well, you best be off then. The training might help you get your mind off things."

Elina and Haven parted ways with Elina heading off to meet some friends, while Haven attended her training session.

When Haven arrived at the Training Center she found Caleb, Zak, and Jonah doing warm-up exercises with Aurora. She approached the group and asked Aurora if she could speak with her friends. The group stopped what they were doing and gathered around Haven.

"I'll give you all a few minutes to have a chat, and then we'll dive straight into training." Aurora stepped aside to give them some space.

"Thank you, Aurora," Haven said as Aurora walked away. "I've just returned from meeting with the Grand Guardian. She gave me some very stern words and a warning not to repeat my stupid actions from last night, ever again. I wanted to say sorry to you guys for getting you into trouble with Mason last night. I hope you can forgive me?"

"Well. Getting yelled at by Jonah's father wasn't a pleasant experience. I feel so deeply troubled in my heart by these events," Zak said, trying not to laugh. "It's going to take time for me to reflect on this incident and to heal these wounds psychologically. Wounds that have so deeply impacted every fiber of my soul and the very core of my being. The sanctity of my existence has been compromised and—"

"You're a jerk!" Haven gently smacked Zak's head.

He erupted into laughter, as did Caleb and Jonah. A moment later, Zak, Caleb, and Jonah embraced Haven in a group hug, which bewildered Haven.

"Get off me!" Haven yelled, pushing the guys away from her with her arms.

This made the guys laugh even more. They stepped away from Haven, respecting her need for personal space.

"It's all good, Haven," Zak said, still laughing at Haven.

"Oh really? So, you're 'psychologically' healed now?" Haven asked.

"That's never going to be possible," Caleb teased.

Zak grabbed Caleb in a headlock and tackled him to the ground, which led to the two wrestling each other. Haven and Jonah stood back. Haven rolled her eyes while Jonah looked on, urging the guys to put a stop to their antics.

Strangely, this event brought the group closer together. They had this unique bond of friendship that was unmistakably growing and developing exponentially. An inexplicable comradery was forming amongst them—something Jonah had never experienced before on Earth. It certainly wasn't something he'd ever expected to find in Concordia.

It made him feel like he belonged somewhere and that he was part of a family. Jonah felt like, for the first time in his life, he had found some like-minded people he jelled with who not only understood him, but just as importantly, he understood them.

Caleb and Zak eventually stopped wrestling each other as Aurora came back and ordered them to regain their decorum. They completed warm-up exercises and continued with their grueling workout, which lasted several hours.

CHAPTER 15

The Middle Astral Realm

E lder Ezekiel and Elder Baldel went to check in on how Master Jakeel (Jonah) was progressing on his life journey. They approached his Spirit Guides—Ondasha and Rumshana—who were busy watching his every move in Concordia. Ondasha and Rumshana were in a separate room of the temple known as a Life Monitoring Room. They watched Master Jakeel from a live stream being projected onto a white wall of the viewing room.

"How is Master Jakeel progressing on his life journey?" Elder Ezekiel asked Ondasha and Rumshana as he and Elder Baldel entered the room.

Spirit Guides, like all beings in the Middle Astral Realm, had soul bodies that resembled transparent human beings. They could also transform into any shape or form they wanted as required.

"We can report that he's now living in Concordia as planned," Rumshana said. "He's undergoing training to become a Guardian, so in that regard, he's doing well and is on schedule. However, he's fallen short in dealing with the loss of his grandfather. If you recall, Master Jakeel wanted to explore grief during his lifetime, and I'm afraid he isn't dealing with it effectively. He's barely shed a tear since his grandfather's loss, which has stunted his emotional progress and growth.

"As it stands now, it's not going to change anytime soon on his current trajectory. This is going to be a problem, as he has other more advanced grief lessons to deal with in the future, which can't happen until he has dealt with this first. So, we believe something needs to change. It may be time for an intervention."

The Elders both looked at Rumshana and Ondasha for a moment, contemplating if what they were saying had merit. In the Middle Astral Realm, the Elders had the ability to move through time and space with ease and to watch someone's life events instantaneously. This was done, by moving their hands left or right over the stream to move backward or forward in time.

The live streams also had the ability to project multiple alternative time-lines at once. The Elders were powerful enough to view this information simultaneously, so they could determine the most optimal timeline for Jonah, that would allow him the greatest growth as a soul.

After going over the events since Master Jakeel lost his grandfather, they looked at each other and nodded. The Elders reached a decision.

"We concur with your findings," Elder Baldel said. "It's time for Master Jakeel to face his grief. From what we determined in the life scan we just carried out, he has an emotional block in his aura. He's had this for some time. If left unchecked, it will get worse and lead to illness in his physical body. And as you mentioned earlier, there's no change ahead, based on his current timeline, that will lead to a greater awareness of his hidden sorrow or its release. We must therefore enact an event that will unblock his aura and trigger the clearing of his emotional trauma. This will, in turn, elevate him to a higher timeline that will enable him to grow and undertake the more advanced lessons he has chosen."

"How do you think we should do this?" Ondasha asked.

"I think it's time for Master Jakeel to visit the Akashic Records, where he can consult his universal record and review his behavior," Elder Ezekiel said. "One visit there, and he will have no other choice but to face his grief."

"Very well," Rumshana responded. "We'll begin orchestrating the events for that to happen."

"Thank you, Rumshana," Elder Ezekiel said. "We'll return and get an update in due course."

While the Spirit Guides began preparations for Jakeel's visit to the Akashic Records, the Elders left the Life Monitoring Room and went to check in on some other souls to see how their lives on Earth were unfolding.

CHAPTER 16

The Physical Realm

In the early morning, Aurora was in her room, getting ready to head off to the Training Center for another session with Jonah and his friends. Mason was still in bed, wide awake. He didn't have any work in the Observatory to do and had the day to himself for rest and relaxation.

"Is there something on your mind?" Aurora looked at Mason and could see he was pensive.

"I was just thinking that today is four months since Dad passed away. I still miss him so much."

"It's perfectly normal, my love. Grief can be a long, bumpy ride."

Aurora looked at Mason with compassion, knowing he still had a long way to go on his grief journey.

While Mason and Aurora were getting on with their lives and dutifully carrying out their roles as parents and Guardians, it didn't stop Mason from missing his father. Although he was a grown man in his mid-forties, he wished his father was still around. Mason had an enormous amount of love for Luke, despite their relationship being difficult at times.

"What's your plan for today?" Aurora asked as she was tying her hair up into a bun on her head.

Mason grinned. "To not move from here."

"You know, I've got an idea." Aurora jumped onto the bed and lay next to Mason. "How about you go to our house on Earth to sort out your father's belongings?"

As Aurora asked the question, Mason's grin disappeared. He immediately felt listless. He had spent the last few months avoiding having to do anything about his father's personal effects. A part of him didn't want to let go of them.

"You've been shying away from that chore for months. The sooner you do it, the sooner I will stop nagging you about it," Aurora said through gritted teeth as she put her hand on Mason's shoulder and jolted him a few times.

"Okay, okay. I'll go." Mason laughed.

Aurora stopped shaking Mason and looked at him briefly with a smile.

"It'll be cathartic for you."

Aurora adoringly rubbed the tip of Mason's nose with her finger. Shortly after, she gave Mason a parting kiss and left to attend her training session.

Meanwhile, Mason slowly tumbled out of bed and got dressed in Earth clothes. He teleported to his home on Earth, initially appearing in the kitchen. Mason purposely landed there so he could have a few extra moments to stall the inevitable.

He stood for a moment, taking in a deep breath. As he trudged to his father's bedroom, Mason's stomach churned and his heart began beating a little bit faster. As he reached the bedroom door, he stopped for a moment.

"Do I really need to do this?" Mason asked himself out loud, pausing for a few moments. "I suppose I have to at some point."

The bedroom door was closed. It hadn't been open since the day Luke passed. Mason slowly opened the door. Everything was exactly the way it had been left on the day of Luke's passing. Luke's bed hadn't been made up from the last night he had slept in it. There was a pile of dirty clothes still sitting on one corner of the bed, that Luke had intended to put in the washing machine after breakfast the day he died.

Photos littered his dresser. Some were of Luke's wife, Evelyn, while other photos were of Luke, Mason, and Evelyn when Mason was in his late teens. Then there was a photo of the day Aurora and Mason got married. Luke and Evelyn were both in the photo, standing next to Aurora and Mason.

He picked up the photo to look at it closely. It put a smile on Mason's face. His father looked so young; Luke's hair hadn't turned grey yet. His mother looked so happy and beamed with joy. He remembered that day so vividly. It had been a perfect wedding, and it was one of the happiest days of Mason's life. He and Aurora got married in May when it was late spring. The weather was a perfect warm day with not a cloud in the sky but plenty of family and friends that loved and supported them.

After staring at the photo for a few minutes and reminiscing about some of the fond memories he had of his parents, Mason put the photo down and got straight to work sorting Luke's clothes into piles. One had clothes he thought were in good condition that could be donated to a local charity, and the other pile were clothes that needed to be thrown out.

"Seriously, Dad, you kept this old, tattered shirt?" Mason said out loud, shaking his head before tossing the shirt into the throw-out pile.

After about an hour of sorting out the clothes and putting them neatly into bags to take to charity, he started going through his father's bedside drawers. Most of it wasn't of much value, just scraps of old papers and various knick-knacks. However, he did find his father's beloved pendant.

The pendant was oval-shaped and made of a green apatite gemstone encased in a thin gold frame with a hexagonal-shaped cavity in the middle that only went halfway through the pendant; the pendant was attached to a long gold necklace. Mason grabbed the pendant and looked at it for a few moments.

Wow, I haven't seen this in years, Mason thought to himself.

He had forgotten his father even had it. However, Mason did remember Luke telling him many times over the years that when he passed away, the pendant would need to be given to Jonah. After taking one final look at it, Mason put it in his pocket for safekeeping to take back to Concordia, so he could give it to his son when he saw him next.

In the meantime, Mason continued clearing out his father's belongings and tidying up Luke's bedroom. Mason threw what he considered rubbish in the trash while he put the clothes to be given to charity in his car. The family photos Luke had on his dresser were left where they were. Mason couldn't bear to move them, or throw them out, or even put them away in a box for safekeeping. He felt the need to leave something behind as a reminder that this was once Luke's space. Mason closed the door as he took one last look at Luke's room.

Later that day, after dropping Luke's old clothes off at a charity, he arrived back in Concordia, where he spent time alone in his room. Mason sat on his bed for a while, thinking about what he had done. After delaying it for so many months, he had finally let go of his father's belongings. As he came to that realization, he began to cry. It was as if a weight had been lifted off his shoulder. Although Mason had grieved for his father many times since his passing, a small part of him hadn't completely let go. Clearing his father's personal effects was the final action he needed to release his emotional pain.

After crying for a few minutes, Mason took a couple of deep breaths and wiped his tears away. Feeling a little tired, he took his shoes off and decided to take a short nap.

Mason woke up an hour later feeling refreshed. Remembering he had Luke's pendant to give to Jonah, Mason got up to see if Jonah had gotten back from his training session with his mother. As he was about to leave his room, he decided it would be best to speak with Guardian Ishwa instead. Mason needed to let Ishwa know about the pendant first.

He telepathically contacted Ishwa and asked to see him. Within a matter of seconds, Ishwa appeared in Mason's room.

"Mason, this is a nice surprise. It's been a while since we've spoken."

"Yes, it has. Thank you for seeing me on such short notice."

"Is everything okay, Mason?"

"Yes, I'm fine. I just wanted to let you know I was going through my father's belongings earlier today and found his pendant. I thought I would let you know I'm planning on giving it to Jonah tonight when he gets back from his training."

Mason took it out of his pocket and showed Ishwa. Ishwa took hold of it for a moment and looked at it.

"At last, Mason, you found it. It's good timing, too. I really think Jonah is ready for a visit to the Akashic Records. I might pay him a visit after you've passed it on to him."

All Guardians had these pendants passed down to them in their families. They were for the purpose of being able to astral project into the Upper

Astral Plane to visit the Akashic Records. Ishwa knew of Luke's pendent as he had seen it several times before. They both had travelled together to the Akashic Records on a few occasions over the years. Visiting the Akashic Records was usually to help with an individual's growth, so they could see things about themselves that they weren't willing to see.

"I'll let you know once I've given it to him."

"Please do Mason."

The two continued talking like old friends that hadn't seen each other in years. Mason talked about his experience clearing out his father's belongings on Earth, while Ishwa listened patiently and imparted some much-needed wisdom that Mason appreciated.

CHAPTER 17

During the four months since Luke's passing, Jonah hadn't been to university. He chose to postpone his studies to focus solely on his training as a Guardian. He was training five to six times per week fervently with Aurora. The intense training, however, was paying off. Jonah's fitness had improved tremendously. His physique looked noticeably different, evidenced by his increased muscle mass and tone. Jonah's combat skills had advanced considerably during that time also. Aurora was more impressed with Jonah's progress with each passing day.

As for his new friends, their friendship had matured during that period. For the first time in Jonah's life, he had friends that he cherished and felt a genuine sense of belonging to a group.

After completing another punishing training session during the day, Jonah walked to his room alone. It was early evening, the sky was turning dark purple, and the millions of parallel dimensions surrounding Concordia were starting to become visible, like pale orange lines of light. People were still out and about in the main center, enjoying the last bit of light before the sun went down. Jonah, on the other hand, was physically spent. His only desire was to eat a good meal and get a good night's sleep.

When Jonah entered his room, he manifested a mouthwatering dinner —that consisted of a hearty serving of lasagne, a side salad and some garlic bread—which he devoured in next to no time at all. After he finished his meal, he was about to have a rest when he heard a knock on the door. As he got up to see who it was, the door opened—it was his father.

"Hey, Jonah. Can I come in?"

"Of course, you can, Dad."

As Mason walked inside, Jonah glimpsed at the pendant dangling in his hand.

"What's that?" Jonah pointed to Mason's hand.

"I was on Earth earlier today, and I was going through your grandpa's things. I found this pendant that belonged to him. He always told me that when he passed away, he wanted you to have it. So here you go."

Mason handed the pendant over to Jonah. As Jonah took hold of the necklace attached to the pendant, it triggered a moment of nostalgia where he recalled seeing his grandfather wearing it on many occasions.

"I hope you remember him every time you look at his pendant," Mason said, his voice quivering as tears welled in his eyes.

"Thanks, Dad."

"You're welcome, Jonah."

Jonah started getting a little emotional too, remembering his grandfather, whom he missed dearly, especially now that he was in Concordia. He longed to be by his grandfather's side and to have a heartwarming conversation. Jonah would've loved nothing more than to be able to have his grandfather help guide him through this journey and share stories about his experiences. Sadly, Jonah's reality was something different now, which he had slowly adapted to.

"Anyhow . . . I need to get going. I've had quite a day on Earth. Goodnight, Son."

"Goodnight, Dad."

As Mason left Jonah's room, Jonah put his grandfather's pendant into a drawer in one of his bedside tables for safekeeping. He didn't want to wear the pendant, as he was combat training regularly and thought it might get damaged during one of his training sessions.

After Mason left Jonah's room, another knock rapped on the door. Jonah approached the door and opened it, finding Ishwa standing before him.

"Greetings, Jonah!"

"Oh . . . hi, Ishwa. I didn't realize you were coming tonight."

My favorite hippie is back, Jonah thought to himself as Ishwa stood there with long matted hair that went past his shoulders and wore all his beaded necklaces and bracelets as he usually did.

"As I always say Jonah, I will appear when you least expect it, but when you're completely ready."

"Right. Well, I certainly wasn't expecting you."

"That's okay young man. I wanted to have a chat with you. I wasn't interrupting anything, was I?"

"Nope."

"Great. Tonight, rather than going to Amabilia, I'm going to take you somewhere different. I want to show you something quite unique, which I guarantee you've never seen before, Jonah. At least, not in your current incarnation."

"Okay. I'm intrigued."

"It's nothing to be afraid of. But to get there, we'll have to go in a special way. And by that, I mean we need to use your grandfather's pendant."

"How did you know about my grandfather's pendant?"

"I am the embodiment of eternal wisdom; I know everything." Ishwa pretended to be serious and enigmatic at the same time.

After a brief pause, Jonah looked at Ishwa with a cheeky grin.

"In other words, my father told you."

"He sure did." Ishwa's serious face eroded into a huge smile before he laughed, followed by Jonah.

"Okay. So why do you need the pendant?" Jonah asked.

"This is no ordinary pendant. This pendant unlocks a gateway to somewhere very special you can't get to easily. Not even our teleportation powers can get us there without this pendant."

"Where is this place?"

"It's a little difficult to describe. It's best if I take you there and you can see for yourself. Please go grab the pendant, and I'll show you how to use it."

Jonah retrieved the pendant from the drawer in his bedside table. He handed it to Ishwa, who also pulled out a green apatite, crystalline object in the shape of a small hexagonal tower from one of his pockets.

"Now, this green key locks into the front of the pendant, like this." Ishwa inserted his key into the hexagonal cavity of the pendant. "You twist it once clockwise, then once counterclockwise, and then hold on for the ride of your life. Are you ready?"

"Okay. I guess," Jonah said, even though he wasn't sure he was ready.

"But first, it would be a good idea for both of us to sit down on the bed so we don't get injured."

"Injured?" Jonah looked at Ishwa, anxiously.

They both sat on Jonah's bed before Ishwa continued.

"There's nothing to be afraid young man. All right, here we go." Ishwa took a deep breath.

Ishwa rotated the key in the pendant once clockwise and then once counterclockwise while they both held onto it. Their astral bodies were instantly transported onto the Upper Astral Plane, while their physical bodies collapsed on the bed in Jonah's room.

Jonah and Ishwa's astral bodies found themselves outside a temple-like structure. The exterior of the building was constructed of a sand-colored stone with pillars made of gold that resembled an ancient Roman temple. As Jonah looked around the building, he was unable to see anything but white light surrounding it. Jonah turned to Ishwa with a puzzled look on his face.

"Where are we exactly?" Jonah asked.

"We're standing outside the Temple of Wisdom. This place . . . it's quite special. And for many reasons which I won't go into now. However, one of those reasons is that it contains the library that holds all universal knowledge, as well as The Akashic Records."

"The what?" Jonah asked.

"The Akashic Records."

"And what exactly are these 'Akashic Records?'"

"These records are unique, Jonah. They're a record of every action, thought, or feeling that every soul has ever had across all dimensions, time, and space. The past, present, and future—all of your incarnations from every dimension you've ever existed in, are in those Akashic Records."

"Really? Every soul, every incarnation . . . aha." Jonah was a little overwhelmed by Ishwa's explanation.

"I know that sounds a little extraordinary, but once we go inside, you'll get a better sense of the Records' power. But before we go inside, I want to lay some ground rules. Firstly, you need to be respectful of the Records. Although anyone can go inside, it's a privilege and you must treat it as such. Don't do anything stupid and do exactly as you are told. Got it, Jonah?"

"Yes, of course."

Ishwa and Jonah approached the temple's front door, which began opening by itself. The door was exceptionally large and looked quite heavy, which made it slow to open. Once it was opened sufficiently, they proceeded inside.

Jonah and Ishwa walked into a long foyer that had shimmering lights on the walls, which then connected to a library. The walls had inscriptions; for Jonah, it brought to mind Arabic writing. Lights in the ceiling lit up the inside of the building. These lights were not generated from light bulbs; instead, huge spheres of autogenic light radiated from the ceiling.

This library was never-ending, containing what appeared to be an infinite number of bookshelves storing books that emanated a brilliant golden light.

There were only a few people around, examining records from what Jonah could determine, as they had books open that emitted light into their foreheads. As they continued walking, Jonah noticed he had a silver cord attached to him, as did Ishwa. The cord was located on his lower back; it extended all the way to the entrance of the library and beyond.

"Ishwa. Why do we have silver cords attached to us?"

"These cords keep us connected to our physical bodies back in Concordia. We are traveling on the Upper Astral Plane, which means we are only traveling with our astral bodies, not with our physical bodies. The vibrational frequency of the Upper Astral Plane is very high, and our physical bodies wouldn't cope with the intense frequencies. They would disintegrate if we brought them here. That's why we can't teleport here directly.

"Your grandfather's pendant helped us astral project into this realm. His pendant and my key work together to unlock the power to project over here. Our physical bodies are still back in Concordia in your room. These silver cords will allow us to return once we've concluded our visit here."

"I see." Jonah was flabbergasted. "You know, I've heard of people on Earth having astral projections. Is that the same thing?"

"Yes, it is. Most people don't know how to astral project at will on a conscious level. Everyone can do it subconsciously when they sleep. It takes a lot of practice to learn how to do this at will, which is why we use the pendant. It's a gateway into here that bypasses the lengthy training it takes to learn how to astral project consciously."

"I see," Jonah said.

They continued walking through the Hall of Records for some time until they came across a section Jonah felt drawn to. Although he couldn't hear anyone speaking to him directly, he felt an energetic pull toward one of the bookshelves, which he was unable to control.

"Ishwa! I'm not sure what's happening, but I'm being drawn to something and I can't pull away."way."

"That's okay, Jonah. Don't be afraid. It's exactly where you're meant to go." Ishwa walked behind Jonah to where he was being lured.

Ishwa continued following Jonah until he eventually came to a halt. They stopped at a location in the library that was a long distance away from the entrance. Jonah felt an incredible magnetic connection to that section of the bookshelf as he stood in front of it. The connection was somehow familiar to him, yet he couldn't remember ever being there.

The bookshelves were not like the bookshelves that Jonah was accustomed to seeing at his university on Earth. The shelves were not very tall, like some of the ones Jonah had seen in the past. They weren't solid timber or metal either; they were made from marble, which Jonah found unusual, having never seen a bookshelf of this type of construction before.

"What's going on, Ishwa? Why was I dragged here?"

"Jonah, I think you've found your Akashic Record—or should I say, your Akashic Record found *you*."

One of the books levitated off the shelf and opened before Jonah. The book automatically scrolled through hundreds of pages until it eventually stopped on one particular page. A luminous gold light radiated from the book and focused on Jonah's forehead, right between his eyes. He felt warmth from the light. Jonah couldn't explain it, but there was a certain familiarity with this light as if he somehow knew what was being conveyed by it. Jonah closed his eyes, and in doing so, he saw images from his past as if he was watching a movie.

"Ishwa, I don't quite understand what's going on. I'm seeing certain scenes and events from my life."

"Jonah . . . this light will show you certain things about yourself from any of your lives, past or present. Maybe even your future. The Akashic Records will reveal to you what's appropriate for you to see right now. You won't be shown anything it believes is irrelevant. Don't question what is being presented; just view it without judgement. Have faith that everything you're watching is what you need to see."

Jonah stood in silence and watched what was being presented to him. Ishwa listened telepathically to what was going on in Jonah's head. He heard everything the Akashic Records were presenting to Jonah. Jonah saw flashbacks from his childhood and teenage years. He recalled moments where he was having conversations with his grandfather, laughing with him, eating meals with him, road trips they had taken together, and many heartwarming moments Jonah had almost forgotten about. Ishwa saw Jonah smiling as he watched all of this in his mind.

Jonah's smile slowly diminished into a frown. Tears soon flowed down his face. Jonah was watching flashbacks from his grandfather's funeral. First, he was shown his grandfather's casket, adorned in a floral wreath. Moments later, an image of himself sitting at the front pew of the church as the priest was performing the service. This was followed by Jonah watching his father give the eulogy and struggling to talk during the speech. His mother cried while Jonah sat beside her, emotionless. He was continuously shown images of his parents weeping, contrasted by visions of himself not crying.

"Why am I being shown all of this, Ishwa? I can't deal with this right now. Stop. Please stop."

A few tears began flowing down the side of Jonah's face. The Akashic Records were trying to tell Jonah to acknowledge his grandfather's passing, to finally be courageous enough to feel his pain, something Jonah had neglected to do.

Jonah began to cry uncontrollably. The golden light beaming onto his forehead ceased, and he collapsed onto the floor in utter sorrow. The book closed and levitated to its original position on the shelf. For the first time in Jonah's life, he felt a deep emotional pain unlike any other. He'd never been forced to look at his emotions like this. The Akashic Records compelled Jonah to bring his emotions to the forefront of his consciousness to be examined and healed. However, this was proving too much for Jonah to handle; he was having difficulty breathing.

Ishwa could see Jonah was overwhelmed with emotion. He decided it would be best to take him somewhere else to process his grief. Ishwa grabbed Jonah's pendant and inserted his key into it, twisting once clockwise and then once counterclockwise. They disappeared from the Hall of Records and left the Upper Astral Plane, going back to Jonah's room in Concordia. After regaining consciousness, they teleported straight to Amabilia, which Ishwa felt was somewhere safe where Jonah could release his repressed grief.

They landed in their usual spot, in the clearing with grass and a river nearby. Jonah cried for over an hour. Ishwa held Jonah and tried to comfort him. When Jonah eventually stopped crying, he curled up on the ground, feeling empty. Jonah had nothing left inside him. He lay on the ground for a few minutes, taking several deep breaths as Ishwa instructed him to. Jonah then sat up and wiped away tears with his sleeve. Ishwa sat on the ground opposite Jonah.

"That was so intense," Jonah said, his voice still shaky from the acute emotional outburst. "How did that happen? Did the Akashic Records do some 'voodoo' on me?"

"The Akashic Records didn't do any 'voodoo' on you. They helped you connect to your emotions and aided in their release. You were in dire need of emotional healing. The Akashic Records reminded you of something critical you had overlooked: grieving your grandfather's loss.

"When you visit the Akashic Records, it always knows exactly what you need to see at that moment. You needed to express your grief and release it, as it was trapped inside your energy field. Up to this point, you had never given yourself permission to mourn and feel the emotions of loss. Even at your grandfather's funeral."

Jonah sat on the grass with his legs crossed, listening to Ishwa intently.

"This is a great lesson for you. Don't ever judge your emotions or yourself for feeling this way. You think because you're a man, you can't be allowed to grieve? What purpose does that serve other than blocking your energy field? A whole lot of nothing, that's what. That belief system does not serve your highest good. It only serves Ego."

"Did you ever meet my grandfather?" Jonah asked.

"Yes, I did. We knew each other quite well, which is why I was so sad to hear of his passing."

"I didn't realize you knew each other."

"Yes, I met Luke over thirty years ago. We fought in battles together. I also gave him counsel many times over the years."

"Wow, it's so cool to know someone that knew my grandfather." Jonah paused for a moment. "When I was given my grandfather's necklace tonight, it reminded me of how much I really miss him. I wish he were here to share this experience with me. Is there any way to stop feeling these emotions?"

Jonah broke down into tears again.

"No, Jonah, there isn't. And you know why? Because you loved your grandfather. Love is an emotion. You are pure unconditional love at the very core of your being, your soul."

"Our soul is nothing more than pure love?" Jonah asked.

"That's right. If you ceased feeling emotions, you would cease to feel love. If you cease to feel love, you stop existing, not just in your physical form, but your soul would cease to exist altogether. It's as simple as that.

"You don't remember this because when you incarnated into your human form, you forgot who you really were. It's one of the more painful aspects of being born human. And part of your journey as a human is to overcome the illusions of Ego and remember who you really are. Pure, unconditional love."

"Okay. But what I meant was that I'm never going to see my grandfather again. That is why I am so unbelievably heartbroken. How do I get over that Ishwa?"

"Jonah, here's the thing you need to understand. We are immortal souls having a temporary human experience. Our souls chose to temporarily come into human form to experience life in a manner we couldn't in any other way. To do so, we created a soul contract before we incarnated into human form, with a list of experiences and missions to complete. We then entered our bodies, which are the vessels we inhabit to have this human experience."

"We choose to be born? But why would we do that? Especially when it involves losing people we love along the way. Why would we go through the pain of losing people we love?"

"For our souls to experience life and to grow," Ishwa said. "But let me tell you, those vessels aren't the totality of who we are. When we experience death of our human form, we don't stop existing. It's simply our souls leaving our bodies because we have completed our soul contracts. Our souls are energy, and energy cannot be created or destroyed. It can only change form. So, our souls don't die. They simply shift into a higher form of being. Having said all that, your grandfather still exists."

"You mean my grandfather is still alive? Where?" Jonah asked.

"Yes. His soul is still alive, but his body obviously isn't. He's in a different form now. He has ascended into a higher plane of existence. He completed his soul contracts and completed his life purpose. You can't communicate with him because he now exists in a much higher vibrational frequency that you are unable to resonate with.

"Our Ego sees this as a form of separation. And that is what makes it so traumatic for those left behind. Our Ego makes us believe death is final and we will never see our loved ones again. Nothing could be further from the truth, Jonah. When the time comes to leave your body, you will be reunited with him and all your loved ones who have gone before you. That won't be for a long time yet, though. You have a lot of living to do and many lessons to learn."

As Jonah listened, he looked over the clearing at some trees.

"I think I understand what you're telling me. But it's still sad not to have my grandfather with me and to see him every day."

"There's no need to be sad, Jonah. Of course, it's important to process your grief and feel your emotions of loss. However, understand that death is nothing more than a transition of our souls to a different existence. An existence of pure love and a higher state of consciousness. So your grandfather still exists. You will see him again someday.

"Another thing to keep in mind, is that grief can be a journey. So you may find yourself feeling sad unexpectedly for many months to come. One minute you might be happy and another you're crying. Something might trigger it like seeing a photo of him, or eating one of his favorite foods, or hearing a song that reminds you of him, or something similar. It's perfectly normal. There is no set time limit on grief. Give yourself some grace. Be kind to yourself and make sure you give yourself permission to feel the loss and hurt, or whatever other emotions that might come up for you."

After Ishwa finished speaking, a moment of silence lingered. Jonah was overcome by everything that Ishwa said.

"This is a lot to take in. I need some time to absorb what you've said. And also, what happened with the Akashic Records, the Upper Astral Plane. All of it. My mind is so blown."

"Of course, Jonah. Let's head back to Concordia, and I'll give you some time and space to think."

Ishwa held out his hands, and Jonah put his hand over them. Within moments, they were back on Concordia in Jonah's room.

"You've had a very intense evening, and you're emotionally exhausted, so I suggest you get a good night's sleep. It will help you integrate what you have learned tonight. Good night, Jonah."

"Good night, Ishwa." Jonah waved goodbye as Ishwa left.

After Ishwa left the room, Jonah climbed into bed.

In his room, alone, Jonah's soul felt much lighter, like a crushing burden had been lifted from it, and he had been set free. He went to bed knowing that although he had to do something that made him feel uncomfortable, he was better off for it.

CHAPTER 18

"I think that's enough wine for you, young lady!" Jordan said to Lucy at the dinner table, while he pulled away the wine bottle.

"Oh . . .you're no fun!" Lucy responded with laughter.

Jordan and Lucy were having lunch with Aurora, Mason, and Jonah at the Community Center in Concordia. They were seated in a booth that was U-shaped and covered in a cozy royal blue microfiber material. The table was large and covered in numerous empty dishes. They had just completed eating a large banquet of Indian dishes: saffron rice, naan bread, dhal, butter chicken, samosas, chana masala, and beef korma.

It had been a while since they all caught up for a meal together. On Earth, the two families would regularly spend time at each other's homes or at a restaurant. Going out to a restaurant often meant visiting one of their favorite local Indian restaurants, Dhalicious, which they all loved very much. Not only for the great food but the wonderful staff. Today, they were all feeling a little nostalgic and had decided to replicate one of their old favorite pastimes, in Concordia.

Aurora and Jonah weren't doing any training that day, as Aurora had decided Jonah could do with some rest and relaxation. He had been working hard over recent days with his training. Aurora also knew about Jonah's visit to the Akashic Records and his experience releasing his grief, so she figured he deserved a little time off.

Jonah had shared with his parents what had happened with Guardian Ishwa the day after it happened. Both Mason and Aurora were glad he'd had a breakthrough, as they had been worried about Jonah's emotional well-being due to him not expressing his sorrow. After hearing of his adventure, they were relieved.

"So, Jonah, how's everything going for you? Are you settling in okay?" Lucy asked.

Lucy's blonde hair was glistening since she was sitting by a window and was facing the sun. It also made her blue eyes sparkle. She was trying to divert attention away from her empty wine glass, which had red lipstick stains on it.

"Everything has been okay so far. It was all a bit of a shock at first and a little overwhelming at the beginning, but so far, so good. Apart from mom's brutal training." Jonah smirked.

"I've trained with your mother, so I know exactly what you mean!" Jordan said.

"My mom trained you?" Jonah was surprised.

"You bet I did. And he turned out to be one hell of a Guardian!" Aurora boasted.

"I suppose I have to give your mother some credit." Jordan rolled his eyes and grinned at the same time.

"Yes, you do." Aurora threw her napkin in Jordan's face in jest. Lucy sat there and laughed, as did Mason and Jonah.

Jonah was really enjoying the time he was spending with his parents and Lucy and Jordan. It reminded him of the times they would all go out and have dinner together on Earth. It was so good to relive some of the normal times he had at home before he became a Guardian. It gave him a small sense of normality and a distraction from his life in Concordia.

"The only thing that's missing from this table is Max. How's he doing?" Jonah asked.

"He's good. He finishes high school this year and is thinking of going to college. He wants to study mathematics. How did I give birth to a child that wants to do something like that?" Lucy laughed.

"I love math, too!" Jonah scoffed, unable to understand why it seemed so weird to Lucy.

"Yes, but you had to learn it as part of your engineering degree. It had a purpose. But what's he going to do with straight math?" Lucy quizzed.

"Let him figure it out. And besides, he'll eventually have to come here anyway. Let the boy do what he wants to do on Earth. Let Max have some fun," Jordan said.

"You call math fun?" Lucy asked as she wrinkled her eyebrows.

"For him, it is. Let him enjoy his time on Earth and stop judging him. He's going to be just fine." Jordan said.

"You should go down to Earth and see him sometime. He's been asking about you," Lucy said.

"Next time my boss gives me a day off from training, I will." Jonah pointed to Aurora.

"That might be a while. You've still got a lot of work to do." Aurora pointed back at Jonah.

As Mason was listening in on the conversation and laughing, a telepathic message came through. It was Wyatt from the Observatory: *Mason, sorry to be a bother, but I need you to come over to the Observatory immediately. We have a potential new threat I would like to discuss with you.*

Alarm tinged Wyatt's voice, alerting Mason.

I'll be there shortly, Mason responded.

Mason looked at Aurora and said aloud, "Sorry, darling, I need to head on over to the Observatory. Wyatt just spoke to me. He wants to see me urgently to discuss a new case."

"Can I hope you'll be back before midnight? Or am I asking too much?" Aurora asked with a smile.

"I'll try my best." Mason kissed his wife and teleported over to the Observatory.

"That Wyatt certainly keeps Mason on his toes," Aurora said to everyone at the table after Mason left.

Mason and Wyatt had worked together for many years. Wyatt was in his mid-forties, like Mason. They knew each other very well and were also good friends. Wyatt had trained Mason and taught him everything he knew about all the inner workings of the Observatory. As such, he knew that for Wyatt to sound a little panicked during his earlier message meant something was imminent. This made Mason a little nervous on his approach.

When he arrived outside the Observatory, he entered the building and quickly made his way to Wyatt's workstation. Mason spotted Wyatt taking notes as he observed some footage from another dimension coming through on his screen.

"Hey, Wyatt. What's up? You sounded a little agitated in your earlier message."

"Yes. For good reason. I've been observing a new Infringer threat for the last few hours, which has slowly escalated to a critical threat that needs some attention."

Wyatt's blue eyes were a little bloodshot from spending a lot of time observing his screen. His long, curly blond hair was a little scruffy from the bad habit he had of playing with his hair when he was stressed.

"Tell me more," Mason said.

"It originates on Planet Zareet, located in the Hyperion System."

As Wyatt spoke, he pointed to a map of the planet on his screen.

"I see. And what's going on there?" Mason asked as he studied the map.

"There is a large army of people being led by someone named Governor Ragnar. He plans to take his army and cross into another dimension known as the Occulus System. There, he is targeting a planet called Ebris. From what I have seen so far, from files we have on him, this man is evil. He is a dictator obsessed with power and control. He has already overthrown several planets in the Hyperion System and is now intent on crossing over into the Occulus System, I'm assuming to overtake even more planets. This man is extremely dangerous and needs to be stopped, which is why I called you here. We need to take action immediately."

As Wyatt was speaking, he showed Mason the live feeds coming in from Zareet and pointed out Governor Ragnar.

"So Wyatt, do you know how he is trying to cross dimensions?"

"I believe he is building a teleporter that can open portals into other dimensions to allow him and his army to cross over. He has a team of people designing and building the teleporter as we speak."

"In that case, we need to gather more information before we can present this to the Grand Guardian. We need to know what capabilities they have in terms of technology and weaponry. But more importantly, what is their motive? Why are they trying to cross over? What are they trying to achieve?"

"Of course, Mason. I'm currently gathering as much information as I can for you. Once I have everything, I'll let you know."

"Please do."

As Mason finished speaking, he walked away from Wyatt's workstation and left the Observatory.

Wyatt remained for the rest of the afternoon and evening, gathering more intelligence. His work continued well into the night. By the time he had finished, it was quite late and he was exhausted. He figured Mason would've been asleep at that late hour anyway, so he decided it would be best to retire for the evening and brief him the following morning.

The next day, after getting up early and having breakfast with his family, Wyatt went back to the Observatory to review his findings. After evaluating all the amassed evidence, he sent Mason another telepathic message.

Mason, can you please come over to the Observatory? I want to have a follow-up discussion about the matter we talked about last night.

Sure thing, Wyatt. I'll be there shortly.

Mason made his way over to the Observatory and found Wyatt at his workstation with all the information he had compiled. Mason noticed that Wyatt—who was of average height and had a solid physique and good posture—was a little slumped that morning due to his lethargy, and his eyes were a little red.

"Gee, you look a bit tired," Mason said as he looked at Wyatt's fatigued face.

"I was up until late compiling evidence about the new Infringer."

"You really need to take a vacation, my friend."

"How's that old saying go? There's no rest for the wicked," Wyatt said.

"Wicked? You drink green tea and watch beagle puppy videos on social media!"

"What's wrong with beagle puppies? They're the best!" Wyatt said, making Mason burst into laughter.

"I don't deny that beagle puppies are adorable. They are. I used to have one myself. I just don't think they make you wicked, that's all." After they both laughed for a moment, Mason's wide grin slowly shrank, and he started getting serious. "Anyhow, back to yesterday's discussion. Have you got an update?"

"Yes, I do. From what I've been able to piece together, Governor Ragnar is trying to invade Planet Ebris for a reason. The planet has an abundance of a compound called Chrimatide, which his planet uses for power generation. They've almost run out on Zareet and throughout the entire Hyperion System. So now the governor wants to invade the Occulus System, to extract what he can from there and take the compound back to his own planet."

"But how do they know Planet Ebris is rich in Chrimatide?" Mason asked.

"He has a psychic adviser—if that's what you want to call him. This man, known as Master Sinai, apparently has the ability to view other dimensions remotely. He was the one that found the mineral on Planet Ebris."

Wyatt pointed to an image of Master Sinai on his screen.

"I've heard of remote viewers," Mason said. "It's similar to what we do here in the Observatory, but these people can do it with their minds rather than looking at the screens. I think we need to take this to the Grand Guardian. She can take this information to the Executive Council and let them decide what to do next. We'll need to act fast. Let's contact Ezra to see if she is available."

Ezra, it's Mason from the Observatory. Is the Grand Guardian available for an audience? Wyatt and I need to see her urgently regarding a new Infringer threat that has been discovered.

Moments later, Ezra responded.

Mason, she's currently in a meeting with someone. When she's finished, I will let her know you both need to see her, and if she agrees, I will contact you to come over and speak with her.

Thanks, Ezra.

Thirty minutes later, Ezra sent another telepathic message: *Mason, the Grand Guardian is ready to see you now.*

Wyatt and I will be there soon.

"Hey Wyatt, Ezra just sent me a message. The Grand Guardian is ready to see us now, so let's go."

Wyatt grabbed his light-pad from his workstation and took it with him. Light-pads, similar to a tablet machine found on Earth, were made of a lightweight material resembling a small glass sheet. They were about the size of a piece of paper and had the ability to store information, such as the data Wyatt had gathered for the Grand Guardian.

As they didn't want to keep the Grand Guardian waiting for too long, and due to the importance of the situation, they both teleported to her chambers once they left the confines of the Observatory. When they arrived at their destination, they were greeted by Ezra, who let them inside. He announced their arrival as they walked in.

The Grand Guardian greeted them with a warm smile and motioned for them to sit in front of her desk so they could have a discussion. As Mason and Wyatt sat, she could see the alarm on their faces and instantly became solemn. Ezra remained standing.

Mason and Wyatt noticed the Grand Guardian was already a little tired, having had several matters to deal with that morning.

"Ezra advised me earlier that you wanted to see me regarding some intelligence you've gathered about a new Infringer. Can you please elaborate?" Grand Guardian Omiya asked.

Wyatt began briefing the Grand Guardian about the new threat he had discovered on Planet Zareet and Governor Ragnar's intentions to invade another dimension to steal Chrimatide for his planet.

As Wyatt spoke about the location of the threat and the whereabouts of each dimension and planet, he projected their locations with holographic images using his light-pad. The images looked so lifelike it almost felt like you were there. These images included Governor Ragnar talking to Master Sinai and Professor Lyndon, as well as some of the stunning pictures of each galaxy that Zareet and Ebris resided in.

When Wyatt finished speaking, the Grand Guardian paused for a moment, thinking.

"Thank you for that information. If what you're saying is true, then I concur: he needs to be stopped. What I also find disturbing is that instead of focusing his efforts on finding an alternative energy source, he is willing to terrorize other dimensions and kill people to mine for primitive methods of power generation. Other dimensions have successfully found alternative sources of power and are thriving. You know, the more I think about this, the more evil he sounds. How far along is he in building his teleporter?"

"He is about three quarters of the way through the process. While it isn't a state of emergency just yet, we need to start making decisions soon and create a plan of attack," Wyatt said.

"What we also need to keep in mind is the governor is also getting advice from a remote viewer, Master Sinai. While Sinai doesn't appear to be dangerous, he may be able to see us coming and warn Governor Ragnar," Mason said.

"I wouldn't be too concerned with Master Sinai," the Grand Guardian said. "Remote viewers cannot see into Concordia. It's one of the lesser-known secrets of this dimension. I assure you both; we are well-fortified from prying eyes."

"So, what should we do next?" Mason asked.

"Our next step should be to go on a reconnaissance mission," Grand Guardian Omiya said.

The Grand Guardian got up from her seat and approached the images to get a closer look. She walked around the holograms and studied them well for a few moments, thinking about her next move.

"We need to send some of our best operatives to take a closer look. Once we have physical evidence confirming his activities, I'll take it to the Executive Council. For now, don't tell anyone of this until we have more evidence."

"You have our word, Grand Guardian," Mason said.

"Good. I'm going to ask one thing of you, Wyatt, and that's to provide information to our operatives once I have briefed them on their mission. I will ask them to confer with you regarding the location of Planet Zareet. Also, please share any other necessary intelligence to aid them in planning their mission."

"Of course. I will be happy to assist in any way possible."

"Thank you. I will now have to ask you both to leave so I can take care of the arrangements for the reconnaissance mission. As always, I thank you both for your good work."

As she finished speaking, Wyatt shut off his light-pad, and both he and Mason got up from their seats and left. The Grand Guardian turned to Ezra. She asked him to gather three of Concordia's best operatives and send them to her chambers. He, too, left the chambers and went about fulfilling her request.

It was not uncommon for the Grand Guardian to send spies to investigate potential threats first, except in extreme emergencies where swift action was required, which was rare. In this instance, while there was potential for great danger ahead, there was time available to undertake some additional investigative work.

About an hour later, Ezra returned with the Concordian operatives the Grand Guardian had asked for. They were Guardians Aiden, Logan, and Skylar. These three were experienced spies and had undertaken many reconnaissance missions in the past. All three of them looked physically fit, with strong muscle tone, and ready to take action on any battlefield.

Grand Guardian Omiya had an enormous amount of trust in them. When they entered her chambers, they sat. She then proceeded to explain their mission details.

"I need to emphasize that it is vital you do not engage with anyone on Planet Zareet. This is a fact-finding mission only. At the first sign of trouble, you must teleport here. From what I understand, Governor Ragnar is dangerous, and I don't want any of you hurt. Gather as much intelligence as possible and get out of there swiftly. Is that understood?"

"Yes, Grand Guardian," Skylar said.

"Very good. Before you go to Zareet, you'll need to visit Wyatt in the Observatory. He'll be able to give you information about Planet Zareet's location. I have also asked him to share with you whatever information he deems relevant to assist you in this mission. Ezra will escort you to the Observatory and provide you with access. Please take care. I'm counting on you."

As she finished speaking, all three operatives exited the chambers, along with Ezra. All of them made their way to the Observatory. Once they arrived, Ezra guided everyone inside until they managed to find Wyatt and Mason.

Wyatt and Mason proceeded to give each of the operatives a light-pad containing the information that had been gathered about Planet Zareet and Governor Ragnar. The light-pads could be folded into the size of sugar cubes, making them highly portable. All three of them folded the light-pads and put them in their pockets to be used later. From there, the operatives planned their mission and decided what they would do next. Once they had everything planned, they left the Observatory.

On departure, all three operatives went their separate ways, melting into the shadows, so that they could gather the equipment needed for their mission. About an hour later, the group reconvened and teleported to Planet Zareet, where they spent the next twenty-four hours on their mission.

CHAPTER 19

When the three operatives arrived on Planet Zareet, they spent a few minutes trying to get their bearings. They had to figure out where they were and where they needed to go.

The point where they had landed on Planet Zareet was far from where Governor Ragnar and most of the planet's inhabitants resided. It was a clearing, in a forested area that was a long distance from any townships—an ideal location to spend the night and safely store their backpacks and equipment if needed. There wasn't any fear of being discovered by any inhabitants, satisfying one of the Grand Guardian's main directives.

For this mission, they were dressed in their combat outfits, which were khaki-colored and made of a spandex-type material that covered most of their bodies, except their necks and heads. These were both comfortable and strong outfits that enabled them to carry out their mission duties with ease.

All three operatives knew each other, having worked on prior missions together. As such, they had developed a great comradery amongst each other and worked well as a group. They were able to adapt to any situation or mission very quickly. Everyone knew what to expect from each other and who was in charge.

"Whenever you finish your assignments, return here and telepathically let everyone else know you've finished. Agreed?" Skylar asked her subordinates.

"Agreed," Logan said.

"I think we should split up and complete our tasks individually to help save time. Aiden, I need you to obtain a sample of Chrimatide we can take back to Concordia. Logan, I want you to plant listening devices in Governor Ragnar's chambers so we can record some of his conversations. I will track where the teleporter is located and photograph it to get as much detail about it as possible. Understood?"

"Understood," Aiden said.

"Excellent. Now let's get a move on!"

On Skylar's instruction, they dispersed and went about completing their assignments.

Skylar and Logan needed to covertly infiltrate Governor Ragnar's headquarters. They teleported to a location outside the compound. The position where they emerged was far enough for them not to be seen by anyone but close enough to observe what was occurring outside. Since it was late into the night, the headquarters' exterior was heavily guarded. The main entrance was surrounded by several luminous lights. Everyone and everything going in and out of the compound, as well as all the soldiers patrolling it, could be observed clearly.

Seeing all those soldiers guarding Governor Ragnar's headquarters made them a little nervous, as the numbers were considerably more than they had anticipated. Skylar and Logan figured they had to be prepared for an ambush in the event they teleported inside and were met with a similar set of circumstances.

After monitoring what was going on, they decided to make a move and teleport into the compound's main building. Entering at the same time, they each went into different parts of the compound to complete their missions separately.

For Skylar, getting a glimpse of the teleporter and photographing it was going to be challenging. While teleporting into the building would be easy, being able to look at the teleporter discretely, without being noticed by soldiers, would be problematic.

Once Skylar teleported inside, she was surprised to discover there weren't as many soldiers patrolling the corridors as she had imagined. This meant she could focus her attention on finding the teleporter. She had to walk down never-ending walkways and peer through multiple rooms by opening numerous doors. Some doors were locked, so Skylar had to teleport inside certain areas to find what she was looking for. To add to all of this, she almost got caught by a few soldiers patrolling the corridors. She managed to evade them just in time by hiding behind an unlocked door.

Eventually, Skylar found the machine when she teleported into the final room, known as the Engineering Room. As she did, Zakia, who worked for Governor Ragnar's surveillance unit, was in the control room monitoring the security cameras of the entire building. Looking at the footage, Zakia was taken aback by what she saw. Did she see a strange shadow, or was the camera playing tricks on her? By searching the security cameras, Zakia spotted a nearby soldier to send over to inspect.

"Yando, I need you to investigate the Engineering Room immediately. I saw a strange figure going inside. It could be an intruder. I'm not sure if they're armed, so approach with caution," Zakia said, her voice carrying into Yando's earpiece.

"Copy that. I'm on my way," Yando responded as he rushed toward the Engineering Room.

Meanwhile, Skylar had a good look around where the teleporter was located. Still under construction, it was much larger than she had expected. After inspecting the machine for a few moments, she stood in one corner of the room and placed a device—known as a Silver Eye—on the ground.

A Silver Eye was a round camera device that could take a three-dimensional image of an area. Once Skylar was satisfied with the camera's positioning, she pressed a button on it and walked away, standing out of the camera's field of view. After a few seconds, the camera began scanning the entire area with laser beams. They captured thousands of minute images, which were fed back to the camera and pieced together into a large, three-dimensional image. The process only lasted a few seconds.

As the Engineering Room was being scanned, Skylar noticed a table near the teleporter. Once the Silver Eye finished scanning the room, she retrieved the device and approached the table. Its surface was covered with blueprint designs. Skylar presumed they were for the teleporter; as such, she thought it would be a good idea to photograph them as well.

Skylar took a good look around to make sure no one was watching her. Just as she was about to take some photographs, Skylar heard someone unlocking the entrance door. Her heart raced in angst. She had to act fast. Glancing around quickly, Skylar spotted a small enclosure within the Engineering Room. It was a storage facility with a locked door, that was also fitted with a small window. Without hesitation, she teleported into the enclosure. As she reemerged inside, the Engineering Room was unlocked and the entry door swung wide open. Yando walked in to check for any intruders, as Skylar peered through the window of the storage facility door.

His footsteps trudged across the floor in the backdrop of silence, which magnified Skylar's anxiety. Yando walked around the teleporter and the table with blueprints to see if anyone was hiding. When he approached the storage facility, Skylar hid out of direct view from the entry door behind some metal shelves.

He put his hand on the door handle, ready to twist it open and walk inside. Skylar's heart raced. As Yando was about to open the door, a second soldier, named Vazky, entered the Engineering Room.

"There you are! I've been looking for you. We need to head toward Governor Ragnar's chambers now! Hurry!" Vazky motioned for Yando to follow him.

Yando let go of the handle and retreated from the door. He ran out of the Engineering Room, closing and locking the door behind him. Their feet pounded the floor, heading away from Skylar's location. A moment later, she took a few deep breaths to calm down.

Once she regained her composure, Skylar promptly teleported out of the storage facility and returned to the table where the blueprints were. The design was complex, requiring someone with highly advanced knowledge of mathematics and engineering to understand. Although she didn't have the expertise to comprehend the design, she photographed the blueprints anyway in the hope that someone in Concordia would be able to understand them. Once she had finished, she teleported out of the building and went back to the meeting point in the forest.

Aiden and Logan. I've taken photos of the teleporter and returned to our base camp. I will stand by and wait for both of you here, Skylar projected to the other operatives.

Copy that, Skylar, Logan said.

Skylar made herself comfortable while she waited for the other two to return.

In the meantime, Aiden went about looking for one of the planet's power plants. He was able to find it promptly by studying the planet's heat signatures. To do this, he used the light-pad Wyatt had provided him with, which he pulled out of his backpack.

The pad scanned for temperature patterns across the planet using built-in sensors, which it then used to generate a heat map. The assumption was that power plants using primitive power generation methods created vast amounts of heat. Once completed, Aiden uncovered a few areas on the map with intense heat signatures, the closest being several miles away from Governor Ragnar's headquarters. He teleported to that location to investigate.

Upon arrival, Aiden was able to ascertain within moments that his assumption was correct due to all the smoke being emitted from the power station.

A truck pulled up at the main entrance as Aiden stood at a distance from the power plant. It was stopped by soldiers who performed numerous security checks to ensure it was a legitimate delivery of Chrimatide. As it was heavily guarded, Aiden thought getting inside to grab a sample of Chrimatide was going to be an arduous task.

As the truck waited to enter the power plant, Aiden noticed it was exposed at the top, which meant the Chrimatide was readily visible and accessible. In a split second, he decided to seize the opportunity.

Aiden teleported behind the truck, where no soldiers were standing. When he reemerged there, he levitated to the top of the vehicle. As he ascended onto the truck, a few soldiers caught a glimpse of him and raised the alarm. They climbed toward the top of the vehicle to see who it was. As the commotion erupted and soldiers rapidly began climbing the truck, Aiden quickly grabbed a piece of Chrimatide and teleported away—right as one of the soldiers reached the top and fired a shot with his gun. Aiden evaded the bullet by a fraction of a second. The soldier on the truck was left bewildered.

"What the heck was that?" asked a sergeant from the ground.

"I thought it was a person, but they somehow disappeared!" the soldier yelled back.

As he shouted, additional soldiers reached the top of the vehicle and concurred with what the first soldier said. Each of them stood on the truck, puzzled. Had they really seen someone climbing on the truck, or was it just a shadow of the night?

Aiden, meanwhile, had returned to the meeting point and found Skylar waiting there. He let Logan know telepathically he had returned to base camp and was waiting with Skylar.

As the two waited for Logan, they studied the sample of Chrimatide that had been extracted. It wasn't an appealing compound to look at. It appeared similar to coal on Earth; however, it was a dull blue color. Also, it was denser and a lot harder.

"They find this valuable?" Aiden asked.

"Apparently." Skylar held the sample in one of her hands and rotated it around a couple of times.

"That's hilarious," Aiden said, mocking the idea.

What they didn't realize was that it wasn't valuable because of its visual appeal; rather it was prized because of the energy it provided to power the planet and its people. That mere sample was able to power someone's home for a day when harnessed correctly.

Logan was inside Governor Ragnar's headquarters, trying to find his chambers. He eventually located it; he recognized it from holographic images he had been shown by Wyatt, hours earlier. On his approach, he spied a soldier patrolling the surrounding area. Logan quickly hid from view by turning the corner into an adjoining corridor, just managing to avoid being noticed.

Logan took a deep breath and thought about what to do next. He initially decided to teleport inside the chambers, but as he was about to, he realized the chamber walls were made from glass. This meant the soldier patrolling outside would be able to observe him planting the listening devices inside. He had to wait in the hope that the soldier would leave momentarily, so Logan could sneak inside to complete his assigned task.

While Logan waited for a period of time, Zakia from surveillance talked to the patrolling soldier's earpiece.

"Yando, I need you to investigate the Engineering Room immediately. I saw a strange figure going inside. It could be an intruder. I'm not sure if they're armed, so approach with caution," Zakia said, her voice carrying into Yando's earpiece.

"Copy that. I'm on my way," Yando responded as he rushed toward the Engineering Room.

Logan watched as Yando left the area, waiting until he was out of view. He seized the moment and teleported into the chambers.

There were two listening devices he needed to set up, which were designed to be quick to install. He just needed to find somewhere to hide them discreetly so they couldn't be detected. After surveying the office for about a minute, he found two suitable spots to plant the devices, one under Governor Ragnar's desk, the other behind a book on a shelf.

While Logan installed the devices, Zakia spotted him from a camera outside the chambers. She couldn't understand what he was doing. She asked another soldier to investigate the area.

"Get to Governor Ragnar's chambers immediately. Someone has broken in," Zakia said to Vazky, who was located at the opposite end of the building.

"Copy that," Vazky said.

"On your way there, collect Yando. He's in the Engineering Room where the teleporter is being built. You might need backup."

"Copy that also."

Minutes later, as Logan installed the last listening device, footsteps approached. Just as they were about to come into view, Logan teleported out of the chambers and back to base camp, where Aiden and Skylar were waiting for him.

"There's no one here," Yando said to Zakia as he and Vazky stood outside and looked through to the inside of the chambers.

"Copy that," Zakia responded, shaking her head in disbelief. She wondered if perhaps a lack of sleep had her seeing things.

Having returned to base camp, Logan sighed in relief. This was followed with a brash grin. He found it amusing how close he'd come to being discovered by soldiers. It gave him an incredible adrenaline rush.

Now reunited, they gave each other high fives, grateful they'd managed to make it back to base camp without being harmed. They needed to stay on Planet Zareet for another twenty-four hours so they could record Governor Ragnar's conversations in his chambers. Hopefully, they'd gather useful information that would assist the Executive Council in finding out what he was up to.

In the meantime, they set up a temporary camp, using a smaller version of a light-pad known as a base generator. Skylar pressed a few buttons on the device and placed it on the ground. Within seconds, it was able to generate a large tent with mattresses for each Guardian, some tables and chairs they could work from, as well as cooking facilities and a bathroom. There was no manual assembly required, saving significant time and effort.

They spent the rest of the night getting plenty of rest for the next day.

The next morning after they woke up, they had something to eat and drink using provisions they'd brought with them. Logan listened in on Governor Ragnar's discussions. Even though the devices were recording everything Governor Ragnar was saying, Logan took copious notes to encapsulate some of the more critical points of his conversations.

Logan listened for many hours and captured a significant amount of intelligence about what Governor Ragnar was planning to do. Logan ascertained the governor was planning a journey to Ebris to steal Chrimatide and that construction of the teleporting machine was nearing completion. Logan pieced the information together to paint a picture of what was about to ensue. This reinforced what Wyatt had hypothesized earlier in Concordia.

Later that evening, Logan ventured back to the chambers to retrieve the listening devices. He did this while he was still at base camp, sitting in the tent, eavesdropping on a conversation. When he heard Governor Ragnar leave his chambers later in the evening, Logan took the opportunity to teleport inside and remove the two pieces. He then teleported back to base camp.

Their mission was now complete. They had gathered crucial evidence for the Grand Guardian. All three Guardians gathered their belongings, being meticulous to ensure they hadn't left anything behind. Skylar deactivated the base generator. Within seconds, the tent, mattresses, kitchen, bathroom, and furnishings—created the day before—disappeared. After a quick final spot check to ensure they hadn't left anything behind, they all returned to Concordia.

On their arrival, they wasted no time informing Ezra of their return. He was glad to see they had returned safely and without incident. Skylar then asked to see the Grand Guardian to discuss their mission findings. After Ezra had a quick telepathic chat with the Grand Guardian to advise of the operatives arrival, he escorted them into her chambers, where Grand Guardian Omiya was waiting to greet them.

"Welcome back," the Grand Guardian said as she stood behind her desk.

"Thank you, Grand Guardian. Fortunately, we weren't met with too much danger on this mission," Skylar said.

"That's good to hear. Now, please tell me more about your findings." Grand Guardian Omiya sat on her chair, while she directed the group to be seated in front of her desk.

"In simple terms, we concur with Wyatt's initial findings," Skylar said. "Governor Ragnar is definitely building a teleporter that can open portals into other dimensions. In addition to taking photos of the teleporter, I also managed to get a copy of the machine's design, which would require someone with engineering knowledge to interpret."

"We also brought back a sample of Chrimatide." Aiden lifted up the sample he had acquired.

"And from what I have determined, he is extremely dangerous and willing to kill to get that ugly piece of rock. It's all in the recordings we captured on the mission," Logan said.

"I see." The Grand Guardian sighed. "Very well. Please leave all the evidence you have gathered on my table. I will present your findings to the Executive Council so we can devise a plan to stop Governor Ragnar. In the meantime, do not discuss this mission or your findings with anyone. As always, you have my deepest appreciation for your efforts. Thank you. You may now leave and get some much-needed rest. Consider your mission completed."

"Yes, Grand Guardian," Skylar said before she and the rest of the group left the chambers.

The Grand Guardian turned to Ezra—who was stroking his grey beard as he was listening to her—and asked him to arrange an Executive Council meeting for the next day, as it was too late in the evening to summon everyone into her chambers. Since the operatives had confirmed Wyatt's findings, it was time to make some serious decisions. Whatever the Executive Council decided, the next phase would be fraught with danger.

While she was confident Concordia could defeat Governor Ragnar and his army, the Grand Guardian was uncertain of the cost to Concordia and its people. She knew there would be a cost. There always was. This weighed on her heavily. The Grand Guardian was painfully aware of the sacrifice that came with the role of a Concordian. The passage of time, however, never seemed to make this aspect any easier for her.

Chapter 20

E arly the next morning, all fifteen members of the Executive Council convened in the boardroom. As this meeting was unexpected, they were a little nervous about why they had been summoned at such short notice. The Grand Guardian never assembled them so abruptly unless there was a dire reason. They all sat at the boardroom table—a long glass table with a metallic frame—and waited for the meeting to begin.

The Executive Council members were adorned in yellow robes that had a golden infinity symbol emblazoned on them, located on the front upper body. These robes distinguished them from other Guardians in Concordia.

To qualify as a member of the Executive Council, members had to be at least fifty years of age. This was due to the responsibilities of the council; members needed to have a certain level of maturity and life experience in order to make complex decisions about missions and matters that concerned Concordia at large.

Once everyone was seated, the Grand Guardian commenced the meeting. "Firstly, thank you, everyone, for attending this meeting. I will get straight to the point. I've brought you all here to discuss an emerging new threat that was discovered recently by Wyatt, who works in the Observatory. I've had operatives go out into the field to verify his findings and bring back evidence."

As she spoke, a holographic projection appeared in the middle of the table with a map of all known dimensions in existence. The map focused in on the Hyperion System and then zoomed in on Planet Zareet.

Grand Guardian Omiya went on to explain details about Governor Ragnar and his intentions for invading Planet Ebris. As she continued speaking, the hologram projection displayed images of the governor, the Occulus System, and Ebris.

Throughout the presentation, the Grand Guardian projected copies of the blueprints obtained during the reconnaissance mission. One of the Executive Council members, Guardian Kandara, was able to look at the designs in detail. Before becoming a Guardian, Kandara had studied engineering at university level on her home planet of Raku in the Aristaseus System. She'd also worked as an engineer for several years prior to taking on her role as an Executive Council member. Using her expertise, Kandara was able to analyze the schematics and explain how it all worked.

The last piece of evidence presented was excerpts from the recordings obtained in Governor Ragnar's chamber. During the playback of the recording, the Executive Council were able to get an insight into his malevolent character and, ultimately, verify what his plans were. This was the final piece of evidence they needed in order to act.

Once the Grand Guardian finished presenting all the evidence, the Executive Council members' faces formed anxious expressions. They knew they had to act quickly to stop Governor Ragnar and spare Planet Ebris from destruction. The question was, how?

Although he was yet to commit any crimes on Planet Ebris, the fact that he was planning on crossing dimensions and potentially killing millions of innocent lives was reason enough to act.

"We must decide what we are going to do to stop him," Grand Guardian Omiya said. "I personally think he needs to be captured and taken to Planet Skepsis. This is the only way to ensure he is stopped and can never try this again. I don't believe Governor Ragnar has the capacity for redemption. He's well past the point of no return. He's a monster. Do any of you have any other suggestions?"

Planet Skepsis was located in the Vandirian system. It was the place where the most problematic Infringers were sent. These were Infringers that could not be reformed and needed to be put away, to stop them from causing serious harm to people in other dimensions. This planet was a place where Infringers had to spend the rest of their lives, contemplating the crimes they had committed.

"Can't we just destroy the machine and leave it at that?" Guardian Danzlo asked as he pulled back his silver-blue matted hair behind him.

"We could do that. However, nothing would stop him from building another one, which we would have to destroy again. And then it would just be one continual cycle after another of build and destroy," the Grand Guardian said.

"I would prefer we capture him and make him answer for his crimes on Planet Skepsis. I think destroying the machine alone doesn't go far enough. He needs to be brought to some sort of justice," Guardian Kandara said.

Two other council members agreed with the Grand Guardian. Some of the other Guardians agreed with Guardian Danzlo, while others were indecisive.

The debate continued for some time, with every Guardian giving their opinion. Some sided with the Grand Guardian, others with Guardian Danzlo. The vote was split down the middle. While the meeting didn't descend into a shouting match or get physical, voices did get raised throughout the discussion, and the situation got tense at times amongst some of the Executive Council members.

Under these circumstances, when the vote was split down the middle, the Grand Guardian had the final say in the matter. Although she listened to all the arguments for and against, the choice was made to arrest the governor and send him to Planet Skepsis. She felt this was the best way to deal with him and to protect the long-term safety of Planet Zareet and Planet Ebris.

It was rare that the Grand Guardian would make such a decision. Typically, she would try and find a way to thwart an Infringer's plans to cross dimensions, with minimum interference of the Infringers free will. Her first preference was to always stop Infringers from crossing foreign dimensions and to leave them in the dimension of origin. In this instance, she felt that wasn't possible due to Governor Ragnar's evil disposition and the potential for great harm on Planet Ebris.

The Grand Guardian knew this mission was going to be a difficult and dangerous one. Governor Ragnar had amassed an enormous army. This would require a lot of planning and the best of Concordia's legion of Guardians. Concordia's Chief Defense Strategist, Guardian Jamari, would oversee the logistics and plan for the mission. Jamari—who was also a member of the Executive Council—voted with the Grand Guardian to put an end to Governor Ragnar's regime.

"Guardian Jamari, I am going to ask you to start planning the mission to Zareet and to come back here when your plans are finalized to present your proposal." Grand Guardian Omiya looked at Jamari with high expectations.

"Yes, Grand Guardian. I will get started immediately and advise you once I'm done." Jamari excused himself from the meeting and went to the Observatory to speak to Wyatt.

As a Chief Defense Strategist, he was very tall and had a solid build. He was in his fifties but in excellent physical shape. Jamari's immense stature was such that no one dared to mess with him. He had short dark hair with a small number of grey patches on the sides of his head, above his ears. His eyes were silver in color, accentuated by a dark beard starting to go grey.

"This meeting has now come to a close. I will recall you all back once we have a plan in place. Thank you for your time." Grand Guardian Omiya motioned for everyone to leave.

The Executive Council adjourned to allow time for Jamari to devise his strategy. Jamari estimated that this would require hundreds of the best Guardians Concordia had to offer. Fortunately, he had a large arsenal of Concordians at his disposal, ready to go to battle at any given moment.

Jamari reviewed the map of Planet Zareet with the assistance of Wyatt. Since his initial investigations, Wyatt had acquired a substantial amount of information about the planet, which he'd subsequently used to create a planetary map.

"So where is Governor Ragnar based?" Jamari asked.

"It's over here." Wyatt pointed to the location of the governor's headquarters on his map. "I've also marked where the teleporter is being built."

Using this information, Jamari was able to plan a step-by-step course of action. This was one of the more complex missions Jamari had needed to prepare for in some time. He worked many hours on this and well into the night. There were many things he needed to factor into his plan—one of those being the level of sophistication in Governor Ragnar's defenses. There was also a need to prepare for any mishaps if things didn't go to plan and a retreat strategy if things got out of control. The main thing, however, was to ensure that whatever they did was done quickly and anonymously.

By the time Jamari had completed his plan, the sun was beginning to rise. He didn't realize how quickly time had escaped him. After completing his proposal and reviewing it, he went to his room to get some sleep. He needed as much rest as possible so he could coherently present his plans to the Executive Council. He had to be prepared for anything, as there was a good chance the Grand Guardian would give the order to proceed as early as the next day.

When Jamari awoke a few hours later, he showered and got dressed, then manifested a big cup of coffee. Still feeling tired, he needed something to wake him up. Taking his time, Jamari drank the coffee while he stood and looked out the window of his apartment and into the tranquil Concordian city. Residing on the fifteenth floor of his building, he was fortunate enough to have a stunning landscape view of Concordia that he loved to gaze at, especially on a charming sunny day like it was that day. Jamari tried to savor the peace and quiet before the storm he was about to enter. After taking his last sip, he began making his way to see the Grand Guardian.

"She is now ready to see you," Ezra announced before Jamari entered the chambers.

"Jamari, welcome. Ezra advised me that you have finished planning for the next mission. Let's discuss it." The Grand Guardian pointed to her desk, motioning for Jamari to sit.

Jamari went over his strategy, discussing the details at great length. As he spoke, Jamari saw the Grand Guardian looking intently at him. He saw a determined leader who had agency and was in full control of her authority.

Jamari never questioned her governance; he didn't need to, as he had full confidence in her ability to lead and make the best decisions possible.

Guardian Jamari was thorough, describing his reasons for everything and justifying all that was required for his plan. As the Chief Defense Strategist, he had a wealth of experience to draw on. He could anticipate the Grand Guardian's and the Executive Council's questions, so he was prepared to answer anything asked of him. She seemed pleased with the plan and the details provided.

The Grand Guardian clasped her hands and smiled. "Jamari, as always, I'm pleased with your strategy and the preparation you've done thus far. I would like you to go over all of this with the remainder of the Executive Council. I will ask Ezra to convene a meeting for later today. In the meantime, do not share this information with anyone. Once the details are explained, I'll convene a General Assembly with the rest of Concordia to announce what's happening. Please return later."

"Certainly, Grand Guardian." Jamari got up from his chair and left.

Later that day, the Executive Council reconvened in the Grand Guardian's chambers to discuss the mission. Jamari arrived and sat before the rest of the council, ready to start his presentation. Grand Guardian Omiya led the conversation and then allowed Jamari to continue.

"As you can all see from these holograms, the teleporter is located at this end of the compound."

Guardian Jamari expanded the map of the Governor's headquarters and pointed out where the machine was located.

He went over the specifics again, as he had done earlier that day, explaining all the intricate details of his plans and what was required. When he finished explaining everything, the Grand Guardian put the proposal to a vote.

"All those in favor of Jamari's strategy?"

All Executive Council members raised their hands. It was unanimous.

"This Executive Council officially endorses your plan, Jamari. You may now proceed with preparations."

The Grand Guardian gave the final approval needed to begin arrangements for the mission. Still, Jamari felt an underlying sense of fear for what was about to happen. The Executive Council members were nervous.

Normally a vocal group, they sat in silence. Given the scale of this mission, the real possibility of bloodshed seemed certain, as was the likelihood that some of Concordia's army would not return.

All that was left was to put their plans into action. Grand Guardian Omiya instructed Ezra to arrange a General Assembly. The time had come for the rest of Concordia to learn of this new mission.

The Grand Guardian was anxious, though she didn't show it. She couldn't, as she was Concordia's leader. She had to be the determined strength that led the charge toward defeat, which she did effortlessly time and time again. This came at a personal cost. She often spent many hours combating angst and fear about the final outcome of battles she had sanctioned and what the price would be in terms of lives lost. It was an anguish not seen by anyone. As far as the Grand Guardian was concerned, no one needed to. This was part of her role as a leader, which she'd previously come to accept—over thirty years ago—when she first became the Grand Guardian.

CHAPTER 21

L ater that afternoon, Jonah, Haven, Caleb, and Zak participated in another rigorous training session with Aurora. They had been in the Training Center for several hours, and Aurora knew they were beyond fatigued.

"Okay, everyone, I think that's enough. Let's call it a day," Aurora said.

Their faces drooped with relief, especially Jonah's.

"About time!" Jonah shouted.

Jonah collapsed on the ground. He lay there trying to catch his breath, while the others did the same standing up. Their bodies ached with pain, and they were drenched in sweat, begging for relaxation and something hearty to eat. After a brief period of rest, they decided to go their separate ways for the night.

As they were walking out of the Training Center, without warning, a telepathic message transmitted inside their heads. Everyone paused and stood to attention.

Attention all Concordians: Grand Guardian Omiya has requested a General Assembly. Everyone needs to make their way over to the Council Stadium immediately for some important announcements. Thank you.

The message came through loud and clear from Ezra, who had a serious tone in his voice and a sense of urgency in his delivery. To call a General Assembly on short notice meant something serious was about to transpire.

"Okay everyone, let's proceed to the Council Stadium. You heard what Ezra said, we need to get there quickly. Dinner and rest will need to wait until later," Aurora said.

Too tired to walk, they teleported to the General Assembly. When they arrived and landed in the Council Stadium, thousands of other Guardians were already seated, with many more entering at a rapid pace. They managed to find seats together and sat, waiting patiently. The stadium filled to capacity in short order, and soon enough, the noise level had reached resounding heights. People were chatting away, wondering why they had been invited to an Assembly at such short notice.

Minutes later, Grand Guardian Omiya entered the stadium, followed by the Executive Council. She walked onto the stage and approached the podium while the remaining Executive Council members sat in their chairs behind her. Grave expressions twisted their faces. Jonah and his friends sensed something serious going on. The arena became silent as it appeared the Grand Guardian was about to speak.

"Thank you for coming so promptly. I will keep this as brief as possible. In recent days, we have gathered intelligence regarding a new Infringer threat discovered in a dimension called the Hyperion System. In this dimension, there is a planet called Zareet, which is governed by a menacing individual by the name of Governor Ragnar. We have strong evidence to suggest he is building a teleporter so he can open a portal into another dimension called the Occulus System. In this dimension, he is specifically targeting a planet called Ebris so he can steal a compound known as Chrimatide."

As the Grand Guardian continued to speak, a map of Planet Zareet projected into the stadium above where the Grand Guardian spoke. This was followed by various other images of Governor Ragnar, Planet Ebris, a sample of Chrimatide, and an image of the teleporter. As these images appeared in the stadium, audience reactions such as "Ooh" and "Ahh" could be heard in the background.

Grand Guardian Omiya went on to explain why Governor Ragnar was so interested in stealing Chrimatide—for energy synthesis—and why she believed he was so dangerous.

"Guardian Jamari, Concordia's Chief Defense Strategist, has devised a plan to fight off Governor Ragnar. Make no mistake—this will be a dangerous mission. We believe he is a treacherous individual. This is going to require an enormous number of Guardians to help defeat him and his immense army.

"Jamari has selected the clusters of Guardians that will be going into battle. If your cluster has been chosen, you must be prepared to go into battle tomorrow. Your cluster leader will be given instructions on what is required and all other relevant details. For those participating in tomorrow's mission, I leave you with Concordia's motto: with infinite bravery comes infinite rewards. That's all for now. Thank you for your time this evening. This General Assembly is now adjourned."

The Grand Guardian hurried away from the podium and left the stadium. The Executive Council followed behind her. People started talking, which raised the noise level in the stadium again. Jonah, Haven, Zak, and Caleb looked at each other. Suddenly, it all became real. Aurora had spent many hours preparing them and giving them the necessary skills to become elite fighters. Now, it was time to put all of that into practice.

Jonah's heart raced. A level of fear he had never experienced overcame him. He had never participated in war on Earth, let alone a war in a parallel universe. He was afraid of the unknown. Terrified of being seriously hurt or, even worse, dying. Jonah felt he was too young to die. His life had just begun. Only recently had he discovered who he really was and his place in the universe.

Jonah had only been in Concordia for a short while and had recently managed to make some friends. What if they never saw him again? What if Jonah's parents never got to hug him one more time? Jonah's parents had lost his grandfather. That in itself was emotionally devastating for Aurora and Mason. If Jonah were to go, it would be overwhelming. His parents would be beyond heartbroken. Being their only son, Jonah was a long way from becoming the Guardian he was supposed to be. His parents envisioned a long future for him, one in which he was a well-adjusted Guardian and took his role seriously. What if that was now to be cut short?

Haven, on the other hand, was ready. Combat was a far too familiar occurrence for her. While she was a little nervous, she wasn't plagued by fear like Jonah. For Haven, fear was a long-forgotten notion. It had to be. On Fasmeon, only the fearless survived. From an early age, she'd had to learn to fight for her existence and for her place in the world. This impending battle on Zareet was merely repetition for her.

As for Caleb and Zak, they couldn't wait. They were ready to grab their batons and teleport anywhere they were required. They were eager to be embroiled in battle and to show off their remarkable warrior skills. For these two, the fear of brutality was long-lost on them and replaced with the hunger for success and adulation.

"So, what happens now? Do we just wait to be called upon?" Jonah asked.

"It isn't certain if any of us will end up going or not," Haven said.

"I don't care if we get called up or not; I'm going. Period!" Caleb threw some punches in the air.

Haven disagreed. "We can't go unless we're specifically told to go. That would be against the rules. And you can't go disobeying the rules just for the sake of it. I've already been in trouble with the Grand Guardian once for doing the wrong thing. It wasn't fun, and I assure you, I don't want to go through that again."

"We'll see about that! Look, if you don't want to go, that's fine. But I'm going, one way or another," Caleb responded with a mischievous smile.

Caleb and Zak were determined to go to Zareet and fight, no matter what. For Haven, it was different. While she was not afraid of going into battle, she was a little more reserved about the matter. She didn't feel the need to fight to appease an egoic urge. She fought when necessary. Caleb and Zak wanted to fight for adoration. On the other hand, Jonah had little desire to fight.

Aurora was anxious for Jonah. Even though he had been in training for the last few months, she was afraid he wasn't ready just yet. In actual fact, though, he was. It was Aurora who wasn't ready to send Jonah into battle; deep down, she was hoping he wouldn't be chosen for this one. She feared that his chances of returning were slim at this point. Aurora was not prepared to lose him just yet.

People started leaving the stadium. Aurora, Jonah, and the rest of his friends all rose from their seats and made their way out of the stadium.

They pondered what the next day would bring. Whatever it was, they were guaranteed not to be the same afterward.

CHAPTER 22

"**H**ell, yes!" Caleb shouted.

He and Zak each threw a fist pump into the air before they gave each other a high five. Their respective cluster leaders had just told them they had been selected for the mission to Planet Zareet. Caleb and Zak were excited to be a part of the upcoming battle. It was going to be their first. Not having been to war before, they viewed this first battle as an initiation into their Concordian duties—their final step on their journey into adulthood.

Haven, whose cluster had also been selected, didn't share Caleb and Zak's enthusiasm. No doubt, she was ready for war and prepared to go and give it her absolute best. She was willing to play her part as needed. However, she didn't view this as a transition into adulthood. Haven understood war quite well. She knew of its brutality. Its anguish, sorrow, and mortality. Although she had respect for its resolve to bring about a desired outcome, Haven knew better than to walk into battle with enthusiasm. Someone always suffered a loss. What's more, Haven was painfully aware she or one of her friends could very well be the subject of loss.

On the other hand, Jonah was advised by his cluster leader that he and his cluster were not going to participate in the upcoming battle. While he felt some relief in hearing this, as did Aurora, he also felt a little left out. He had heard Haven, Caleb, and Zak had all been selected to take part in the forthcoming mission. This made Jonah feel a little excluded.

"Why do they all get to go, and I have to stay here?" Jonah asked his mother as she stood in his room, while he sat on his bed.

"Jonah, not everyone is able to go. They only need a certain number of Guardians for this mission. They can't send everyone, as that would be excessive. Also, Concordia would be left with no one to send to other battles, should the worst happen and we end up being completely annihilated. Besides, I don't think you're ready for war just yet. You need a lot more training before you can engage in combat this dangerous, which is what Haven, Caleb, and Zak have."

"Is that what this is all about? My supposed lack of training? So, were you involved in me not being selected?" Jonah demanded to know.

"I don't have any influence in cluster selection for battles. However, I'm glad you weren't chosen for this mission. You're not ready yet."

Jonah wasn't pleased with Aurora's answer.

"Yes, I am ready! *You* know I'm ready; *you* just don't want me to go! Am I meant to sit here and do nothing while my friends go risk their lives for 'the greater good?'"

"Yes, Jonah, that's the way it works. The Executive Council don't send everyone into a conflict all at once. Sometimes your friends might go in, and other times it will be you. Sometimes none of you will go—or it might be all of you. You just never know. All you can do is be patient. Don't worry; your time will come and when it does, you'll wish you didn't have to go into battle."

"I still feel useless sitting here, doing nothing. Surely, there's something I can do to help. If not in battle, then maybe I can help in some other way. I'm going to speak to Dad."

Before Aurora could say anything, Jonah teleported away to try and find his father. He began his search in his parent's room. As Jonah emerged into their room, he found Mason, who was about to leave for the Observatory. Jonah stopped him just in time.

Mason was required to do intense surveillance work for the impending conflict. While he was no longer involved in direct physical combat these days, his surveillance work in the Observatory was crucial for Concordia—especially prior to a mission, as it was the basis for making key decisions in battles, even putting a stop to a mission in some rare instances.

"Dad, is there something I can do for this upcoming mission? My cluster wasn't chosen. I just don't want to sit around doing nothing while my friends are out there on the ground fighting and potentially getting hurt. It makes me feel a bit useless. There must be something I can do?"

"Jonah, apart from surveillance, there isn't much else I can think of. And I can't let you do any of that work, as it takes a lot of training. You might have to accept that you'll need to sit this one out until next time."

"No, I don't want to sit this one out until next time!"

At that point, Jonah thought back to what Grand Guardian Omiya had said during the General Assembly. Something about a teleporter Governor Ragnar was building so he and his army could cross over into other dimensions.

If only I could gain access to the design of the teleporter and see how it worked, perhaps I could find a way to exploit a vulnerability in its design, Jonah thought to himself. *Something that could be used to destroy or, at the very least, disable the machine.*

With his engineering knowledge, Jonah had a good understanding of machine design and was familiar with reading schematics. He was confident he could figure something out if he could access the teleporter's design.

"Dad, do you know if there's a copy of the teleporter's schematics somewhere? Do you or the Executive Council have anything that shows how the teleporter works?"

"Wyatt has a copy of the schematics. Why do you ask?" Mason looked at Jonah with apprehension.

"If I can look at the design, I can hopefully figure out some flaw that could be used to destroy the teleporter."

"Jonah, I don't think it's a good idea. I'm sure the Executive Council has explored all of that. The reason I say this is because Guardian Kandara used to be an engineer on her home planet of Raku. I guarantee she's examined the schematics and figured all of that out."

"Okay. So what harm is there if I have a look as well? Seeing as I'm not going anywhere, it wouldn't hurt. It will help me pass the time while my friends are off to war. And it'll help me feel useful. And I can stop bugging you."

"You want to feel useful? Pity you didn't have those feelings on Earth, when your mother used to ask for help with the dishes."

Jonah put his hands on Mason's shoulders and gave him a sly grin. "Dad, we need to stop living in the past and just live in the moment. That's what Guardian Ishwa always says."

"Oh so now you've decided to get all spiritual?" Mason paused briefly. "Anyhow . . . let's go see Wyatt in the Observatory."

Mason brushed Jonah's hands off his shoulders and they both teleported over to the Observatory.

They both arrived at the Observatory and minutes later found Wyatt.

Mason asked Wyatt for the schematics Jonah was looking for. Wyatt handed them to Jonah, albeit hesitantly, as he thought similarly to Mason—that it was a waste of time. However, Wyatt didn't have the time or the energy to argue the point since he was so busy with his work.

After grabbing a copy of the blueprints, Jonah sat in a quiet corner not too far away from Wyatt. He manifested a large cup of caramel latte to sip on as he analyzed the design in detail and tried to interpret what it all meant. Although some of the mathematical notation was a little different from what he knew on Earth, Jonah was able to make sense of it reasonably quickly.

As the hours passed, Jonah gained an understanding of how the teleporter functioned. In fact, he was having a lot of fun trying to figure out the teleporter's components. For the first time since leaving university, he was able to use his engineering studies for something useful—something he'd never imagined doing in Concordia.

What? Are you serious? Jonah thought to himself.

He couldn't believe something so simple had been overlooked by the engineers on Zareet who had designed the teleporter.

Jonah checked it again to be sure. *Yes. I'm right.*

During his analysis, Jonah figured out there was a component at the core of the teleporter that, if overloaded with power, would potentially blow up the entire machine.

How could the engineers that designed this be so reckless? Jonah thought.

In all fairness to the engineers, Governor Ragnar had forced them to design and build the teleporter quickly. As such, the engineers had to overlook certain elements of the teleporter and not design it as well as they could have. It still worked as intended; however, it left the teleporter vulnerable to security attacks and prone to malfunctions. Given the size of Zareet's army, security wasn't of great concern to the original designers of the teleporter.

Jonah went to speak to his father about his findings.

"Dad, you're not going to believe what I just found."

Jonah was so excited. Without warning, he forcefully dragged his father over to the schematics to discuss what he'd uncovered. Mason was a little irritated by Jonah's abruptness and pushed his arm off when they reached the diagrams.

Jonah explained, in broad terms, how the teleporter worked and revealed the vulnerability he discovered that could destroy the machine. Jonah's father listened with an open mind and realized Jonah knew what he was talking about. Mason was quite proud Jonah was able to put his engineering skills to good use.

"Dad, do you want to explain this to the Grand Guardian and the Executive Council? I mean, as far as we know, do they have any plans to destroy the teleporter?"

"I don't know. But I'm sure the Executive Council has considered this and has some sort of plan in place to demolish it."

"So, can you go and ask the Grand Guardian?" Jonah asked with great tenacity.

"No, Son, I cannot. I don't want to disturb her in the middle of combat preparations. She's got a lot of work to do and wouldn't want to be interrupted."

"Then, if you don't want to ask, I'll ask."

"Jonah don't be so stubborn. You can't see the Grand Guardian, and that's that," Mason said, furious at Jonah's obstinance.

"Dad, the Grand Guardian needs to know this. It's important. Maybe no one has thought of it. I'm going whether you like it or not!"

As Jonah couldn't teleport out of the Observatory due to its tight security, he marched out of the Observatory with conviction, heading toward Grand Guardian Omiya's chambers. Mason followed close behind. He figured if Jonah was going to see the Grand Guardian, at the very least, he should be there to control the situation in case Jonah said or did something foolish.

Within minutes, they arrived at the chambers and were greeted by Ezra.

"Mason, how lovely to see you again," Ezra said. "Oh, and young Jonah, it's good to see you too. I almost didn't recognize you without the lipstick and Wonder Woman outfit."

Mason and Ezra erupted in laughter. Jonah kept a straight face and didn't say anything. He didn't appreciate being the butt of Ezra's joke.

"We were wondering if we could see the Grand Guardian." Mason paused for a moment and looked at Jonah. He thought twice about asking Ezra for an audience with the Grand Guardian, as he didn't want to interrupt her during preparations for the next mission. He continued anyway. "There's some important information Jonah has regarding the impending mission, which could prove to be useful."

"I see. Wait here a moment, and I'll check if she's available," Ezra said before he went to consult with the Grand Guardian.

"How did he know about me wearing lipstick and the Wonder Woman costume?" Jonah asked.

"He was the one who brought you to Concordia the night you passed out drunk at your university," Mason said.

"You never told me that. I thought you and Mom brought me here."

"Oh, didn't I tell you? Yes, we all came together to your university and picked you up and brought you here. Ezra was the one that knew where you were. Wyatt from the Observatory told him. And along with your mother and I, poor Ezra got to see you in all your glory."

He saw me dressed as Wonder Woman! How embarrassing, Jonah thought.

A few moments later, Ezra returned.

"The Grand Guardian can see you now. Come this way."

Ezra escorted them inside, where the Grand Guardian was waiting to greet them. As Mason was there, she was willing to take the time to listen to Jonah. This is because she knew Mason quite well due to the surveillance work he had done over the years. The Grand Guardian had enormous respect for his work and how seriously he took it. Not many people in Concordia enjoyed the same luxury.

The Grand Guardian, who was standing behind her desk, gestured for Jonah and Mason to be seated. As they all sat, Jonah noticed a large sculpture of a beagle dog lying on her desk. He had a fondness for beagles from a young age, as his parents had bought him a beagle puppy, Benny, when he was five years old. Benny was a great addition to the family but passed away when Jonah was seventeen. Seeing the sculpture on the desk brought back some fond memories for Jonah; it helped put him a little at ease as he sat before Grand Guardian Omiya.

"Thank you, Grand Guardian, for seeing us on such short notice. My son, Jonah, has some important information that may be of use for the upcoming mission."

The Grand Guardian looked at Jonah very astutely for a moment, wondering what a new Guardian had to say that was so important. She could see drops of sweat on his forehead and could tell he was nervous.

"What is it, Jonah?" the Grand Guardian asked in a gentle, patient manner.

"I've looked at the teleporter's schematics and found a weakness that we could use to sabotage it. I've studied the design at great length and have found a component that has some vulnerabilities. With a little tampering, it could be manipulated to destroy the teleporter."

"And how do you know this, Jonah?" the Grand Guardian asked.

"When I was on Earth, I studied aerospace engineering, so I have a very good understanding of machinery and how to interpret schematics. I am very confident that if you let me teleport to Zareet, I could exploit this flaw and sabotage the teleporter. It won't win us the battle, but it will be a good start."

The Grand Guardian pondered over what Jonah had said. She needed a little more convincing before she could decide to go ahead with Jonah's proposal.

"That all sounds very interesting, Jonah. Thank you. Here's what I'm going to do. Let me call in Guardian Kandara, and you can discuss the matter with her. She, too, has extensive engineering experience and knowledge. If she concurs with your findings, we can consider creating a plan to destroy the teleporter."

She turned to Ezra and asked him to summon Guardian Kandara into the meeting. Ezra teleported out of the chambers and went about finding her. A few minutes later, Ezra returned with Kandara, who entered the chambers and sat next to Jonah. After the Grand Guardian briefly explained to Kandara why she had been summoned, Jonah proceeded to describe what he had discovered earlier about the teleporter.

Kandara was initially skeptical about Jonah's idea.

"I'm not sure this is going to work, but I'll have a look at the schematics anyway," Kandara said, as she began examining the design once again.

Kandara took her time to consider what Jonah had said. She wanted to be sure before giving her approval. There was a lot at stake here, and Kandara wanted to be certain that Jonah's idea was valid.

After spending about thirty minutes studying the schematics, Kandara was able to agree with Jonah's findings. She was quite impressed. Kandara appreciated that there was someone else in Concordia with some engineering knowledge like herself whom she could confer with.

"Grand Guardian, I believe what Jonah is saying is correct. And I'm of the view that what he has discovered will work, and we should give it a try," Kandara said with authority.

"Very well, then. Jonah, I'm going to send you to Planet Zareet on a specialized mission to carry out your plan. I will provide you with other Guardians to assist you in case you get into trouble. There's safety in numbers. That way, you can concentrate on destroying the teleporter, and the other Guardians can focus on protecting you."

Grand Guardian Omiya gazed at Jonah in a strong, authoritarian manner, her piercing eyes not willing to accept any answer other than a yes.

"As you wish, Grand Guardian."

Jonah became excited and anxious at the same time.

The Grand Guardian ordered Ezra to call Jamari into her chambers. She realized Jamari had a lot of work to do with organizing the fast-approaching battle. However, the Grand Guardian also realized Jonah was onto something, and Jamari needed to assist in organizing a mission to do something about it.

Jamari arrived within minutes, at which point the Grand Guardian explained everything. As Jamari looked at Jonah with his silver eyes, he was astounded by his idea. It was ingenious.

After considering Jonah's plan, Jamari concurred with the Grand Guardian that the best way to tackle this was to arrange a smaller, specialized mission. His initial thought was to pair him with Guardian Skylar.

"She is an experienced and highly skilled operative who has been on several missions for the Grand Guardian in the past," Jamari explained to everyone in the room. "More recently, Skylar was on an assignment to gather intelligence for the battle on Zareet. As such, she is familiar with the planet and can help guide Jonah around Zareet."

Jamari also decided to use Caleb, Zak, and Haven. Although they had been assigned to work on the bigger battle on Planet Zareet, he figured this mission would be a great experience for them and help the group develop some new skills. He was aware they had all been training together with Jonah and thought since they all knew each other, they could easily work together on this mission.

The Grand Guardian approved the plan. Jonah was thrilled his friends would be working with him. It would make the task that little bit easier. Jonah was also excited to work with Skylar, whose experience as a Guardian was something that he and his friends could utilize for their mission.

Jamari left the Grand Guardian's chambers to meet with Skylar, Haven, Zak, and Caleb's cluster leaders. He explained the plan to each of them and what was required. They all agreed. However, Caleb and Zak weren't too thrilled with the idea at first, when their cluster leader explained the change in circumstances.

"What?" Caleb cried to his cluster leader, Guardian Wanaki and Zak's cluster leader, Guardian Mibano.

"There's been a change of assignment for both of you—" Guardian Wanaki said before being interrupted by Zak.

"Change of assignment! Caleb and I are happy with the current assignment. This new mission sounds like we're bodyguards for Jonah. We want a real battle, not a frolic with Jonah to blow up a teleporter!"

By now, Guardian Wanaki's lips were pursed and his eyes bulged. Both he and Guardian Mibano had lost their patience with Caleb and Zak and were not going to tolerate their insubordination.

"This is a directive from the Grand Guardian and Jamari" Guardian Wankai said. "And at this point in time, I really don't care what you think or how you feel. It's irrelevant to me. You're both going on this new assignment. Period! Now move!"

Caleb and Zak, infuriated by the decision, walked off. They felt the new assignment was a demotion. Their egos didn't allow them to see the importance of the new task and what Jonah's mission could potentially achieve. They managed to calm down by the time they found Jonah, Haven, and Skylar. As they entered Jonah's room, they gave Jonah a dirty look, which Jonah noticed; it made him a little uncomfortable.

"Apparently, we've been assigned to babysit you and help you blow up a teleporter," Caleb said with a sharp tone.

"C'mon, guys. We're all friends here. There's no need to be angry. Trust me, this is an important mission and could help us potentially win," Jonah said, trying to diffuse the situation with a smile.

"Whatever, man. So, what's the story with the teleporter?" Zak asked.

"Before I get to that, this is Guardian Skylar."

Jonah pointed out Skylar to everyone. Skylar was of a similar height to Haven with red hair and freckles on her face.

"From what I've been told, Skylar has been on a previous mission to Zareet and has some knowledge of the planet, which is why she's also been assigned on this mission. And she's also got a lot of experience as a Guardian and could be quite a valuable asset."

"Yes. I've been to Zareet before and seen the teleporter, so I'll be able to help navigate us all there," Skylar said.

"Now, getting back to Zak's earlier question about the teleporter," Jonah said. "I've looked at the machine's design and found a flaw in one of its components. It will help destroy the teleporter and stop Governor Ragnar from getting to Planet Ebris."

As Jonah spoke, Caleb and Zak calmed down. They went from being incredulous to impressed as Jonah continued to explain what he wanted to achieve and why. Haven didn't mind her assignment being changed. She was happy to help in any way possible. Jonah also knew how strong and fit they were, besides being great fighters. He was confident they could protect him while he did his best to sabotage the teleporter.

"What's the plan, then?" Skylar asked.

Jonah directed them to his desk, where he had holographic images on display of Zareet and a schematic of the teleporter.

"I need to reach the machine so I can tamper with it," Jonah said, pointing to the location on the holographic image. "I can only guess there's going to be tight security around that area. This is where you all come in. It sounds easy, but it could get very dangerous depending on how many soldiers occupy the surrounding area."

"From what I saw on my last mission, there were a lot of soldiers patrolling outside Ragnar's headquarters, but not many inside. I can't guarantee it will be the same when we get there," Skylar said.

"I don't care if there's a lot of soldiers. The more, the merrier. We'll take them down with our eyes closed!" Zak quipped as he demonstrated his fighting moves.

This put a smile on Caleb's face, which in turn helped ease the tension in the room. Caleb, not wanting to be outdone, showed his moves and eventually started play-fighting Zak. Haven, Skylar, and Jonah watched until they got bored.

"Guys, that's enough!" Haven yelled, breaking up the fight. She glanced at them with a piercing stare. "C'mon. This mission is critical. A whole planet's destiny is at stake here, and you two are wrestling each other. Be serious for once."

Caleb and Zak stopped fighting and composed themselves, sporting mischievous smirks. Now that they'd gotten that out of their systems, they discussed how they were going to get in and out as quickly as possible.

Jamari was waiting on Jonah and his friends to complete their mission with the teleporter, before sending out his army of fighter Guardians to take on Governor Ragnar and his military force.

"I think we should go to Zareet tonight and complete this mission. There will be fewer people around, and we can get in and out easier. Also, Jamari wants to send his army tomorrow for the big battle, so we need to get this done before then. Let's all get some rest and meet back here this evening around midnight; then we'll head over."

Haven, Caleb, and Zak retreated to their own rooms to get some sleep. Skylar stayed behind.

It dawned on Jonah how important this undertaking was to the overall success of the bigger mission Jamari was planning. His hope was not to disappoint, especially when he was the one who instigated this.

"Amica, please set an alarm to wake me up at 11:30 p.m. tonight," Jonah instructed.

"A reminder has been created in your schedule for 11:30 p.m. tonight, Jonah," Amica said.

"Thanks, Amica."

"You're welcome, Jonah."

"Jonah, before you get any rest, I think we should go to the Observatory and speak with Guardian Wyatt. He can give us some further details about Zareet, which might be useful for this assignment," Skylar said.

"Sounds like a great idea. My dad works in the Observatory with Wyatt, so he can get us in there."

"Well, that's handy to know." Skylar raised her eyebrows, surprised by the revelation.

CHAPTER 23

*H*ey, Dad, where are you? I urgently need to speak to you, Jonah said telepathically. There was a brief silence before Jonah got a reply.

What is it, Jonah? Mason asked.

It's about the mission. I need to see Wyatt to get some details about where Planet Zareet is and some information about the teleporter.

I'm actually in the Observatory with Wyatt right now. Come over, and I'll let you in. I will wait for you outside.

Thanks. I'm on my way. I'm also going to bring Guardian Skylar with me, who's been assigned to help me out on this mission.

Jonah and Skylar teleported to the Observatory, where Mason waited for them outside as promised. They all walked in together and meandered through the building's security checkpoints until they found Wyatt, who was away from his desk chatting to another guardian.

"Hey Jonah, your dad mentioned you and Skylar wanted to see me," Wyatt said.

"Yes that's right, Wyatt. I was wondering if I could have a chat with you. I just need some information from you regarding my upcoming mission to Zareet."

Jonah explained that he was going on a mission sanctioned by the Grand Guardian to sabotage the teleporting machine Governor Ragnar was developing.

"What do you need to know?" Wyatt asked.

"I need to learn more about where Planet Zareet is and if you have any further details about the location of the teleporter."

"Follow me," Wyatt said as he turned around and walked back to his workstation and brought up a hologram. "Over here, you have the outer edge of the Hyperion System. Now, if we zoom in over here, you can see Planet Zareet."

As Wyatt was zooming in and expanding the hologram, Jonah marveled at the vastness and majesty of the universe. Witnessing the towering nebulas, the quasars, pulsars, star clusters, and even a supernova happening in real time; Jonah was captivated. These were phenomena Mason and Wyatt had observed many times before, due to the work they did in the Observatory and the thousands of hours they spent studying so many different universes.

Mason admired how Jonah was in awe of what he was seeing for the first time. He had this childlike curiosity as there was much he had yet to discover about universes and how glorious they were. After spending a few minutes admiring the holograms, Jonah realized he had to focus on the task at hand and prepare for his mission.

"If you have a look over here on my screen, you can see some live footage from Zareet." Wyatt pointed to the monitors at his workstation.

From what they could see, the area was heavily guarded by soldiers and had some very sophisticated security. While this added to Jonah's anxiety, it was valuable information for him and Skylar to have. It gave them some added insight that could be used to prepare for their journey and to create a better strategy for accomplishing the end goal.

"Now, before you both leave, I want you to take this." Wyatt handed Jonah a light-pad. "This device is similar to a tablet computer you would've used on Earth. I've downloaded information onto it that might be useful, such as the teleporter's schematics and a map of Zareet.

"A light-pad also has the capability to work as a GPS device so you can navigate the planet. I've programmed a few locations of interest to you, the main one being where the teleporter is located. Make sure you take it with you. Otherwise, you and Skylar will be wandering around the planet aimlessly trying to find the teleporter."

"Thanks, Wyatt!"

Jonah appreciated Wyatt's generosity and willingness to help. Wyatt also spent time showing Jonah how to use the light-pad, including a few sophisticated enhancements he'd added. He even demonstrated how the light-pad could be folded into a small cube the size of a die for easy transportation.

After being there for about an hour and gathering as much information as they could, Jonah and Skylar decided to leave the Observatory and head to their respective rooms to get some rest. As they were leaving, Mason stopped Jonah.

"Son, please be careful out there. This is your first mission, so please don't do anything stupid." Mason put his right arm on Jonah's shoulder.

"I won't, Dad. Besides, I've got Skylar, Haven, Caleb, and Zak coming with me. They'll look after me and make sure I return safely. I trust them."

"It's not that I don't trust your friends, Jonah; it's just that you're all new Guardians and this will be your first mission. Please promise me you'll take care out there."

"I will, Dad. I promise."

"Don't worry, Mason, I'll take good care of Jonah, you have my word," Skylar said.

Mason breathed a sigh of relief. "I'm so glad you're going on this mission. It helps alleviate some of my anxiety."

Mason gave Jonah a big hug and wished him well. Jonah and Skylar walked away from the workstation and left the Observatory. Mason's eyes filled with tears. *I hope he comes back safely.*

Wyatt, who sat nearby at his workstation, sensed Mason was uneasy and tried to comfort him. Wyatt was also a parent and understood Mason's apprehension.

"He's going to be all right, Mason. My gut instinct tells me he'll be back to fight another day," Wyatt said with a comforting smile.

"I hope so, Wyatt."

Mason faced away from Wyatt. He didn't want to show his tears, so he kept his back to Wyatt for a moment while he dried his eyes. As he composed himself, Mason continued with the mountain of work he had before him. He hoped it would help distract him from thinking about Jonah and his mission ahead.

Later that evening, just before midnight, Skylar, Haven, Caleb, and Zak congregated in Jonah's room.

As she had previous experience participating in missions, Skylar advised everyone what to wear. It consisted of combat outfits that were designed to have storage for gadgets, including their batons. They were skintight and covered their entire bodies, apart from their neck and heads. Resembling the training outfits they used, they were made of a spandex-like material and were khaki in color. All it took was the press of a few buttons on their wardrobe generators to change into their combat outfits.

"Skylar and I went to see Wyatt earlier. He works over in the Observatory and has been following the situation on Zareet. He gave me a whole bunch of information about the planet and where it is."

Jonah went on to explain some of the other details Wyatt had provided them. He also demonstrated the light-pad device he was given and how to use it.

"Wow, that's pretty cool." Zak hadn't seen a light-pad before; he thought they were fascinating.

"Wyatt also showed us some live footage from Zareet. There are a lot of soldiers around that teleporter and some really sophisticated security. We are going to have to be on our A-game to get through all that and return safely. This is where we now need to get serious. We can't afford to slip up. This mission is vital to the success of the bigger mission that Jamari is preparing for. We can't disappoint him."

Jonah showed everyone images of where the teleporter was on Planet Zareet and the plan to find it. Jonah proposed to split up into two groups, with one group being Skylar, Caleb, and Haven and the other being Jonah and Zak. Jonah figured it would be best not to pair Caleb and Zak together to avoid them acting out.

"I want you three to be the first line of defense," Jonah said, pointing to Skylar, Caleb, and Haven. "I want you to be able to deal with any soldiers we encounter who try to resist us. And I want you to lead us to the teleporter."

Zak and Jonah would be next in line if things got out of hand. Jonah envisaged that the other three would be strong enough to handle anything that came their way, so he and Zak wouldn't need to fight off too many soldiers. Having seen the earlier footage, though, he realized his hands would need to get dirty eventually.

Jonah didn't go into any details with the group about what he needed to do to the teleporter to hamper with it. He felt they didn't need to know, as it was quite technical in nature and would take far too long to explain. Jonah thought it would be best for him to be the brains of the operation, while the others would be the muscle.

Once Jonah finished explaining everything, they were ready to go. He folded the light-pad into a cube and tucked it into a pocket of his combat outfit.

"Okay. I think it's time to go. So, everyone knows what they're doing?" Jonah asked one last time.

"Yes," they all responded.

"Okay, then. Let's do this," Jonah said as they all joined hands to form a small circle.

Since Skylar knew more about the location of Planet Zareet, Jonah let her lead the way. Skylar closed her eyes and focused on where she wanted to land. Within seconds, she teleported everyone out of Jonah's room and moments later, she opened her eyes and saw everyone standing next to her in a circle, safe and sound on Planet Zareet.

Jonah took a moment to get his bearings. His immediate surroundings looked familiar. They were in a corridor, which Jonah felt he had seen before in the Observatory, when he was looking at the live feeds from Wyatt's workstation. Jonah pulled out his light-pad to pinpoint exactly where they were. Within seconds, he confirmed his initial assumption was correct. They had landed in Governor Ragnar's headquarters and were only minutes away from finding the teleporter.

Jonah handed Skylar the light-pad. As she had travelled to Zareet previously on her last mission, Jonah felt it would be a good idea for Skylar to navigate the rest of the way, due to her experience.

Everyone remained quiet. They proceeded in a crouch-run across the building, keeping to the walls. As they were about to turn a corner, Haven noticed soldiers up ahead. She stopped and quietly turned back. Haven gestured for everyone to stop and remain silent. Fortunately, the soldiers didn't see her.

Soldiers up ahead! Haven said telepathically to all of them.

Caleb briefly poked his head around the corner to look for himself. He spied eight of them standing around, talking to each other.

Okay, here's what we're going to do, Caleb projected to the others. *Skylar, Haven, and I will use our batons to knock them unconscious. But first, we'll need to wait for them to turn around and look away from us. Then we can catch them by surprise. Jonah and Zak, when you see us run, you two wait here until we give you the all-clear. Understood?*

Understood, Jonah said.

Everyone waited patiently. Caleb and Haven kept a watch on the soldiers, looking for an opportune time to charge in. Finally, there came a time when the soldiers were looking away from their direction.

Skylar and Caleb, now! Haven commanded.

Jonah and Zak remained behind and looked on while Skylar, Caleb, and Haven quietly charged from around the corner with their batons. As they approached, one of the soldiers saw them and raised the alarm.

"Watch out behind you!" one of them shouted.

Before the soldiers could draw their weapons, Skylar, Caleb, and Haven knocked them out with their silver batons—that flashed against the lights from the ceiling—one by one, until they were all lying on the ground unconscious.

Zak and Jonah were impressed by what they saw and how efficient the other three worked together. After a moment of admiration for their fellow Guardians, they both ran out and raced toward the other three.

That was awesome, guys! Jonah projected with glee.

Glad to be of service. Caleb boasted, standing in his finest superman pose, proud of his good work.

That's enough of your sycophancy, Caleb, we need to keep moving, Haven said, not wanting to waste time with Caleb's thirst for adoration.

They had to move quickly, as they all knew the effect of the baton was temporary. When they regained consciousness, the soldiers would most likely sound the alarm.

They continued down another long corridor. The light-pad indicated the teleporter was only minutes away. They kept moving until they encountered another group of soldiers. This time, there was a greater number of them, and they seemed prepared. Little did Jonah and his friends know that security cameras were watching them. When they had knocked out the other soldiers, one of them managed to send an alert to the control room just before he was struck. From there, someone in the control room tracked what was going on and alerted the next group of soldiers to be ready for a group of rebels.

Standing before them now were over forty soldiers; many were taller than average and were well-built, with intimidating faces. Within seconds, they had surrounded Jonah and his friends. One of them smirked at Jonah.

"You're outnumbered. There's no escaping, so don't even try," the soldier said.

The guard's arrogance fueled Jonah and the rest of his team's fire. As one of the soldiers attempted to handcuff Jonah, Haven pulled out her baton and struck him. He fell to the ground.

The other soldiers looked shocked. They weren't sure what Haven had used. It was advanced technology they hadn't seen before. The fact that a baton-like object could knock someone out cold with a single touch left some of the soldiers with their mouths wide open. Some grabbed their own belted weapons, which resembled pistols. Regardless of what Jonah and his friends were capable of, the soldiers had to fight back. After a moment of silence, carnage ensued.

The soldiers ran toward them. Jonah's team each had batons in their hands, ready to inflict pain. Haven and Skylar began the assault. They made it look effortless. Haven rotated in a circular fashion, knocking her enemies out, one by one. Skylar was equally quick, striking out soldiers with ease.

Caleb and Zak followed suit, wiping their opponents out one at a time. For these two, it was a sport. The soldiers attempted to punch and kick Caleb and Zak, but they proved to be too quick. With one touch of their batons, they were able to impede the soldiers' attempts by putting them to sleep.

Jonah was able to defend himself more adequately than his friends expected, easily defeating soldiers with his non-stop baton assaults. Every now and again, Haven would glance out the corner of her eye to see what was happening with Jonah. It surprised her how well he was able to handle his fair share of soldiers.

After a few minutes of intense fighting, all of Governor Ragnar's soldiers ended up laying unconscious on the floor. While taking a moment to rest, Jonah thought about what to do next. They had to get to the teleporter quicker than ever before. Jonah didn't know what kind of resistance they would continue to encounter, which heightened his sense of urgency.

We have to keep going until we find that teleporter. Not sure what's up ahead, but we need to be prepared for anything. You've all done well so far, so just keep up the great work. Now, let's go, Jonah said.

Skylar didn't need the light-pad device anymore, as she had figured out where they all needed to go, so she gave it to Jonah, who folded the light-pad and put it away in one of his pockets.

As they were about to head off, all five of them felt a small, sharp jab in their necks. Within seconds, Jonah's vision began to blur, and he slowly collapsed on the ground. He saw a soldier running toward him from a walkway, holding a tranquilizer gun. Jonah quickly realized what had happened before he became unconscious—they had all been shot with tranquilizers.

After they collapsed, several soldiers converged around them. They made sure Jonah and his friends had been knocked out cold, before picking them up and transferring them to underground prison cells located in the same complex.

They locked each of them in separate cells with thick walls so they wouldn't be able to see or hear each other once they were awake. They each lay in their cells, paralyzed. As soon as they regained consciousness, an interrogation awaited them.

CHAPTER 24

An hour had passed since Jonah and his team were shot down by soldiers. Jonah was lying on a bench in a prison cell. As he awoke, subdued voices emanated from the corridor, their words muffled and inaudible.

While Jonah lay on the bench, he was unable to recognize his surroundings. His mind foggy, he tried to remember what had happened but struggled to do so. The tranquilizer he'd been shot with was extremely potent. In addition to forgetting where he was, the drug made him drowsy. His body felt almost paralyzed, and he had a pounding headache. Jonah lay there, trying to breathe deeply and regain his wits.

After a few minutes, he recalled where he was. Planet Zareet. Jonah remembered that he was on a mission, travelling with Skylar, Haven, Caleb, and Zak. He couldn't see any of them in his cell and wondered if they were locked up in other cells like his. Jonah tried to speak to them telepathically, but a sharp pain lanced his brain every time he tried. It was as if the messages were bouncing back to him in his head. Jonah also attempted to teleport back to Concordia but wasn't able to.

He remembered feeling a sting in his neck and seeing a soldier with a gun as he collapsed on the floor before becoming unconscious.

Was that a tranquilizer gun? And is that what they shot us with, which made us unconscious? Is this why my powers are failing? Jonah thought to himself.

This gave him a sick feeling in his stomach. Afraid of what would happen next, Jonah grew anxious.

Governor Ragnar was in the control room looking at footage of his captives in their respective cells. Skylar, Haven, Caleb, and Zak were still unconscious, but the governor could see Jonah was starting to wake up. He ordered two of his soldiers to move Jonah into an interrogation room. Aghast at what had happened earlier, the governor wanted to get to the bottom of who these renegades were.

After the soldiers dragged Jonah into the interrogation room, Governor Ragnar walked in and saw Jonah sitting on a chair. It was a dark room with scant lighting. A vexed look contorted the governor's face. Jonah and his friends had knocked out a multitude of the governor's soldiers. He wanted to know why.

"What is your name?" Governor Ragnar asked.

Jonah still felt drowsy. He kept going in and out of consciousness and was unable to answer the question. Governor Ragnar's patience was running out. He grabbed Jonah by his shoulders and lifted him up from the chair.

"I *said*, what is your name?" He shook Jonah a few times to wake him up.

Jonah opened his eyes and looked at the Governor briefly. He saw a decrepit old man with a malevolent look on his face.

"Mickey. Mickey Mouse," Jonah said.

"What kind of a name is Mickey Mouse! Are you trying to be funny?" The governor threw Jonah back into the chair.

"Who put you up to all of this?" Ragnar asked, as he put his face close to Jonah's and stared at him, eye to eye.

"Donald, of course. Donald Duck," Jonah quipped, his head lolling about.

"Where is this Donald Duck you speak of?"

"Not sure. Maybe Disneyland?"

"I've never heard of this 'Disneyland.' You're lying to me." Frustration built within the governor. "I suggest you start telling me the truth. Otherwise, you will find my patience is *very* thin. I'm going to ask you again:

what is your name, and who put you up to this? How many more of you are there?"

"My name is Green Lantern."

Governor Ragnar struck Jonah's face with a heavy hand, splitting his lip and causing it to bleed. It stung and took Jonah by surprise, which he tried to hide.

"Take him back to his cell!" Governor Ragnar barked at his soldiers. "And this time, hang him upside down from the ceiling. Perhaps it will encourage him to remember who he is."

Two soldiers returned Jonah to his cell. As Jonah was being hauled back, he went past another cell and glimpsed Caleb through the cell's window, lying unconscious on a bed. It gave him some comfort knowing that at least one of his friends was still alive.

As instructed, Jonah was hung upside down, with ropes, from the ceiling inside his cell. By this stage, he began to feel less drowsy. He attempted to teleport out of Zareet again but was unable to do so. The effects of the tranquilizer hadn't completely worn off yet.

Minutes later, Jonah heard some soldiers dragging someone else down the corridor toward the interrogation room—it was Haven, who was demanding to be let go. She tried to put up a fight, but she too was affected by the tranquilizer and still didn't have her full strength or powers back.

Once in the interrogation room, Governor Ragnar attempted to question Haven. He figured she was a soft target because she was a woman. However, he had never encountered a strong woman like Haven before. She knew how to fight back with words and stand up to him, even though she didn't have her full strength.

"You've got mommy issues, haven't you? You can't handle a strong woman like me. Yeah, that's right. You're basic!" Haven shouted.

After attempting to grill her for some time, the governor eventually gave up and ordered his soldiers to return Haven to her cell and hang her upside down as well.

Haven and Jonah both hung for some time. Jonah drifted in and out of consciousness until a faint voice awakened him.

Jonah. Can you hear me? Haven asked telepathically.

Yes, I can, Haven! Jonah answered with excitement.

As he responded, Jonah realized he had just spoken to Haven telepathically. Did this mean the effects of the tranquilizer were fading and he had regained all his powers? Jonah attempted to teleport out of his cell and back to Concordia. However, it didn't work.

Haven, are the others awake yet?

I'm not sure Jonah. I haven't been able to reach them.

Okay. So, how do we get out of here? I just tried teleporting and it didn't work. I think it's going to take a bit of time for our powers to be fully restored. Jonah sighed

You might be right Jonah. I can't think of any other way. But we have to come up with some sort of plan to get out of here once we get our powers back.

Yes, but Haven, I still need to get to the teleporter to try and tamper with it. I need some sort of distraction while I'm doing that, so they don't notice what's going on.

I think I can provide one. But we first need to get all our powers restored so I can create a distraction and you can do whatever you need to do to complete the mission.

Okay then. That sounds good to me, Haven. Let's just be patient. Our telepathy is working, so I'm sure our teleportation shouldn't be too far off. I'm not sure what they shot us with, but it was very powerful.

I think they shot us with some sort of tranquilizer to knock us out. I remember seeing one of the soldiers firing something at Caleb just before I got knocked out.

Yes, I think you're right, Haven. I vaguely remember seeing one of the soldiers holding some sort of tranquilizer gun before I collapsed.

Jonah stared at the dark concrete walls trying to piece together what had happened before becoming unconscious.

Minutes later, without warning, an electric shock pulsed through Jonah's entire body. It felt like the day Grand Guardian Omiya had unlocked his powers.

Haven, I just felt an electric jolt throughout my body. I'm not sure if that means my powers have been restored and I can teleport again.

I just felt the same thing, Jonah. Did you want to try teleporting out of here?
Okay. Here I go.

A few seconds later, Jonah teleported out of his cell. He ended up back in Concordia in his room. Jonah was so relieved and thrilled at the same time. At that moment, he really came to appreciate his powers. He would never take them for granted again.

After teleporting back to his cell on Zareet, Jonah confirmed to Haven he could teleport again, and to go ahead with their plan.

"Hey, bush pig!" Haven screamed to the soldiers outside of her cell. "Take me to Governor Ragnar! I give in! I will tell him whatever he needs. Just get me out of here!"

Two soldiers entered her cell with caution and began to untie Haven. Tall and brutish looking, the soldiers dragged Haven to the interrogation room. On the way, she walked past another cell and caught a glimpse of Zak—through the cell's window—as he lay on the bed. From what she could see, he was still asleep.

Meanwhile, Jonah—who was still in his cell—pulled out the light-pad from his pocket to try and determine his current location in relation to the teleporter. Once he figured out where he needed to go, he teleported out of his cell and into a corridor near the engineering room. When he reemerged in the corridor, Jonah could see soldiers standing outside the room and swiftly hid in a corner, escaping their view.

His next challenge: getting into the engineering room. While Jonah could easily teleport into the room, the problem was he didn't know what to expect once inside. Would there be more soldiers or other workers that he would need to deal with on his own?

After thinking about it momentarily, Jonah decided the best thing to do was to teleport into the engineering room and levitate up to the top of the ceiling. The ceilings in the building were lofty, so floating up high was going to be a good way to go unnoticed.

Remembering the training he got from his mother on levitation, Jonah started imagining he was an oscillating wave and vibrating very quickly. Within seconds he was levitating in the corridor. He then teleported into the engineering room and continued levitating in there. Jonah struggled a little, levitating haphazardly up and down, left to right, as he hadn't practiced it much since his mother taught him months earlier. However, after a few moments, he got the hang of it and managed to steady himself, so he could observe if anyone else was around.

Jonah noticed two people working on the teleporter in the distance. He figured they were technicians enlisted to construct the machine. After a few minutes of Jonah being there, the two technicians finished their shift and started getting ready to leave. Jonah waited patiently until they left the room.

Haven, I found the engineering room with the teleporter. I shouldn't be too much longer. Just hang in there.

Jonah, for goodness sake, be as quick as you can. I don't know how much longer I can stall the governor, Haven replied.

Jonah lowered himself to the ground next to the teleporter. He used his light-pad to retrieve a copy of the machine's schematics. It took a few minutes for Jonah to study the teleporter and correlate it back to the design on the light-pad. After doing so, Jonah found what he was looking for. He rearranged the wiring as planned, until he had finally turned the teleporter into a ticking time bomb.

Haven, I'm finished. We can head back to Concordia.

About time, Jonah!

Haven was relieved. Governor Ragnar was coming toward her in a threatening manner. She feared he was about to do something drastic.

Okay. Haven, you pick up Zak, and I'll pick up Caleb and Skylar, and we will teleport each of them back to Concordia.

Copy that Jonah.

When Governor Ragnar faced away from Haven, she teleported out of the interrogation room. She entered Zak's cell and grabbed him, then teleported him to Concordia.

Governor Ragnar turned toward where Haven previously sat and shouted a question at her. She wasn't there. He stood there for a few seconds, wondering where she had gone. Looking around the cell, he couldn't find her anywhere. *Where could she have gone? What kind of sorcery is this?* Governor Ragnar didn't know what to think. All he could do was wander around with an incensed look on his face, followed up by thunderous rage.

Meanwhile, Jonah teleported to Caleb's cell, grabbed Caleb's hand, and teleported him back to Concordia. They ended up in Jonah's room with Haven and Zak. Once he dropped off Caleb, Jonah returned to Zareet and picked up Skylar and returned her to his room in Concordia. Although Caleb, Zak and Skylar were still a little dazed and confused, everyone returned intact.

After looking at each other for a moment, they all let out a huge sigh of relief. None of them could believe what they had just been through. Except for Skylar, it was the group's first mission, which also gave them a small victory.

They were relieved that they had made it back safely. However, Caleb and Zak began to recognize that these missions weren't as glamorous and as fun as they'd once thought. They came to the realization that this work was truly dangerous.

Like many their age, they'd thought they were invincible. Especially because they were Concordians and could teleport anywhere, in any universe at any time. They also had their powerful batons, which could render their opponents unconscious in milliseconds. Despite all of that, they'd still managed to get captured for some time. Caleb and Zak were now starting to understand that they were vulnerable and had to take care not to get hurt during their missions. This particular exercise taught them not to take anything for granted.

After they had composed themselves, the group discussed how grateful they were to be back and retreated to their rooms. They were exhausted—they still felt some side effects from the tranquilizer—and needed time to fully recover.

Jonah still had to report the mission results to Jamari. As it was the middle of the night, he didn't want to wake Jamari, so Jonah decided to jump into bed and get some rest instead.

CHAPTER 25

Aften having slept for a few hours, Jonah woke the next morning feeling refreshed. The effects of the tranquilizer had finally worn off. As he lay in bed, reflecting on everything that occurred during the mission on Zareet, Jonah thought about how close he came to danger and how grateful he was to be back in Concordia, with his powers completely active again.

It was his first mission, so his pride was at stake. His ego urged him to make his mark with the Executive Council. Jonah not only wanted to make his parents proud, but he also wanted to prove he was worthy of his position in Concordia. In Jonah's mind, he was on his way to prove he was. The reality, though, was that he wasn't required to prove himself. The Executive Council had no benchmark he had to achieve to be a Guardian. Being Concordian was his birthright. However, the human side of Jonah wanted to excel in everything he did and felt compelled to attest to his worthiness.

"Amica, what time is it?" Jonah asked as he stretched his arms out on the bed.

"High time you got out of bed, Jonah."

"Well gee Amica, aren't you cute this morning."

"I'm programmed to have a sense of humor. But all jokes aside, I've been monitoring your vitals and can see that you are back to normal now. Your heart rate and blood pressure have recovered after your mission last night, so you are free to resume your normal activities."

"I didn't realize you monitored my vitals."

"I'm always doing that while you sleep Jonah. I gather the information from your wardrobe generator. It's all part of the service. I'm rather caring like that."

"Well, that's good to know, Dr. Amica!"

"Now look who's being cute."

Jonah laughed. Moments later, he decided to finally get out of bed and make a start on his day. He needed to visit Jamari and the Grand Guardian to report the outcome of his mission. After quickly showering and getting dressed, Jonah manifested a quick bite to eat. As he was almost finished and ready to leave, there was a knock on his door.

As he was about to open the door, Aurora and Mason entered the room and were noticeably glad to see their son. Aurora ran to Jonah and gave him a big hug. She squeezed Jonah so hard that he found it difficult to breathe.

"I hear that breathing is a vital function of human existence," Jonah said, after he escaped his mother's embrace so he could catch his breath.

Aurora laughed. His parents knew he had returned and couldn't wait to see him.

Jonah went on to explain what had happened on the mission and the calamity he and his friends had encountered by being detained and tranquilized. Aurora and Mason—with jaws wide open—were understandably stunned by what he said.

"Oh, Jonah, I'm so glad you're back from your mission in one piece," Aurora said. "I was so worried for you last night. I didn't really get much sleep. I kept thinking about you and if you were all right. I know I'm a warrior and a trainer, but I'm also your mother first. I will never stop worrying or caring about you. You know that, right?"

"Yeah, I know, Mom. But I made it back, and apart from some mishaps, the mission was successful. And you should have seen me with the baton; I was slaying like a master! Oh, and Skylar, Haven, Caleb, and Zak were pretty awesome, too. Without them, I wouldn't have succeeded. I am so grateful they came along on this mission."

"Well, I did train them!" Aurora boasted.

Mason looked at his wife and rolled his eyes while Jonah laughed.

"The other good thing is I managed to modify the teleporter. Which is the main reason why we all went to Zareet in the first place. So, when Governor Ragnar tries to use the machine, the teleporter won't work in the way he expects."

"That's great news. You really deserve a pat on the back for all of your hard work," Mason said. "Your work will save an entire planet from potential death and destruction from an evil man. I hope you understand the enormity of what you have done, even though Planet Ebris will probably never understand how much you've helped them.

"That's the way it is with a lot of the work we do as Guardians. It often goes unnoticed by the people we help. It's a thankless job. Nonetheless, it has a lot of value and is so rewarding. You'll begin to understand this more and more as time goes on and you undertake more missions."

"I think I'm starting to already, Dad. Anyhow, I need to get going. I must see Jamari to give him a status update on last night's mission. I'll see you both later."

Jonah left his room and started making his way to see Jamari. Jonah eventually found him as he was in the midst of preparing for the bigger mission to Zareet. As Jonah approached, Jamari spotted him from a distance. He was quite pleased to see Jonah, as he was eager to know how everything had gone on his assignment. He was also interested in hearing any information Jonah could provide which might be useful for the next mission.

"Jonah, I'm so glad to see you made it back. How did everything go?"

"The mission was a success. I was able to alter the teleporter, which should hopefully put a stop to Governor Ragnar's plans. But I really need to talk to you about the trouble we faced during the mission."

Concern tinged Jamari's voice. "Trouble? What happened?"

"We ended up getting captured by Governor Ragnar's army."

"What! And then what happened?" Jamari asked.

"While we were trying to get to the teleporter, we came across several soldiers. We managed to fight them off, for the most part. But just as we finished knocking out a whole bunch of them and were about to move on, we passed out. All I remember is feeling this small, sharp jab on my neck. I think we got shot by some sort of tranquilizer."

"A tranquilizer?" Jamari asked. "Wow! I don't ever recall seeing something like that used on any of my missions before."

"Yes, a tranquilizer. Or something similar. Whatever it was, it knocked us all out. Next thing I knew, I woke up in a jail cell with a bad headache and I couldn't use my powers. They eventually came back, but it took a bit of time."

"You couldn't use your powers?"

"That's right Jamari. I couldn't teleport or speak to the others telepathically," Jonah said. "It was really scary. Then I got cross-examined, and when I wouldn't answer Governor Ragnar's questions, his soldiers hung me upside down in my cell. Shortly after that happened, my powers returned and I was able to continue with the mission."

"I see. This changes things a little. Our combat outfits are obviously not equipped to handle these tranquilizers, so we need to take this into account for the next mission. I'm glad you told me about all of this. We need to prepare ourselves."

Jamari could not afford to send Concordia's Guardians into known danger. He thought about it for a moment and came up with an idea to adjust the combat outfits using the wardrobe generators. Only some minor changes were required. Namely, the addition of protective headgear to keep most of their heads covered, apart from the eyes and mouth.

The headgear was made of the same material as the combat outfits, which was a spandex-like material but stronger and impermeable to many sharp objects. Strong enough to at least withstand tranquilizer shots. After testing the headgear a few times, he managed to get it right. He was confident the changes would make a difference to the Guardians on the next mission.

"Well, Jonah, thanks to you, our Guardians are going to be better protected. It's a good thing you and your friends went to Zareet first and were able to give us this vital information. Unfortunately, you had to find out the hard way. But it's great, nonetheless. Thank you."

"Glad we could help. So, Jamari, now that we're back and we are all okay, can we help with the bigger mission?"

"That won't be necessary, Jonah. You and your friends have done so much already that you won't need to participate in this bigger battle. You've earned your rest from this one."

"But wait. We've had sufficient rest and are more than capable of going back and fighting again."

"It's not needed, Jonah. We've got this under control. You and your friends have done enough. The other Guardians we're assembling are more than sufficient to complete this mission. Don't worry; there'll always be another mission for you and your friends. There's never a shortage of battles to fight; I can promise you that."

"But, Jamari, having gone there before surely gives us some advantage that could be used to your benefit?"

"Jonah, that's enough! You will stay put on Concordia and leave the rest of the mission alone. I don't have time to argue with you. End of discussion."

Jamari turned around and walked away. Jonah wanted to scream. He was frustrated. He and his friends were more than capable of participating in the next mission, but Jamari thought otherwise. Jonah couldn't understand why.

There was too much at stake in the next mission to just sit by on the sidelines. Jonah needed to see how the others felt. Certain they would agree with him, Jonah chose to round them up and discuss what Jamari had decided.

CHAPTER 26

"**I** can't understand why Jamari won't let us go on this next mission!" Jonah was pacing his room, furious with Jamari's decision. "We've been to Zareet before and know a little bit about the planet. I thought our presence would be to his advantage. I don't want to sit here and do nothing while the rest of Concordia goes out and fights!"

"Agreed," Zak said.

"So, what are we going to do?" Caleb asked.

"I hope you guys aren't thinking of defying Jamari's orders." Haven stood next to Caleb and stared at him briefly. "I've already gotten into trouble from the Grand Guardian after what happened on Planet Kenarios, and I'm not willing to go through that humiliation again."

"C'mon, where's that warrior princess we saw on Planet Kenarios? She was fierce!" Caleb smirked as he did fist pumps near Haven's chin.

"You're an idiot!" Haven snapped and grabbed Caleb's fist, before she pushed him away. He burst out laughing as he tried to steady himself from falling backward.

"I'm pretty sure we could go incognito so no one would know we're there. The new outfits Jamari designed cover most of our heads, so we can probably go without being noticed. We should be able to blend in," Jonah said.

"It's risky. Very sneaky and totally unexpected from you, but I like it kid. I'm impressed." Zak looked at Jonah, amazed that he would make such a suggestion.

"I'm full of surprises." Jonah said.

"I think we should do it," Caleb said. "It's the only chance we've got of taking part in the battle. Besides, we know where Zareet is located, so we can go there whenever we want without anyone knowing."

"If we're going to do this, we need to find out when the other Guardians are leaving so we can go with them," Jonah said.

"Everyone going on the mission has been told to gather in the Council Stadium, from what I was told by someone else in my cluster. And I think they'll be leaving fairly soon, so we need to hurry and get ready," Haven said.

"We?" Caleb asked Haven in a curious fashion. "By 'we' do you mean you're coming?"

Haven paused for several moments. She looked at Caleb in silence for a moment, not knowing what to say.

"You ask too many questions." Haven turned around and walked a few steps away from Caleb.

Caleb laughed.

Meanwhile, Jonah left the group. He teleported to the Council Stadium, and as he reemerged inside, he saw hundreds of Guardians seated in a large section on one side of the stadium. Jamari was standing on the ground, facing them as he spoke. Jonah teleported to a part of the stadium close to the other Guardians to hear what was being said. It was an area with dim lighting that enabled Jonah to sink into the shadows. His intention was only to stay long enough to find out when they were leaving.

As Jamari spoke, numerous holographic images were projected into the middle of the stadium, such as maps of Zareet and images of Governor Ragnar, for everyone to see. Jamari explained the main objective of the mission. He then gave detailed information about their assignment and what was expected of them. He also told the audience about Jonah's previous mission to alter the teleporter device.

While Jonah was listening, he felt an arm grip his shoulder, which startled him. He turned to see who it was—and saw his mother.

"What exactly are you doing here, Jonah?" Aurora asked.

"Ah ... nothing in particular. Just listening in. I thought it might be interesting to hear what Jamari had to say," Jonah whispered.

"Jonah, you're *not* part of this mission; you shouldn't be here!"

"Okay. You make a valid point."

"Then why are you here, Jonah? Are you planning on going on this mission? Even though you haven't been selected to go? Even though you've been instructed *not* to go?"

"Aarrhh . . . I plead the fifth."

"Jonah, you are in Concordia; there is no fifth amendment for you to hide behind!"

Jonah had to think quickly. After Aurora finished speaking, he instantly grabbed her arms. He teleported himself and his mother to their home on Earth, ending up in their living room.

"Now, we're on Earth, Mom. I plead the fifth. I don't have to answer your questions."

Aurora's jaw dropped. "Now, you listen here, Jonah—"

Just as Aurora was about to scold Jonah, he teleported back to his room in Concordia. On his arrival, he took a deep breath and laughed. Jonah was initially impressed with how quickly he could think on his feet. However, he soon realized he hadn't been completely honest with his mother and would have to deal with the consequences of his deceit at some point. In that moment, though, he had to put that to the side as there was a mission to focus on.

Jonah's friends were still in his room talking to each other. He told them what had happened in the Council Stadium and about the encounter with his mother. They now had to think about how else they would obtain the information they needed.

"Would your father know anything? Can you go and ask him?" Caleb asked.

"He'd probably know, but I doubt he'd say anything, knowing I'm not meant to be going. Besides, my mother has probably already spoken to him."

"I have an idea." Zak gave them a coy smile. "I may know a 'lady friend' that's in one of the mission clusters. I might be able to convince her to give me some details."

"Is this one of your supposed 'lady friends' you keep telling me about?" Caleb asked.

"No, no, no. It's one of *many, many* 'lady friends' that I have," Zak bragged.

Haven rolled her eyes. "Oh, please!"

While Haven had heard Zak talking to Caleb about his womanizing nonsense before, it made her nauseous. Zak saw Haven's reaction, which made him laugh even more before he went about searching for his friend.

Zak returned around twenty minutes later. While Haven, Jonah, and Caleb didn't hold much hope, Zak did, in fact, come back and relay the information they needed. He knew exactly when the clusters were heading to Planet Zareet—which was only an hour away—as well as how they were going to get there and the plan of attack.

Haven's eyebrows arched in astonishment. "Well. It appears you *can* be useful sometimes."

"You bet I am," Zak boasted.

Now armed with the knowledge they needed, they prepared themselves for the mission ahead. They put their battle outfits on and got their batons ready. No time was wasted going to the Council Stadium, where they sat near the back, hidden from view.

They could see all the clusters ready to transport themselves to Zareet. They all had their outfits on, just like Jonah and the rest of his friends, as well as their batons. The clusters were being called into the middle of the stadium, one at a time. Once there, they would teleport over to Zareet.

During one of the cluster movements, Jonah and his friends crept into a cluster that was waiting to be called up to the centre of the stadium. They managed to blend in without being seen. With the new outfits, their faces were mostly covered, so no one took any notice of who they were. They sat patiently, waiting for the cluster they were sitting in to begin the mission journey. Not long after, the cluster was given the signal to make its way down to the center of the stadium.

Once they got to the center, they were instructed to create a circular formation and hold hands. In a split second, the cluster leader teleported the entire group over to Zareet. They reemerged in an empty field not too far from where the teleporter was being built.

Jonah and his friends couldn't see any of the other clusters. This is because they'd been spread out in and around Governor Ragnar's headquarters, as per Jamari's plan. They were spread out strategically to ensure there were enough Guardians to surround the main building inside the headquarters complex, as well as all the main entrances into the complex.

Inside headquarters, Governor Ragnar's army monitored what was going on. One security team member, Zakia, reviewed footage from various cameras around the compound. She glimpsed several groups of people wandering around the exterior of their headquarters, as well as the main building inside the complex. Zakia alerted her supervisor, Lieutenant Lomar, who, in turn, informed Governor Ragnar.

"One of my subordinates has warned me of a security breach. It appears we have more of those rebels who attacked us the other day. They've grown in numbers and there are now hundreds of them. We need to do something quickly," Lieutenant Lomar said.

"Them again! How did they breach our perimeters? Where are they at the moment?" Governor Ragnar asked.

"They are circling the perimeter of this compound as well as this main building, getting closer by the minute. Governor, we need to act fast to keep them at bay and then get rid of them."

"Lomar, seal every entrance into this building and ensure there are plenty of soldiers stationed at each one! We need to safeguard the teleporter with as many troops as possible. *Nothing* better happen to that teleporter. Also, make sure our troops have tranquilizers on them. That will knock out the insurgents until we can figure out what to do with them. Now move!"

The governor became increasingly anxious and ready to go to war. A lot was at stake. The future of his planet's energy supply was in jeopardy. Only a limited supply of Chrimatide remained, which could keep them going for a few weeks at best. They needed to get to Planet Ebris as quickly as possible so they could rapidly replenish their Chrimatide inventory. For this plan to work and guarantee his planet's survival, he needed to annihilate anything that got in his way and threatened his plans.

Governor Ragnar didn't know with any certainty who these people were. He guessed they were somehow connected to the renegades from his encounter the day before.

Who are these people? They must be militia intent on fighting my regime, Governor Ragnar thought to himself.

The governor assumed they were inhabitants of his own world, completely oblivious that they were from another dimension.

As directed, all entrances into his building were blockaded with soldiers. With at least thirty soldiers at each entrance, they were armed with tranquilizers, ready to shoot the invading insurgents. The teleporter was ready to be tested, and Governor Ragnar was eager to send his army to Planet Ebris. He had come so far and couldn't afford to have the machine ruined. Nothing was going to destroy the teleporter now.

CHAPTER 27

Jamari finished transporting his selected clusters to Planet Zareet. Concordian Guardians now surrounded every entrance into Governor Ragnar's headquarters, as well as the main building within the compound. Jamari had decided which cluster would lead the charge into the central building. The entrance chosen was the farthest away from the teleporter.

Dakani, on my instruction, you are to break open the entrance door and send your cluster inside to begin the attack. Be aware that there might be soldiers ready to strike back. Do you copy? Jamari projected to Dakani, one of the cluster leaders under his command.

Copy that, Jamari, Dakani responded.

After a few tense moments, Jamari gave the signal to Dakani to begin the attack. He, in turn, gave the word to his cluster to instigate the charge.

One of the Guardians in the cluster attached a small disc-like object to the entrance door. As she attached the disc, she pressed a button to activate it. Within a few seconds, the entire door started disintegrating.

Jonah and his friends watched from a distance. They hadn't seen that particular disc before in any of their training. It amazed them how something so small could disintegrate such a solid object. The door was constructed of a heavy, thick piece of metal, which was quite strong by any standard of measure—yet it was now being reduced to a pile of dust.

As the door disintegrated, the Guardians standing in front of it glimpsed a group of soldiers behind the door. The soldiers' eyes and mouths were wide with terror as they watched the door crumble. They'd never witnessed anything like it before.

The Guardians charged toward them at full force. Not knowing what to expect next, the soldiers decided to take their chances and fight as best they could.

They shot their tranquilizers at the Guardians with no effect. The Guardians' suits repelled the tranquilizers, falling to the ground like water drops from the sky. Horror filled the soldiers' eyes as they realized their most powerful defense against these insurgents was now futile. Three of the soldiers fled while the rest remained behind to fight on.

The next line of defense for the soldiers was to use their batons. The soldiers' batons weren't anywhere near a match to that of the Guardians' batons, due to their lack of strength and power. The best the soldiers could do was attempt to defend themselves. The Guardians began their assault on the soldiers with relentless vigor. After several minutes of combat, the governor's soldiers ended up unconscious on the ground.

Governor Ragnar observed the battle from his control room through security cameras. He was shocked to see how a part of his army had fallen. Even more startling was that the tranquilizers seemed to have no effect on the Guardians. The governor could see that their suits somehow protected them from being shot.

Although Governor Ragnar didn't show it, he grew nervous, suspecting that his plans were about to come undone. As he tried to formulate another strategy, he witnessed another blockade of soldiers being attacked.

The second blockade was getting pummeled just as badly as the first. His soldier count was dwindling. At this rate, he wouldn't have an army left by the night's end. He came to the stark realization that he would not win this battle. He had to do something drastic.

"Lieutenant Lomar, find Chief Engineer Komaro and tell him to activate the teleporter. We need to start moving to Planet Ebris immediately!" Governor Ragnar shouted.

Lieutenant Lomar fled the control room and raced to the teleporter. On the way, he came close to the second blockade of soldiers being attacked but managed to evade them.

When he finally arrived and entered the engineering room, Lomar was unable to find Komaro. He looked around the room in a frenzy. There was no one else there. He began to panic. *Where could he be? Has he been attacked by the insurgents?* Lieutenant Lomar ran out of the engineering room to continue his search for Komaro.

In the meantime, Jonah, Haven, Caleb, and Zak were still outside, waiting to attack the soldiers inside. They stood amongst the cluster they'd snuck into Planet Zareet with. As the cluster leaders waited for instructions from Jamari, Caleb motioned for Jonah, Haven, and Zak to follow him. They broke apart from the cluster and ran a short distance away so they could discuss their plan.

"I say we attack Governor Ragnar and his army on our own. There's no point in waiting to be called up to fight," Caleb whispered as he fidgeted with his baton.

"Can we not get carried away and break every possible rule? Why can't we just wait here until we're required?" Haven asked.

"Well, you all can do that. I, for one, am not waiting around doing a whole lot of nothing like a chump!" Zak exclaimed.

"Keep your voice down . . . Can we think about this before you do anything?" Haven asked.

Before she could discuss the issue any further, Caleb grabbed her arm and Zak grabbed Jonah's. They all teleported inside the main building. After they reemerged inside, Haven gave Caleb an intense stare.

"What the hell!" Haven whispered furiously to Caleb. "We better not get expelled from Concordia because of this!"

"Calm down, will you? We'll be fine," Caleb whispered back.

After a few tense moments, the group walked down a corridor inside the building until they reached a corner. As they were about to turn the corner, they came face-to-face with a tall, blond man. His green eyes gave away how startled he was to see them.

The man drew his rifle, loaded with tranquilizers. Haven, who led the group, managed to push the weapon away from everyone. Within a matter of seconds, she seized his rifle and struck him with her baton. He collapsed to the ground. It was Lieutenant Lomar.

"That was close," Jonah said with a panicked voice.

"He didn't stand a chance," Haven said. "Now, let's keep moving."

They continued through another corridor and approached an alternate entrance. Haven noticed a huge blockade of soldiers manning the entryway. She stopped and whirled to face her friends, preventing them from going any farther. She put her finger to her lips, signaling to them to keep quiet. Haven then pushed the group into a dark corner, out of the soldiers field of view.

There's a large number of soldiers further down, Haven said telepathically. *So, are we ready to play?*

Let's do it! Caleb answered.

Let me go first. Just wait here and then follow my lead. Haven said.

Haven then teleported into the middle of where the soldiers were stationed. They gasped, astonished by what they'd just seen.

"Hey, boys, you all look a little bored," Haven said. "Want to play with me?"

She struck the nearest soldier with her baton and knocked him to the ground before anyone could comprehend what had just happened. An onslaught ensued.

Caleb, Zak, and Jonah teleported to join Haven in the ambush. The soldiers used their batons to strike Jonah and his friends, putting up a valiant fight. However, they didn't stand a chance against the Concordian batons.

The conflict continued for a few minutes until the soldiers were all on the floor, unconscious. As the soldiers lay there, the group tried catching their breath.

Meanwhile, Governor Ragnar watched them from his control room. His brow furrowed and his lips pursed as he started breathing rapidly. What he'd just seen bewildered him, and he had to think quickly. This reinforced his previous assumption: he wasn't going to beat these insurgents. It was just a matter of time before his whole army was annihilated. There was only one last thing he could do to guarantee his survival.

"Is the teleporter ready yet?" Governor Ragnar screamed at Zakia, who monitored the security cameras.

"It doesn't look like it's been turned on," Zakia said in a diffident tone.

"What do you mean? Where is Lieutenant Lomar?" Governor Ragnar shrieked.

Zakia showed Governor Ragnar an image of Lieutenant Lomar lying sprawled in one of the corridors. The governor's face filled with horror. He quickly thought about what to do next. He turned to Amani.

"Amani, round up as many troops as possible and tell them to meet me in the underground bunker. We must get to Planet Ebris!"

The governor ran out of the control room and hurried to the bunker—located underneath the Engineering Room—while Amani raced across the building, stopping at each of the still-standing blockades. She instructed everyone to meet Governor Ragnar in the bunker, which the soldiers obeyed without question.

During this time, Jonah and his friends continued their quest. While they found a few more soldiers and were able to take them down effortlessly, most of the soldiers managed to evade Jonah and his friends, arriving at the bunker unharmed.

The bunker stored many large vessels, similar to shipping containers, that included various machines and equipment they would need to excavate Chrimatide from Ebris. The containers also included a large supply of food, tents, and medical supplies to help during the initial phase of settlement on the new planet. In addition to all of this, they included a large arsenal to help fight the inhabitants of Ebris, in case Governor Ragnar's army encountered any resistance.

The bunker was connected to the Engineering Room via a secret passageway. This passageway was conveniently created to be used during haulage of the containers to the teleporter, ready for subsequent transportation to Ebris.

Governor Ragnar had been preparing for the trip to Ebris over the last few days to begin mining for Chrimatide. He had ordered the stockpiling of equipment, weapons, and supplies into the bunker so everything would be in place when the time came. The time, however, had come a little earlier than anticipated.

This was not how Governor Ragnar had planned to go to Ebris. He had hoped to complete a few trial runs with the teleporter before crossing over. Circumstances had now changed, and he had to adapt rapidly to the situation. He had to go to Ebris quickly, whether he liked it or not.

"You two, I want you to run down the corridor and distract those insurgents. Make sure they don't go anywhere near the teleporter," Governor Ragnar said to a pair of soldiers.

The two soldiers ran out of the bunker. The governor hoped the soldiers could distract Jonah and the rest of his friends long enough for the teleporter to be turned on, so he could escape with his remaining army to Ebris.

Governor Ragnar and a few of his other soldiers ran to the adjoining Engineering Room where the teleporter was located and began locking the entrance. The remainder of his army transported equipment up from the bunker in preparation for the transfer over to Ebris.

Just as the doors were about to be closed and locked, Chief Engineer Komaro returned—a short-statured man in his sixties with grey hair and glasses.

"Where the hell have you been?" Governor Ragnar asked Komaro.

"I went to get something to eat, and when I came back, I couldn't get back into the building due to those damned renegades. But I managed to sneak in eventually and make my way back here without getting hurt," Komaro said.

Governor Ragnar grabbed Komaro by the neck and threw him to the teleporter controller.

"Start up the teleporter now! We must get to Ebris immediately. We have no more time to waste!"

Komaro's heart pounded at the sudden outburst. He was petrified of the governor. Komaro knew what he was capable of and lived in constant fear of his visceral outbursts. He pulled himself together and initiated the teleporter's startup sequence. Komaro felt the weight of being observed, so he thought twice about everything he did. While he was usually very good at his job, on this occasion, he was visibly tense due to the presence of Governor Ragnar, which diminished his capacity. Komaro was the only one in the building at that time who knew how to operate the machine, which only added to his anxiety.

As the teleporter started up, Komaro noticed it sounded a little peculiar. It had an unusual grinding noise and he wasn't sure why. He didn't say anything and tried to keep a straight face out of fear of what the governor might do. Komaro continued with the startup sequence and hoped the noise would disappear. Everything else seemed fine, so he didn't think the noise would be of any consequence.

While the machine was still going through its startup sequence, more containers were moved into the engineering room. Before long, the room had been filled with all the equipment from the bunker. Now, they were only minutes away from Ebris.

As the containers were moved closer to the teleporter, Governor Ragnar started rethinking his plan. He thought about whether he could return to Zareet, considering insurgents were overtaking his planet. The governor believed there was a strong possibility he wouldn't have much of a planet to come back to.

His son, Zyaire, was also in the Engineering Room, ready to head over to Ebris with him. He had arrived just before the doors to the room had been locked. Taking Zyaire with him meant there was nothing left behind for the governor to return to.

Would it be better to stay on Ebris and overthrow its leader? To take over the planet and start over again? The more he thought about it, the more he began to like his idea. In his thirst for power and lust for supremacy, Governor Ragnar thought this would be a great new challenge for him. He had no loyalty to his planet and thus didn't care about whether it was destroyed or not. All he cared about was ruling over and dominating the masses.

The teleporter was almost ready. A portal opened, which began as a small fluorescent orange ball of light that expanded into a huge sphere thirty feet in diameter. This was the gateway between Zareet and Ebris. The strange noise the teleporter had started making earlier now became more obvious to everyone inside the Engineering Room, including Governor Ragnar.

"Komaro, what the hell is that awful noise?"

"It's nothing, Governor, it's standard functionality. It always sounds like this."

Komaro knew something was wrong. He had to hide his concerns, as time didn't allow him to investigate the cause. Being under a lot of pressure to get everyone over to Ebris, Komaro had to do whatever was necessary to carry out Governor Ragnar's orders.

Jonah and his friends were still in the building, trying to battle any remaining soldiers they could find. As most of Governor Ragnar's soldiers were now on standby near the teleporter, ready to head over to Ebris, Jonah and his friends were struggling to find any soldiers to attack. As time passed, the group wondered what was going on and began speculating Governor Ragnar was up to something.

Hey, guys, does it seem a bit weird that there aren't any more soldiers around? Haven asked the others telepathically.

You're right; something seems a little bit off, Jonah said.

I think you're both right. Caleb said. *At the start, we were being ambushed at every entrance, but now, there are none to be seen. I think Governor Ragnar is up to something.*

As they turned a corner, the group came face-to-face with two soldiers. These were the two who'd been sent to distract them during teleportation to Planet Ebris. The soldiers took out their weapons, and before they could even think of striking, Haven charged and knocked both weapons from their hands. She grabbed their necks and slammed them to the ground, face first. Haven didn't want to use her baton because she figured they might have useful information.

As they lay shocked by what had just happened, Haven stared down at them with a ferocious look, determined to get answers.

"Where is Governor Ragnar? Where are the rest of the soldiers?" Haven screamed.

They didn't answer. The soldiers tried to remain silent and ignore Haven, thinking they could withstand her aggressive questioning. Haven kicked each of them in the stomach, causing both soldiers to scream in agony as their bodies flinched. They still didn't say anything.

"Where is he?" Haven shouted again.

"As if . . . we're going to . . . tell you," one of them answered.

Haven gave each of them another swift kick.

Caleb pulled Haven away from the soldiers, as he could see her aggression was becoming excessive. Concordians were not meant to torture their combatants. Caleb knocked them out with his baton to put them out of their misery.

"What did you do that for?" Haven asked.

"You were way out of line, Haven. Sometimes you don't know when to stop. We don't torture people. This is not Fasmeon!"

"Caleb, I wasn't trying to torture them. I was trying to extract some information out of them to help us locate the other soldiers and Governor Ragnar."

"Haven, that looked way more like torture to me than fact-finding!"

"Cut it out, you two!" Jonah stood between Caleb and Haven, forcing them apart. "Now isn't the time to be arguing. We should go straight to the teleporter as I don't think we're going to find any more soldiers to attack. It's way too quiet out here, and I don't like it. C'mon, let's go!"

They rushed to the teleporter. When they arrived, the doors to the Engineering Room were locked.

"We're going to have to teleport inside," Zak said.

"Let me go in," Jonah said. "I need to see what they're doing with the teleporter. If they have started it up, it could very well explode any minute now, in which case we need to leave and warn everyone else."

Jonah immediately teleported into the Engineering Room. He was able to hide in a corner without being seen. He could see in the distance the teleporter had been started, and a fluorescent orange portal was open, presumably to Ebris. Numerous soldiers and containers were standing by, ready to go through the portal.

As Jonah stood in the corner, a strange noise came from the teleporter. He figured his sabotage had worked. That meant the teleporter was going to explode. The noise became unbearably loud, and the floor started shaking. He had to get out of there and tell the others to evacuate. He teleported back to Haven, Zak, and Caleb to warn them.

"We need to get out of here immediately!" Jonah yelled. "The teleporter is about to explode. We need to warn the rest of the Concordian army about the impending explosion. We need to tell Jamari."

"If we tell Jamari, we risk being found out," Caleb said.

"We also risk half of Concordia getting killed if we don't. We need to do something," Haven said.

"I've got an idea. But we need to get out of this building first and find other Concordians," Jonah said.

They teleported out of the building near one of the Concordian clusters on standby, ready to enter the building. Jonah approached the cluster leader.

"This building is about to explode. We need to evacuate. Please let Jamari know right now!" Jonah screamed.

He teleported away from the cluster and reappeared in another location, where he could still observe what was going on. Caleb, Haven, and Zak followed him in quick succession.

The cluster leader didn't know who Jonah was. He was a little confused by what had just occurred. It had happened so quickly he didn't get a chance to ask Jonah any questions. However, he didn't want to take any chances, so the cluster leader telepathically informed Jamari about what he had been told.

This is Guardian Jamari. To all Concordian Guardians, I have been advised this building is about to explode. Everyone, abandon this mission and teleport back to Concordia. Now!

A loud blast emanated from the teleporter's location within seconds of his announcement. The ferocious explosion caused the entire building to ignite, sector by sector. The sound could be heard miles away from the compound. The force of the explosion reverberated through the ground like an earthquake. It shook homes in nearby townships. The sky lit up. A remarkable ball of fire could be seen far and wide. Everything inside the building, was destroyed.

Meanwhile, all Concordian clusters teleported back to Concordia's Council Stadium. They all arrived simultaneously. Jonah and his friends, however, teleported back to Jonah's room instead.

Each cluster leader performed a quick count—everyone was accounted for. Jamari declared the mission a success. The entire stadium erupted in a raucous cheer.

Their mission was finally accomplished.

CHAPTER 28

"That was way too close!" Caleb shouted, on the tail end of an adrenaline rush.

Having just returned from Zareet, right after midnight, Jonah and his friends were standing around his room, scrambling to catch their breath and comprehend what just happened. After a couple of minutes, Caleb and Zak gave each other a high five. This was immediately followed by Zak getting Caleb into a headlock and the two wrestling each other like a couple of teenage brothers. Jonah laughed as he stood nearby, watching the two act out their adolescent impertinence. Caleb managed to get out of Zak's grasp and put Jonah into a headlock so he didn't feel left out.

Zak approached Haven, but he took one look at her ferocious gaze and thought better of it. No words or telepathy were required to read Haven's aversion toward the boys' behavior. While Haven felt a great sense of achievement and pride in her work on Zareet, she didn't feel the need for any immature expressions of accomplishment.

"Your plan worked, Jonah. Whatever you did to that teleporter was genius," Zak said.

"Thanks, Zak," Jonah said with humble pride.

"You sure gave Governor Ragnar a blasting he'll never forget. Get it? A blasting? *Kaboom*!" Everyone looked at Caleb, unimpressed with his humor. Zak smacked him in the head in jest for his lame attempt.

"Have you got children we don't know about? Because that sounded like a dad joke to me. And not even a good one." Haven giggled briefly.

"What the hell? Did you just . . . did you just make a joke? And you even laughed." Caleb laughed ever so faintly and squinted his eyes in disbelief, as he looked at Haven.

"Yes. And it was better than yours," Haven snapped back.

Everyone was surprised Haven had made a joke. They all laughed in unison with her. In that moment, the guys saw her hard exterior crumble ever so slightly. It warmed their hearts to see Haven wasn't so serious all the time.

For Jonah, it gave him faith that Haven would eventually find some happiness. It also gave him hope that she was far more than just a great Guardian with a tough exterior. Jonah began to see there was a greater level of complexity to Haven, far more than he had ever imagined.

"So, who wants to grab something to eat?" Caleb asked.

"Hell, yes, I'm starved." Zak grabbed his empty stomach with his hand.

"How about some Shankani from Kenarios?" Caleb looked at the group with enthusiasm.

"It's a bit late for Shankani; they're probably closed. How about we order in? I hear room service on Concordia is pretty good; it's a twenty-four-hour service!" Jonah quipped.

"Oh, look at you, trying to have a sense of humor. You and Haven should do a comedy show together," Zak said.

"Or we could just shut up and eat!" Jonah snapped back.

Jonah conjured some tables and chairs in his room and some mouthwatering pizzas. There was a whole range of different pizzas to try and cater to everyone's taste.

"Okay, I see your point," Zak said, licking his lips at a pepperoni pizza.

After racing to the tables and sitting down, they began devouring the pizzas with an unstoppable appetite.

"Why is there pineapple on that one?" Caleb pointed to one of the pizzas on the table.

"It's a Hawaiian; it's meant to have pineapple on it," Jonah said.

"Pineapple on a pizza? That is so wrong." Caleb shook his head in disbelief.

"Don't you have this type of pizza on your planet?" Jonah asked.

"Hell no! We don't put pineapple on a pizza. We use blueberries instead," Caleb said before taking a large bite of pizza.

Everyone stopped eating momentarily and looked at Caleb, baffled by the words that came out of his mouth. Moments later, they continued eating again as if nothing had happened. They were too hungry to think about the issue anymore.

After eating everything Jonah had manifested, they were still hungry. Caleb conjured some more pizzas, which they all consumed in next to no time at all. This time, however, they were finally full.

They sat slumped in their chairs with their hands on their stomachs, feeling like they had eaten way too much. They were at the point where they almost felt sick. As they laughed and tried to digest the mammoth amount of food they'd eaten, Jonah's mother walked in. The group sat up straight and took on a solemn demeanor.

"Well, here you all are. How lovely. What have you been up to tonight?" Aurora asked.

"Ah, we've just been eating pizza," Jonah said with a nervous tone.

"Is that right? I was looking for you all earlier and couldn't find you. And now you're here. It's fairly late to be eating pizza, don't you think?" Aurora asked.

"Well, we were feeling a bit restless and couldn't sleep. So we decided to hang here with Jonah and have a bite to eat," Zak said.

"And you decided to do this in your warrior outfits?" Aurora asked as she raised one eyebrow.

Jonah was familiar with his mother's eyebrow raise. It meant she wasn't in the mood for any nonsense.

"We decided to have a dress-up party. It's Halloween on my home planet of Kenarios?" Caleb said.

"You celebrate Halloween on Kenarios?" Aurora asked.

"We sure do!" Caleb said.

"Wow, that's amazing. You know I love Halloween. Jonah and I used to love to dress up when he was younger and go trick-or-treating. Brings back a lot of good memories, doesn't it, my darling son?"

"Yes, it does, my sweet mother."

"You know what, I'd love to go to Kenarios right now and have a bit of fun. Just for old-time's sake. See how you crazy Kenarians celebrate Halloween. How about it, kids?" Aurora asked with a conniving smile.

Everyone sat there momentarily, not saying anything.

"Well, it's getting late," Caleb said. "All the trick-or-treating would've finished by now, so there's no point going. I'm off to bed. Good night, everyone!"

Caleb waved his right hand and teleported out of the room.

"Yeah, I'm feeling a bit tired myself. Later, dudes." Zak waved goodbye and teleported away, followed by Haven.

"Well, Mom, I'm feeling a bit sleepy," Jonah said, yawning. "I'm hopping into bed. Thanks for the chat. Nighty night."

"I know you went to Zareet. Do not insult my intelligence and deny it. If you ever go on a mission again that you have not been chosen for, I will have no hesitation in reporting you to the Grand Guardian. Consider this your first and final warning!"

Aurora was beyond furious. She turned around and exited the room, exasperated with Jonah's misconduct.

Jonah was stunned. He hadn't anticipated his mother finding out about his covert expedition. *How did she find out?* Jonah thought to himself. He was too tired to think and went to bed, leaving the analysis for another time.

CHAPTER 29

Shortly after celebrating the success of his mission, Jamari visited the Grand Guardian's chambers to give his report. Although it was late at night, Jamari knew the Grand Guardian would want to be updated, no matter the hour. The chambers were silent; the only noise that Jamari could discern was the sound of Ezra's footsteps.

"Jamari, the Grand Guardian will see you," Ezra said as Jamari waited in the chamber foyer. Walking into the chambers, Jamari saw Grand Guardian Omiya standing near the entryway with a smile.

"I believe you might have some good news to share?" Grand Guardian Omiya asked as they both approached a couch in her chambers and sat, facing one another.

"Yes, Grand Guardian," Jamari said wearing a triumphant smile. "I am happy to report our mission was a success. I'm also delighted to advise we had no casualties from our side. The teleporter exploded and was destroyed. This lead to Governor Ragnar getting killed, as well as a significant portion of his army. So although we didn't capture him as planned, he will not be of any consequence to Ebris or his people from now on."

The Grand Guardian breathed a sigh of relief. "I couldn't be more delighted with your accomplishments and that of our army. And the fact that you came back without any casualties is even better news. So please tell me more about what happened on the mission."

Jamari continued explaining the events of the mission in detail. During that discussion, Mason and Wyatt entered the chamber foyer and spoke to Ezra.

"We need to speak to the Grand Guardian. It's very urgent," Mason said with a dire face.

"At this hour? Why? What's going on Mason?" Ezra was mystified.

"It has to do with the mission on Zareet. Governor Ragnar is still alive and has made it to Ebris. We need to let the Grand Guardian know so she can send Guardians to deal with him—before he wreaks havoc on Ebris."

"I see. Very well, follow me." Ezra led the way to the Grand Guardian's chambers, with Mason and Wyatt behind him.

"Please forgive the interruption, but I have Mason and Wyatt here, who need to speak to you urgently about the mission," Ezra said.

"Very well then. What is it, Mason?" the Grand Guardian asked as she and Jamari got up from the couch.

"It has come to our attention that Governor Ragnar and some of his army have made it across to Ebris."

As Mason uttered those words, Jamari's expression changed from delighted accomplishment to disbelief and disappointment.

"It appears that before the explosion, he and some of his army managed to escape, by going through a portal that transported them over to Ebris," Wyatt said. "They took a wide range of weaponry, supplies, and machinery with them. And from what we can see, they've started setting up a base camp on Ebris already."

"I see." The Grand Guardian sat down slowly. After taking a slow deep breath, a look of discontent came over her, which was glaringly obvious to everyone in the room.

"We fear the governor will continue with his plans, regardless of what has happened," Mason said.

Jamari looked disappointed. "But, I thought he died in the explosion."

"That's what we thought too until we saw footage of him on Ebris. As you can imagine, we were quite shocked, to say the least," Wyatt said.

"How many of his soldiers made it through?" Jamari asked.

"There wouldn't be more than about one hundred. However, the significant amount of weaponry and machinery they took makes his small army quite dangerous," Wyatt said.

"That means we have more work to do," Grand Guardian Omiya said.

Although the Grand Guardian was disappointed to hear Governor Ragnar was still alive and on Ebris, she wasn't entirely surprised. In all her years as Grand Guardian, she knew battles weren't always straightforward and easily won. Sometimes, many battles were required to win a war. This was one of those occasions. Nonetheless, her resolve to see this through to the end was unflinching. The Grand Guardian was determined to continue the fight to the end.

"Jamari, we will need to send another cluster of Concordian Guardians to Ebris. We cannot let him take control of another planet. What he did on Zareet was shameful enough. He cannot be allowed to repeat his evil dictatorial behavior on Ebris."

"Very well, Grand Guardian, I will start making plans immediately."

"Please do. And I cannot stress enough how quickly we must act. The people of that planet do not deserve to be the subject of his wrath and malevolence. While devising your plan, I will speak to the Executive Council to obtain their endorsement."

Jamari left the chambers so he could commence preparations for the new mission to Ebris. Mason and Wyatt stayed behind, along with Ezra.

"Guardians Wyatt and Mason, please continue to monitor what's happening on Ebris. Keep me abreast of everything that happens from now on and let me know if you see him committing atrocities on the planet or its people. I feel we have limited time to prevent him from causing any mayhem. After everything we have seen him do already, I fear nothing but the worst from him."

"Will do, Grand Guardian," Mason said.

Mason and Wyatt hurried out of the chambers. Meanwhile, the Grand Guardian turned to Ezra, who stood beside her.

"Ezra, convene an Executive Council meeting immediately. I need to update them about what happened on Zareet and the new mission to Ebris. It's going to be a long night."

Ezra contacted the Executive Council members telepathically and invited them to an urgent meeting with the Grand Guardian. They arrived shortly after the invitation was made and sat in the meeting room. Since it was the middle of the night, they were visibly tired. Some were muttering to each other about why they were having a late-night meeting.

The only one absent from the meeting was Jamari, who had been excused to make new arrangements for the next mission. When the meeting began, the Grand Guardian explained the situation on Zareet and how Governor Ragnar was now on Ebris with some of his army. The council members were taken by surprise.

The Grand Guardian called for a vote on the next mission to Ebris. This was a mere formality required by the Executive Council to endorse the mission. The vote was unanimous, and the mission was officially ratified. Ezra was told of the outcome and asked to let Jamari know so the mission could proceed.

Jamari was sitting at a desk in the Observatory, feeling dejected from what he had been told. He was with Wyatt and Mason, who were monitoring events on Planet Ebris. Jamari felt responsible for not delivering the expected outcome. As Concordia's Chief Defense Strategist, he felt immeasurable disappointment. He couldn't believe Governor Ragnar was able to slip through his fingers and find his way to Planet Ebris.

He thought of an infinite number of 'What if?' scenarios and how he could have done things differently. After some time, though, he realized that type of thinking wasn't doing him any good. Dwelling on what he should have done would not help him in the now. In fact, it was hindering his ability to focus on the task ahead.

"Jamari, you need to stop beating yourself up," Wyatt said. "I don't think any of us could have predicted the outcome of what happened on Zareet. You managed to destroy a big part of his army. That, in itself, is a great feat. It will go a long way to subvert his power and his ability to inflict further damage to both Zareet and Ebris.

"And now the teleporter has been destroyed, so he has no way of getting back to Zareet. That means the people of Zareet are now free from his tyrannical rule. Hopefully, they can now move toward a more democratic system of governance. Provided another dictator doesn't emerge to continue his rule."

"That's right, Jamari, you can't beat yourself up," Mason added.

"I guess you're both right. I still feel responsible, though. Anyhow, I'm not going to dwell on it. I need to move forward and come up with a new plan. This time, on Ebris."

Jamari, Mason, and Wyatt spent the next several hours monitoring Governor Ragnar. From what they could gather, he had set up base camp outside one of the planet's main cities. It was in a forested area with no other inhabitants. They'd set up makeshift tents and an office so they could bunker down and prepare their plan of attack on Ebris.

As they monitored him, Governor Ragnar made preparations for his attack. His plan was to divide and conquer. This meant attacking small cities and forcing all the healthy men and women to join his army. If they didn't comply, death would befall them. This was his failsafe plan to rebuild his lost army until he eventually became the planet's new ruler. He had a sufficient stockpile of weaponry he could use to accomplish this easily. This gave him a certain amount of solace, which also gave him the confidence he would soon be the new ruler of Ebris.

Wyatt, Mason, and Jamari watched this unfold through the surveillance feeds coming into the Observatory. Jamari constantly tapped his fingers on the desk he sat at.

"We need to act swiftly," Jamari said to Wyatt and Mason.

Jamari continued gathering intelligence about Ebris, including details about what was left of Governor Ragnar's army. However, there was one critical piece of information that Jamari already knew without the surveillance: the teleporter had been destroyed, thanks to Jonah. This meant there was nowhere to escape. To this end, Jamari felt that he had the upper hand in this situation.

Jamari's strategy would only require a few clusters of Concordian troops, unlike the previous mission. He believed it wasn't necessary to send as many Guardians to fight this time around, as the army they were fighting was now diminished.

He needed to present his plans to the Grand Guardian so she could endorse them. Once approved, Jamari could send Concordian clusters to Planet Ebris while Governor Ragnar still hid from the main city. Jamari's intention was to catch him by surprise to encounter less resistance.

It was now morning. Jamari hadn't slept all night; he had been up working on his strategy. He proceeded to the Grand Guardian's chambers and was greeted by Ezra, who ushered him in to see the Grand Guardian.

"Please take a seat. Ezra mentioned you wanted to discuss a plan for the new mission to Planet Ebris," Grand Guardian Omiya said.

"Correct." Jamari sat on a chair in front of the Grand Guardian's desk. "Governor Ragnar is camped just outside a major city with his army, away from any of Ebris's people. I think we should get a few clusters of our own Guardians over there. As he is isolated from the main population of the planet, we can avoid encountering any of its inhabitants, which in turn would help minimize any casualties."

"I couldn't agree with you more," Grand Guardian Omiya said. "Now, tell me more about what you're planning."

Jamari spent some time describing his plan to the Grand Guardian. She considered his proposal carefully and decided she was happy with the strategy and sanctioned it.

"Jamari, please gather the necessary resources to execute this mission. I will have a meeting with the Executive Council to go over what you have discussed with me and obtain their endorsement. Hopefully, we can stop him this time. Once and for all."

"That is my intention, Grand Guardian."

"Very well. I wish you success. Please be careful out there."

"Of course, Grand Guardian." Jamari walked out of the room, eager to get the mission underway.

Afterward, the Grand Guardian called for Ezra. She asked him to reconvene a meeting with the Executive Council to discuss the new mission with them. He did so immediately. Within minutes, the Executive Council had assembled in the meeting room again, where the new mission was discussed and unanimously endorsed. Now, it was up to Jamari to make this mission a success.

CHAPTER 30

After Jamari chose the clusters he wanted to send on the next mission, he gathered the cluster leaders to brief them on the new assignment. He asked them to start preparing their Guardians immediately. Jamari emphasized the need to do this promptly, so they could get to Ebris that evening. Governor Ragnar had to be stopped.

One of the selected clusters was Haven's. Haven's cluster leader, Guardian Angara, summoned everyone for an urgent meeting. She telepathically asked all of her cluster members to meet her at their muster point. Within a matter of moments, Haven and the rest of the Guardians teleported to the required location for a briefing.

"I've asked you all here to let you know we've been selected to go on a new mission, which will be to Planet Ebris. A short while ago, I was informed by Jamari that during the previous mission on Zareet, Governor Ragnar escaped. He and some of his army traveled over to Ebris, prior to his teleporter exploding. It was assumed during the explosion that he was killed; however, that is not the case. The Observatory has been monitoring Governor Ragnar on Ebris. He and his army have set up a base camp, waiting to make their next move."

Guardian Angara paused, taking on a solemn expression. Haven was alarmed by what she just heard. She, too, was under the impression that the governor had been killed, ending his regime and tyranny on Zareet.

"Our mission now is to stop him, no matter the cost. Meet in the Council Stadium at 10:00 p.m. and be ready for battle. Are there any questions?"

Haven, along with the other cluster members, remained silent.

"Cluster members dismissed." Guardian Angara signaled for everyone to leave.

All cluster members left the muster point while Guardian Angara continued with her preparations. Haven teleported to her room, dumbfounded.

How did Governor Ragnar escape death and get to Ebris? Haven thought to herself.

Hearing the governor was still alive unsettled her. She became determined to put an end to this evil man's plan.

Haven telepathically invited her friends to her room; they all noticed that there was a sense of urgency in her request. Within moments, Caleb, Zak, and Jonah appeared in front of her, where she went on to explain the situation on Ebris.

"What? I can't believe Governor Ragnar is still alive. I thought for sure he would've died during the explosion. How could this have happened?" Zak asked.

"Somehow, the teleporter must have worked long enough for Governor Ragnar and some of his army to get through before the explosion. We all assumed he died in the blast, but he obviously didn't," Haven said.

"So, now we need to go to Ebris and stop him from causing further harm," Caleb said.

"We? Has your cluster been asked to go on the mission?" Haven raised her eyebrows, knowing full well what the answer would be.

Caleb tried to skirt the question. "Well, not exactly."

"And by 'not exactly,' you mean 'No?'" Haven looked at Caleb straight into his eyes.

Caleb gave Haven a cheeky grin. "Well, kinda."

"C'mon, we're not going to sit here and do nothing." Zak looked at Haven, annoyed with her suggestion they should sit this one out.

"Well, I think you should. This is a much smaller mission, and I don't think you guys need to get all heroic and break the rules again. You should stay put," Haven said.

"Since when have we been known to do nothing?" Caleb was shocked that Haven would even suggest such a thing.

"This may be a smaller mission, but it's important. We finally get the chance to get rid of Governor Ragnar. I'm going, and I don't care what anybody says." Zak turned his back on the group and left no room for argument.

"And what about you, Jonah? Are you in?" Caleb asked.

Jonah considered it carefully. His mother knew about him going to Zareet the night before, when he wasn't supposed to. Aurora was very clear that if he went on another mission without Concordian authority, she would report him to the Grand Guardian without fail.

"I'm in."

Jonah knew his parents wouldn't approve of his participation in the mission. Especially his mother. However, a big part of Jonah was more concerned with doing the right thing. He felt morally obligated to fight for what he believed in.

"When are we going?" Jonah asked.

"We've been told to meet in the Council Stadium tonight, at 10:00 p.m," Haven said.

Caleb made a group decision. "All right then, let's get ready and meet in Haven's room at 9:30 p.m. Then we'll head over to the Council Stadium together."

They all left to prepare for the mission. Once Haven was alone, she thought about what was happening. She felt uneasy about the others joining. As their involvement wasn't sanctioned, she knew there would be an added risk.

Their participation in the previous mission wasn't endorsed either, but this time around, she felt since it was a smaller mission with fewer clusters involved, there was a greater danger of her friends being discovered. It wasn't clear what the consequences would be for their insubordination.

None of them had been in that position before, so she could only speculate what would happen. She knew from her own experience, with what had happened on Kenarios, that at the very least, they would be given a stern warning from the Grand Guardian. However, this felt like a far more grievous breach that could potentially lead to a serious punishment. Only time would tell what would happen.

All Haven knew for certain was she couldn't be held responsible for their actions. They were solely responsible for their decisions. They'd decided to ignore her advice. So now, it was all on them.

CHAPTER 31

A fter spending a long day building their base camp, setting up their operations, and settling in, Governor Ragnar and his army sat and had their evening meal. It was in a forested area away from one of the main cities on Ebris.

Afterward, Governor Ragnar walked over to his tent so he could relax for a while before getting some sleep. Zyaire followed him close behind.

As he walked to his tent, the governor paused to look at the night sky. The sky was crimson with small patches of blue interspersed throughout. He could also see one large moon surrounded by three smaller moons on the horizon. As it was getting darker, the sky began to fill with brilliant unfamiliar stars and constellations. Governor Ragnar hadn't seen a sky that color before.

"That sky looks awful!" Governor Ragnar rolled his eyes and continued walking over to his tent.

I think it's stunning, Zyaire thought to himself.

As Governor Ragnar was filled with hate, it didn't surprise Zyaire that his father lacked any sense of wonder or appreciation for something so beautiful.

The governor's tent also doubled as a makeshift headquarters. He sat and poured himself a drink—a glass of mandasky, similar to whiskey—from a secret stash under his desk. He knew drinking alcohol would upset his stomach, but he didn't care. The governor wanted to celebrate crossing over to Ebris.

Alongside him were his assistant Amani, Lieutenant Yanzuro, and his son, Zyaire. He invited them over to have a private discussion about his plans for Ebris. He didn't offer any of them a drink, not that they expected him to. Besides, Zyaire wasn't a drinker, so he didn't care.

Governor Ragnar addressed everyone with apathy. "After the events on Zareet, it has become clear we will not be returning to that planet ever again. The teleporter was destroyed, and we have no way of getting back. I suggest you get used to the idea. Any family you had back home are now history. You'll never see them again."

Amani and Lieutenant Yanzuro looked at Governor Ragnar with indifference as if what he'd just said was inconsequential. However, it wasn't. Although they were concealing their feelings, both had families on Zareet they missed terribly and yearned to see again. They masked their emotions so the governor couldn't see their weakness, out of fear for what he might do.

As for Zyaire, it was just another reason to hate his father after what he did to Levi.

Governor Ragnar continued. "Now that we have that out of the way, we need to focus on the future. I am going to rule this planet. That's something you all need to make happen. We need to overthrow the current ruler and make the people of this planet bow to me and pledge their allegiance."

Lieutenant Yanzuro was unconvinced. "That's going to take some time. We don't really know much about this planet or its people."

"We will shortly. I sent out spy drones to gather some intelligence about this planet. I expect the drones to return soon." Governor Ragnar was confident that the drones would give him the answers he was looking for.

"And then what?" Amani asked.

"We divide and conquer." Governor Ragnar took a sip of his drink and savored every drop.

Lieutenant Yanzuro was intrigued. "What do you mean by that?"

"We attack their army first. We defeat them and force them to pledge their allegiance to me. We coerce them into submission, and if anyone doesn't comply, we execute them. We show them what we are capable of. Then, once we have taken over their army, we get rid of their leader. This will make way for me to rule. I will lead this planet. Just like I was born to do."

Everyone in the room felt sickened by the governor's words.

"Do we know what capabilities they have? How advanced they are?" Lieutenant Yanzuro asked.

"We will once the drones return to us. I can't imagine they are more advanced than we are," Governor Ragnar said.

Lieutenant Yanzuro listened to Governor Ragnar's plan, thinking he had perhaps underestimated the situation. The Lieutenant had served in the army for many years, all the way back to the time when the governor's father was a ruler. However, Yanzuro had only been promoted to Lieutenant earlier that day because his predecessor, Lieutenant Lomar, had been killed in the explosion on Zareet. Given Yanzuro's years of experience, he felt the governor's strategy was too simplistic. What if Ebris was more technologically advanced and could annihilate them in an instant? Time would tell, but somehow Lieutenant Yanzuro felt a little uneasy about the governor's scheme.

Zyaire, who stood listening to his father speak, was sickened by what the governor was saying. His stomach twisted as his father spoke of taking over Ebris and executing anyone who didn't comply with his demands. It was disturbing. How could the man who raised him and always treated him with warmth and kindness be so cold and calculating? Why did he have no respect for human life? How could he execute someone at a whim if they didn't follow his orders? All of this from the man who took pity on Zyaire when he became an orphan as a small child. The man that adopted him and looked after him as his own son.

While Zyaire had known for quite some time that his father's kindness was nothing more than a charade, hearing Governor Ragnar being so overtly cruel distressed him. Now, like never before, a deep loathing festered within Zyaire for his father, which he tried to hide. All of this, combined with what the governor had done to Levi, showed him what a monster his father really was.

"What about mining Chrimatide? Are we still going to do that Governor?" Amani asked.

"That will still happen. Once I become ruler of this planet, we can survey the land for Chrimatide. We can then use the people on this planet to excavate it."

Governor Ragnar hadn't forgotten about the Chrimatide. In fact, it was his most pressing issue. All his other plans led to the search and excavation of this beloved mineral. This was where his power lay. Not only to provide power to the people of Ebris but to use it as a form of control over its people. Just like he'd done on Zareet, he planned to use Chrimatide as a power source its people relied upon, thereby creating a demand for it that could be monopolized.

This was all Governor Ragnar could think about: continuing his desire for domination. As things stood, he no longer had authority over any people besides his small army. This left his ego feeling a deep sense of weakness. To be devoid of power was something foreign to him. Something he hadn't felt in a very long time. Since the time of his father's rule, when his father ruled over him and he had no autonomy. Something he loathed immensely.

As the governor discussed his plans, the drones he'd sent to gather intelligence about Ebris returned. While the governor couldn't wait to see what information the drones had collected, it was getting very late and he was tired. He stored the drone's data in a metal cabinet to be looked at the next day. The governor then asked everyone to leave so he could retire for the evening.

CHAPTER 32

Haven was in her room, dressed in her combat outfit, ready to head to the Council Stadium. Zak teleported into her room as she practiced defensive moves, followed by Caleb and Jonah in quick succession. They were also dressed in their combat outfits, which included the headgear from the last mission. All of them were eager to get to the Council Stadium, so they could teleport over to Ebris as quickly as possible for the battle.

"Is everyone ready?" Caleb asked.

"You bet I am!" Zak threw a few punches into the air as he spoke.

"Are you guys sure about this?" Haven asked. "It's not too late to back out. I know I'm probably wasting my breath saying this, but you don't have to go."

"You're right; you are wasting your breath," Caleb said with an unabashed smile.

Haven rolled her eyes and sighed, not only because of Caleb's predictable response, but also because she couldn't understand why she'd even bothered to ask the question.

"Let's go," Haven said. "Guys, do me a small favor. Stay away from me when we get into the Council Stadium. I don't want to be associated with your delinquency."

"Delinquency! Now, that's a bit rich. I just got one word for you—Kenarios," Caleb said.

Haven pursed her lips at Caleb and took a deep breath. She pretended to ignore what he said; Haven didn't want to let Caleb's remark get the better of her, so she teleported away.

Caleb burst out laughing, proud he'd managed to frustrate Haven. Zak and Jonah stood there grinning. As Caleb was still giggling, Haven reappeared in front of him. She quickly smacked him on the head, and teleported away. Caleb's face instantly took on a more somber look while Zak and Jonah laughed uncontrollably. Haven had gotten the last laugh.

After they finished laughing and composing themselves, Caleb, Zak, and Jonah teleported to the Council Stadium. Haven joined her cluster, while the others tried to blend in and not be obvious standouts.

Everyone was slowly arriving and making their way into the Council Stadium. Jamari directed everybody to be seated so he could make a few announcements before they ventured to Ebris.

"It was discovered overnight that Governor Ragnar is still alive and that he and his army are on Ebris. So, this mission is about finally putting a stop to his evil rule"

As Jamari continued speaking, a massive holographic image appeared in the middle of the Council Stadium. It showed an image of Ebris and a map of the planet. It also showed live footage of where Governor Ragnar and his army were currently situated and what they were up to.

Key to Jamari's strategy was to use the element of surprise. The plan was to attack late at night when Governor Ragnar and his army were sleeping. Doing so would increase their chances of success. Jamari didn't want to take any chances this time around. He felt the success of this mission was his responsibility.

Although he had the assistance of Concordia's Guardians, he was ultimately responsible for the end result. For this reason, he couldn't bear the thought of not succeeding. To fail would mean devastation for Ebris and its people. Governor Ragnar had already devastated his home planet; he could not be allowed to repeat that on this new planet.

Jamari instructed each cluster group to approach the center of the stadium, one at a time. Each cluster leader had been provided with directives on where to congregate on Ebris. The location was a few miles away from Governor Ragnar's base camp, in another forested area away from one of the main cities. Once all clusters had arrived, they would advance with their attack plan.

After all clusters landed on Ebris, Jamari telepathically instructed everyone to wait at their current location. He then asked two of his cluster leaders to approach the base camp to observe what was going on. More specifically, Jamari wanted to know if they were asleep.

The two cluster leaders teleported closer to Governor Ragnar's army as instructed, making sure they were close enough to see what was going on but not too close to get noticed.

Can someone give me a status report? Jamari telepathically asked the two cluster leaders.

Yes, Jamari. We can see that most of the camp is asleep now. There are some soldiers that are awake and patrolling the area. So we need to proceed with caution.

Copy that, Jamari said.

With that, Jamari turned to the rest of the clusters standing next to him.

Everybody, listen up. I've just been advised the base camp is quiet, and most of its people are asleep. They have some soldiers patrolling the area, so we need to proceed with caution. We will now begin our approach toward the base camp, but you all need to keep quiet. Once you get there, don't do anything until I give you further instructions.

One cluster at a time, they moved closer to where the other two cluster leaders were located. When Jamari eventually got there, he spent some time observing what was going on in the area. He wanted to see if it was an appropriate time to strike or whether they should wait a little bit longer. After a few minutes, he began focusing on the soldiers that were on patrol. They carried weapons with them resembling rifles.

They look different from the weapons they had on Zareet, Jamari thought to himself.

These were much larger, and the barrels appeared to be wider. Jamari thought twice about striking.

After some consideration, he decided to attack anyway but chose to select only one of the clusters to begin the attack.

On my command, I want you all to teleport into base camp. Begin by attacking the patrolling soldiers. Once you have dealt with them, we will assault everyone else, Jamari told the cluster.

After waiting for about thirty seconds, Jamari turned to the chosen cluster.

Now!

After they received the command, the cluster teleported into the camp as instructed. The Guardians in the cluster prepared to strike with their batons. As they materialized in the base camp, the Governo's soldiers seemed dumbfounded.

Where did they come from? How did they appear out of thin air? one of the soldiers thought to himself.

As one of the Guardians—Kaiden—was about to strike a soldier, the soldier fired shots from his rifle. One of the rifle shots struck Kaiden's arm. The strike was painful; it made him scream and start bleeding. He teleported away to where Jamari and the remaining clusters were.

"I've been shot!" Kaiden cried.

Jamari rushed to examine Kaiden's wound. A metallic bullet had penetrated his skin, partially protruding from the site of the injury.

"Brace yourself, soldier. I need to get this out of your arm. It's going to hurt," Jamari said.

As Jamari pulled it out of his arm, Kaiden screamed for a moment. Jamari took a closer look at it. The bullet resembled the tip of a spear. It was triangular in shape and lightweight—but very strong. It was able to penetrate the outfit Guardian Kaiden wore and was capable of doing substantial damage.

As Jamari inspected the bullet for a moment, another Guardian assisted Kaiden by covering his wound with a cloth, as he was losing a lot of blood. At that point, Jamari took notice of Kaiden's bleeding and telepathically spoke to the Guardian that was assisting him.

Take Kaiden back to Concordia and have a doctor look at him!

The two Guardians teleported back to Concordia as instructed. As they teleported back, a few more Guardians returned from battle, also seriously wounded. Some had been shot in the leg, others shot in the arm, while one was critically shot in the abdomen. They were all bleeding heavily, the Guardian shot in the abdomen collapsing in agony. Jamari sent each of them back to Concordia to receive emergency medical care.

Concordia had its own hospital with some of the best doctors working there. While they were especially advanced in their medical technology, Concordia's doctors still had their limitations. They could not prevent death and could not always revive someone who had died.

Jamari had to think fast. Their weapons were more harmful than anticipated. He asked some of his cluster leaders to go back to Concordia to retrieve some hand shields.

These shields were unique in many ways. Firstly, they came in the form of a metal glove that a guardian could wear on their hand. By clenching their glove-adorned hand, to form a fist, a shield would appear within milliseconds. The shield generated would be big enough to secure a guardian from head to tow. To deactivate the shield, a guardian would clench their hand again and it would disappear.

The other interesting thing about them was that they had one-way transparency. This meant that when a guardian held a shield in front of them, they could see through them like glass. However, for someone who faced a Guardian holding a shield, it appeared opaque.

While the cluster leaders retrieved the shields from Concordia, Governor Ragnar—who was asleep—was abruptly awakened by the commotion outside. He went to find out what was going on by peering through a small window in his tent. His soldiers were being attacked. As he looked closely at the assailants, he stood with his mouth wide open, bewildered. He couldn't believe what he saw—the same insurgents from Zareet. He recognized them by their uniform.

What the hell are they doing here? Governor Ragnar thought to himself.

When his soldiers had fought the Guardians on Zareet, Governor Ragnar presumed they were insurgents from his home planet trying to fight against his regime. Now, however, he was second-guessing who they were.

How did they get here? Governor Ragnar asked himself.

They couldn't have come through the teleporter. The machine was destroyed, and only his army had managed to get through. They must've arrived on Ebris another way. If so, how? Did they come from some advanced civilization that had well-developed teleportation technology? If that was the case, perhaps these insurgents weren't who he thought they were, leading him to speculate on their true origins.

Although the insurgents intrigued Governor Ragnar, his curiosity had to be put to the side in that moment. His base camp was being attacked; he had to act at once. He hastily got dressed and grabbed his rifle.

In the meantime, Caleb, Zak, Haven, and Jonah stood by, watching the horror unfold. Jonah became increasingly anxious, as did Caleb and Zak. Unlike Jonah, Caleb and Zak tried to hide their angst. As they watched the wounded soldiers being sent back to Concordia for medical treatment, they were confronted with the reality of war for the first time. It wasn't quite as glamorous as they had once thought. Sometimes, people were injured. Occasionally, it was critical. Haven, on the other hand, wasn't bothered by it. She had experienced war before and knew its harsh reality. Haven had grown painfully accustomed to it.

CHAPTER 33

The patrolling soldiers at the base camp had raised the alarm. They managed to wake everyone and ordered them to defend the camp.

The two cluster leaders who'd gone to Concordia to retrieve some shields had returned. Jamari telepathically instructed all Guardians to grab a shield. Caleb, Zak, Jonah, and Haven grabbed one each and put it on their hands. They had used the gloves a few times before throughout their training with Aurora, so they were familiar with how to use them.

After all clusters had been armed with shields, Jamari instructed everyone who hadn't gone into battle to get ready. On his command, all Guardians would be directed to teleport into base camp and surround the patrolling soldiers.

"Now!" Jamari screamed. Within seconds, all Guardians teleported into base camp.

By the time Jamari and all the clusters had dropped into base camp again, all of Governor Ragnar's soldiers were awakened and primed for combat.

Haven, Zak, Caleb, and Jonah led the charge, each attacking numerous soldiers and defeating them. When Jonah was in the midst of an attack, about to strike a soldier with his baton, one of Governor Ragnar's soldiers aimed his rifle at Jonah's back. Before the soldier could fire, Haven took care of the situation, storing it in her memory bank for later use on Jonah.

Caleb and Zak were not far away, taking down soldiers with the greatest of ease. The soldiers didn't stand a chance against them, as they simply could not compete with Caleb and Zak's endurance and agility. Like

Haven and Jonah, Caleb and Zak seemed to work together in perfect harmony, each managing to have the back of the other. They seemed indestructible.

Zak! I've been shot! Caleb screamed telepathically. An incredible, sharp pain radiated from Caleb's left leg.

Zak turned around to have a look and noticed a copious amount of blood streaming down Caleb's leg. Caleb tried to push through the agony and the bleeding but soon realized he could not continue. He began to feel faint and eventually collapsed to the ground. Zak shielded him from getting shot again. He grabbed Caleb's arm and teleported him back to Concordia. The soldiers in close proximity saw Caleb and Zak disappear before their eyes and were at a loss to understand what had just happened.

Caleb and Zak teleported into Concordia's hospital, where Zak carried Caleb into an emergency room and tried to catch the attention of one of the doctors on duty.

"Doctor, I've got someone over here who's been shot! He needs help!" Zak said frantically. The doctor took one look at Caleb and tended to him, trying to stop the bleeding. A nurse rushed to the doctor's aid soon after to assist. Once Zak knew Caleb was being well looked after, he teleported back to Ebris.

As the battle continued, Wyatt and Mason were in the Observatory, monitoring everything happening on the battlefield. During his observations, Wyatt noticed someone from Governor Ragnar's camp appeared on the screen in a red color.

"Mason. Come and have a look at this." Wyatt pointed to the screen and the red man.

They looked at each other and knew what that meant.

"We have to stop him from getting hurt," Mason said.

"I'll head off to Ebris now and bring him back," Wyatt said.

Wyatt changed into his combat outfit using his wardrobe generator. He promptly left the Observatory and teleported to Ebris.

On his arrival, Wyatt approached the battlefield and attempted to find the person he'd spotted in the Observatory. Within minutes, he found him in the midst of a battle with Guardian Randu. He ran desperately toward both of them. As he advanced, Wyatt watched Randu paralyze the man with his baton. He dropped to the ground and lay there, unconscious, with Randu standing over him. Wyatt grabbed Randu's arm and pushed him away.

Guardian Randu looked at Wyatt, aghast by his actions.

"What the hell are you doing?" Randu asked.

"We have reason to believe he might be Concordian," Wyatt said.

"What?" Guardian Randu looked at Wyatt, baffled by what he'd just said.

"There's no time to explain. I'll take care of him; you continue with the battle."

Wyatt didn't bother to elaborate, as he needed to act quickly to get out of harm's way. He handcuffed the soldier and teleported him back to Concordia. On arrival, Wyatt placed him into a holding cell in Concordia's jail.

As Wyatt processed the soldier's admission into jail and performed various tests, the fight on Planet Ebris continued. Governor Ragnar's soldiers were being defeated steadily and gradually shrinking in numbers. The Governor knew this and felt a strong sense of entrapment. All he could think about in that moment was his survival.

Governor Ragnar gathered some basic supplies and necessary weapons. There was a vehicle parked outside of his tent that he could use to escape; a hovercraft that could travel incredibly fast to somewhere where he would be safe. It was time to escape.

"Going somewhere?" Jamari asked as he entered the governor's tent.

Governor Ragnar looked at Jamari, seeing a tall soldier with a spear-like weapon and a frightening look on his face.

"Who the hell are you people? Why are you doing this to me?" Governor Ragnar asked.

"You don't need to know who we are. All you need to know is that your regime of fear and tyranny is about to end. You have committed some of the most heinous crimes on your own people on Zareet. Just now, you were ready to do the same to the people of Ebris. Your ego has no shame. You are abhorrent and devoid of empathy."

"Everything I have ever done is for the good of my people. They have homes and jobs. Food, water, and everything they need to live their lives. Why are you hunting me?" Governor Ragnar asked.

"You rule over your people with fear and intimidation," Jamari said. "People are not free to do as they please, only to do what pleases you. That is not how to lead. You impinge on people's free will. And now, you want to do the same on this new planet to a group of people you don't know. People who don't know you or have ever heard of you. We won't let you do it."

"What would you know about leading? I've had to make sacrifices for the good of my people!"

"You are delusional. The only people who have made sacrifices are the innocent people who have served under your disgusting regime. As long as you have all the power, everyone else is damned. That ends tonight."

As Jamari spoke, Governor Ragnar slowly and discreetly grabbed a pistol from his back pocket. Once he grabbed it, he quickly drew the weapon and fired a shot at Jamari. Jamari was wearing his hand shield and managed to activate it and block the bullet in time. Governor Ragnar fired several more shots in an attempt to break through the shield, but to no avail. The pistol eventually ran out of bullets, leaving him defenseless.

Jamari deactivated his shield. The two stood there looking into each other's eyes intently. Across from him, Jamari saw a man approaching the end of his life as he knew it. Governor Ragnar was looking at someone who was about to cause him great harm. He couldn't comprehend what had led him to this point in his life journey. In his mind, he blamed everything and everyone around him. The governor behaved like a victim. The truth was that he was the mastermind behind it all. He had no one but himself and his ego to blame.

In that moment, Governor Ragnar ran toward Jamari and attempted to ambush and tackle him to the ground. Before the governor could make physical contact, Jamari took his baton and struck the governor. The strike was quick and sharp. Governor Ragnar's body crumpled to the ground like a rag doll.

An immediate calmness filled the air. Jamari stared at Governor Ragnar's body, contemplating what had just happened. Jamari came to the realization he had just captured Governor Ragnar. He handcuffed the governor in readiness to transport him to Planet Skepsis. The governor was no longer going to be of any consequence to Ebris.

As he walked back to the base camp where the fight had begun, Jamari could see the last of Governor Ragnar's remaining soldiers had fallen. The war was finally over. As the Guardians all tried to catch their breath, Jamari felt a sense of accomplishment. He was not only proud of the Guardians for defeating Governor Ragnar's army, but he was also satisfied he had finally defeated a malevolent leader. This time around, he was able to put an end to his tyranny. He had achieved his goal.

Job well done, everybody. Everyone, except for the cluster leaders, please head back to Concordia. This war is finally over, Jamari said telepathically to all Guardians.

As instructed, all Guardians, except for the cluster leaders, teleported back to Concordia, returning to the Council Stadium where they'd commenced their mission.

All cluster leaders, I need you to transport Governor Ragnar's army, who are still unconscious, back to Planet Zareet. Drop them off at the governor's old headquarters. They don't need to be punished for their leader's malevolence. They can go back to their families on Zareet and hopefully live better lives than before, Jamari said.

On his instructions, all cluster leaders began teleporting the fallen soldiers back to Zareet, a few at a time, until all were returned to their home planet. Once the task was complete, they teleported back to Concordia.

Jamari went back to Governor Ragnar's tent. He grabbed the governor and teleported him to Planet Skepsis. On arrival, Jamari carried the unconscious governor and presented him to Warden Nakuno.

Planet Skepsis was a prison for Infringers that were captured during Concordian battles. It was for Infringers that were considered too dangerous to be taken back to their dimension of origin. On Planet Skepsis, once they were imprisoned, Infringers would live out the rest of their natural lives there.

However, Planet Skepsis was not the typical prison of other dimensions. It wasn't cold, dark and gloomy. Rather, it was filled with light, green pastures, beautiful architecture and breathtaking nature. People held captive there would participate in activities such group therapy, spiritual counseling and meditation. They were encouraged to take on artistic hobbies like painting and music, as well as physical pursuits such as sports and other fitness activities. Planet Skepsis was more about rehabilitating an Infringers soul and asking them to reflect on their past actions, in the hope that they could change their behaviors moving forward.

"Welcome Guardian Jamari. Who do we have here?" Warden Nakuno asked.

"I have a new Infringer for you to take in. Governor Ragnar from Planet Zareet. I have a feeling he is going to be your most challenging prisoner yet."

"There isn't a prisoner I can't handle. I've seen them all." Warden Nakuno gave a coy smile.

Jamari explained to the warden the reason for his arrest and why he had been brought in. The warden then began processing the governor and put him into a cell, while Jamari teleported back to Concordia.

After Jamari reemerged back in the Council stadium and was satisfied everybody had returned safely, apart from those that had gone to hospital, he dismissed them from the mission. All Guardians, except for the cluster leaders, left the Council Stadium to return to their rooms, exhausted.

The cluster leaders remained behind for a debrief with Jamari. Once that had been completed, they too left the Council Stadium, while Jamari decided to visit the Grand Guardian to give her a status report.

"Welcome, Jamari. I believe you have an update regarding the mission to Planet Ebris. Did everything go as we'd hoped?" Grand Guardian Omiya asked.

"Yes, Grand Guardian." Jamari said. "I am happy to report the mission was a success. Governor Ragnar and his army were defeated. We all returned just a short while ago. Some of the Guardians who participated in this mission were injured. However, I have been informed they will all make a full recovery. Fortunately, we didn't suffer any losses this time around.

"Also, Governor Ragnar has been taken into custody on Planet Skepsis, while his soldiers have been returned to Planet Zareet. Oh and by the way, Warden Nakuno sends his regards."

"Oh that's lovely. It's been a while since I've spoken to him. Well, that is great news. Congratulations on a successful mission and a job well done." Grand Guardian Omiya said. "Now, I will let you go get a good night's sleep. You've earned it. We will meet again tomorrow and have a debrief with the Executive Council on what happened."

Jamari left the Grand Guardian's chambers and teleported to his room to get some rest. His wife was sound asleep in bed. He slowly crept under the blankets and gently wrapped one of his arms around his wife, and gave her a loving kiss on her shoulder. Jamari was glad to be back holding the love of his life in his arms once again. He felt like the luckiest man alive.

CHAPTER 34

After Zak returned from battle, he headed to the Concordian hospital to see how Caleb was doing. When he arrived, he found Caleb asleep on a hospital bed. He had survived his injury and had bandages applied to the wound. He appeared to be recuperating well. Zak approached Caleb and went to his bedside.

"Is Caleb going to be okay?" Zak asked one of the nearby doctors, who was treating another patient.

"Yes, he's going to be fine. He lost a lot of blood, but we gave him a transfusion, which took care of that. His wound will take a few weeks to heal, and he might limp for a little while, but other than that, he should feel great in no time."

"That's good to hear, Doctor. I'm so relieved."

"I'm glad you're so relieved by Caleb's well-being, Zak," Mason said, as he seemingly appeared out of nowhere.

"Mason. I didn't see you there."

"But I saw you and Caleb—on Ebris—when you weren't supposed to be there. Your clusters were not asked to participate in the mission. You will both need to explain yourselves to the Grand Guardian and me. As will Jonah. I know he was also there."

"What are you talking about? We weren't there. I think you must be mistaken—"

"Yes, you were! And don't even attempt to waste my time denying it," Mason said with a fierce look. "I don't appreciate having my intelligence insulted. Save your explanation for tomorrow. It's late, and everyone is tired. We will discuss this in the morning when we meet with the Grand Guardian. For now, I suggest you have a delightful evening."

Zak watched Mason leave. Suddenly overcome with a gut-wrenching feeling, Zak sighed and thought about how much trouble he was going to be in the next day. He was also terrified by the thought of having to confront the Grand Guardian.

"We are in so much trouble," Caleb said with a frail voice. He opened his eyes and looked at Zak, while Zak looked at him in disbelief.

"Were you awake when Mason was here giving me a lecture?"

"Sure was. I was pretending to be asleep so that I wouldn't get yelled at." Caleb laughed faintly. He had been given pain relief medication, which made him drowsy.

"If you weren't a patient, I'd whack you in the head!" Zak said.

Caleb gasped in pain.

"Caleb, are you okay?"

Caleb motioned for Zak to lean in a bit closer. Caleb gazed at him for a few moments with a serious expression. When Zak wasn't expecting it, Caleb whacked him in the head.

"You mean like that? Is that how you'd whack me?" Caleb asked.

Zak took a step back and regained his composure. His immediate instinct was to retaliate and give Caleb a nice return, but Zak thought twice about it.

"I will temporarily let that slide. And I emphasize the word 'temporarily.' Just wait until you get out of hospital. I'm going to be the reason why you come back! Yeah—you laugh while you can, boy." Zak stared at Caleb with an intense look.

After a few seconds, Zak—whose lips were pursed tightly—burst into laughter.

After chatting for a little while, Zak decided to leave so Caleb could rest and recuperate. Zak teleported to his room, ready to get some sleep. Exhausted from the mission, he jumped straight into bed. His head had barely touched the pillow before he was sound asleep.

The next morning, Caleb was released from the hospital and returned to his room. Although he was limping, he was in good health otherwise.

Before lying on his bed, Caleb grabbed some extra pillows and stacked them up high so he could lay his back up against them and sit up right. He slowly lay on the bed and made himself comfortable, then threw a blanket over his legs. Caleb was ready to be pampered. He was feeling hungry and decided to manifest a hearty breakfast to eat. Within seconds, he created a plate consisting of a tall stack of French toast that was drowning in maple syrup. It was surrounded by a mixture of fresh berries and plenty of vanilla-bean-flavored whipped cream on the side. He also manifested a large cup of coffee to quench his thirst.

The perfect cure for my hunger! Caleb thought to himself, as his mouth started watering.

Caleb took his knife and fork and cut a piece of toast. He dug the fork into the toast, followed by a plump strawberry. That was then coated with a thick layer of cream and maple syrup. As Caleb was about to put it into his mouth and devour it with unapologetic pleasure, someone gripped his arm and smacked the fork out of his hand, which then crashed onto the plate. Within a split second, he was in the Grand Guardian's chambers.

"Good morning, Caleb," the Grand Guardian said.

"Ah . . . good morning, Grand Guardian," Caleb said, a little shaken.

He was dumbfounded at how he had gotten there. Then he noticed Ezra holding his arm. Ezra had teleported into Caleb's room, grabbed him when he wasn't looking, and teleported him back into the Grand Guardian's chambers.

Beside him were Zak and Jonah, as well as Mason, Wyatt, and Jamari.

"Now that you're all here, we can begin," the Grand Guardian said, seated behind her desk. "It has come to my attention that the three of you went on the mission to Planet Ebris last night, without sanction. Is that correct?"

Everyone in the room could see that the Grand Guardian was not impressed. She had a look of calm on her face that was just about ready to explode into rage.

"Yes, Grand Guardian," Zak responded on behalf of himself, Caleb, and Jonah. He didn't bother trying to argue or evade the question. With evidence from the Observatory, it was futile trying to deny it.

"That was a huge mistake!" shrieked the Grand Guardian. The three of them were taken aback by the Grand Guardian's outburst. "I'm really disappointed in all of you. Under no circumstances are you ever to repeat this. We cannot tolerate this type of behavior.

"When Guardian Jamari selects clusters, the selections are to be adhered to strictly. We cannot have Guardians going rogue, doing what they please, and going off on missions without the express consent of Concordian authority. Otherwise, it makes a mockery of everything we do here and our existence. It is also disrespectful to Jamari's authority.

"You are not a law onto yourselves. We have rules that need to be honored. What if something had happened to you and we didn't know about it? Did you think of that before you recklessly decided to go on a mission you were not chosen for? Obviously not! And look at Guardian Caleb. He was hurt. Fortunately, his injuries weren't serious and he has lived to tell the tale."

The Grand Guardian's eyes erupted with disappointment, anger, and frustration at their stupidity.

Zak, Caleb, and Jonah sat in silence, feeling the wrath of the Grand Guardian's fury. Every word she uttered felt like lashings to their ears. It was incredibly painful to listen to. As the Grand Guardian spoke, repentant looks crossed their crestfallen faces.

"When I was told about this earlier this morning, I thought long and hard about how I was going to handle this. I cannot let this behavior go unpunished. After careful consideration, I have decided to lock down your powers for the next two weeks," Grand Guardian Omiya said.

All three of the young Guardians had stunned looks on their faces.

"What does that mean?" Caleb asked.

"It means I will immediately suspend your powers for a period of two weeks," the Grand Guardian said. "You will not be able to teleport, communicate telepathically, or levitate during this time. And you won't be able to leave Concordia for the duration of this suspension. Consider it a form of detention.

"The only thing you will be able to do is manifest food to eat. That's it. And another thing, your training will be suspended as well. I have already advised Guardian Aurora not to continue your training during this time. Have I made myself clear?"

"Yes, Grand Guardian," Jonah responded with humility, as did Zak and Caleb.

"If you ever do this again, if you ever go on an unsanctioned mission without Concordian authority, you will be expelled next time. That means you'll be removed from Concordia and stripped of your powers for a significant period of time. You won't be able to stay in Concordia and enjoy all it has to offer like you can this time. I mean it. This is not a game! Do you understand?"

"Yes, we do." Zak stared at the floor, too embarrassed to look at the Grand Guardian.

At that point, Grand Guardian Omiya got up from her seat and approached all three of them. She put her hand over their heads, one at a time, and locked down their powers. They each felt a brief jolt throughout their bodies before returning to their normal selves.

"I have now locked your powers. You may leave. And I strongly suggest you think very carefully about what I've told you here today."

Jonah, Caleb, and Zak all stood and left the room. Walking out of the Grand Guardian's chambers, it felt like they had each been given a savage beating across their faces. They all thought they were doing the right, honorable thing and fighting against evil. However, in the Grand Guardian's eyes, it was a violation of the rules.

Even though Concordians had powers and could come and go as they pleased, they still had a code of conduct they needed to abide by. There were limits to what they could do, and if they went beyond those limits, there were consequences.

CHAPTER 35

The Middle Astral Realm

E lder Ezekiel and Elder Baldel returned to speak with Master Jakeel's (Jonah's) Spirit Guides—Ondasha and Rumshana.

"Greetings, Ondasha and Rumshana. We want to get an update on how Master Jakeel is doing. More specifically, how he went with handling his grandfather's passing," Elder Baldel said.

"He has definitely made huge progress in that regard. We helped guide him to the Akashic Records. Through that, he was able to break through his emotional block, which in turn helped him release a significant amount of his grief," Ondasha said.

"I see." Elder Ezekiel turned to Jakeel's stream to view his most recent events. Elder Baldel followed suit.

Both Elders took some time to review Jakeel's visit to the Akashic Records and his subsequent visit to Amabilia, where he spent some time crying over his grandfather's loss. They could feel his intense pain and sorrow being released as he lay on the ground with Guardian Ishwa by his side, supporting him.

Although in the Middle Astral Realm the Elders—along with all beings of light—never experienced sadness or intense pain like Jakeel had during that event, they had enormous empathy for him. They understood the gravity of what Jakeel felt and the courage it took to go through the grieving process.

Ezekiel and Baldel had both spent considerable time on Earth in human form, over many lifetimes, prior to becoming Elders. They understood the intensity of grief and the many aspects of its nature. Looking at Jakeel displaying his vulnerability to Ishwa, the Elders felt nothing but love for him. Watching him lying on the ground, they wanted nothing more than to embrace him and let him know he would be okay. However, as Elders, they weren't allowed to interfere unless Jakeel requested it or they could see he was heading off course from his planned life. All they could do was witness this event with compassion and oversee his growth as a soul.

"You've both done wonderful work to guide him to this point on his life journey," Elder Ezekiel said as he turned to Ondasha and Rumshana after completing the review. "He's come a long way. And he's got a lot more to accomplish. But we are proud of the work he has done and the guidance you have both given him. Well done to both of you."

"Thank you," Rumshana said.

"His life is only going to get more interesting from here. Keep up the great work," Elder Baldel said before both Elders left and moved on to the next review.

CHAPTER 36

The Physical Realm

After he returned from his meeting with the Grand Guardian, Jonah was greeted by Ishwa, who patiently waited outside his room. Following his encounter with the Grand Guardian and listening to her damning sermon, the last thing Jonah wanted was a visit from Ishwa. He just wanted to be alone.

"Hey, Ishwa. I wasn't expecting you." Jonah tried not to look too annoyed at Ishwa's unexpected visit.

"As I said last time, I always come when you least expect it, but when you're completely ready."

"Yes, I think I remember you saying something like that." Jonah gave a polite smile.

"Anyhow, Jonah, I'm here to have a chat with you if that's okay?"

"Do we have to do this now Ishwa?"

"Judging by the look on your face, I think we do."

Ishwa's piercing eyes studied Jonah. He sensed Jonah was not in a good mood, which was all the more reason for them to sit down and have a conversation.

"Is it that obvious?"

"It sure is, Jonah."

"Okay then, Ishwa. Let's go."

"Great. Hold onto my hands, Jonah."

Ishwa put his hands out in front of Jonah's. Jonah sighed and grabbed Ishwa's hands; within moments, they were on Planet Amabilia. They landed in the same spot they'd sat on during their previous visit. Jonah took in the fresh air and basked in the planet's hypnotic atmosphere—the perfect antidote to the Grand Guardian's blistering reprimand he'd received only minutes earlier. Jonah began to appreciate this visit even though he'd been a little ungracious toward Ishwa moments prior.

"Sorry if I came across a little rude earlier. I've just had a bad morning," Jonah said, repenting for the way he acted toward Ishwa back in Concordia minutes earlier.

"All is forgiven Jonah. Now that you've relaxed a little, let's talk." Ishwa motioned for Jonah to sit on the ground and make himself comfortable. "So, what's bothering you, Jonah?"

"I kind of did a bad thing and feel really guilty now. And I wouldn't mind your opinion on it." Jonah paused for a moment, reluctant to tell Ishwa. However, rethinking the issue, Jonah felt compelled to let Ishwa know and get his view on the matter.

"Absolutely, Jonah. What is it?"

"I went on a mission last night to Planet Ebris to help fight against someone by the name of Governor Ragnar, who had illegally teleported into another dimension. The mission was a success. But the problem is I went with some friends of mine, and we kind of weren't supposed to be there. Our clusters were not selected to go, but we went anyway."

"Aha. You kind of weren't supposed to be there, or you just plain *weren't* supposed to be there? You need to be really clear with me, young man." Ishwa had an interrogative gaze that remained glued to Jonah.

"One could say in a roundabout sorta way that we weren't supposed to be there," Jonah bashfully replied.

"Jonah—"

"Okay, okay. We were *not* supposed to be there."

"I appreciate your honesty, even if it took a 'roundabout sorta way' to get there." Ishwa laughed.

"Anyhow, the Grand Guardian found out and gave us . . . let's say . . . a *really* strong talking to. It was humiliating. So, now I'm in the bad books with the Grand Guardian. And she's locked down my powers for the next two weeks. And it's not my fault."

Jonah sat there picking at some grass, trying to avoid eye contact with Ishwa. As he spoke, he began to feel a little embarrassed. He knew he had done the wrong thing but didn't want to admit it to himself.

Ishwa let out a deep breath. "Wow! She locked down your powers. For her to do that, she must have been furious with you and your friends. That's not a punishment she hands out very often, and when she does, it's *very* serious. So, Jonah, my question to you is: what made you go to Planet Ebris without authority?"

"Well, Caleb and Zak asked me to."

"But what *made* you go?"

"Caleb and Zak asked me to go. They can be very convincing—"

"Jonah, you were asked to go, but you were not forced to go, were you?"

"Well, no. Not exactly."

"Jonah, you were asked to go by your friends, and *you* decided to go. *You* made the decision. Yes?"

"Well . . ." Jonah paused to think about his answer. "Yes."

"Then you are responsible for that decision. You made that choice. Not your friends. You didn't have to go. You could have stayed in Concordia and let them go and get into trouble on their own.

"Your friends are accountable for making their own decisions. Each and every one of you is responsible. Separately and collectively. You all co-created this experience, which led to you all getting into trouble with the Grand Guardian—collectively.

"You see, Jonah, when you were trying to blame Caleb and Zak for everything, you were actually playing the role of a victim. Your Ego was trying to deflect responsibility onto others for what you very consciously decided to do. The Ego is very good at doing this. Go and blame everyone else around for your problems except yourself. That is classic Ego at its very finest. But here's the thing, Jonah—I don't see a victim when I look at you. I see a Master. You are the Master of your existence. You chose to break the rules. Then you must accept responsibility for it. And at the same time, you need to forgive yourself for that decision."

Jonah looked at Ishwa with a certain knowledge that what he was saying had much truth to it. It was starting to sink in for Jonah, where his responsibility lay in all of this, which made him feel a little uncomfortable.

"Here's another thing you're not consciously aware of. Just as you made a choice that was out of alignment with your highest good, you also have the power to make choices that are. Choices that will help you grow. That will lead you to a greater level of consciousness. Choices that will guide you to discovering the core of who you really are.

"This negative experience you created is now in your past. You can't change that. And it does not need to define who you are in the present moment. Again, that is a choice you need to make. Ask yourself this, Jonah—does living in the past and dwelling on your errors serve your Ego or your Highest Self?"

"Ego, I suppose," Jonah said.

"You suppose?"

"Okay! It's Ego!"

"You bet it is!" Ishwa laughed. "To serve Ego is to be a victim. To let go and to be in the present moment, to learn from your mistakes and to use them as lessons to grow from—to not let your mistakes define you until the end of time—that is honoring your Highest Self. And that is what your spiritual journey is all about. Honoring your highest self."

Jonah looked at Ishwa in wonder. He was right. Jonah had acted irresponsibly and was accountable for his actions. The group were all responsible for their actions. Individually and collectively. A few tears ran down his face as Ishwa spoke. Jonah was in such awe of his wisdom and his kind nature.

When they'd first met, Jonah thought he was some meditating hippie he had to meet because his mother told him to. Now, though, he was really enjoying spending time talking to Ishwa. He appreciated listening to his wisdom and sharing an incredible journey of discovery. Ishwa spoke to Jonah with such honesty and a truthfulness he had never experienced before—honesty spoken with compassion. It was eye-opening.

They continued to talk for quite some time. Jonah enjoyed the chat and was not even paying attention to the time. Rather, he was paying attention to what Ishwa had to say.

"So, Ishwa, how do I conquer Ego once and for all and get more in touch with my Higher Self?"

"Well, Jonah, it's not about completely conquering Ego only so you can live a life based on your Higher Self. It's a matter of understanding how to balance the two and learning about the traps of Ego and overcoming them. Remember, you exist in physical form, and to continue to exist in your physical form, you need your Ego. To do away with Ego, you need to strip away your physical body. It means your body dies. And you cease to exist in physical form. So, let's not do away with the Ego entirely. Okay? Let's aim to overcome the trappings of Ego."

"Got it. So, Ishwa, why do I keep feeling like everything you say makes perfect sense on some level, even though my brain doesn't fully comprehend it?"

"Because, Jonah, it does make perfect sense. To your soul, your Higher Self. But to your brain, which forms part of your Ego, it doesn't. The fact you can acknowledge that can only mean one thing: *Jonah's awakening*."

The two continued talking for over an hour before they left Amabilia and returned to Concordia. During their time on Amabilia, Jonah forgot that his powers had been locked. On his return to Concordia, while he was alone in his room and trying to telepathically talk to Zak, Caleb, or Haven, Jonah remembered his powers had been shut down.

Damn it! Jonah thought to himself.

Jonah was too tired to go and find his friends and talk to them in person. He went and sat on his bed thinking about what to do next. As he sat there, he decided there was only one thing that would help cheer him up; to manifest some quesadillas. There was nothing that a few good quesadillas couldn't fix. At least in Jonah's eyes.

CHAPTER 37

"Do you have any information about him yet?" the Grand Guardian asked as she looked at the captured soldier lying unconscious in a prison cell. There was a certain familiarity about him that she couldn't quite pinpoint.

"Yes, I do," Wyatt said. "A little earlier, I took a sample of his DNA and tested it against our database. It turns out he is an exact match for someone by the name of Zyaire."

"Zyaire?"

"Yes. According to our records, his mother's name was Ugabe, and his father's name was Chidike. They were both killed many years ago on their home planet of Madibu. As it turns out, they were both killed by Governor Ragnar when Zyaire was a young child."

Wyatt showed the Grand Guardian images from his light-pad of Ugabe and Chidike. She was immediately overwhelmed by what she saw.

"Do you remember them?" Wyatt asked.

"Yes. I remember them . . . Ugabe was my sister."

"Oh. I didn't realize," Wyatt said, shocked at the revelation. "Zyaire is your nephew?"

"Yes. His parents' death was tragic. My parents and I were so heartbroken. And I remember we couldn't find Zyaire. He went missing. We searched for him so many times over the years and never found him. And I always wondered what happened to him. There hasn't been a day that's gone by that I haven't thought about him. And now . . . we have our answer. He survived."

The Grand Guardian gazed at Zyaire in wonder.

"How did he survive, and how is it that Governor Ragnar raised him?" The Grand Guardian looked at Wyatt, aghast.

"That, I don't know."

Grand Guardian Omiya looked at Zyaire for some time before teleporting into his cell to see him up close. He looked just like his father. There was no question in her mind it was her nephew.

"Welcome home, Zyaire," she whispered as she gently took hold of his hands, choking back tears. "Welcome home."

About the Author

 John Darous was born in Melbourne, Australia as the son of a Greek/Syrian mixed race family. After graduating with a Science degree from Monash University, John went on to work in various roles in the insurance industry. It was during this time that he began writing as a form of escape from his unfulfilling day job. Soon enough, it had become a true passion. This passion eventually led him to pen his debut novel, "The Concordian Chronicles: Jonah's Awakening." When he's not busy crafting new tales, John can be found whipping up delicious meals or wrestling with his furry friend Bonnie for control of the TV remote (which she often wins).

If you would like further information about John, or if you wish to sign up to his monthly newsletter, please scan the QR code below, or, alternatively go to www.johndarous.com

www.ingramcontent.com/pod-product-compliance
Lightning Source LLC
Chambersburg PA
CBHW020349120726
47904CB00002B/520